SCREAM BLUE MURDER

LINDA COLES

Blue Banana

All rights reserved. This book or any portion thereof may not be reproduced or used in any manner whatsoever without the express written permission of the publisher except for the use of brief quotations in a book review. This is a work of fiction. Names, characters, places, brands, media, and incidents are either the product of the author's imagination or are used fictitiously. Any resemblance to actual events or persons, living or dead, is entirely coincidental.

Copyright © 2019 Blue Banana

CONTENTS

Chapter 1	1
Chapter 2	5
Chapter 3	9
Chapter 4	13
Chapter 5	17
Chapter 6	21
Chapter 7	25
Chapter 8	29
Chapter 9	33
Chapter 10	37
Chapter 11	41
Chapter 12	45
Chapter 13	49
Chapter 14	55
Chapter 15	59
Chapter 16	63
Chapter 17	67
Chapter 18	71
Chapter 19	75
Chapter 20	79
Chapter 21	83
Chapter 22	87
Chapter 23	91
Chapter 24	97
Chapter 25	101
Chapter 26	105
Chapter 27	109
Chapter 28	113
Chapter 29	119
Chapter 30	125
Chapter 31	129
Chapter 32	133

Chapter 33	139
Chapter 34	145
Chapter 35	149
Chapter 36	153
Chapter 37	157
Chapter 38	161
Chapter 39	165
Chapter 40	169
Chapter 41	175
Chapter 42	179
Chapter 43	183
Chapter 44	187
Chapter 45	191
Chapter 46	195
Chapter 47	199
Chapter 48	203
Chapter 49	209
Chapter 50	215
Chapter 51	221
Chapter 52	227
Chapter 53	233
Chapter 54	237
Chapter 55	241
Chapter 56	245
Chapter 57	251
Chapter 58	255
Chapter 59	259
Chapter 60	265
Chapter 61	269
Chapter 62	273
Chapter 63	279
Chapter 64	283
Chapter 65	287
Chapter 66	291
Chapter 67	297
Chapter 68	303
Chapter 69	307
Chapter 70	311

Chapter 71	321
Chapter 72	325
Chapter 73	329
Chapter 74	333
Chapter 75	337
Chapter 76	341
Did you enjoy Scream Blue Murder?	345
Acknowledgments	347
Also by Linda Coles	349
Also by Linda Coles	355
About the Author	357

Chapter One

The wind whipped through Melissa's blonde hair as they sped down the leafy lane on a hot Sunday afternoon. Callum was at the wheel. A somewhat immature and invincible twenty nine-year-old, he pushed the accelerator to the floor a little more each time his fiancée squealed with excitement. He was a show-off. And he liked people to watch him, notice him, in everything he did. Even sex. He turned towards her. Her head was thrown back, her hair flying behind them like a cream silk kite being beaten and jostled in the whip from the wind. The speedometer on the walnut dashboard read seventy, a full thirty over the limit, but what did Callum care? They were having fun. He laughed and squealed along with her, the effects of his lunchtime G&T pumping through his thin veins and firing his adrenalin even more.

He took the tight corner with ease; he'd done it so many times in the past and knew the road well enough to trust it. There was a long, straight stretch ahead, and he pressed the pedal down further, feeling the power of the V8 engine as they raced forward. Eighty. Eighty-five. Another corner ahead, and he was confident. Melissa urged him on, squealing, laughing, hair still whipping as they raced towards it. Callum touched the brakes of his Ferrari and slowed it a little to take the bend, turning towards her to receive her appreciation of his skilled driving. Her dark shades were a stark contrast to her Colgate mouth. Overly white teeth had been a present for her birthday, her mouth important to him. Turning his attention back to the road, he took the upcoming S-bend with skill, using both sides of the narrow lane like a switchback ride at the fairground. Melissa whooped and squealed like a child at Thorpe Park, without the candy floss. The Rosso red car sparkled in the afternoon sunshine like a cherry on top of a trifle as they sped out of the final bend and back along the flat.

"Faster! Faster," Melissa shouted above the raucous tones of Freddie Mercury urging them not to stop him now, as he belted his soul through the stereo system and out into the vapour trail behind them.

Melissa was having such a good time. Callum was having a ball.

He turned again to her dazzling smile as Freddie gave the performance of his life. They both shouted the chorus along with him as they approached another bend. Callum turned back to the road and took it wide, crossing the centre line as the car swung out around the curve. He glanced back at Melissa and saw, as if waking from a dream, that her rapturous expression had changed to horror. She screamed out hysterically and he swung his head around to the front again, following her wide-eyed gaze. Fully alert now, he yanked the steering wheel hard to the left in an effort to avoid the oncoming car turning left out of a driveway. The other driver tried to swerve out of harm's way as Callum barrelled towards them; he was almost sideways to it now. It wasn't going to be enough. He yanked the wheel again, struggling to keep the Ferrari away from a collision that was now impossible to avoid.

It wasn't enough.

The few seconds immediately after a car crash are eerily quiet. Callum first checked himself then glanced across at Melissa, who was dazed but conscious. Neither spoke. Through the smashed windscreen, Callum watched as the driver's door opened on the other vehicle, a navy-blue Golf, and an elderly male staggered out, hand to his forehead. Red oozed through his fingers; he'd cut his head badly. Further up the road, a man who had probably been out walking off his Sunday lunch had turned and was racing towards the carnage, no doubt to see if he could be of assistance. Still Callum didn't move. Melissa whimpered; Callum ignored her. He wiggled his toes; nothing broken. Opening his door, he staggered out and headed straight for the other driver, gathering his strength and balance as he did so.

"Are you blind!?" he screamed. "Did you even look? Look at my car!"

The old man's milky grey eyes widened in fear as Callum raged at him, not caring in the least that the man was obviously hurt.

"Are you deaf too?" Callum screamed again.

The old man's mouth opened and closed helplessly; he looked like a fish, Callum thought. *Stupid old bastard.*

Callum squared up in front of the old man and let loose a torrent of obscenities that questioned the man's parentage and sexuality, spittle flying from his ashen lips. The man cowered, terrified. Callum's eyes were bulging; a vein in his neck thumped hard, his face was red as a beetroot.

Suddenly there was a shout from behind them.

"Hey!" The man who had been running along the road towards them arrived now, out of breath. He placed a protective arm in front of the older man, shielding him with his body, and whirled on Callum. "Leave it out, eh?"

"What's it to you?" Callum shrieked. "Did you see what happened?"

"I did, actually. So back off, eh?"

"So, he was in the wrong! Look at my car!" Callum said, turning to look. Melissa was still in the passenger seat, moaning and crying, not that Callum was about to help her anytime soon.

"What about your friend? Is she alright?" the man asked, taking a step forward and turning away from the old man for a second.

"She's fine," Callum snapped. "Leave her."

"I'll just take a look; she doesn't sound fine."

The young man stepped forward obstructing his path as the first punch landed on his jaw, jerking his face awkwardly to one side.

"What the—?" He put a hand on his face for a split second, then, quick as a fox, formed a fist of his own and landed a savage punch on Callum's chin. Callum sprawled backwards onto the grass verge, where he lay catching his breath for a moment. Chastened, he had the sense to stay silent.

The old man looked on in disbelief as the Samaritan went to check on Melissa; he had his phone in his hand and was already dialling an ambulance. He talked alternately to both the operator and Melissa and was assured that help was on its way.

Melissa herself was largely unharmed, save for being in shock, and had climbed out of the car. She sat on the grass bank, rocking backwards and forwards to comfort herself. A little blood trickled from her forehead; she would probably need a stitch.

The passerby went back to the old man and sat him down in the passenger seat of his own Golf; this was a better option for his older body than the grass.

Callum was still in the ditch, though he'd got to his knees and was preparing to scramble out. Nobody was in a rush to help him.

The ambulance arrived a few minutes later. The paramedics treated the old man's head wound on site and decided to take him on to the hospital to check him for concussion. Melissa was largely unharmed; no stitches would be needed. She declined to be taken to hospital.

Callum had stumbled out of the ditch and was standing beside the wreck of his car, arms folded and a dark expression on his face. He was still angry, but had simmered back to below boiling point. He had called a tow truck to remove his beloved Ferrari, and arranged a ride back to his parents' house.

All seemed well.

Chapter Two

Melissa Ross had been driven home alongside her fiancé in the back of Mr Parker Senior's Jaguar. Callum had finally calmed down and, having regained his usual bluster, had regaled his father with the whole story, embellishing each detail for good measure. Callum, too, had refused to go to the hospital, and Melissa began to feel much better as soon as she was seated quietly in the Jaguar.

Mr Parker had called his wife to tell her they were on their way, and, via speakerphone, she had voiced her displeasure at Callum and Melissa's refusal to get themselves checked out properly, a scolding that had made Melissa smile at and Callum feel like a child again. But mothers did that, they both knew; their sons and daughters were always and forever eight years old, no matter their current age or what they were doing. Mr Parker Senior, for his part, hadn't much else to add—his wife had said more than enough for them both—and as they turned up the long shingle driveway to their house, which stood majestically at the end. Mrs Parker could be seen standing in the doorway, jiggling from one foot to the other as if the stone step was burning the underneath of each foot in turn.

Clad in a formal skirt and silk blouse, she looked like a member of the Royal Family.

She descended on them, full of anxiety, as soon as they got out of the car. "Why don't you go and get checked out?" she asked again.

"Because it's Sunday and I don't fancy sitting in an A&E department for the next six hours," Callum moaned. "Plus, the fact, we're both fine—a couple of scratches each, nothing more. So, stop fussing, Mother!" He carried on past her and into the coolness of the hallway. Melissa followed suit, not wishing to rile her man up any further, even though his words had sounded downright rude. His mother was concerned; she could understand that.

"I don't like it," Jean Parker said, turning to her husband.

"His choice. He's a grown man. And he's not hurt."

"But still."

They both fell in behind Callum and Melissa and headed through to the lounge, where Callum was helping himself to another gin and tonic. Ice clinked in the tumbler as he sat back in one of the wing chairs, the wing itself almost hiding his face as he closed his eyes, savouring his drink in silence. Everyone else took a seat and collected their own thoughts after what had just happened. Mrs Parker quietly made sure that their future daughter-in-law, Melissa, was truly alright, then changed the subject to lighten the mood, breezily enquiring about where they'd ended up for lunch. She cooed her approval at their choice, a local hotel and a long-standing favourite of her own.

Callum hadn't said another word. He'd finished his drink and had dropped off to sleep, so Brian and Jean Parker, along with Melissa, left him be.

"It must be the shock. Best to let him sleep it off," Mrs Parker said, taking Callum's drink from his hand and putting it on a nearby table. They headed outside, where a huge umbrella shaded a table and chairs on the patio. A retired greyhound slept peacefully in the shade of a bush hanging over the far corner. His ears pricked up as they settled in, indicating he wasn't actually asleep at all, but his eyes stayed closed. Familiar voices were nothing to get bothered by.

"So how are the wedding plans going?' Jean Parker said brightly, happy for something else to chat about while her grumpy son had forty winks inside. She hated rudeness.

"Terrible!" Melissa complained. "The hotel is being super silly over the menu and letting us have the *whole* of the gardens for our party because there's another wedding on! Can you believe it? Why they can't simply tell the others to find another venue, I've no idea. It's causing Mummy and me a lot of stress. As if we haven't enough to worry about!"

"Oh dear. How annoying for you. What will you do?"

"Mummy is going to go and tell the other people they can't have the gardens. She's found out who they are, so once she's told them, it'll be fine, I'm sure. They'll just have to find another venue, and we'll have the gardens to ourselves!"

Jean watched as Melissa helped herself to the jug of lemonade that stood in the centre of the table. She didn't offer anyone else a glass. Rather than say anything, Jean filled a glass for herself anyway, and then poured another one for Brian, who had tuned out of the wedding arrangement conversation and was watching the dog sleep. Melissa was turning out to be a proper Bridezilla of gigantic proportions. At least she looked the part, though, Jean thought, and would fit into their lifestyle on looks alone. And as for their future grandchildren, with Callum and Melissa's natural good looks, they would produce a couple of beautiful children between them. That would be nice to share with the bridge club ladies.

She was conscious Melissa was talking to her; she'd tuned out herself.

"Sorry, Melissa. I was elsewhere."

Melissa scowled and repeated herself. "I said one of the bridesmaids has put so much weight on, the seamstress has had to make a whole new top half of the dress because she couldn't squeeze in! I'm telling you, if she gets much fatter, I'll tell her she can't be a bridesmaid. I don't want her ruining the photos because she can't keep control of her food."

"Oh dear," said Jean again. It was all she could think of saying. She glanced over at Brian, who was still intently watching the dog and showed no signs of rescuing his wife from the conversation. It was all right for him; he could simply turn the TV on or potter in his tool shed and avoid the drama. Even if Jean went inside, Melissa would almost definitely follow her, yammering away as usual about some other self-created drama. She sipped her lemonade and, needing some reprieve from Melissa's whining, asked, "Why don't you see if Callum is awake, take him some cold lemonade?" Her smile was as sweet as the saccharine she'd made the drinks with.

Melissa pulled her bag onto her lap and reapplied her lipstick, then ran her fingers through her hair like a wide-toothed comb. Jean wondered if she did the same things before Callum woke up in the mornings, so she could be ready before he saw her bed-head. When Melissa was happy with her lips, she ran her tongue over her teeth, shook her head like a long-haired dog and went in search of Callum.

Jean breathed out a deep sigh of relief.

"Thank goodness for that," Brian said in a near whisper. "Nice girl, but heaven give me strength," he added, tilting his chin to the sky. Jean smiled and was about to add that the wedding would be done and over with soon when a woman's shrill scream shattered the quiet.

Even the dog looked up in alarm.

"What the blazes has happened now?" Brian said, standing.

Chapter Three

Melissa was almost hysterical when Jean and Brian rounded the lounge door. It wasn't obvious at first what they were looking at. Melissa stood with her hands covering her face, fingers splayed, screaming and crying all at the same time. Callum was as they'd left him when they'd gone out to the shade of the patio. But Jean knew her boy, and Callum didn't look right. His eyes were still closed, despite the noise that was emanating from Melissa's lungs. Jean rushed to her son and held the back of her hand to his forehead like she'd done so many times when he was a young boy. He didn't feel hot this time; no, he felt cool, and cooler than she would have expected given the warm day. She patted his face, and called out to him.

"Callum, Callum—wake up, Callum," she said urgently, but there was no response. Something was dreadfully wrong. "Call an ambulance, will you, Brian?" she directed. He reached for his phone and punched in 999 as Jean carried on trying to wake their son.

Crying now, she felt for a pulse on her son's neck. Nothing. She moved her fingers slightly higher up; nothing registered. She tried his wrist but got the same result: nothing. She turned to Melissa, panic written on her face.

"Melissa! Help me lay him on the floor!" she demanded, but Melissa, still in shock and crying uncontrollably, stood rooted to the spot behind her future mother-in-law.

Realising Melissa was not going to be much use and that Brian was on the phone with the emergency services, Jean heaved Callum down to the floor and on to his back and started CPR. Somebody had to take charge, she thought, pushing down rhythmically in the centre of her son's chest.

Brian rang off with the emergency services, shoved his phone back in his pocket and knelt beside his wife.

"Ambulance is on its way. Move over, love. I'm a bit stronger."

Jean sat back on her haunches, her shoulders aching, and let her own tears flow in earnest now that her husband had taken charge. She watched as he pressed overlapping palms to the spot where Callum's St. Christopher usually hung; it now rested in the creases of his neck. She could hear Brian counting to thirty, over and over again, his compressions regular and evenly spaced. Each time he reached thirty, he released his hands, pinched Callum's nostrils shut and administered two deep breaths.

Then back to his chest.

Counting.

Thirty.

Two deep breaths.

Still no response.

Jean and Melissa sobbed as Brian persevered, not willing to give up yet, not willing to give up hope. Now they could hear a siren in the distance.

"Go to the front, Melissa. Show them where to come! Hurry!" Brian said, panting, not breaking his rhythm.

Melissa didn't move.

"Melissa! Go! Now!" he shouted. That did the trick; she fled towards the front entrance as the siren groaned to a stop outside. There was the sound of the door being flung open, then heavy footsteps, and then the paramedics were there, a man and a woman. Brian was still straddling his son, still pushing at his chest. One of the crew gently placed his hand on Brian's shoulder for him to move over and let them get to work. Quickly and on auto pilot, the two made basic checks and took stock of what they were dealing with. The female directed questions to Jean, sensing she was a little more coherent than the younger woman.

"How long has he been unresponsive?"

"We've just found him like this. We were all outside and he was having a sleep."

"When did he go to sleep?"

"About half an hour ago, maybe."

The look on the woman's face told Jean it wasn't a good sign. CPR was generally futile at this stage.

"Stand clear, please."

Jean, Brian and Melissa stood back as the woman attached wires to a machine, ready to shock Callum's heart back. Jean crossed her fingers and said a silent prayer. There wasn't anything else left for her to do.

After a few minutes, the paramedics transferred Callum to a stretcher and rushed him out to the ambulance; the female paramedic was still working on his heart with her hands.

Melissa, Jean and Brian stood in the doorway watching the ambulance pull away, sirens wailing again. They would follow on to the hospital together. It didn't look good, they knew. Silence filled the hallway until Jean spoke quietly.

"I'll get my bag. Brian, are you alright to drive us all?"

He nodded, unable to comprehend what had just happened only moments ago.

Callum Parker's heart never did beat in his chest again. He was pronounced dead on arrival.

Chapter Four

Amanda Lacey hated working Sundays, particularly when the sun was making an appearance and Ruth was pottering in the garden, but such is life. She tossed her phone onto the wooden outdoor table and sighed. The wood needed a coat of preserver before the winter months took their toll on it, or else they'd be buying a new one next year. She filed the task away for another day and thrust her head into work mode, processing her next steps. She glanced over at Ruth, who had turned instinctively to her when the phone had first rung; she knew full well what was coming. Amanda shrugged, frowning.

"Better go and change, then," Ruth said. "The sooner you go, the sooner you'll be back." She smiled.

"I suppose so. Sudden death, though. I may be a while," Amanda said, standing. "I'll let you know when I'm on my way back. Sorry!"

"No need to apologise. It comes with the territory; I know that." Ruth set down her trowel, walked over to Amanda and put her arm around her shoulders. They walked up to the house together. "I can finish that bottle of red off by myself now. No need to share." She gave her partner a cheeky grin.

"Well, I'm glad you benefit from my working hard," Amanda said, elbowing her gently as they went into kitchen through the back door. The air was a couple of degrees cooler inside, perfect to help her switch from lazing in the sunshine to work mode.

Ten minutes later, she was in her work clothes and heading out to meet the Parkers. Harry Styles cooed quietly in the background as she navigated through a relatively quiet Croydon and on to Stanstead Road in Caterham. The route was familiar to her; she'd driven it many times when Ruth's father had lived nearby. He had recently decided to move on after the death of his wife, Madeline Simpson, a couple of years ago.

Amanda had interviewed Madeline during the course of an investigation into a missing landscaper; at first, she hadn't realised Madeline and Ruth were related, since Ruth had kept her birth mother's surname, McGregor. Something had always seemed off about that case to Amanda, but the feeling had dissolved and the enquiries had halted when Madeline had died in an accident. The investigation had turned up no evidence of her involvement in the landscaper's death, and his body had never been found. The police had concluded that he'd gone missing of his own free will, and the case had been officially archived as a misper.

After Madeline's death, Gordon Simpson had rattled around the five-bedroom family home all on his own; then, a month ago, he'd sold it and moved into a flat closer to his work in town. It made more sense all round, though Amanda and Ruth both knew it hadn't been an easy decision. He'd enjoyed Madeline's gardens as much as she had, but he hadn't the time or the patience for the upkeep. His new place had a small courtyard out back, big enough for a few choice pot plants. The following week, he was having a small flat-warming party for his family and close friends.

Driving past the old house now, Amanda flicked her indicator and turned into the shingle drive of the Parkers' house.

The big black front door looked stylish but from a different era, not 2019, and so Amanda assumed the Parkers would be in their late 50s or 60s. As she stood by the car, the door was opened by a man wearing knee-length chino shorts and a formal short-sleeved shirt, no doubt his attempt at dressing down on a warm summer's day. Even a stranger could see his face looked drained, tired, and pale—unsurprising, since he'd lost his son only a few short hours ago.

Amanda knew all too well that, as the man of the house, he'd be bottling his emotions up until he could let them out in private. She'd seen it too many times before: the female open and grieving, the male stoic until later. "Big boys don't cry; be the man; stay strong for your family"—it was all a load of bollocks, really. She shut the car door and went up to greet Brian Parker, her warrant card at the ready.

"DS Amanda Lacey. Mr Parker?"

"Yes. Please, come through."

Amanda followed him into the lounge, which looked exactly like Amanda had imagined it would, given the old-fashioned front door. While it was nicely done, it wasn't to her own taste; she preferred a less formal look and feel when watching the TV.

There wasn't a TV.

Perhaps it was behind the huge gilt mirror adorning the chimney breast, hidden away so as not to spoil the Tudor-themed room. Or perhaps they had a TV room elsewhere. Either way, it didn't much matter.

Jean Parker stood now to meet her, and Brian did the introductions. There was another, much younger woman who introduced herself as Melissa Ross, Callum's fiancée. The words caught in Melissa's throat as she realised there would be no wedding now he was gone, and another older woman rushed over to comfort her as howls like a tomcat's pained their way from deep inside. She looked like an older version of Melissa, Amanda thought; there was no need to ask who she was. Melissa's mother and father introduced themselves anyway. Confirmation complete. Everybody sat now, except for Melissa.

"He killed him!" she screamed at the room. "He hit him!"

Melissa's mother touched her daughter's shoulder in comfort, cooing to her like her daughter was a twelve-year-old, as tears made fresh streak marks down her cheeks. Melissa's father encouraged her to sit down; she did his bidding and quietened somewhat.

When everyone was settled, Amanda suggested they start at the beginning so that she could take everything down in order. She turned to Brian Parker and asked him to start.

"Actually, it might be best to start with Melissa," he said. "She was with Callum when they had the accident. It could be related."

"'Could'!" Melissa stood and screeched the word like a banshee. "He's dead because of that man hitting him!"

"Melissa, please! Try and calm down so we can get this down in some sort of order," pleaded her mother. The room waited once again for the young woman to compose herself. When Melissa had once again settled into her chair, Amanda prodded gently.

"You were out driving? Where had you been and where were you both going?"

Melissa Ross told the story, in minute detail, of how they'd been out for a quiet drive and Callum had accidentally hit another vehicle. There had been an altercation. The traffic police had come and taken everyone's details, and then Brian Parker had picked them up and driven them home.

The man who had hit Callum was to blame, she said huffily. Amanda was to arrest him immediately.

"Do you know the man's name?" Amanda asked. Surely Melissa or Callum would have taken it for the insurance claim, as he was a witness to the accident.

"Yes. He lives along the same road where the accident happened," she said sullenly, as if she'd finally run out of steam.

Amanda's pencil was poised on her pad as she waited to jot it down.

"It's Mr Laurence Dupin."

Amanda felt her face grow pale. *Oh, shit!*

Chapter Five

The front door to Laurence Dupin's house was already wide open when he returned from his walk. A woman filled it, arms crossed. He was late back.

"I was getting worried; thought you'd fallen off a cliff. Where've you been all this time? I was about to send a search party out."

It came out in one long sentence with no real pause for breath. Everything she said came out the same way. How she managed to speak like that all the time he never knew, but after twenty years of marriage, he'd got used to her ways. And to hardly getting a word in edgeways. It was easier to keep quiet, generally, but there was no escaping her enquiry this time. And since she was blocking the doorway, if he ever wanted to see the inside of his house again, he knew he'd better speak up.

"There was an accident. I had to stop and assist."

She relaxed her arms to her side and let him through, satisfied but needing more information.

Gossip.

"Oh? What happened? Anyone hurt? I thought I heard a siren. Did you see it? Where was it exactly?"

One at a time, please.

"A car travelling too fast hit another coming out of his driveway. The chap who got hit was an old guy; he was pretty shaken up but ended up with just a head wound, nothing too serious, I expect. There was a young couple in the other car, and he was driving. Started throwing punches and I intervened." Laurence was searching for a glass in the kitchen cupboard while he babbled out what he knew, quenching her need for details. He filled it from the tap and drank it straight down, then refilled it again. He turned back to her. "Fancy lashing out at the old man when *he* was the one in the wrong. What a prick."

"Huh. The world's full of them. And trust you to get involved, on your day off, too." Her hands were back on her hips, matron-like.

"I couldn't very well leave them to it, now, could I? I was first on the scene. Anyway, it's all cleared away now."

"Yes, but you'll be pulled in for a statement, won't you? Wasting your time."

"That's hardly a hardship, now, is it?"

"Still." She grunted disapprovingly. He watched her amble out of the back door and down into the small garden out the back. 'Her' chair was placed in the shade of an old plum tree that straddled their property from their neighbour's garden. It never produced any real quantity of plums, but the green coverage was appreciated on sunny days. She picked up her *Woman's Weekly* and resumed reading. Laurence watched her from the window. He wondered when his wife had turned into an old woman. She was 45 going on 65 and had a sour spirit with it. He couldn't imagine what she'd be like when she did reach 65.

"Heaven help us," he said to no one in particular, and went in search of his book. His thoughts drifted to the woman in the car —Melissa had been her name. When she'd finally recovered herself, he couldn't help noticing she was a bit of a looker, though about half his age. In her prime. Even during the melee, he had been rather surprised to realise that his desire for a sweeter woman in his life had been on his mind. It wasn't the first time he'd contemplated finding someone a bit more appealing, but he'd stayed true to his marriage vows and never acted. Not that an opportunity had ever come his way since Lyn had staked her claim on him. He doubted anyone would want to cross her if she ever found out.

He was making himself comfortable in the lounge when his mobile phone rang. He got to his feet and scrabbled around for it; he found it lying under the pile of newspapers that were still on the sofa from before lunch. He'd yet to finish them, though the Sunday supplement was already wrapping the vegetable peelings in the compost heap at the end of the garden. He'd asked her repeatedly to use a tray for the job until he'd read it but had given up reminding her. Reading the tiny screen, he groaned.

"Some day off this is turning out to be." He swiped to accept the call.

"DI Dupin," he said flatly. "What can I do for you, Amanda?" The joys of caller ID. There was no escaping even if you wanted to.

"Sorry to bother you, sir. Are you at home, by chance?"

His left eye twitched involuntarily, something that plagued him when he got wound up. His hopes for a relaxing Sunday were diminishing fast.

"I am, yes. Is there a problem?" He knew there was, or else why would she be calling him at nearly 3 pm?

"Hopefully not, sir, but I need to pop over right away. I'll tell you more when we get there."

There was a pause as they both realised what she'd just said.

"We?" Did he detect a groan on the other end of the line? "Who is 'we'?" A moment passed before Amanda spoke; her annoyance at being caught out was audible now.

"DCI Japp will be meeting me there, sir. It's a bit of a delicate matter. So as long as you're home, please stay there and we'll be right over." It was obvious Amanda was trying to get off the line and avoid any more stupid mistakes. "See you shortly, sir."

And then she was gone, leaving Dupin staring at his phone. It was warm; there were traces of grease on the screen from his sweating temple and sticky fingers. He hadn't realised how hot he'd found himself during the strange conversation.

"What the hell can Amanda and DCI Japp want?"

"I've no idea. What does he want? And why is he calling on a Sunday, for heaven's sake? And don't tell me he's coming here? Why?"

He hadn't realised Lyn had been listening in on the other side of the doorway. He looked up at her as she continued to barrage him with questions, registering the damp, sweaty patch across her top lip. He wiped his own as if that would remove hers. The woman looked like a double-handled tea pot, with a spout to match.

"Well, I've no idea either, but he's on his way round. I guess we'll both find out soon enough." He looked down at his T-shirt front. There was a small patch of blood on it, from the old man's head, he assumed. "I'd better go and change my shirt."

What did Japp want, indeed? The only possible reason he could think of was the accident he'd just witnessed. Maybe they'd take his statement while he was at home, get it out of the way. That must be it.

But on a Sunday? Was it that important? And the DCI coming to do it?

He hoped the old man was okay.

Chapter Six

DCI Jim Japp had the same moustache as his Agatha Christie namesake, but stopped short of wearing a trilby. Having both Japp and Dupin in the same station had caused a ripple of laughter when the more well-read detectives and staff realised they now worked with famous namesakes in the same profession. Not that their surnames were commonly used, as in Dupin's case. Dupin was slyly referred to as 'Dopey' behind his back.

As for Japp, his nickname was 'Jim-lad', after the character in *Treasure Island*. He'd picked up the name when the movie had first come out and was well used to it now in his 50s. Right now, he, Dupin and DS Amanda Lacey were sat in Dupin's lounge waiting for Lyn to bring mugs of tea through, though on this warm Sunday, they all would have preferred a cold beer. Japp was attempting small talk until they could talk without fear of interruption, though Dupin would no doubt tell his wife later. Having met Lyn on several occasions, he wanted to avoid the burst dam of questions that would no doubt spew from the woman's mouth as they always did. He pitied Dupin sometimes.

When the tea finally arrived, and Lyn had got the message to leave and not to linger, DCI Japp cleared his throat and did his best to look Dupin straight in the eye as he spoke. The swirl on the green carpet underfoot was distracting.

"You're wondering, I'm sure, why we're both here on a Sunday and interrupting your time, so I'll get straight to the point," he said, then paused, choosing his words. "You'll recall the accident you attended earlier on this afternoon."

"Yes. Is that what this is about?" Dupin felt relieved, even though he'd figured the visit was likely about that—though why the DCI, he'd still no idea. Yet.

"Can you run me through what happened, exactly? From the beginning?"

Dupin looked at Amanda, then back at his DCI, and then, receiving no clue from either, started his story from the beginning as instructed, from leaving the house to witnessing the collision. Nobody said anything while he spoke, until he got to the part where he said he'd thumped the male driver because he'd tried to attack the older man. Amanda and Japp exchanged glances silently.

"What?" asked Dupin. "I was protecting the old guy; otherwise, he'd have been in a far worse state than he already was."

"And what happened after you hit Mr Callum Parker, the younger male?"

"He fell back into the grass, then nursed his ego and scrambled back up. The ambulance arrived shortly after that."

"Was he talking? Walking about?"

"Yes. Why? What's this about?"

Japp avoided Dupin's question and asked another.

"How did he seem to you?"

"Again, fine. Why?"

Japp and Amanda exchanged another glance then DCI Japp turned back to Dupin.

"Because about an hour or so later, Mr Callum Parker was found dead."

Dupin's eyes flicked rapidly from side to side as he tried to comprehend what they were telling him. Dead? How could he be dead? He'd scrambled out of the ditch, hadn't he?

"He was fine! How can the man be dead?"

Nobody spoke, and then it twigged in Dupin's head what they were getting at. "You think *I* killed him?" he said incredulously. "I was trying to keep things calm, not kill him! I was protecting the old man!" His voice had risen with his outburst, and Lyn hurried back into the room. Dupin ignored her; his mind was reeling. He was aware of Lyn's voice asking questions, but there was too much to take in without worrying about her.

"Try and calm down, Laurence," Japp was instructing him. "We don't know much at the moment, save for the statement from the woman who was with him." He looked at his notebook for clarification. "Melissa Ross says you threw a punch and knocked him over. Now, that might be true, but somewhere, somehow, along the way between the accident site and his parents' house, something happened. We know he went for a nap, and when his fiancée called in on him, he was dead. Now, at the moment, they don't know who or what you are, but they will find out. And when they do, we have to be whiter than white. Everything in this investigation will need to be by the book. All the way. Because, mark my words, they'll think it's mates looking after their mates, a cover-up, and all hell will let loose. Do you understand, DI Dupin?"

Dupin nodded, stunned. Lyn had the common sense to stay quiet in the background.

Amanda carried on where her DCI had left off. "So that means a thorough investigation, without you as part of it, I'm afraid. As of now, you're under arrest until this is sorted out. By the book, remember. A man has died."

DI Dupin stared at his boss as the man read him his rights. By the book or not, it had suddenly become a good deal more serious all of a sudden. Amanda gave him a weak smile as he sat stony-faced, trying to comprehend all that was being said.

Dead. The young man was dead. But how? Was he responsible?

He was beginning to sound like Lyn with so many questions, he chided himself; he shook his head in an effort to dislodge them.

"Do you understand, boss?" Amanda said.

"Yes."

DCI Japp stood to leave. "I'll leave you with Amanda, then, Laurence. I'm sure this is a formality, but until we know what we're looking at for sure, as I said, everything by the book." His moustache lifted at both ends over a slight smile that was probably meant to encourage. It didn't.

Laurence Dupin could think of better things to be doing than worrying about a manslaughter charge hanging over him.

"I'll see myself out," said Japp, leaving Amanda to do the necessary.

Dupin glanced at Japp's retreating back and was reminded of the Grim Reaper. He only hoped his scythe wouldn't swing his way.

Chapter Seven

Monday morning and Amanda was in the office before anyone else, a mug of steaming hot frothy coffee in one hand, a mouse in the other as she scrolled down a web page. It was the best time of the day to work without interruptions, and since Ruth had risen early for her run, Amanda had prized herself out of bed too. Once she was up, she was fine; it was the act of actually getting out from under warm covers that was the hard part. She'd been the same all her life, and at 42, she knew the struggle was something that would never leave her. The silence was broken by the sound of the coffee machine chugging in the nearby 'cupboard' kitchen, accompanied by a few choice aggravated words.

Jack Rutherford had entered the building.

She smiled to herself; it was impossible not to. They'd had the coffee machine for two years, and still it flummoxed him. Either he forgot the coffee capsule itself, making frothy milk with no caffeine, or he forgot to fill the water tank and no coffee erupted from the spout. By the sound of it, it was the former this morning—no coffee capsule.

"It needs a capsule," she shouted through.

"All right. I know," he yelled back, clearly annoyed with himself.

Amanda sipped her own and then stood to peer around the door frame.

"I can see you watching me," Jack said testily.

"Just browsing."

"Yeah, right."

"You're in early for a Monday morning. Couldn't sleep?"

"Au contraire."

Jack was taking French lessons and now had a habit of dropping odd phrases into his daily routine for practice. "Slept beautifully, thanks. If you want to watch the sunrise, you have to get up to see it."

Amanda cocked her head. "Are you taking deep spiritual lessons now as well as French?"

"Nope. But if you must know, I'm making more of an effort to fill my spare time with things other than work. Hence the lessons. And I've taken lawn bowls up again. It's called broadening one's horizons. You should try it sometime." He raised his eyebrows at her. When his mug was finally filled with coffee and milk, he asked, "What are you working on so early?"

"I'll be filling the team in soon when everyone's here, but you may as well know now. DI Dupin got into a scuffle at the scene of an accident yesterday afternoon; smacked the guy in the face, apparently. All was well when they parted ways, but not long after, the man died at his parents' home. Dupin's in custody."

"Oh, shit."

"Yeah, that's what I thought, too. Not the best position to be in. As yet, I don't think the family are aware that Dupin was an off-duty police officer, but they will find out. Apparently, Callum Parker, the young man who was driving, hit an oncoming vehicle driven by an elderly gentleman. No one was badly hurt, but Parker tried to attack the old man, saying it was his fault. Dupin was out walking, saw the accident and intervened to stop the older man getting hit. He punched him. Parker fell, but got back up and was walking and talking. He was also a bit mouthy, apparently. He'd been drinking, but was just under the limit."

"How's Dupin?"

"How you'd expect. Worried, mainly, and embarrassed he's in custody. And the shit pile that could fall down on him, as well as the station, when the press find out won't help. All in all, a torrid time ahead."

"Poor old Dopey. I wouldn't wish that lot on my worst enemy."

Amanda frowned at him. "Let's stick with his proper name, eh? Keep it all friendly. I'm sure he could use our support right now. DI Dupin to us all from now on."

Jack mock saluted, adding, "Yes, boss."

The rest of the team slowly filed in over the next half hour, and a low chatter of conversation filled the room. Tales of the weekend, what was on the telly, the cricket results. Exciting times around the Croydon region for most. Still, it was better than what Dupin now found himself in, Amanda thought grimly. She called them all to order and broke the news. The gleeful, relaxed faces quickly turned serious. While no one particularly liked or respected Dupin, they were all concerned for their colleague.

"The pathologist will know more when the autopsy is completed," she said, closing her notebook. "Any questions?"

"Who's doing the autopsy?" It was DC Raj Atwell, soon to be a DS if he ever took his sergeant's exam.

"Faye Mitchell, I believe. And right now, she's no idea who she is autopsying and why. This is just another sudden death to her. And that's on purpose, so strictly hush- hush, right? All she knows is it's her priority case first off this morning.

"Also, DCI Japp will be in attendance."

The officers looked at each other in puzzlement.

"I can see from your expressions I need to explain," she said. "The doc doesn't know, so she can't be biased in any way. DCI Japp feels he needs to witness the process for that same reason, though it's highly unusual, as you've already deduced. No doubt, the doc will wonder herself, but she won't be told until after her findings."

Heads nodded sagely, and murmurs filled the air.

"What can we do to help?" asked Raj.

"Liaise with the traffic cops who attended, see what they can tell us. Until we know what we're dealing with from the mortuary, we don't know if this death is connected to a simple traffic accident or not, but let's be prepared."

Amanda wrapped up the briefing and doled tasks out to various officers; one by one, they split off back to their desks.

Jack turned to Amanda and quietly asked, "What's our next move?"

"Well, that depends on whether Mrs Stewart made you a full English breakfast or not this morning. How strong is your stomach?"

Chapter Eight

Jack was wishing he hadn't eaten the extra sausage; the faint herb flavour repeated in his mouth each time he stifled a belch. He also wished he was outside, alone, where he could get his wind up with one long, noisy gust. And he wouldn't have to see Dr Faye Mitchell peel back the flesh of Callum Parker's chest to get to his organs. The site of human intestines was making it a real possibility that his breakfast would be returning back up his oesophagus. How anyone could perform autopsies on a daily basis he couldn't compute. But someone had to do it. Of course, people said the same about his own job—being spat at, punched and kicked, as well as witnessing the macabre and horrific things humans inflicted on each other; it wasn't a job for butterflies. He focused on a fleck of something on a nearby tile, praying his breakfast would stay put.

"Everything looks about normal so far," Dr Mitchell was saying, "but I'll know more when I look at the organs in turn." She turned to Amanda. "Tell me what happened again?"

Amanda cleared her throat; maybe she was struggling too, Jack thought.

"Callum here was in a collision," she said, "and he later threw a punch at the other driver. He missed, but a passerby stepped in, there was a scuffle and the passerby hit Callum full in the mouth. That's it."

Dr Mitchell looked at her quizzically; it was obvious she knew there was more to the story but wasn't being told.

DCI Japp took it up now, maybe to give himself something different to focus on for a moment. "The fiancée is now making a huge fuss, saying the passerby is responsible for Callum's death, and the family appear to be gathering behind her."

Again, the doctor waited, but there was nothing else forthcoming. "Let's crack on with it, then," she said briskly. "And I can tell you straight away there is no sign he was hit in the mouth, nothing here that would lead me to believe that. I've noted the few superficial abrasions down the nose and chin area, as well as the bruising lying diagonally over the right lower neck. That's from the seatbelt, I expect."

Japp looked at Amanda and Jack, but nobody spoke.

Faye caught the look but carried on; she began to take the organs out of the chest cavity. Placing each organ in turn on the scales to weigh it and examine it, she said, "His heart is slightly enlarged, and his liver is fatty. These are probably signs of significant alcohol intake. The man liked to party." She directed the photographer to take closeups for her records; the snap of the shutter was the only sound apart from their own beating hearts.

With the organs taken care of, she prepared to open the top of Callum's skull. "Hopefully the brain will tell us more," she said.

That sent DCI Japp fleeing from the room with his hand over his mouth. Jack smiled and Amanda glared at him. Faye raised her eyebrows and then returned to the task at hand.

One detective down, two more to go.

Jack and Amanda watched as Faye removed the top of the man's skull, made a few deft cuts, and took the brain out.

"The brain is full of blood. Interesting."

"How so?" asked Jack.

"I'll be able to tell you more later, Jack. You know I hate to speculate before the facts are all in. But this is interesting. I may get a colleague to look a little closer, just to be sure. He's a whiz at brain pathology."

She busied herself once more with the autopsy. A taste of herbs filled Jack's mouth again, and he swallowed hard.

"Since Mr Parker here may have suffered whiplash, I'm going to remove the neck and accompanying arteries so I can do a more detailed examination on those parts specifically. I've a feeling that this, along with the brain, holds a clue to what happened to the young man." She looked up at the two remaining detectives now and smiled; their faces were almost drained of colour. "It never gets easier for you, does it?"

"It was the brain that did for me," admitted Amanda. Jack gently nodded his agreement.

"Well, there's little for you to see now, so you may as well get some air. I'll take a closer look at the neck and see what we find, and ask for my colleague to assist with his brain. It might be tomorrow before I have anything for you, though." Faye smiled again at the almost motionless duo stood before her and urged them out. "Now, unless you want to watch me dissect in detail, go!" she said, flicking the fingers of both hands outwards as though shooing chickens off the doorstep.

They didn't need asking twice. As they fled out of the mortuary and through the corridor of offices back to reception, Jack let out a resounding belch.

"Jack!" exclaimed Amanda. "Gross!"

"Well, it's better than the alternative," he said.

As they rounded an aquarium full of tiny brightly coloured fish and stepped into the reception area, a woman at a desk screwed her face up with disgust.

"Sorry—I didn't know anyone was about," Jack offered.

"Clearly," said the woman primly.

"I'd better call DCI Japp," Amanda said as they passed back out into fresh air. She dug into her bag for her phone.

"No need. He's still right here," Jack said, pointing to the far end of the car park. As they approached, they could see Japp's colour had reappeared, though he looked tired out.

Even though it was an unspoken rule that you never ribbed your boss over something that could affect your own self, Jack went in and took the opportunity anyway; he wasn't looking for promotion at his age.

"You missed a trick in there, sir, when she took the neck out. Lots of dangly bits." Jack mimicked the loose arteries with his fingers.

"Ignore DC Rutherford, sir," Amanda said, glaring at Jack.

"I am," Japp said caustically. His face had gone pale again.

She went on, "Dr Mitchell might have something for us tomorrow. She wants a closer look at the neck and brain. Interesting, don't you think, that there was no evidence of Callum's being hit in the mouth? Has Melissa Ross got this wrong, I wonder? There was a scuff on his chin and bruising on his neck from the seatbelt, but the chin is hardly 'full on in the mouth,' as she stated. It's a swipe on the chin."

DCI Japp let out a long sigh. "Well, let's hope Dr Mitchell can fill in some gaps tomorrow. I could do with a proper night's sleep."

Chapter Nine

❦

"You don't do yourself any favours, do you, Jack?"

"What do you mean?"

Jack and Amanda were walking back to his car, having left DCI Japp looking at the view and clearing his lungs. At least his colour had returned.

"I mean teasing him, dangling your fingers pretending they're arteries—he was as green as the grass on my back lawn. Why do you do it?"

"Just for a bit of fun, and because I can. It doesn't matter to me. Promotion prospects and I parted ways many years ago. I'm not out to impress anybody."

"Well, if you want to keep your police pension and not get sacked before you retire, you might want to rein it in a little." Amanda was always the voice of reason, Mrs Sensible. Jack unlocked the car and they climbed in; the air was thick with the trapped heat from the sun. He started the engine and pumped the air-conditioning button; the fan roared like a plane engine.

Raising his voice over the noise, he said, "It's not that long ago that we didn't even have air-conditioning in cars. Do you remember that, Amanda?" Sunlight glinting off the roofs and bonnets of the other parked cars.

"I'm not as old as you are, Jack. We didn't start our cars by cranking them with a lever at the front, either."

"Now you're being cheeky," he chided. "Seriously, though, I remember what twenty or twenty-five years ago you had to manually wind the window down, never mind having air-conditioning. And my hair would blow all over the place," he said, smiling and turning her way.

She raised her eyebrows at him questioningly. "Was that during your rocker period, before you were left follically challenged?"

"Harsh."

Jack pulled out of the car park and headed back to Park Lane and the station. They fell quiet for a few moments before Amanda spoke again.

"Interesting, don't you think, that the doc said he hadn't been hit in the mouth, whereas the fiancée specifically said he *had* been hit on the mouth?"

"Maybe, but he was hit on the chin—there was evidence of that—and the chin and the mouth are not that far away. So maybe she just got it wrong in the heat of the moment."

"Maybe. She seemed surprised that the brain was filled with blood, though. That's not normal in anyone's book; even I know that," said Amanda.

Jack grunted, trying to shut out the image of Faye taking the top off Callum Parker's head. "She won't be pushed for an opinion, though; not until she's certain. There is no informal review with Dr Faye Mitchell—more's the pity."

"Keeps her from getting in trouble, I expect. Anyway, let's see what she comes back with tomorrow. And I hope it's good news for Dupin."

Traffic was building and a dirty halo of exhaust fumes surrounded the car now. Jack was glad his windows were up and the air-conditioning was finally cooling the inside of the car. He turned the fan down so he didn't have to raise his voice over it again.

"You probably wouldn't remember—it was way before your time —but there was a case many years ago of something similar to what's happening to Dopey Dupin now. It wasn't a police officer it happened to, but it was similar circumstances."

"Oh?" said Amanda.

"I'll have to get the case file out, but the guy went down for life. I thought it harsh at the time, I remember that, but it wasn't my decision; that was the judge and jury. But I often thought about that case afterwards because it seemed a bit rough. From memory, the guy was a bit of a rogue anyway, but he didn't deserve such a long sentence, not for that. I must look it up when we get back."

"Why would you bother?" asked Amanda. "What good will that do?"

"Call it curiosity, just out of interest. Bedtime reading."

"Well, if the guy did get life, I wouldn't go telling everybody else, especially Dupin. It's not going to make him or the team feel any better. The poor guy looked worried sick when I delivered the news to him yesterday, as you would, too."

"I'll keep it to myself. Like I said, idle curiosity and bedtime reading." He turned into the car park of the station pulled into an empty space beside a gleaming BMW. If the other cars parked in the yard were anything to go by, his colleagues were earning a good deal more salary than he was, he thought ruefully. Maybe he should have worked harder on that promotion when he'd still got the energy.

He followed Amanda in through the back entry and checked his watch at the same time. It wasn't far off 12 o'clock. His stomach gurgled but he wasn't entirely sure if that was the remains of the full English repeating and giving him grief or the sign of needing more. He'd wait another hour.

The cooler air indoors was welcoming.

As soon as they entered the squad room, it was obvious something was afoot. The room was almost silent except for a telephone call going on over by the window; an officer was deep in conversation, leaning back in his chair with his feet up on the ledge. He ran his fingers through his full head of hair as he spoke; Jack wondered idly if it was self-soothing. Everyone else had their heads down, like a classroom full of frightened children. Amanda was about to ask what was up when DCI Japp made his appearance behind her. She startled slightly at his firm voice.

"DS Lacey, a word please."

She gave Jack an uneasy sideways glance; he simply shrugged. She had no choice but to follow Japp through to his office.

"Shut the door," he instructed, looking at a piece of A4 in his hand. "I'll get to the point," he said. "It seems the Parkers now know that it was an off-duty policeman that hit their son, and as you can imagine, they feel we are covering something up—or about to do so. How the hell they know, how they found out so soon is a mystery, but since DI Dupin lives just down the road from the accident scene, I suspect a neighbour said something. Either way, however, they found out, and now we have to deal with it." He sighed. "I don't need to remind you that this could now become quite a circus for the team—for the whole station, in fact."

"Right," said Amanda, sounding deflated. The distraction coming from the media and from the family would now ramp up significantly. "Is there anything specifically you'd like me to do, sir?"

"I'll be calling a press conference for later on this afternoon, simply because we can't ignore them. May as well face it head on. But the rest is business as usual. This case is no different from any other just because it involves one of our own. We will investigate it with as much resource and vigour as we would any other case."

He was beginning to sound like his own press release already, Amanda thought grimly. Maybe he was practising for later.

Chapter Ten

After the official news of Callum's death had been delivered, Melissa's parents had collected her and taken her back to their home, where she'd spent the night. All plans of her future with Callum Parker were now dashed, and she had sobbed as though her heart would break. She'd drained most of her father's vodka and had finally fallen asleep on the sofa. Her father had carried her up to her old room and covered her over with her favourite quilt, which had baby rabbits on it.

Bevan Ross looked down at his daughter now and smiled slightly. Even though she was going through hell, he was silently pleased the wedding wouldn't now be going ahead. Neither he nor his wife Nicola had liked Callum Parker; he had been too inconsiderate in too many ways, and they both knew Melissa could do better. Lashing out at an old man after a car accident was typical of Callum, Bevan thought with disgust; the boy could never do wrong in his own book and had always been quick to point the finger of blame at others. They'd hoped he'd never do it to their Melissa. Now, thank god, he'd never get the chance.

Bevan and Nicola had talked about him for hours when Callum and Melissa had first got engaged, about how they both hoped it would never go through, never last. Their concerns had been raised during the winter just gone when Melissa had fallen on the icy pavement and hurt her knee badly, and Callum had thought it the funniest thing, telling his friends he was engaged to Jayne Torvill in training. Melissa had told her parents and had then silently seethed; not wanting to look like a poor sport, she had never confronted Callum—about this or any of his other "jokes." Instead, she'd put up with his selfish ways and grown accustomed to them—and, perhaps inevitably, some of that spite had rubbed off on her. Over the following months, Melissa had grown to be a precocious young woman who had wanted everything Callum Parker and his money could buy her. And that meant spending his money in style. If she was going to be his trophy wife, she'd do the best job she could, starting with doubling her cup size and getting her lips filled.

As her father looked down at his sleeping daughter now, he hardly recognised her. He left the mug of tea he'd taken up to her on the bedside cabinet, next to a stuffed pink rabbit who had seen better days. Its glass eyes stared at Bevan like something from a horror movie. He returned to join Nicola in the kitchen feeling heavy inside. He wanted only the best for Melissa, and he was sorry she was hurting inside. He hoped she'd get over her fiancé quickly.

"Still asleep. I left the mug with her," he said at Nicola's enquiring look.

"She'll be exhausted, I expect. Stress and shock will do that. And the vodka wouldn't have helped."

Bevan slid onto a bar stool and Nicola filled his mug with coffee. She sat next to him, sipping her own, and they enjoyed the easy silence. They'd both talked long after Melissa had fallen asleep the previous evening, and there really wasn't much left to say. Conscious that their daughter could appear at the door at any moment, they'd vowed not to mention his name further unless Melissa brought it up. Their thoughts were interrupted by the landline ringing.

"I'll get it," Nicola said, reaching for the handset. She looked at the caller ID and groaned. Taking a breath, she answered, trying to balance her voice somewhere between sadness and resolute cheerfulness.

"Morning." There was no point adding the 'good' part, because it wasn't a good morning for whichever Parker was on the line now.

"Yes. Morning, Nicola." It was Brian Parker. Unsurprisingly, he sounded tired; his words were slow and weak, not like his usual upbeat delivery. Nicola pressed her lips together tightly in sympathy for the man. Whatever she and Bevan had thought of Callum, they'd always found Jean and Brian to be decent people; Brian in particular was a gentle soul.

"I thought..." He cleared his throat. "I mean, *we* thought we'd see how Melissa is this morning. Did she manage to get some sleep?"

"Yes, thank you. She's still sleeping now, actually. Do you want me to give her a message when she wakes?"

"No, just wanted to check on her." Brian Parker fell silent for a moment or two, and Nicola waited patiently, feeling there was more to come.

Finally, he spoke again. "Actually, there is something else."

"Oh?"

"We had a visitor last night. Someone from near where the accident took place. I guess he lived along the way somewhere. Anyway, he found us."

"Yes?"

"Well, he knows the man who lashed out at Callum. That's what he wanted to tell us."

Nicola wasn't picking up what he was skirting around, what he was trying to say. "I'm sorry, Brian. What were they trying to tell you?" Bevan looked at her in concern and then moved closer to her, trying to listen in to the conversation.

"The man who hit Callum. He was an off-duty police officer. A detective, in fact."

"Right." Nicola still wasn't sure what he was trying to spell out to her.

"Well, that means a cover-up, wouldn't you say? Mates together, looking after their own?"

"Ah, I see what you're saying now. And you're worried."

He was like an old Morris Minor setting off from a set of traffic lights, slowly accelerating. By the time Nicola had caught up with his meaning, he was full throttle and powering on ahead.

"Damn right we're worried! They'll make it look like Callum was over the limit, crashed his car and died of his injuries. Meanwhile, their man gets to keep his job and pension, and Callum gets to lie in a coffin. Mark my words, that's how it will go! But I'll not let them get away with it!"

He was shouting down the phone now, and Nicola held the handset away from her ear. Bevan had no trouble hearing him now, and he and his wife looked at each other in concern.

Would that really happen?

Chapter Eleven

Brian Parker was shaking with rage as he replaced the handset back into its holder. It bleeped to let him know it was charging. Glancing impatiently at it, he wanted to tell it to go to hell, but what good would it do? The phone wasn't responsible for his angst; if only it were that simple, he'd crush it under his foot. He let out a loud sigh and stood stooped over, his heart racing, trying to calm his breathing. If he wasn't careful, he'd need another blood pressure tablet. Jean was hovering nearby and he sensed her wanting to say something.

"Say it, then."

"I don't need to, do I? You already know."

He stood up straight, forcing his shoulders back with a crunch. His bones and sinews sounded like twigs on a forest floor being trampled over by walkers. He needed to see the osteopath again; the stress from Callum's death was adding to his discomfort. He yawned to get some oxygen into his lungs.

"I'll get you a glass of water. Go and sit down," Jean said, putting a comforting hand on her husband's forearm. He did as she instructed and plopped himself onto the hard chair by the kitchen table. It scraped loudly over the tiled floor as it moved a couple of inches under his weight. Jean rejoined him, holding a glass for each of them.

"We should contact Bryson," he said. "He should be able to suggest who can help with this mess. We'll need more than a trust lawyer if the police start looking out for their own. They'll not be damned about the loss of our son, mark my words." He was staring at a fly that had landed on the corner of the table and was now rubbing its legs together, cleaning itself. The bristles on its body twitched as it sensed the world around it. Maybe it would pick up on the sombre mood in the kitchen. Having tasted whatever it had landed on, the fly lifted off with precision, propelling itself forward at breakneck speed for something with a body and inner engine so incredibly small. Brian watched it soar into the air and out the open back door, where it had presumably flown in from in the first place. He felt like flying away somewhere himself, somewhere he wouldn't have to deal with the shit storm that could well be ahead. There was no way they were going to accept anything but the truth, he vowed: the name of Callum Parker was not going to be buried, tainted or disrespected by dirty police officers.

"How do you think he knew?" Nicola said. "I mean, that chap who came around last night and told us? And who was he?"

Brian rubbed his chin. How indeed had he known?

"Did he leave his name or contact details?" he asked her. "Do you remember? I was in a fog last night, still am really, as I'm sure you are. It's been a hell of a twenty-four hours for us both."

Jean's chair scraped on the tiles as she stood and walked to the pin board on the fridge. If she'd written it down, it would be clipped in place; it was the only way to keep track of things. He watched his wife scan the bits and bobs held in place with tiny plastic clips, but she didn't pull anything off.

"There's nothing hung here," she said, "so that means no. It would be here if they had."

She moved to sit back at the table, and the repeat shrill sound of the chair on tile made Brian wanted to yell out. His nerves were frazzled at the ends, but there was no point upsetting Jean with his own wants and needs; she was acting like a zombie herself.

"I do have the name of the detective that came around, though," she told him. "Perhaps I can call her. Perhaps she'd know who was involved?"

It was a long shot, and Brian couldn't see it being of use, but he had no better idea. Why on earth would the police know who had come to their house and informed them the man who'd killed their son was a police officer? It didn't make any sense. A more sensible approach would be to return to the scene of the crime and knock on doors in the vicinity to find the visitor from last night.

To pacify Jean, he said, "I'll ring her, but first I'm going to get some air. I need to clear my head a little. Will you be alright on your own for an hour?" He looked at her puffy pink eyes and wished he could ease her pain, as well as his own. They'd clung to each other in grief when they'd returned home from the hospital, and he knew she also hadn't slept much. No doubt they'd both collapse and take a nap together later.

"I'll be fine. You go. You look as exhausted as I feel. It will do you good."

With a weak smile, he gathered his car keys off the work surface and headed out into the morning air. It was still cool, but the day had high hopes of being another warm one; the sun was already working on burning through the puce-coloured clouds. He'd be back home by the time it did.

It didn't take Brian Parker long to arrive at the crash site. He pulled over onto the grass verge and got out and stretched his legs. The lane was covered with a canopy of leafy overhanging branches, the sunlight sparkling through as the breeze caught them and created gaps wide enough to give an almost magical light show. On another day, he'd have appreciated Mother Nature's spectacle, but not today.

The road was cleared of debris, though there was spray marker paint still visible on the tarmac; broken glass had been swept onto the side of the road, and it glinted as the sun caught it. Whose car it had belonged to he didn't know. Maybe it was from a previous collision on another day. It didn't look much like a crime scene; simply a crash scene. Nobody had died here; there was no blue and white police tape cordoning it off. Not now, at least. He stood by the grassy ditch and listened to the wind rattling in the leaves above. Taking a deep breath, he closed his eyes. Not a religious man, Brian found himself saying a prayer anyway, even though he knew it wouldn't bring his son back. It did, however, bring fresh tears to his eyes, and he let them slip down his face unchallenged.

Then, just like the fly earlier, the bristles on his own body sensed that the world around him had changed.

Somebody was standing next to him.

Chapter Twelve

After Amanda had been taken off by DCI Japp, Jack took the opportunity to dig out the case file on the one he had been reminded of; he didn't have anything else pressing. He was entitled to a lunch hour, wasn't he? And who knew how long Amanda would be. He entered the details he knew of into the crime reporting information system, CRIS for short, and waited for it to do its thing. Since the case in question was around fifteen years ago, he didn't need to go digging into dusty archives in the bowels of London. He was thankful; he hated mice. Several cases filled the screen and he scrolled down to find the one he was after. He made himself comfortable as he browsed through the scanned documents, clicking the print icon for the interesting or useful pages. He kept one eye on the door for Amanda, or worse, Japp, reappearing.

He was about finished when he spotted Amanda entering the squad room, her cheeks flushed. He doubted she'd been having a good ol' time in the broom cupboard, so that meant one thing. She caught his eye and waved backwards with a flick of her head for Jack to follow her. He hastily grabbed a manila folder off a nearby desk, scattering its contents onto the floor as he dashed to the printer and stuffed his freshly printed bedtime reading into it, all in a roundabout way of walking over to his boss. He didn't want others knowing what he was interested in—not yet, anyway.

Amanda raised a tweezered eyebrow in question at the mess he'd created in his wake, clearly wondering what he was doing with the folder. Jack ignored it. He caught her up as she left the room. In the corridor, she took a couple of loud, deep breaths and headed towards the canteen, Jack in tow like an obedient Labrador. Eventually she'd fill him in, he knew, so he didn't bother asking what was afoot. The double doors were still swinging from someone else entering or leaving, and he caught them with his foot for Amanda. She still hadn't said anything, though her obvious temper was dissipating. He held a plastic chair out for her and she flopped down like a sack of spuds. Designer suits didn't maketh this woman. Amanda preferred functional clothing, including the Dr. Martens she wore each day, come rain or shine. You could, however, see your reflection in their gleaming, polished finish.

"Tea or coffee? And are you having lunch in here?" he asked. There was a welcoming smell of pie and chips wafting from the kitchen, and Jack hoped she'd be joining him.

"Tea, thanks, and whatever you're having."

Jack grinned and headed over to place their order, carrying back two steaming mugs of tea. Fighting irons were in a metal holder in the centre of the table, and he took out two sets of knives and forks, placing one in front of each of them.

"Thanks. Are you playing Dad?"

"Mrs Stewart is training me well," he said, and smiled.

"I can see that. She was a good buy, then, was she?"

Amanda and her partner Ruth had organised for a housekeeper when Jack had found himself in hospital with appendicitis and they'd realised he needed a little assistance in the homemaking department. He'd never remarried after his Janine had died, and he'd desperately needed the guidance of a woman's touch. Mrs Stewart was that woman now, though only on an employed basis. They did, however, go to lawn bowls together. But as Mrs Stewart was a good fifteen years older than Jack, Amanda didn't think they'd become lovebirds anytime soon. She had made Jack happier at home, though, as well as more presentable and better fed.

"I don't know how I've managed all these years, looking back. I hope she's not thinking of croaking it and leaving me for a while yet. Call me selfish, but it's a pleasure to spend time at home again. The fridge is always full of goodies, like in the movies."

Amanda had relaxed a little, and Jack figured he could broach the subject of what had been rattling her after Japp's summons.

"What's Jim-lad have to say, then? There was more steam coming from your ears than that kitchen behind me." He figured he might as well give her a nudge.

"The Parkers know about Dupin," she said. "Don't ask me who told them, but it's out there. Japp has a press conference organised."

Jack had figured as much; it would have been only a matter of time anyway. Now it was out, though earlier than expected.

"A neighbour, by chance?"

"I'd say so. Or a leak. I'd prefer the former."

"I'll find out who lives near the accident scene. It was bound to be a witness or a nosey neighbour." He made a mental note to look up the inhabitants of that stretch of road after his pie and chips. He opened the manila folder by his elbow now and flicked through the top sheets, scanning the text and reacquainting himself with the case. It had taken place some years ago. Amanda sat silently, watching.

"What's the case about, then? I'm assuming it's the one you mentioned earlier."

"It is. It goes back to my earlier days, long before you arrived on the scene. A rather different time to be a cop back then, the way we did things. Couldn't get away with it now," he said almost longingly. "Though sometimes I wish I could give the odd one a good slap or shake their bones until their teeth rattle."

When a pervert or murderer was sitting opposite you with their brief advising 'no comment,' shaking their bones was only the beginning of what you'd like to do to them. Especially if children had been hurt or lost. Holding the file up in the air, Jack announced, "This is the file of a man still inside eighteen years on. And he was in the exact same circumstances as Dopey Dupin is in now."

Their pie and chips arrived. Jack reached for the brown sauce and squirted a dollop onto the side of his plate. He picked a chip up and dunked it. "Allow me to tell you the story," he said, biting into it.

Chapter Thirteen

A little over 15 years ago

DC Jack Rutherford watched as DS Eddie Edwards threw Michael Hardesty up against the wall – for a second time. Spittle collected at the corners of Edwards' mouth as he shot accusations at the man cowering in front of him, his face clenched up tightly, eyes firmly closed. He looked to Jack like a kid who was waiting for a slap from the back of a parent's hand. Eddie had always had a short fuse, but of late had found it even harder to control his temper. He knew he needed to work at it to keep it in check, and so did his team.

Jack was going to give the man five seconds more before he stepped in himself. He counted backwards in his head from five down to one before he lurched forward to stop his sergeant from doing something he'd later regret. And to save the suspect from a bloody nose.

"You've made your point. Let the man sit back down," he ordered. Even though Eddie was his superior, he sat.

The two of them had worked together long enough for Eddie to know that Jack was usually right in situations like this. For the life of him, Jack couldn't figure out how or why Eddie had been promoted. Although he wasn't complaining about still being a DC himself, he chafed at how Eddie took advantage of his new title and regularly offloaded on his team instead of showing leadership and drive to get things done. Fortunately for Eddie, his direct boss was no different than he was: DI Will Morton preferred the racing pages and a lunchbox of ham and mustard pickle on white to putting his mind to police work. He therefore never saw the need to keep Eddie Edwards in check; why bother? Retirement loomed in the near distance for the DI, after which his successor would take over. Whoever that would be. So, for the time being anyway, Eddie was safe from being picked up and reprimanded for his behaviour; it was too much like hard work for Morton to contemplate.

Eddie sat back in his chair now, glaring at the suspect in front of him. Jack glared at Eddie in return and then interjected to give Eddie some time to calm down; he was getting nowhere with the man.

"Mr Hardesty," he started, calmly. Comfy cop to Eddie's 'in your face' cop. "Everyone knows you hit that driver. There are witnesses, and I understand you're not disputing it, either. But that poor man is now lying in the mortuary because of that thump, and that puts you in a good deal of trouble."

Michael Hardesty kept his head hung low, listening but exhausted. He'd been either in the cells or the interview room being grilled for almost 24 hours, and tiredness was catching up with him. He knew he'd be charged soon enough, and remand was not somewhere he'd want to spend the next six months. But the manslaughter charge was looking more like a murder charge, as Eddie Edwards was arguing he'd planned it.

"There is plenty of evidence pointing towards you. We've done our homework, you know," Eddie went on. "You and the victim go back a long way, and we've had you both in here for various spats in the recent months. Now he's dead and you expect us to believe that it was an accident, that it was manslaughter? Well, I'm telling you, Hardesty, you're going down for murder, and if I have my way, you'll get the maximum."

Jack watched, without saying another word; it wasn't his place. Eddie was in charge of the interview. It was his gig; he held the authority of the two of them. But that didn't mean it felt right in Jack's stomach. While it was true that Michael and the man he was now accused of killing had a long and sometimes violent history together, it was unfortunate that Michael Hardesty had now killed his arch-enemy. He'd picked a bad family to deal with.

The McAllister family had a rough and torrid reputation, and had ruled parts of London for as long as Jack could remember. The Hardestys weren't quite in the same league, but the two families allowed each other to exist as long as they didn't get too cheeky and overstep territory. It also helped that they were in slightly different lines of criminal business: the McAllisters focused on illegal gambling and money-laundering, while the Hardesty family complemented their services with pills for the clubbing scene. But the previous evening, the two men had come to blows, quite literally, when their cars had collided at a junction in the centre of Croydon.

Even though it had been nearly midnight when the crash happened, there had been plenty of eyewitnesses who could corroborate the story that Chesney McAllister had struck first, but it had been Michael Hardesty who had thrown the punch that had stopped everything. Thinking he had merely knocked the man out, Hardesty had then left the scene, leaving McAllister lying on the pavement unconscious—or so he thought. When McAllister hadn't come back round, someone had called an ambulance and he'd been taken to hospital, where he'd been pronounced dead on arrival. An hour later, the police had knocked at Hardesty's house. And that was how he'd found himself in the interview room at Croydon police station with DS Eddie Edwards and DC Jack Rutherford.

"I'm sure you realise the trouble you're already in, Hardesty, and this isn't going away," Eddie continued. "There will be an autopsy in the morning, and no doubt that will confirm what we already know. You threw the killer punch, and he was probably dead before he hit the pavement. But let me ask you this: why didn't you check for a pulse before you just walked off? Like any other decent human being would have done?"

"I thought I'd simply knocked him out, that's all. I hadn't planned on killing him, as you suggest. Why would I?" It was the longest sentence Hardesty had uttered during the repeated hours of questioning.

"Because your two families have been warring for the last ten years, to my knowledge. That's why."

"We coexisted. We each knew where the line in the sand was. We had our spats, but we worked things out. And do you not think that I would be safer if Chesney McAllister was alive rather than dead?" Hardesty's eyes were bloodshot with exhaustion, but his words made sense. To Jack, anyway. Why would he risk the shit-fest that would fall on him and his family? It didn't make sense. The McAllister brothers were hardcore—Mac and Cheese, they were affectionately called.

Jack grunted that he had a point. "Well, you're in one sticky position now, then. I wouldn't want to be in your shoes. The McAllister family have long tentacles, and those tentacles reach into all sorts of sweaty crevices, whether you're home sleeping with Barb in bed or safely bunking with your new best friend in a remand centre." Jack put air quotes around the word 'safely,' knowing full well that a remand centre was far from safe. He looked at his watch—they didn't have much time left. Jack wondered what would happen in the time they had. Could they charge him, or would they have to release him? How much evidence did they have that wasn't circumstantial? A couple of witnesses to a fight was not enough to show premeditated murder. Regardless, he wondered if maybe Hardesty was better off in the police cell downstairs for protection, because Mac McAllister would be out on the prowl looking for the killer of his brother. And when he found him ...

Eddie stood to stretch his legs for a moment. He'd also seen the time. It gave him an opportune segue.

"So, Hardesty," he said, "what would you like us to do with you? Send you home, where you can risk a grisly visit from Mac McAllister and maybe some of his other family members, or keep you here in the police cells where we can talk some more? And before you answer, I suggest you think about Barbara and Cassy and how they fit into this one."

Hardesty rested his grimy forehead on the Formica table. Jack could see that his hair was stuck to the back of his neck with sweat; there was a damp patch on his shirt between his shoulder blades. It wasn't particularly warm in the room, but Hardesty had clearly been feeling the heat nonetheless.

"I'm going to give you some time to think about what you'd like to do," Jack told him, "so it's back to your cell for you for the time being. Then, in half an hour, you can let us know what you decide." He looked across at Eddie, who nodded slightly in agreement. It wasn't up to Jack to decide, of course, but Eddie was used to his ways. Jack had more authority in his pinkie finger than Eddie had in his whole body; he just wasn't allowed to officially use it.

Jack stood and waited for Hardesty to summon some energy and get himself right. His face was flushed and clammy, his five-o'clock shadow looking more like two-day-old stubble. Eddie opened the door and the three men filed back out. As Eddie escorted Hardesty back towards the holding cells, Jack ordered the man a sandwich from the custody sergeant.

Important decisions were best made on a full stomach.

Chapter Fourteen

His feet hung over the end of the narrow mattress in the cell. Hardesty was well over six-foot against Jack's 5 foot 10 and expanding girth, and he kept himself trim working out in the gym most days; his philosophy was "a healthy mind in a healthy body." The youngsters who had taken his party pills over the years and had ended up in hospital, or worse, died, would probably disagree.

The harsh blue plastic crunched as he turned over on to his side and then, unable to find comfort on the skinny bed, turned onto his back, arms by his side, and stared straight up at the ceiling. An orange glow emanated through the tiny window at the top of the concrete wall, from the street lamp outside. He had no idea what time it was—sometime between midnight and dawn, probably. He had to give them a decision when they came knocking. There was no way he was going to put Barbara and Cassy in harm's way. They'd been there before, and it had terrified not only them but Michael himself. When it was over, he'd sworn that it would never happen again: he would keep his business interests totally separate and if anyone had beef with him, they could come for him—and only him.

But pleading guilty to murder wasn't right, either, because he hadn't done what they said he'd done; not exactly, anyway. Ches McAllister had gone down like a sack of rocks, and he hadn't hung around to check his pulse. Perhaps he should have done, but would McAllister have done the same for Michael had he knocked him out? He doubted it. And so, he'd left him lying on the pavement and walked, figuring he'd get up on his own soon enough. Alas, he hadn't.

He was exhausted. He needed a shower desperately. The police cells were no place for a good night's rest, his mind on overdrive. If he admitted it, pleaded guilty, then Barbara and Cassy would be safe—it was the only saving grace. He was a big, strong man and a businessman with a reputation, so he knew he could handle himself in prison. He'd had a taste of prison life some years before, when he was just getting his business going, and while he couldn't recommend it to anyone, he knew it was doable. He just had to make sure he stayed on the right side of the lads who were running the wings—and that didn't mean the screws.

But the prospect of 15 years to life daunted him, and he knew the cops were not going to give up easily. They'd been after him for years, though never for murder, and nothing had ever stuck. Murder wasn't his modus operandi, however: a strong word with a hard fist or a crowbar was usually enough for people to see sense if it needed dishing out.

The orange glow was getting dimmer; finally, it disappeared altogether as the timer on the street lamp outside clicked off. A dull grey seeped in now, into the walls and into his bones, like a damp fog. This was going to be his life from now on. He rubbed his arm. Cassy's name was intricately tattooed on the inside of his forearm, where it was more visible to him than anyone else. He loved his girl.

The jangle of keys on a ring out in the corridor broke into his thoughts, but he didn't stir. There was no rush. The lock was opened and the door pushed a draft of fresher air towards him as an officer approached with his breakfast tray. It was a long way from room service.

"Breakfast," the officer said, and left, locking the door behind him with a firm clunk. It could have been Prince Phillip that had delivered his food; Michael hadn't turned to look. He shifted now and looked at the tray of food on the floor—it was all the same colour. White bread, pasty cereal and white milk, all delivered on white paper plates, plus a Styrofoam cup of pale tea. He could have pissed stronger. But he knew he'd better get used to it, because prison food wasn't going to be any better.

He swung his long, lean legs off the mattress and rubbed his eyes with the heels of his hands. He rotated his neck to alleviate the cricks that had gathered during his sleepless night, then rolled his shoulders to loosen them. Finally, he got down on his hands and knees on the grimy concrete floor and cranked out twenty perfect press-ups.

Afterwards he made his way to the stainless-steel sink in the corner, which supplied cold water in short bursts if he kept his hand on the tap. There, he refreshed his face to rid his gritty eyes of what the Sandman had delivered as he'd dozed. There were no paper towels, so he dried his face as best he could on the tail end of his shirt. He could feel the sharp stubble thickening on his face.

He glanced at the tray of pasty food and picked up the tea, which was still faintly warm. He drank it down in one go to avoid it hitting his taste buds, then started on the bread. It had a dry feel to it; clearly it was meant to be toast. He forced himself to chew; he knew he'd need to keep his strength up, although he didn't feel much like eating. He prized the soft cereal down after the bread, then rinsed his mouth as best he could in the sink using his finger as a make-do toothbrush.

His teeth felt furry; his mouth tasted sour.

He turned at the sound of voices outside his cell. There was the now-familiar sound of keys, then the push of a welcome breeze as the door opened back into his space. His solicitor had arrived. Tall with long greying hair, he looked like an extra from *Lord of the Rings*; he just needed a cape and a horse. His name was Howard King; he looked ready for action in his well-cut navy suit, but his eyes were full of concern. His glasses magnified the effect.

"I wanted to meet you here rather than in an interview room. Hope you don't mind," King said by way of greeting.

Michael shrugged; it made no difference to him where they talked. Howard King sat on the edge of the bed. In the absence of a table and chairs it was the only place to sit. Michael joined him, keeping a little distance between them; he was conscious of his personal hygiene status. Michael would normally have made a joke about having a chat on a bed, but now was neither the time nor the place.

"They'll be charging you today, I'm afraid. Not the news we'd hoped for, but the Crown Prosecution Service feels they have enough evidence for a case against you. Then it's off to the Magistrates court where, because it's murder, they will no doubt commit you, the accused, in custody, to the Crown Court. It's the Judge at Crown Court that has the say on your future. I, of course, will be working on getting you bail, but murder is a serious charge, an indictable only offence and I must warn you not to get your hopes up."

Michael dipped his head in resignation. Despite having prepared himself for the worst during the night, this wasn't the news he wanted to hear.

Chapter Fifteen

Jack met Eddie coming back from the cells; he was grinning like a kid on Christmas morning. Jack had seen Hardesty's solicitor leave and knew that Hardesty had been charged. He should have felt pleased, himself—they'd been after the man for long enough—but it felt a bit like catching Al Capone on tax evasion: it wasn't quite right. While Capone had served a lesser sentence than he deserved, given the 33 deaths he'd ultimately been responsible for, Hardesty would be the reverse. Some would say his murder charge was exactly what he deserved. He had been responsible for the pain and suffering of others besides Ches McAllister, and now he was going to pay for it.

"What a result," Eddie exclaimed, pumping his fist in the air. Jack raised a weak smile. He knew that for Eddie, this meant a nice neat tick against the charge and a hearty slap on the back from higher up. For Jack, though, like the rest of Eddie's minions, it meant simply a pint of bitter at the pub later.

"And he'll be straight off to the remand centre," Eddie carried on, "the magistrate won't be letting him go home tonight, not for murder. A little less scum on the street, and another job well done."

Jack and Eddie walked back out to the fresher air of the car park, where Eddie lit a cigarette. Jack watched on, glad to be out and above the surface again. The bowels of the station felt like being in a submarine at times, and the lack of fresh circulating air made him feel unclean. Prison would be a terrible place to spend the rest of your life, he thought.

Eddie drew on the white, papery stick as though it was his last breath, and Jack watched as the smoke trickled through his nostrils. Eddie licked his lips. They looked cracked and sore and needed some Vaseline. Jack had some in his desk drawer that Janine had given him, but he wasn't going to volunteer it; he didn't want Eddie's germs transferred on to his own lips. He shuddered; Eddie did his bit on the sleeping-around front; for whatever reason, the ladies seemed to like him.

The sun came out from behind a concrete-coloured cloud, and for a few moments it was almost too bright without sunglasses on. Instinctively, both men turned their backs on the glare, making use of the shade their bodies created. Neither of them spoke, each enjoying the feeling of cleansing air wafting around their faces. It had been a long 24 hours. Two motorbikes sped past on the main road out front, weaving dangerously in and out of traffic, their engines spluttering loudly as gears changed. They sounded like phlegm clearing in a mechanical throat.

"So that's that, then," said Jack. "Magistrates next up, then off to the big house to wait it out. The McAllister family will be chuffed, but I do feel sorry for Hardesty's wife, Barbara, and their daughter Cassy. This could hit Cassy especially hard; she's a vulnerable 16-year-old now, and she's quite close to her dad. I think he had designs on her taking over one day."

"A bit of a looker, too. She'll be in hot demand in another couple of years," Eddie said, and leered.

Jack made a disgusted face and ignored him; the man had no class at all. "Aren't you a little surprised at the CPS charging him?" he said. "I didn't think there was much usable physical evidence of him planning the murder. Lots of circumstantial, but not much else. I must admit I'm wondering why; aren't you?"

"Not particularly, and quite honestly, as long as the man's going down, I couldn't really much care."

"Do you think he'll plead guilty or not?"

"If he's any sense, he'll plead guilty. It's stacked against him." Eddie sucked the last of the nicotine out of the stub of cigarette between his fingers, and then flicked it away. It landed alongside a strewn pile of other butts, and Jack watched it as it slowly smouldered, a tiny stream of smoke rising and dissipating. A butt graveyard.

"Did you know it takes near on five years for a cigarette stub to finally degrade? So, you tossing your butt is no different than you tossing your gum paper out the window." Jack turned to meet Eddie's eyes as he said the last words, waiting for a reaction.

"Pick it up, then," Eddie said, and turned to head back inside.

Jack sighed and left the butt where it was. He had a modicum of respect for his direct boss, but that didn't include picking up his rubbish. As they headed back indoors, his thoughts turned to Hardesty again. He would wait for his brief appearance before a magistrate, then would be off and out of the way—and Jack would move on to more pressing cases. Idly, he wondered who the magistrate would be and who Eddie had been dealing with at the CPS. But it didn't really matter; decisions had been made, and the legal ball was rolling. If Hardesty pleaded guilty, it would pass for sentencing and his life would carry on behind bars. If he disputed the charges and pled not guilty, he'd get his time to explain and defend himself in the Crown Court in front of a judge and twelve of his peers.

"Rather him than me," Jack said as the doors shut behind them. "On to the next case."

Chapter Sixteen

Michael sat back on his mattress. His solicitor, Howard King, hadn't seemed particularly hopeful he'd be going home mid-morning, and the prospect of life confined by grimy concrete walls was daunting. Yes, he'd done a stint some years ago, but he'd been younger then. He hadn't had a family to worry about and indeed hadn't had anyone other than himself to think about. But that was then and this was now. He rolled the scenarios, the two possible choices he had, around in his head. If he pleaded guilty, he'd never get bail, but would get a shorter sentence when the judge heard his case for saving valuable court time and costs. It would be all over and done with in the blink of an eye, but he'd be incarcerated for the next who knew how long. He'd be at least ten years older when he got out. But Barb and Cassy would be safe—until he was released at least, though after that they'd have to reassess. Maybe move away, move to another country even, somewhere warmer. Australia was a possibility, or New Zealand even.

On the other hand, if he pleaded not guilty, bail was doubtful, but he would get a trial in front of a judge and jury. Surely, they'd see there wasn't enough evidence to convict him of murder. That it had been an accident, nothing premeditated about it. He could be set free, then run off to start fresh with the two women in his life, maybe run a nice bar in the Mediterranean.

He sighed and rubbed a hand over his face. Either option was frightening—there wouldn't be a man or woman on earth who would find his situation appealing. And so, the turmoil in his head tossed about like washing in a tumble drier, bits and pieces bashing against the metal drum and falling to the bottom of it to be picked back up and tossed around again. In another hour or so, the tumble drier in his head would have to stop, and wherever the thoughts settled, that would be the decision he'd have to choose.

The now-familiar sound of a key turning in his locked door brought his attention back to the stinking room he'd spent the night in. The welcome whoosh of fresh air once again pushed into his space, and Howard King filled the doorway. His hair seemed to be even greyer than when he'd left earlier on, and his expression was even more hopeless, if anything. He did however, hold a clean shirt, a tie and a suit for Michael to change into for his appearance.

Michael stood. "Any chance of a shower and a shave?" he asked.

Howard entered the room fully, and the door closed behind him. "Afraid not. But look at it this way: you're not in a dry cell. At least you've been able to wash your hands and face."

"I'll count myself lucky, then. Do I get my shoelaces back?"

Howard produced them from his own pocket and handed them over. "We leave shortly, so get yourself changed," he said. He handed the shirt to Michael and laid the suit and tie on the mattress behind him.

"Have you come to a decision?" Howard asked. "Only it would really help me if I knew what you were going to plead," he said dryly. "I'm on your side, remember?"

Michael took off the sour shirt he'd been wearing so far, dipped it under the tap and used it as a makeshift wash cloth, wiping it under his arms and around his neck. It wasn't much, but it was all that was on offer. Fragrant hot showers were not part of the en-suite facilities in police custody cells. He tossed the sodden shirt to the floor and slipped the fresh one on; he felt better immediately.

He was conscious he still hadn't answered Howard's question, but he focused on switching his trousers over and then threaded his shoes with the retrieved laces. The tumble drier in his head was still churning.

When he'd slipped his jacket on, he stood tall and, facing his solicitor, took a deep breath before he spoke. "I'm not guilty. I didn't do this. I'm not going to say I did." He sniffed loudly, wrinkling his nose and upper lip like a boxer putting his fight face on before he entered the ring, his neck thrust forward, shoulders back. At his full stature, he could easily be a basketball player, and he towered over Howard King, who had to look up at him slightly when he spoke.

"That's all I need to know. Now, do you understand what will happen this morning?"

"Yes."

"But as I say, a murder charge means bail is unlikely. Your reputation as a party pill dealer doesn't work in your favour, I'm afraid."

"I'm a businessman."

"That might be so, but the court won't like your business model. So, I'll see you in your cell just before you're called, then again at the proceedings, and finally after the ruling. How are you feeling?"

Michael wanted to roll his eyes. What a dumb question. "Have a guess."

Howard looked slightly embarrassed and broke eye contact with his client as he banged on the cell door to be let back out. "I'll see you shortly."

Michael watched as the long grey ponytail receded and an officer entered to escort him to the van for transportation. He was suddenly nervous, and his tongue felt like it had doubled in size in his mouth, causing his breathing to catch. He tried to gulp air into his lungs as panic took over and realisation of this next step took hold. Whatever happened in the courtroom today would determine how his life would pan out. It was literally in the hands of a stranger, a man or woman who had no prior knowledge of or dealings with him, had never met Michael socially or via business, and yet they were to decide what happened to him next. He hoped they were at least educated.

The officer clipped handcuffs onto his wrists now, and Michael Hardesty was dutifully lead down a much cooler corridor towards the back door and waiting van. As he walked the couple of steps across the concrete, he tried to pause and look up at the sun, which had slid out from behind a cloud. It felt warm on his face and he closed his eyes briefly.

"You'd best get used to not seeing much of the old currant bun," the officer said snidely. "You'll be lucky if you get an hour a day where you're headed."

Chapter Seventeen

The cell walls that now surrounded Michael were custard yellow, maybe in an attempt to make them feel cheery. Whether or not that was the case, they still smelt of other people's urine. Michael wondered if the yellow was to cover up the stains or to match them, in some weird form of Feng Shui. *Eau de piss*. The banality of the custard colour took his mind off what was coming. A soggy egg sandwich and a plastic cup of water had been lunch, and he'd forced it down, not knowing when his next meal would come. Or where. While he liked to think he'd be home with Barb, Cassy and fish and chips, he wasn't expecting to be.

He sat back on yet another hard, blue-plastic-covered mattress and put his head in his hands. The loud clank of the metal door opening made him sit up abruptly as Howard King and an officer walked in.

"It's time," King said, as handcuffs were again attached to Michael's wrists. "Remember: stay quiet and calm, and let me do the talking. That's what you're paying me for." He smiled encouragingly.

Michael's face was blank. He felt like he was in a trance; if only he could wake up from it. Putting one trembling foot in front of the other, he walked out of the cell and up the long corridor to the courtroom.

King went on ahead, knowing Michael would be held back for a few minutes until his case was called. It gave him the time he needed to get into the designated courtroom and get ready. He knew Michael Hardesty's chances of being granted bail were slim, and that the Magistrate was unlikely to make an exception just for him. He had to try, though, and he knew the prosecution would strenuously oppose it. Of course they would. Murder was a serious charge.

As he trudged down the hallway, he remarked that the corridors and waiting areas of courts in every town across the land looked almost identical. While the décor differed—some modern, some old-fashioned—their occupants were of the type that could be found in any busy A&E on a Saturday night after closing time: the serial offenders, the petty-crimers and joyriders, all waiting their turn in front of an over-scheduled magistrate. The repeat offenders, those used to making court appearances, knew how the system worked and generally slumped indifferently in chairs or against the walls; those new to it sat nervously forward in their seats or paced up and down in frustration. The speeding ticketers, the weekend addicts and the other white-collar attendees tended to huddle away in quieter corners away from the riffraff to wait their turn; with their expensive briefcases and tailored suits, they stuck out like red Ferraris in a Lidl supermarket car park.

Howard King nodded towards a tall blonde woman, a barrister called Maxine Kipple whom he'd come up against more than once. She nodded back, giving him a slight smile that could have meant either that she was being coy or mocking him. He preferred the first option. He could never be certain with Maxine; she was a rather unique individual in many ways. They'd had a one-nighter six months ago, though she hadn't been back for more. He'd wondered why. Maybe he'd taken the wig thing a bit too far.

The courtroom he was heading for was up ahead, and he could see two nervous-looking women, one older, one in her teens, standing by the door—Barbara and Cassy Hardesty. Barbara spotted him first and held out her hands to him; he took them in his.

"How is he?" she asked urgently. "They won't let me see him."

"He's holding up, Mrs Hardesty."

Her eyes searched his, flickering from one to the other and back again in quick succession, her brow furrowed, tears threatening like storm clouds. Howard hated this part of his job; the grief of his clients coupled with the grief of their loved ones got to him sometimes. Whether he thought Michael was innocent or not was immaterial. His job was to defend him and get him the best outcome he could.

"Let's talk after, okay?" he said, touching her shoulder gently. She nodded, blinking back tears. He opened the door and walked inside, headed to his spot at the front table, files tucked carefully under his arm.

Fifteen minutes later, it was all over. As expected, the bench had huddled together and, after a few short bursts of whispers, committed the accused in custody to the Crown Court. Michael Hardesty would have to wait it out in another cell.

"But I'm innocent!" he'd shouted as he was led away in handcuffs, back to the cells in the bowels of the courthouse. From there, he'd be taken to his new temporary accommodation, more than likely HMP High Down. At least it was a fairly new building and a far cry from the notorious Wormwood Scrubs.

Howard closed his files, gathered his things and headed back out. He'd pop down and see Michael before he left. He knew what he'd be faced with: Michael's disappointment, changing to anger then worry. Everyone reacted the same way: the fear of getting through what was ahead of them, the worry about how they'd cope, how they'd settle in. In the court's eyes, you were technically still innocent until proven guilty, and yet Michael and others like him would now have their liberty infringed. Howard had his work cut out for him. He'd need to get the best criminal barrister Michael could afford.

Buttoning his jacket, he went in search of Maxine Kipple.

Chapter Eighteen

"And he's still inside?" Amanda asked.

"Yep. He was found guilty and is still serving now. I'd have to check when he's due for release, but it can't be far off."

"And all because he whacked someone. How did it become murder and not manslaughter, then? What was the evidence against him?" Amanda was nursing her mug of tea, though there really couldn't have been much left in the bottom.

"I never had much to do with it after they charged him that day. It was all Eddie. He liaised with the CPS. You know what's it like—charge them and move on; another crime solved. There were some threats made, and some witnesses came forward, though I wouldn't have said they were the most reliable of people. Those willing to testify for either McAllister or Hardesty back then would have been desperate or stupid."

Amanda nodded. "And you think it was rigged?"

"I had my suspicions. But Hardesty was a bad lad, and, like I say, we did things differently back then. Not a lot could have been done anyway. What does Jack know?"

Amanda smiled at that; it was Jack's turn to catch on. *Jack shit.*

"Ha, ha. Funny. True, though. He was a convenient statistic—another crime solved, another criminal off the streets." Jack thought for a moment or two before adding, "I might just pay him a visit. He's still in High Down, I think. Only around the corner."

"Why?"

"Call it curiosity, since we've been talking about him. Here's another fact for you to brighten your afternoon. Gary Glitter was an inmate there for a while. And that cricketer, the drug smuggler guy—I forget his name now."

"No point asking me. Do I look sporty?" she said, passing her hand over her torso. Sporty Spice she was not.

"Point taken. Anyway, you finished?"

Amanda nodded, and Jack stood and stacked their plates together to take to the trolley parked by the wall.

Amanda stood. "Better get some work done, I suppose, or Japp will be after my ass." She placed their mugs on the trolley next to their plates. "What happened to your mate Eddie, then?"

"Not a mate. He was a pain in the neck to work with, to be honest. Always skiving off to the pub or climbing into some poor woman's bed. It amazed me how he got away with what he did. But he left suddenly. It would be about ten years ago now, I expect. There one day, gone the next. I didn't keep in touch. He was not my favourite boss to work with."

"Is that my cue to ask who is? Or was?" she said playfully.

"If you like, O favourite boss person," he said, bowing at her with arms outstretched. It wasn't like she needed to dig for compliments; Amanda had a skin as tough as bacon rind. That was the side she showed to the outside world, anyway; she was soft as warm brie on the inside, Jack knew.

They walked together back to the squad room; the sunshine streamed in through the grimy glass doors and windows, highlighting the various rub marks and hand prints.

"We need a new window cleaner," said Jack ruefully. "We're working in a damned petri dish with all that bacteria smeared around. There'll be all sorts of crap breathing alongside us."

Amanda looked at him in surprise. Mrs Stewart's cleaning habits were rubbing off on him.

"What time is the press conference?" Jack asked.

"Around four pm. 'Jim-lad' Japp will be front and centre, and no doubt I'll get roped in alongside him."

"Lucky you. Don't forget your lipstick."

Amanda turned and raised her eyebrows at him menacingly. Jack quickly stepped off ahead to avoid a swift slap. He teased Amanda mercilessly about her looks. She was a good-looking woman but rarely spent the time to accentuate her features. On the odd occasion she did, she looked knockout. It had come in handy when she'd ventured undercover in the past.

Back at her desk, Amanda watched her friend and colleague sift through the file he'd shown her over lunch. Michael Hardesty's file was clearly intriguing him: she watched his body language as he scanned the pages, thumb and finger twiddling the left side of his moustache. His reading glasses needed updating, she mused. He lifted his chin and looked off into the distance, past his colleagues and through the window on the opposite side of the office. She could see the smear marks and streaks he'd referred to earlier. She wondered what he was thinking, what was rolling around in that exquisitely educated, fact-filled head of his. Maybe he was reminiscing about the good old days when a cop could get right up close and in the face of a suspect.

Jack's hunches and keen nose for clues often got him in trouble. But he was also often right. Maybe she'd look at the case herself.

And maybe she'd organise a window cleaner.

Chapter Nineteen

Brian Parker stood at the side of the road, staring at the spot where his son had met his killer, and wiped his eyes with the back of his hand. It felt like leather on the much thinner and finer skin of his face as he brushed the tears away.

He turned slightly at the sound of a male voice beside him.

"I can't imagine how tough this is for you and your wife," the man said solemnly.

Brian turned fully to look at him now; it was the same man who had been in their house only last night.

"How did you find me here?" he asked, surprised.

"I live nearby. I was out for a walk."

The man stared straight ahead as he spoke, not looking at Brian at all. Brian, however, kept watching the man, studying his features as he stood there quietly, like he was a statue in a stately home garden. His nose was huge and bulbous—a drinker's nose, it was called, though the condition generally hadn't much to do with drinking. Brian's father had had the same condition, and he had never touched a drop except at Christmas, christenings or funerals. Tiny red blood vessels burst under the skin, giving it a bumpy, swollen appearance. It had been ugly on his father; it was equally ugly on the man standing beside him now. He was tempted to tell the intruder to get it looked at before he got much older, but he knew he would sound cruel. Besides, Brian doubted he'd give a damn anyway; he was dishevelled and stank of ancient cigarette smoke.

"You came to my house last night. Why?"

"Thought you should know."

"You think there's a cover-up going on?"

"Oh, undoubtedly. Best you're aware so you can do something about it." The man still hadn't turned to face Brian yet; he seemed to be finding the hedgerow across the road of great interest.

"May I ask why you think they'll cover up my son's death? I'm sure there are good coppers on the force these days."

"Some, yes, I grant you. Not like the old days." He smirked at the hedge. "I would know, I guess."

"Oh?" enquired Brian. "Did you have dealings with a bad one back then?"

"You could say that, yes. More than one, actually."

"What's your interest in this, can I ask?"

"History. I'll leave it at that."

The man began to walk back towards the row of houses further along the lane. Brian stood watching as the man faded into the distance and then rounded the bend. It was quiet once again, and Brian sat down on the grassy bank for a while to lament his lost son. He had fallen into the ditch only a few feet away, then got back up and called for a lift home.

And died.

"What happened to you, son?" Brian asked the breeze. "You were fine when you arrived home." He dipped his head and let the tears roll away down his cheeks again. When the natural flow eased, he wondered again about the man and his motive. He silently reprimanded himself for not asking the man's name or getting a telephone number. But he knew he must live nearby; he was on foot, after all, and had said as much. Perhaps he should try and catch him up, get his card, find out who he was. He struggled to his feet and hurried back to his car. He could drive down the lane after the man; he'd soon catch him up.

He climbed inside, pulled the door closed and started the engine, lowering the driver's window to feel the warm air on his face. Winter would be along soon enough; best to enjoy the summer warmth while it lasted. His Jag cruised around the corner, the dappled effect of the sun through the trees dancing on the car bonnet and turning the silver paint almost a deep moss. There was nobody about. Brian carried on, slowly, watching front pathways for the man walking to his door, but there was nothing. Curious, he thought. The man couldn't have got very far on foot in this short time, and there were no other houses on the stretch before the few in front of him now.

He carried on; maybe the man had run on ahead, though he'd been wearing sandals and shorts, not exactly running attire. There was still no sign of him, so Brian pulled in to the side and prepared to do a three-point turn and head home. Jean would be disappointed he'd missed the opportunity to get the man's details; he knew she'd be as curious as he was about why the man was involving himself. Jean was the one with conspiracy theories in her head, though; she had her theories about Princess Diana's death, about the missing airplane with hundreds of people on board, and of course she had her answers to them all.

"I doubt you'll find the answer to this one," he said gloomily as he headed for home.

Chapter Twenty

❦

DCI Japp looked like he had a broom handle wedged up his backside. In immaculate police uniform, buttons gleaming in the afternoon sunshine, he stood on the steps of the station and addressed the nation via the cameras and microphones that were set up before him. Past President Obama would have been proud of his poise and delivery. Jack watched on from the sidelines, keeping cool in the shade of the building as his boss tried not to melt in the heat. The thick fabric of uniform dress was not the most pleasant thing to wear during the summer months, and Jack was glad he didn't have to suffer it.

"Let me make myself crystal clear," Japp boomed to the journalists gathered. "As with every case, we do our utmost to get to the truth. Simply because an off-duty officer has found himself involved does not mean anything will change. Every case gets thoroughly investigated."

"What do you say to those who are crying 'cover-up,' Detective?" It was Dan Smart from *The Courier*, a skinny, nervous-looking man whom Jack knew to have particularly sweaty hands. Even on a warm day like today, Smart kept his sleeves long; his mousy brown hair, which needed washing and styling, hung limply on his collar.

He held a microphone with a smartphone attached to it in the air. "Readers have a right to know."

Jack grimaced at the cliché; why did journalists always haul out the public's right to know? What good did it do? "Ask a proper question, would you?" he mumbled under his breath.

Japp, also clearly annoyed by Smart's statement, raised both hands slightly as if pacifying a large, unruly crowd. "Let me assure you, there is not and never will be a cover-up. The officer involved is cooperating fully, and we are in the process of investigating this terrible event. I am not able to tell you any more at this time, as the investigation is ongoing."

"The Parkers say they'll sue. What do you say to that?" Dan tried his luck again. His whole body seemed to shake as he shouted his question from near the back of the crowd.

"That is up to the Parkers. We'll know a good deal more when the autopsy results are all back and we have the facts to work with. I really don't have much else to say until then."

A barrage of questions flew towards Japp now; he stood stunned for a moment, looking like he'd been slapped. The gathered press were not ready to leave with the little they had. Silvery microphone heads waved erratically in the air like magpies. Jack tittered quietly to himself as he unwrapped a Werther's Original and slipped it into his mouth, sucking on it loudly. The crowd in front jostled, and again Japp did his best to quiet the chatter with his hands.

"Please, one at a time." He pointed to a local female journalist who had a TV cameraman with her. Her bright red lips had caught his attention, though he wasn't sure which channel she was from. He rarely saw anything other than the 10 o'clock news. The lens swung towards the woman as she asked her question.

"Who leaked DI Dupin's name to the family? Did it come from inside? Wasn't he a popular man, Chief Inspector?" The camera swung back towards Japp now, almost hitting another young reporter in the side of his head. Jack winced as he watched and sucked on his caramel.

"We are unsure at this time. Again, it's part of the investigation.

DI Dupin is a popular man." Japp nodded to another reporter, avoiding eye contact with the red-lipped woman and moving swiftly on. "Last question. Yes?"

"DI Dupin is in custody currently. Surely, you'll be sending Internal Affairs in, won't you?"

Japp tugged uneasily on his collar. He needed to end this, to get back into the safety of the building behind him. Sweat was beading on his brow, not just from the sun but from the questions he'd rather not answer.

"That's all I can say for now. We will, of course, update you when we have more information..."

The crowd shouted last-minute questions over his words as he turned to go back inside. Realising the DCI wasn't going to answer any more, however, they began to stow their notebooks and microphones away with a chorus of unsatisfied rumblings. They looked like disappointed concert-goers, Jack thought. They'd driven all the way to see their band and they hadn't played the hit song they'd wanted so desperately to hear. Jack swallowed down the last of his caramel and smiled to himself, folding in through the front doors a few steps behind Japp. Just enough to keep out of earshot and out of his sight.

Watching the whole affair was another man, an ever-present cigarette burning between his cracked lips. He looked like an older version of the nervous young journalist; he was almost 50, not far in years from Jack. Had Jack lingered long enough after the journalistic vultures had packed up and left, he might have noticed him. He was skin and bones now; his face was older but largely unchanged, aside from the hideous bulbous nose. His hair was still mousy and now sported salty streaks courtesy of Mother Nature. He smiled to himself now; he'd fancied a spot of afternoon entertainment, and he hadn't been disappointed. DCI Japp had looked hot and uncomfortable, particularly when questioned about Dupin being arrested.

He sipped from his ever-present hip flask and then slipped quietly away.

Chapter Twenty-One

The early evening sun was still warm as DS Amanda Lacey headed home, windows down, enjoying the rush of air on her face. Traffic was moving for a change, and the light breeze had worked wonders in clearing off the lingering exhaust fumes. Public transport was a godsend, and environmentally friendly, of course, but the black plumes of diesel exhaust from the buses made her gag.

However, it was a necessary component of London life.

Take away the Tubes and buses, and Greater London would grind to a standstill. It was home to nearly 9 million people, Croydon housing 400,000 of them all on its own. Unless scooters were made legal and then weatherproofed with neat little plastic covers like mobility scooters, what was the alternative for getting from A to B? Amanda coughed as a bus pulled out in front of her, as if to prove a point. She wound her window up and turned the air con on, something she detested doing. The temperature was either freezing or stifling hot, without a great deal of satisfaction in between.

"Thanks, Mr Bus," she said sarcastically, wafting her hand in front of her face. The air cooled dramatically within a couple of minutes, and she went back to readjusting the fan speed and temperature to find the sweet spot. By the time she'd arrive home, it would be about right.

Her car filled with Ruth's allocated ringtone now, the familiar bing-bong opening bars of Ed Sheeran's "Shape of You." She smiled as she always did; the song was perfect for Ruth. She had one for Jack too, ELO's "Mr Blue Sky"—his thinking song, he called it. She also had ones for Dupin and Japp, though she knew she'd be in trouble if either one was in her space when the other rang. Disney's "Dopey" was the obvious choice for Dupin, while "Drunken Sailor" was what she used for Japp.

"Hey," Ruth's voice cooed over the speakers. "Are you on your way back or still fighting criminals with your bare hands?"

"They're all tied up with rope and sitting in a cell back at the station. The streets are clear for the next few hours. What do you need?"

"Pi-zza!" Ruth said in a loud singsong voice.

Ruth was definitely the more youthful of the two, although not by much. A talented businesswoman running her own tech company, she enjoyed her down time just as much as her working day. Pizza or crispy pork balls from Wong's were her favourite foods, either to celebrate a successful day or provide comfort when major sustenance or a cheer-up were required. She never worried about what she ate, knowing she'd run it off again the following morning.

Since Ruth had squealed the word "pizza" like a ten-year-old just now, Amanda knew it had to be the successful day option.

"Good day?"

"You bet! I might even open a bottle of wine."

"Eh? On a school night?"

"Why not? Big contracts should be celebrated, and that's what I'm going to do."

"Pepperoni to go with it, then?"

"With extra cheese."

"Must have been a good deal." Amanda smiled. Ruth had been

worrying about getting this contract and hadn't been her normal chirpy self while the details were pored over and agreed. Thankfully, it sounded like normal service had resumed. "Well, I'm glad it's all worked out for you. Extra cheese it is. I'll stop and get it. Where are you?"

"Home. Just walked in and thought 'I fancy pizza.'"

"Great—then I shall provide. See you shortly. Ciao." Amanda rang off and altered her course to the nearby pizza place. She looked forward to relaxing with Ruth tonight; she knew Ruth had been preoccupied lately, not only with the deal but with her father's move to a new flat closer to London. After Madeline had gone, it had made sense for him to downsize a bit, but they both knew it was going to take some getting used to. Now, though, his commute would be halved, the maintenance on his home would be negligible, and his social life might just get a boost. He'd joined a tennis club, and he'd been out for a drink with a woman other than his Maddie. Amanda knew he'd felt a bit weird about it, of course, but a widower had to start somewhere. And drinks didn't have to mean sex, something else Ruth had had a chat with him about. She'd mused about it with Amanda later—"It's usually the dad telling the offspring about the birds and the bees, not the other way around!" To the best of their knowledge, Ruth's dad was still a one-woman man, certainly within the last thirty-odd years. Before that, though, Gordon Simpson had been like any other regular hot-blooded single male, and Ruth had been the result, conceived up a Croydon nightclub toilet wall. Ruth quipped that it made her feel special—at least she hadn't been washed down the loo.

Amanda pulled up outside Peri Pizza. The aroma drifted her way as she stepped out of the car, a good deal more pleasant than the black bus fumes. Hot garlic butter hung in the air, and the side street smelled more like Florence than Croydon. A queue had formed out on to the pavement; it seemed others had the same idea on a nice evening. Amanda wondered if they were celebrating too. She joined the rear of the line and waited her turn, surfing through her phone to occupy her mind and idle away the time.

She didn't hear her name being called at first, but something or someone caught her attention and she finally looked up and refocused, her eyes adjusting after the silvery glare of the tiny screen. An older woman stood before her and was smiling straight at her. She had a pleasant face, though the wrinkles and laugh-lines around her eyes could have held a pencil in place. Her expertly streaked greying hair in a neat bob style told Amanda she was well into her 50s, and she looked vaguely familiar. Whoever the woman was, she knew Amanda. When she spoke, her voice was like whiskey-coated ice cubes—smooth and cool, but with an edge.

"DS Lacey, isn't it?" She held her hand out. Amanda took it politely and the two women shook briefly. The woman had a powerful grip, and she hung onto Amanda's hand for a moment longer than she was accustomed to.

"Yes. Hello."

"I'm a friend of Jack's," the woman said. "Vivian. I met you once when you worked on a case. You were investigating the death of my friend James Peterson, the book club fellow who died a couple of years ago." She waited for Amanda to remember the case and when it registered in her eyes, she carried on. "How is Jack? I've not seen him for a long time." The woman was still smiling; Amanda found it infectious and smiled along with her at the mention of their mutual friend.

"Oh, he's still the same Jack. Loves his bacon sandwiches and his ELO. Not much changes there. I'll tell him we bumped into each other; he'll be pleased, I'm sure."

"Yes, please do. Tell him it would be nice to see him again, too; he knows where to find me." Vivian flashed expensive dentistry and moved off slightly. "Nice to see you again!" she called lightly as she carried on past, on her way home most likely. Amanda waved back cheerfully.

So, Jack had a woman after him? She smiled as the queue moved forward.

Chapter Twenty-Two

Ruth and Amanda had been together for a couple of years but still retained a house each. They had thought long and hard about whether to combine their resources, sell both properties and buy somewhere new, somewhere between them, somewhere they could both enjoy from scratch and maybe even raise a family in the future. But it hadn't materialised yet. While neither of them had any conscious intention of living in separate homes, they naturally referred to Ruth's place as home and the house that they rented out as Amanda's place. Anybody listening to them would think they weren't married at all, that they were two separate girlfriends living in separate houses.

So, when Ruth's father's place had come on the market, Ruth had been keen to buy it. Amanda, not so much. It was just a bit too far out of town, for one thing, and if they were going to spend over £500,000 on a property, she wanted to choose from what was on offer in a more suitable area and not just move into something that had an emotional attachment. Since Ruth had only ever lived in the house as a torturous teenager for a handful of years, she wasn't sure quite where the 'attachment' bit came from, apart from maybe some latter memories of her stepmother, Madeline, when she'd been alive. They had just been getting used to one another, and Ruth had found herself actually quite liking the woman, when Madeline had been killed.

The bottle of red was almost polished off and the pizza box was empty. Amanda and Ruth sat in garden chairs watching birds grab at the remaining pizza crust that Ruth had tossed across the tiled patio. As one starling managed to pick a piece up, another one muscled in. They squabbled for a bit until they eventually managed to break it into a couple of pieces, one for each. More starlings and couple of sparrows had gathered on the sidelines now, perched upon the wooden fence that separated the property from the neighbours' garden next door, each waiting for its turn but not daring to dive in.

Ruth drained the last of the red wine from her glass and slithered down in her chair with her face directed up at the setting sun, which was all but disappearing over the fence at the bottom of the garden. She loved the warmth of summer; who didn't? Amanda picked up the bottle and examined the contents; there were a couple of inches left in the bottom, so she topped Ruth's glass up. She'd had enough herself and didn't want a banging headache in the morning. Since Ruth was celebrating, it belonged to her. Picking up the pizza box and trying to fold it in half, she left Ruth soaking up the last of the day's rays.

"What time have we got to be at your dad's tomorrow?" Amanda asked as she moved away towards the house.

"Straight from work, so any time after six," Ruth called. "Will you be able to make it?"

"I'm hoping so. We're not flat tack at the moment, though with Dupin out of the picture we're a man down, but it shouldn't be a problem. I'm guessing I'll meet you straight there?" she called from the kitchen, only just in earshot.

"Yes, there's no point me coming all the way back here to go back into town again. We can come home together."

Amanda returned and grabbed the empty bottle and her glass and went back into the kitchen to load the dishwasher and turn the kettle on. If Ruth was going to avoid a headache in the morning, she needed to dilute the alcohol.

"I can't believe he's been there a month already," Ruth said when Amanda returned to the garden. "He seems happy enough, so I guess it was the right move for him in the end."

Amanda sat back down at the table and looked across at her. "You know, just because we didn't buy your dad's old place doesn't mean that we can't still find a place between us. I also know that our setup is not quite the norm for most people, but it works for us, and it just kind of makes sense. We've got an income coming in with my old place rented out, and your place here is that bit bigger with a nicer garden. But we can still move. You just need to tell me —just say the word."

"No, it doesn't matter now, and as you say, what we've got here makes sense to us. That's all that's important. I guess I was being a bit sentimental with Dad's old place." She sighed. "I was just getting to like Madeline when she ... when she died." She was quiet for a moment. "Anyhow, it's in the past now. Somebody else lives in their old house, and we're here."

Amanda leaned across and gave Ruth's hand a squeeze.

"I'll go and bring the tea out; it won't be long before it's dark." She stood to go back to the kitchen, feeling strangely ill at ease. Inside, she leaned against the counter, thinking, as she waited for the kettle to boil. Maybe she was missing something; maybe Ruth really had started to get on with Madeline and her father after all the years they'd been separated. Maybe it had all hit her harder than Amanda had realised.

She grabbed the biscuit tin and put the mugs on a tray and took it all out to the patio. The sun was almost down now; there was just a bit of twilight left. The starlings were chirping sleepily amongst themselves, looking for beds for the night in the surrounding trees and bushes. In the quietness of the little garden, she thought, they could have been in any tranquil part of England. Unless Ruth really did want to move to a bigger place, their unconventional ways would do for Amanda. The spot was ideal.

Chapter Twenty-Three

Amanda was glad she'd drunk water during the night; it was a shame Ruth hadn't. She took a mug of tea up to her and sat on the edge of the bed. Ruth rubbed her temples, wincing. Her discomfort was obvious. The wine on its own would have been okay, but the trouble was the vodkas Ruth had later admitted to shooting back at work with the team just before she'd left.

Amanda looked across the room at her now and said, "Vodka, eh? That would explain it. I hadn't realised you'd started drinking before you got home; more fool you." She smiled. "They say don't mix the grape and the grain. Sounds like you're going to suffer," she said teasingly.

Ruth looked at her and said, "ha, ha" with as much sarcasm as she could muster with a stonking headache.

"I'll go and get you some paracetamol," Amanda offered, and went back downstairs.

It was going to be another beautiful day, and Amanda hoped the weather would last for Ruth's father's get-together later on. One thing you could always rely on with the English weather was its unreliability. Nice now didn't mean it would stay nice later. And the weather apps weren't much use in terms of accuracy, either, making predictions futile. She took two white pills and a glass of water back up to Ruth, who was sitting up in bed with her eyes closed. She passed them over and watched Ruth slip them into her mouth and drink; afterwards, she lay back and closed her eyes again.

"You'll feel better when you get up and have got something in your stomach," she said cheerily. Ruth grimaced at the thought of food, but knew Amanda was right. She wasn't much of a drinker—they only tended to share a bottle of wine over the weekend—but the celebration had called for it. And she'd imbibed. Heartily, it appeared.

"Right, I'm headed for the shower. I've got things to do, and you're not normally sat here at this hour. I take it you're not going for a run this morning?"

Ruth opened one eye and gave Amanda a 'You reckon?' look.

Amanda laughed and headed into the shower. As the hot water ran over her, she smiled to herself about both their inabilities to get rip-roaring drunk. Slightly merry was Amanda's limit and while Ruth could drink a little more, she suffered for it the next day—as she was right now.

She rough-dried her short blonde hair, rubbed some gel through it to separate the strands, applied a light covering of make-up and went through to put her work suit on. Amanda wore pretty much the same outfit every day, though with a different shirt; it was her own self-imposed uniform. She made too many decisions daily to need to worry about what to wear each morning; since it worked for Christian Grey, with his array of grey suits and white shirts, it would work for her. She pulled on her Docs and was almost ready. Downstairs, she filled a bowl with muesli and sat down to eat it. She was almost finished when Ruth entered, looking a tad more human than she had half an hour earlier.

"Are you feeling better yet?" Amanda asked.

"My headache is starting to dwindle; I'll be fine soon."

Amanda watched as Ruth filled a bowl with muesli and sat looking at it, willing herself to eat it. She was noticeably quieter this morning, but that was probably the headache. Amanda didn't push any conversation; they rarely ate breakfast together anyway. She stood and carried her bowl to the sink, rinsed it and placed it in the dishwasher. She pecked Ruth on the cheek and grabbed her bag. "I'll call you later, see how you're holding up."

"Ha ha," Ruth said. She still hadn't picked her spoon up and taken a mouthful.

"I'll speak to you later. Have a good one," she called. Amanda was off.

While it was still early, she was leaving later than she normally did. Traffic was starting to build; buses resumed choking out black fumes. Croydon was waking up and going to work. Since it was a clear morning, a few local commuters walked, backpacks slung across their shoulders.

The electric gate at the rear of the station slid back and she pulled into the staff car park. There were already a handful of cars parked up, some from the night shift. Jack's wasn't one of them. She entered the building through the rear entrance and went straight to the coffee cupboard for her morning fix. Tea was her preferred first drink of the day, but as soon as she got into work, it was coffee she craved. The machine chugged into action, sending little pockets of steam into the air as it heated the milk. She dropped her bag on her desk as she passed it and took her mug across to the window to watch the world go by while it was still quiet. Even on a sunny day, Croydon was a town like any other concrete mass. There was nothing particularly nice or particularly nasty; it was a nondescript regular concrete town, with regular people, regular crimes and regular everything else. You could have put the whole town up in the north of England and it wouldn't have looked out of place. Double lines of traffic ferried folks to destinations all over the country.

She focused on a red car below and wondered about its occupants, where they were headed, what their life was like, where they'd been. What was in store for them today? Crime hit the innocent as well as the guilty, and when those innocent folks got caught up in something out of their control, it could be a treacherous time. There was nothing more disconcerting than finding yourself explaining where you were and why you had gone there just because somebody had been murdered or kidnapped or gone missing. If you didn't have an explanation or an alibi, your whole life could be turned upside down. You almost needed to provide one each and every day just in case, and being at home with your loved one was not enough. It happened all the time. She picked out a white van further down the road and wondered the same. Was it legitimate? Was the driver up to no good? Where were they going? She'd never know.

A noise behind her brought her back to the present. It was Raj.

"Morning, Amanda," he said brightly, as always. Raj never seemed to be in a bad mood, which was just one reason why everybody liked him.

"Morning, Raj," she said, turning to face him fully. He always looked smart, and today was no different. Slim and fit, he wore a dark navy suit with a pale blue shirt and his black hair had been gelled back neatly into place. He was a good-looking man, though not Amanda's type, obviously, and he was popular with everyone.

"We might get some news on the autopsy today," he said. "I know everybody's concerned about DI Dupin, and I suspect he'll be relieved at some good news."

"Good news?" Amanda enquired.

"Well, yes. Dupin didn't kill that guy on purpose. It was a freak accident; something must have gone on and I hope the autopsy will show it. Then we can all get back to normal, and Dupin can come back to work."

"I certainly hope so; it can't be easy having that hanging over your head. I'll call Faye later this morning if she hasn't called me. I know she was waiting for some specialist to take a look at some aspects of the autopsy, so that's what's taking the time."

"Well, fingers crossed," Raj said.

And she watched as he walked towards the coffee cupboard for his own morning caffeine fix.

His shoes were almost as shiny as her own.

Chapter Twenty-Four

By the time Amanda had finished her coffee, several other officers had filed in and a gentle hum of conversation filled the room. It was the usual stuff: what had been on the telly last night, what had happened down the pub or banter over the sports match. Did men talk about anything else? She could hear Jack coming through the door, reciting French lines from his learning app. Why he had picked French she wasn't entirely sure. She'd have to ask him.

"Bonjour, Madame," he said with gusto as he reached Amanda's desk. He just needed a beret on his head, she thought, smiling inwardly.

"Ah, bonjour, Monsieur."

"As-tu bien dormi? J'ai bien dormi."

Amanda looked at him blankly.

"That's as far as my French goes, Jack. School was a long time ago, and there's not much call for it around here. Now, Polish or Croatian would be a different matter."

"I asked if you slept well. I slept well." He took out his earbuds.

"Well, that's good to know, and yes, I did, thanks."

He perched on the corner of her desk, one leg swinging. "Tres bien." He smiled and looked like he was about to add to it, but Amanda cut him off.

"I know what that means. Why are you learning French anyway? What's it for?"

"Oh, I plan to go one day. I've never been. I'm quite partial to a croissant occasionally, or a spot of art gallery mooching. I'm not all about bacon sandwiches, you know."

Amanda smirked. "You could have fooled me."

"Well, I'm off to make a café au lait. Need a refill?" Amanda raised her eyebrows at him, knowing full well that café au lait would never materialise. It would be something coffee-coloured, but who knew what. Jack's coffee attempts were random at best.

"I'm good, thanks," she said. She watched him disappear into the coffee cupboard and waited for the cursing to start. Today must have been a good day, though, because all she could hear was the *putt, putt, putt* of the coffee machine and the next thing she knew, Jack was back hovering around her desk, coffee in hand. Mission accomplished.

"So, I did a bit of bedtime reading last night. I took the file home, the one I showed you about Michael Hardesty." He sipped, white foam sticking in his moustache. He must have felt it because he rubbed it away with the back of his hand.

"What did you learn?"

"I didn't learn much, actually, which is the point. Wasn't anything in there that I didn't already know about, but it was good to jog my memory. But something is nibbling away at my gut. Something isn't quite right. Those witnesses, for one: they sounded a bit convenient."

"What do you mean, convenient? There were witnesses at the scene, I assume?"

"Yes, but the McAllister family were well-connected and I can't help thinking that they are behind this somehow. Same with the prosecution solicitor. I don't know, but I'm going to have another look. And it would be better if I could do it with your say- so, boss lady." He wiggled his eyebrows comically at her. They needed a trim.

"That's not really down to me. You know that, Jack. In Dupin's absence 'Jim-lad' is looking after these things temporarily, and I don't want to have to ask him for anything unless I really have to. So, it's up to you. I'll turn a blind eye, but we haven't officially got permission for time to be spent on a case that was put to bed years ago."

Jack sipped his drink, staring off somewhere over Amanda's shoulder.

"I can't see it hurting, though," Amanda went on. "There's not too much going on at the moment. Have you got something in mind?"

"I thought I might go over to the prison and see Hardesty. He's been there a good few years now. Did you see the press conference last night, with Japp?"

"I caught the last minute or two on the news, but other than that, no. Did you?"

"I watched from the sidelines out the front, watched him squirm. Those reporters don't take any prisoners, and I can't say he filled me with confidence. But that's Japp. He looked well-polished in his uniform finery."

Amanda sat back in her chair and tapped her pen against her bottom lip. "Right. If he asks where you are, I'll cover for you. What time are you headed out?"

"I may as well go first off when I finish my coffee. It's only around the corner. They probably won't let me see him without an official appointment, anyway, though I may as well try. I have a cunning plan."

"Well, good luck with that. Oh, and before I forget, I met a woman last night outside the pizza shop—"

Jack's eyes lit up in mock horror. "Don't tell me Ruth and you have had an argument and you're already on the lookout? Though I have to say, it's a strange place to pick up someone."

Amanda waved her hand like she was batting a fly and said,

"Don't be stupid. No, I met a woman who knows you, silly. She said she was a friend of yours from way back and a friend of that man from the book club who died a couple of years ago, Peterson. She said her name was Vivian."

Jack stood open-mouthed.

"Funny, I've never heard you mention a 'Vivian' in all the years I've known you."

Amanda couldn't resist putting it out there and watching for his reaction. She got one. Jack's cheeks flushed crimson. Amanda leaned forward. "Gotcha," she said with a grin. "You've got to tell me more now. Who is Vivian? She seemed really nice. So come on, then. Tell me. Who is she?"

"Like the lady said, we were friends," he said defensively.

"*Were* friends? She didn't say you 'were' friends."

"But I haven't seen her for a long time, so we are more acquaintances now, I guess. In fact, the last time I saw her was after Peterson's death. I interviewed her." He drained the last of his coffee. "Well, I've got work to do. I'm going to see if I can get in and see Hardesty and leave you to your fantastical mind. I'll be on my mobile if you need me."

Amanda sniggered under her breath that she had riled him up a bit about a woman. When he was well out of earshot, she mumbled to herself, "That was a bit mean, Amanda. The guy is allowed a personal life." She stood and stretched and headed back to the coffee cupboard for a refill. From the doorway she could see Jack gathering the manila folder and its contents again before he headed back out to his car.

She frowned. If Vivian had been interviewed during the Peterson case, she'd be on file.

"Worth taking a look," she mumbled to herself. "Out of nosey curiosity."

Chapter Twenty-Five

The prison was situated on the site of the former Banstead Psychiatric Hospital. The ancient, crumbling building had been bulldozed and a modern prison built in its place; it housed all kinds of inmates as well as remand prisoners. The last time Jack had met with Michael Hardesty was when he'd been on remand 15 years ago. Jack navigated his car over the mini-roundabout and headed for the main reception block.

It was a modern-looking concrete building from the outside; it could have been a new hospital but for the enormous chocolate-coloured main doors that reached almost two stories high. They were a bit of a giveaway that something a tad more sinister than a children's ward was behind them. Jack parked his car and made his way to the visitor entrance, a separate building opposite that looked like a cheap motorway motel. He hadn't taken Amanda's advice and called first, but he was hoping that as a serving police officer it wouldn't be an issue and they'd see fit to let him in. He glanced at the plastic Sainsbury's bag in his hand.

He approached the reception desk and a huge, unsmiling man in uniform looked up from one of his many screens. He looked like he belonged to a beanstalk somewhere, Jack thought. He smiled as pleasantly as he could manage. He'd dealt with many prison staff in his time and one thing they all lacked was a sense of humour. It must be a prerequisite at the interview stage that they didn't smile a great deal. The only jokers who operated between these walls were the inmates.

As usual, the officer's smile didn't appear to be working at all, though he did say "Good morning." Jack placed the bag on the counter, and the officer glared at it disapprovingly.

"DC Jack Rutherford," Jack said firmly. "I'm hoping that Michael Hardesty will agree to see me this morning." The officer raised an eyebrow in question and Jack answered before the man opened his mouth. "No, I haven't made an appointment and since I was not far away, I thought I would drop in on the off chance." He opened his carrier bag and pulled out a tin of assorted luxury chocolate biscuits. "But I haven't come empty-handed. I dropped in to Sainsbury's and picked up a little something for you and the boys so your cuppa isn't so wet this morning." He slipped the tin towards the man, who looked down at it with interest. On the lid were images of various delicious-looking chocolate biscuits, and Jack could see it was going to do the trick. The man grunted his approval and pulled the tin closer to his ample stomach.

"So, what do you say?" said Jack. "While you're dunking those with your pals in the tea room, might I have a chat with Mr Hardesty? It's been a good few years since I was last in here." He looked around the reception area. "You've done it up a bit." The man raised his eyebrow questioningly and again Jack wondered if he might actually speak. He pre-empted him just in case. "I'll just wait over here," he said. "If you wouldn't mind telling Mr Hardesty I'm here?" The officer pulled the tin of biscuits closer to himself. Jack wondered if his pals would in fact see any of those chocolate biscuits at all. It didn't much matter, as long as it granted Jack entrance.

"I'll see what I can do," the guard said, running his hand over his heavily Brylcreemed head. He picked up the telephone and turned his back to Jack, who could see white flakes across the tops of his mountainous shoulders. Having seen the man run his hand over his greasy head, Jack wondered what the telephone handset held by way of bacteria. He was reminded of the grubby windows in the squad room and the petri dish of bacteria growing all around them. He bet the man's keyboard was slippery with grease too.

A moment later the call was finished and the guard turned back around to face Jack, who wandered back so the man didn't have to shout.

"He'll be ready in ten minutes."

Jack said his thanks and sat back in one of the plastic chairs alongside the window. As he sat down, he heard the Sellotape being taken off the biscuit tin seal, then the faint tinny sound of the lid lifting. Jack smiled to himself. He knew what breaking bread meant; that's why he'd stopped for the tin of biscuits. It was a nice thing to do, a custom, and the reason you found a chocolate on your pillow in an upmarket hotel—a gift. It had worked back in ancient times, so it should work in a concrete prison near Croydon, he'd reasoned. It was £5 well spent.

Jack was tempted to go back to his French app while he waited, but he'd no doubt get disapproving looks as he repeated the sentences out loud. Instead, he pulled out the manila folder and flipped through the pages like he was a barrister about to see his client.

Fifteen minutes later, the guard called him back over to his desk.

"They've put him in an interview room for you. I'll take you through." Still no smile, no nothing. The man appeared to wear a permanent, flat mask of jowly skin. Jack wondered if he was married. Poor woman, if he was. He followed the broad, dandruff-covered shoulders down through concrete corridors with locked doors on each side, and on to an interview room that looked like any other he'd been in. Its concrete block walls had been painted a depressing pale grey, and the only furnishings in the room were a Formica table and two plastic chairs. He couldn't see any cameras or any audio equipment, but he asked anyway.

"I'm assuming we won't be overheard," Jack said. "This is private between Michael and the police."

The man nodded, which Jack took to mean he was correct, and left the room. Jack sat down in one of the chairs, placed the file on the table in front of him and waited. A couple of minutes later he heard voices approaching from the corridor and he looked up to see Michael Hardesty enter with another officer. His hands were cuffed in front of him, but the first thing Jack noticed was how frail the man now seemed after so many years. While he was still tall, there wasn't much of him. Jack was reminded of a young Rodney Trotter - a walking rack of bones with thin skin holding everything together but without his jovial sidekick. Prison life hadn't been kind to him over the years; he wondered if the man was ill.

Michael sat down in the other chair, his eyes never leaving Jack's. The officer left them to it.

"Why now?" Michael asked, without any preamble.

"Good question," replied Jack.

Chapter Twenty-Six

"How have you been, Michael?" In hindsight it was probably a stupid first question.

"How do I look like the I've been? Let me ask you again," Michael said. "Why now? After all these years, you come and see me. Not that I particularly want to see you, but I'm curious what brings you here now. Has something happened to Barbara or Cassy?"

"No. Not that I am aware of, anyway. I'm here on another matter. It's good of you to meet with me today."

"I've hardly got a busy social calendar." Michael rolled his eyes sarcastically. "You're something to fill the abundance of time with, that's all."

Jack ignored the comment. "There is a case at the moment that we are working on, and it has some similarities to your own case back then. And me being a picky individual, I thought it would be a good idea to come and talk to you about what happened all those years ago."

Michael scoffed loudly. "You're only *now* taking an interest in the sentence that I should never have had, in the fact that I should never have been put away for murder?" he said incredulously. "At best it was manslaughter, but I've been stuck in here almost since the turn of the century—and it feels like the nineteenth century. So, I'm not sure I can tell you much more, DC Rutherford," he said. "But fire away. It will pass the time."

Jack nodded his understanding. He'd be pissed at being in prison for murder, too, if he hadn't done it. "Can we go back to the accident and what happened that night? I know you've been through it a million times, but just humour me."

Michael sat back fully in his chair, his handcuffed wrists out on the table in front of him. He twiddled his thumbs, searching for a place to start. Jack waited patiently; he'd got all the time in the world. When Michael had his thoughts together, he began to speak.

"It was just an accident. The car came out of nowhere and we collided. We both got out to inspect the damage. When I realised it was Chesney McAllister, I didn't think 'This is your chance to kill him.' We might have had our differences over the years, but killing was never on my agenda—though the prosecution would have you believe differently. There was a scuffle, he went down. Then suddenly, a couple of witnesses came forward from nowhere and here I am now. They said our known fractious relationship, and the fact that we were two warring local criminals, gave me reason to want the man dead. I'd threatened it often enough. But then so had he." Jack let the moment of silence between them stay empty until Michael was ready to go on. "I don't think my barrister was the best. I shouldn't be in here, but I've come to terms with it now."

"What do you think happened, Michael?"

"Well, see, I've had plenty of thinking time while I've been here, and as you said at the beginning, there isn't much to do. So, to answer your question I was set up, scapegoated; call it what you wish. Yes, it sounds cliché, but it just happens to be the truth. The accident and Chesney's subsequent death—it was all too convenient to put away a man that the police had been after some time. And that's what I think happened."

"So, you think the police fitted you up? Is that what you're saying, Michael?"

"I am, yes."

"And how do you think it happened? Why don't you think the McAllister family were behind it all?"

"I think they had their place in it. Mac McAllister would have tightened the screw somewhere, maybe provided the last-minute witnesses, but he would have needed it to be something official to get false witness statements, and that's where I think their involvement lies. They were paying, and someone turned a blind eye."

Jack thought for a moment. "I've been looking at the file again, and I wonder about some of those testimonies from some of the people who came forward as witness at the end. I'm sorry to say I didn't pay that much attention at the time; you were one more criminal off the street, and it wasn't up to me what happened." Michael grunted and Jack carried on. "A couple of them seemed a little too obvious for my liking, when I reflected back, and when I spent a little time recently cross-checking those names, I couldn't honestly say they would be what I would call a reliable witness."

Michael grunted again. "So, tell me," he said, "what's brought all this on? Why are you bringing this up now? What's your interest? Has one of them confessed or something?"

"I guess you don't watch the TV much, the news?"

"Can't say as I've got TV in my cell. Why don't you enlighten me?"

"A similar incident happened on Sunday, to our detective inspector, in fact; a man called Dupin. He was off duty at the time, and he attended the scene of an accident nearby. The driver lashed out, and Dupin smacked him on the chin in retaliation. That man is dead now."

"So now it's one of your own you figure maybe it was an accident and not murder?" Michael shook his head in disbelief. "Perhaps if I'd been a police officer, I wouldn't be sat here talking to you now, eh?"

"As you can imagine, there's a bit of grief."

"And the family know it's a police officer and are shouting cover-up, right?" Michael had put the pieces together quickly, he wasn't stupid.

Jack nodded. "The autopsy results from your case say there was blood inside the victim's skull when they took the brain out, which is similar to what happened in this case. We're investigating, though we haven't had the official autopsy report back yet. I only know about it because I attended the autopsy. It says on your file that the blow you delivered could have been the one that killed him. But it was the premeditated angle that the prosecution pushed that drove things up to another level. Your past relationship with your opponent. Had that not been the case, who knows what you'd be in for. Maybe you would have got manslaughter, be home by now."

"Thanks for pointing out the obvious," Michael said wearily. "But nothing's going to change now. I've got two years to go on my sentence, then I've served my time."

Jack knew all this but let the man have his say. He doubted Michael received many visitors other than Barbara and Cassy—if they did indeed still visit. Many families moved on with their lives when a family member was imprisoned for so many years. It was a sad fact.

Jack knew there wasn't much more Michael could tell him at that moment, so he closed the manila folder before he stood up. "I might need to come and talk to you again, Michael. Will that be okay?"

"If it helps me get out of here, yes. I have nothing better to do. But if you're just trying to help your police friend, don't bother coming back."

Jack nodded his understanding and banged on the door to alert the officer he was ready to leave.

"I hear you, Michael. I'll be seeing you."

As Jack made his way back down the concrete corridor and out into the fresh air, he wondered about what had gone on back then—the prosecution, the police involvement, the witnesses, all of it. And who had been behind it, if anyone.

More to the point, could he make a difference now?

Chapter Twenty-Seven

The young prison officer who showed Jack out was a bit more pleasant than the Brylcreemed mountain with dandruff.

"Thanks for the chocolate biscuits, Detective. We have to buy our own around here, and no one ever wants to fork out for anything other than Rich Tea."

Jack turned to the man. He must have been one of the youngest prison guards in the building, likely in his early 20s, and Jack wondered what had driven a youngster to choose a life working as a prison officer. It wasn't a common career choice for young men; prison work was more suited to the middle-aged, those with a bit more life experience. This young man looked like he had hardly started shaving; he still had some fresh acne across his cheeks, and scars from old acne were visible down to his jawline. Being the 'baby' of the unit, he'd probably get the piss taken out of him all the time by his colleagues, and was no doubt taken advantage of by the inmates. His light-heartedness hadn't been ripped out of him just yet, but working with colleagues who'd already lost all sense of humour and seen it all, Jack knew, it wouldn't be long before the young lad would be just the same as the rest of them.

"What's your name, son?" asked Jack.

"Kyle. Kyle Greenly, but my friends call me Mino."

Jack was perplexed. "Why Mino? That's a freshwater fish, isn't it?"

"No, you're thinking of M-I-N-N-O-W." He spelt it out for Jack. "I'm M-I-N-O, as in Kylie Minogue. I swear my mother wanted a girl, hence the Kyle. I guess she got her wish since my mates call me Mino now."

Jack had to smile, and since the kid was smiling too, he didn't feel so bad about the lad's name. Educated in freshwater fish too.

"Well, Mino, you don't often see a young prison officer such as yourself, and I was kind of wondering back there what made you choose this as a profession. Is your dad in here somewhere and you're hoping to get him out? Through a back door, perhaps?" Jack was being jovial as he said it, hoping to get another officer on his side.

"No," Mino said, smiling. "They do background checks on us, so I wouldn't have got away with that, had it been the case. My dad's dead anyway."

"Sorry to hear that," Jack said.

"I just thought it would be interesting, that's all. I wanted to join the police, myself, but I didn't get the grades at school. So, this was my second choice." They strolled slowly through the concrete corridor back towards the reception area. They were in no hurry.

"Well, I guess you meet some interesting folks in this line of work, like I do," Jack said casually.

"Too right you do. There're all sorts in here. Take that Michael Hardesty that you were just visiting—he's not a bad bloke, unlike the other party in his crime."

Jack was confused. "What do you mean, the other party in his crime?"

"I did a bit of research on him, as I do for most of the inmates, so I know what I'm dealing with. The family whose brother Hardesty killed, the McAllisters. Well, Mac McAllister is here in the same prison—over in a different wing, though."

"Oh? Mac McAllister is here? Hardesty didn't mention it."

"Yes, he's been here about a year. He'll be out soon."

Jack remembered McAllister well enough. He'd been done for his part in an organised dogfighting ring that he and Amanda had busted. Remembering the setup in the big old shed—the filth, the suffering dogs—made Jack's stomach roll. People like McAllister deserved to be put away; it was a shame he'd be out again soon. And back to his old tricks, no doubt.

They'd reached the front door again; the main reception entrance was bathed in the mid-morning sun. The two men stood for a moment, enjoying the feeling of the warmth on their skin.

Jack had an idea. "What would you say the chances are of me seeing Mac McAllister now, while I'm here?"

"Got another tin of biscuits with you?"

"No, but I can get one."

"Well, bring another and I'm sure your wish will be granted."

Jack looked at the young lad approvingly. Mino had picked up some smarts working in this place already; he'd go a long way in life. They strolled slowly across the car park toward Jack's car; Jack guessed the lad was enjoying the morning sunshine a whole lot more than being cooped up inside the concrete walls. He took his car keys out of his pocket and turned to him.

"Well, Mino, it's been nice to make your acquaintance. So, you think another tin will do the trick if I come back tomorrow, then?"

"I can almost guarantee it, Detective," Mino said with a smile.

"In that case, I'll see you tomorrow." Jack was just about to get into his car when he had another thought.

"I'd appreciate it if you didn't tell McAllister that I was coming."

Mino tapped the side of his nose and winked before heading back to the building.

Chapter Twenty-Eight

Jack's head was swimming. He'd missed the fact that McAllister was in the same prison as Michael Hardesty, but he'd had no reason to look him up. McAllister had only been there for a year, and Jack assumed that Hardesty already knew. The drums would have been beating loud and clear when the man had arrived.

Jack's stomach was grumbling and while the screws enjoyed their morning cuppa and biscuits, he hadn't been offered one. Since it was coming up to 12 o'clock, he decided he might as well grab lunch on the way back in to the station. He wondered if Amanda wanted something picked up too. It was all too easy to have a big meal every day in the station canteen, and since he'd had pie and chips yesterday, he'd stick to a sandwich today. He'd already put on a couple of pounds of recent, mainly because of Mrs Stewart's cooking and all the things she left stocked in his fridge after her thrice-weekly visits. He liked her, and while she was a good deal older than Jack, she was nice to have fussing around the house when he was there. She liked to start early and finish early. When Jack didn't have to be out with the larks, she'd cook a full breakfast for him, or a boiled egg. He figured she secretly liked to have someone to look after; her own family was now living abroad and, apart from her bridge friends and lawn bowling friends, there wasn't anyone particularly close to her. Jack enjoyed her company like he would his grandma's, had she still been alive.

But back to needing lunch. He dialled Amanda's phone and waited for her to pick up.

"Hi, Jack," she said breezily. "Are you on your way back?"

"I am, yes. I'm going to pick up a sandwich first, though. Do you want something, or are you eating in the canteen again?"

"I'll have a sandwich, thanks. In fact, bring me two, please."

"Two? If you're that hungry, you should go to the canteen. It's lasagne today, I believe."

"First off, how do you know it's lasagne? And second, I need two sandwiches because I'll have one for lunch now and the other later on, because Ruth and I are going to the flat-warming tonight and we won't get to eat anything until later. Is that okay with you?"

Jack chuckled. "Ooooooh. I was only looking after your nutritional needs. No need for the sarcasm. Anyway, whose flat are you warming again?"

"Ruth's dad's, remember? He moved out of the big house and bought a flat in Fulham. He moved in about a month ago and tonight's drinkies in the courtyard."

"My goodness, is it a month already? It doesn't seem five minutes since she told me he'd sold up. I must've been missed off the invite list."

"You hardly know the man. The only time you ever went to that house was when you were investigating the landscaper that went missing."

"Yes, but I met him at your wedding, and I saw him one Christmas."

"Well, if you really want to come, I'm sure he won't mind. Anyway, I thought you were looking Vivian up tonight."

"I have a different hot date tonight, actually," he said matter-of-factly. "It's lawn bowls night, and they're putting a supper on."

"So, there you go—you don't need to gate-crash with us after all."

"I'm perfectly capable of sorting my own social life out, thanks very much. I have hobbies, you know."

"Well, that's good to know, Jack. Now, I fancy chicken salad and a ham salad, if you get the choice. If not, I'll leave it up to you. And a packet of salt and vinegar."

"Right, got it. And before you go, after I had my chat with Hardesty, I was talking to one of the younger screws on the way out and he just happened to mention another inmate in passing. You'll never guess who is in the same prison, though in a different wing."

"Do tell."

"Mac McAllister." Jack let that sink in for a moment.

"The dogfighting ring mongrel," Amanda said, and gave a low whistle. "I didn't know he was so local. So he's in the same prison? That doesn't seem right."

"That's what I thought, but it does happen. The offences were years apart, though, and I guess with Michael out of the picture the family feud died down a bit."

"I guess it did. It was before my time; you'd know better than me. I was just glad to get McAllister off the street and close down that dogfighting mess. I can remember that old warehouse like it was yesterday."

Jack shuddered again, and then indicated to turn left. "Anyway," he said, "I'm about to pull up at the sandwich shop now, so I'll see you shortly."

He pulled into a vacant parking space in front and sat with the engine turned off, just thinking for a moment. He'd forgotten to ask Hardesty if he was unwell, given his deterioration. Not that he could do anything about it, of course, but he wondered about it nonetheless. And McAllister in the same building? Surely, they were aware of each other's presence.

He watched two teenage girls stroll into the sandwich shop. By their ages, they couldn't have been out of school for long; they were probably working their first positions somewhere local. They looked smart in their blouses and skirts, and he watched them through his windscreen as they laughed and giggled with each other, waiting for their lunch order to be made. When they left, he watched them almost wistfully as they headed towards the small park area around the corner. Young and carefree. They made him feel old—maybe because he was getting old, but you had to one day.

He was just about to get out of his car when he saw a familiar, slim figure enter the shop from the opposite direction. She wore her hair in a stylish blonde bob, and she hadn't changed a bit since the last time he'd seen her about five years ago.

It was Vivian.

He debated whether to let on he'd seen her or stay in his car until she'd finished her purchase in the sandwich shop. He opted to stay put, watching her through the plate glass window. It brought back memories of the lonely, empty times after Janine's death when he had occasionally sought Vivian's personal services and companionship. He wondered why he'd stopped. Maybe it didn't seem important anymore; maybe he'd simply needed something at that time. His grief and his anger over Janine's illness and death had been unbearable at times; Vivian had been there when he'd needed somebody. Time heals, though, and Jack had eventually sorted himself out. Seeing her now, however, made him want to say hello.

"What the hell. I liked her," he said to himself. He opened his car door and headed into the shop. He watched as she collected her order and, as she turned in the small space, she came face to face with Jack, who was smiling straight at her. Her pale green eyes lit up with delight.

"Jack!" she exclaimed.

"It's good to see you, Vivian," he said, bending forward to plant a peck on her cheek. Her smile was as big as the chocolate eclair in the cake cabinet next to her. And to Jack, just as sweet.

"Fancy bumping into you today. I saw your friend Amanda last night; did she mention it?" Customers carried on all around them as they stood to talk, blocking a good portion of the small shop. No one seemed to mind.

"She did, actually. She said she saw you at the pizza place, and then she tried to grill me about who you were." Their eyes caught and twinkled; the secret of how they knew one another was only for them.

"Well, if you fancy going out for a drink one night, Jack, look me up. It would be nice to catch up again and see what's been going on in your life. It's been way too long."

"I'll do that," he said with a smile, and watched as she left the shop. He was just about to place his order when he realised he had no idea how to contact her. He babbled his order to the young woman behind the counter, said he'd be back in a moment and ran down the street after Vivian. For a woman in high heels, she could walk surprisingly quickly.

"Vivian," he called as he got closer. "Vivian!" he tried again. She heard the second time and turned as he reached her. She broke into a smile as he spoke. "I don't have your number anymore, and a drink would be nice."

"Give me your phone, Jack," she said.

"What do you want that for?" he said, taking it out of his pocket.

"So I can put my number in it for you, silly," she said, laughing lightly. "I thought you were a detective." He watched as her long, pale pink fingernails tapped her details into his phone. She finished and handed it back. "Call me, soon, Jack."

"I will," he said.

He walked back to the sandwich shop, paid for his order and drove back to the station. It was one of those journeys where you remember absolutely nothing of it, not a thing, and you wonder how you arrived at your destination safely and in one piece.

His mind had been somewhere else completely.

Chapter Twenty-Nine

Amanda could see something was on Jack's mind as they sat in the sunshine eating their sandwiches on a low brick wall in the car park. While there were no park benches or shady trees, it was better to sit outside than in the stuffy petri dish indoors. The building itself gave some shade to their heads, and the sun was welcoming on their arms and legs. Jack chewed thoughtfully on his chicken salad sandwich and pointed to Amanda's boots with a mayonnaise-smeared finger.

"Aren't your feet stifled in those during summer?"

Amanda looked down at her Docs. They shone in the bright light, but they shone in dull light too. Amanda was almost fanatical about polished footwear; it was one of her major gripes with others, particularly her work colleagues. Shoes and how you looked after them said a lot about a person. Hers said "functional, strong, and polished."

"No more than yours probably are right now," she replied. "Talking of which, your shoes could do with a polish. You're letting the side down, Jack."

Jack glanced down. Amanda was right, of course. "I'll ask Mrs Stewart to do them."

"You're a big boy now. Why don't you do them yourself?" She watched as he crammed a couple of ready-salted crisps into his mouth with the remains of his last bite of sandwich. There really wasn't room, and she curled her nose up at him. Crumbs fell to the concrete beneath their feet.

"Mrs Stewart loves looking after me and my things. It gives her joy. Who am I to take that joy away from her?"

Amanda rolled her eyes in disbelief. The thing was, she knew Jack was correct, and he himself loved being looked after. It was the perfect match for them both.

"Pity she's a bit old for you to become romantically involved with."

"I used to wonder what an older woman would be like," he said, deadpan, gazing off into the distance. Amanda stopped chewing.

"When?"

"When I was about twenty, like all young men do, I suppose."

"I was going to say—I thought you meant recently. Anyway, age doesn't matter, though I doubt any woman would want to be in your life as a skivvy only. Even if Mrs S was interested in you, it would change things."

Jack turned to face Amanda full on. "Why are we having this conversation? Mrs Stewart could be my grandmother almost."

"How about your friend Vivian, then? She looked more your age, and you two go way back."

Jack wondered if she'd been sniffing already. How else would she know they went 'way back'?

"And what makes you think that?"

"You said as much."

"No, I didn't."

"Yes, you did."

Jack turned away, pondering, but was saved from any further inquisition by Amanda's phone ringing. The opening bars of Landscapes' "Einstein A Go Go" beep-beeped. It was Faye, the pathologist. Jack smiled at Amanda's choice of ringtone; better than Elton John's "Better off Dead," at least. He finished the last of his crisps and scrunched the packet noisily, earning him a glare from Amanda. He motioned to her to put the call on handsfree and she obliged.

"Hi, Faye. I have Jack with me too. Have you got something for us?"

"Yes, sort of, and hello, Jack."

He waved a 'hello,' not that she could see him.

"What's the 'sort of'?" Amanda enquired.

"It would be better for me to show you. Any chance of you coming over to the lab?"

Amanda looked at her watch. "We'll be there in twenty, if that works for you?"

"Perfect. See you shortly."

Amanda tapped to end the call and put the last of her sandwich in her mouth, passing the remaining crisps to Jack.

"Come on. I'll drive," she said, and they headed over to her car. They flinched as they opened the doors; it was like a furnace inside. They slipped in and Amanda started the engine.

"You can play with the air con. I'm sick of trying to get it right," she said as they headed out, the fan on full bore. "I'll be almost glad when winter comes back. It's easier to manage, temperature-wise. Set it on hot and leave it."

As Jack twiddled with the knobs, they headed across town and back to the mortuary in the lunchtime traffic. As they pulled into the car park almost twenty minutes later, the car was the perfect temperature to sit in.

"Shame it will be like a spit roast again by the time we come back out," she said, tossing her bag strap over her shoulder. They walked up to the double doors and waited for them to slide open. At reception, a pretty woman with long, shiny black hair greeted them. Tiny pearl studs were only just visible on her earlobes; her lips were painted a deep pink. Jack took everything in like she was a crime scene. Details were his thing. His eyes dropped to her name badge—Gloria. She suited the name.

"Dr Faye Mitchell is expecting us," Amanda said as the lift

doors behind them pinged open, revealing Faye in her white lab coat.

"I saw you arrive. Come on up." She held the door and the two walked over to the lift. Jack gave a slight wave to Gloria, ever the gentleman.

Amanda leaned in. "Too young," she whispered, though Faye had no difficulty hearing the comment.

"Are you on the lookout, Jack?" Faye asked, somewhat amused.

"Why is my personal life the topic of discussion for the second time today?" he enquired stiffly.

Amanda and Faye glanced at one another and smirked. Jack kept his back to them as the lift took them up to Faye's office. Thankfully for Jack, it was a short journey, though he could feel sniggering going on behind him. He shook his head in comical disbelief as the doors opened again and waited for the two women to go on ahead.

When they were finally seated in the doctor's office, Faye went through her findings and then sat back in her chair with a questioning look.

"First, why didn't you mention that DI Dupin was the person who hit the victim?" She didn't look pleased.

Amanda took the question, as the senior officer.

"We didn't want your judgement clouded. We figured if you didn't know, it wouldn't sway you in either direction if something wasn't one hundred percent. We didn't want to influence you."

"You wouldn't have. I work with the facts, and only the facts," Faye said sharply. "I work with what the body tells me; it alone gives me the story of what happened. I don't care if it's the Queen on my examination table. And even if I wanted to alter the facts, there is always the chance of another autopsy being done—you know that. So no, you wouldn't, never will influence my decision. Do I make myself clear?" Her voice had risen with the last sentence, and both detectives squirmed uncomfortably.

She went on, "Now that I have that out of the way, I can tell you that Callum Parker's heart and liver were both enlarged, most likely from alcohol abuse. He was a drinker, even if he wasn't over the limit at the time of the accident, the initial crash." Nobody dared to interrupt her. "There was also blood inside the skull from a brain bleed, though that didn't come from the single blow to the chin."

Jack dared to speak now. "So DI Dupin didn't kill him, then?" He looked at Amanda with wide-open eyes, almost a look of celebration.

"No, that blow didn't kill him. If the fight had caused his death, I'd expect a lot more soft tissue injury, and there isn't any."

Jack pumped his fist in the air and Amanda let a long breath out. DI Dupin was in the clear.

"So, what killed Callum Parker then, Doc?" Jack said.

Faye pulled out the autopsy photos from a folder and laid them out in front of them: pictures of the neck and accompanying arteries that she had taken out to show a colleague for further inspection. Jack remembered his remark about "dangly bits" and taunting Japp out in the car park afterwards.

"You might remember I took these out for further analysis." She pointed to the photos as she spoke. "It's an odd thing that's happened. It's called a sub-arachnoid haemorrhage. Let me explain."

"Please do," said Jack. He inched forward in his seat to get a closer look. It was far more pleasant to view photos than the real-life wet and bloody specimens.

"When we drink alcohol, it can raise our blood pressure. Add to that the frantic turning of the steering wheel first one way," she demonstrated, "and then the other to correct the car and avoid collision. By doing that, Callum Parker inadvertently dislocated his spine here," she said pointing. "That in turn ruptured this artery, sending blood into the brain." She stopped to check they were both following. "All the activity immediately after the crash—the aggression, the lashing out and the increase in blood pressure—accelerated that bleeding. Now, it might have only been slight to start with, but by the time he arrived home, it proved fatal. It can take from a few minutes to hours for the blood to spread up to the skull."

"So, let me get this straight," said Amanda. "The punch from DI Dupin was nothing to do with his death?"

"Correct."

"And he died of a freakish dislocated spine that burst an artery and filled his skull with blood."

"Correct."

"Wow."

"Quite. It's not common, but it happens. Occasionally it's genetics. DI Dupin is not at fault here. If Callum Parker hadn't wrestled the steering wheel as he had, hadn't had a couple of drinks and hadn't tried to punch Dupin, he might still be here now. It was no one's fault. Rather, it was a series of moves that ended up proving fatal. Callum was a dying man on the drive back home; he simply didn't realise it. The punch on the chin made no difference whatsoever."

Jack sat back in his chair, thinking. He hadn't got a lot of time for Dopey, but he wouldn't wish a manslaughter charge on him either.

It also raised a question concerning another case on his mind.

Chapter Thirty

"I really can't believe it," Jack said as he and Amanda headed back to the lift and down to reception. "Shall you tell him the good news, or shall I?"

"We should tell Japp first, since he was the one who told Dupin in the first place. What a weird situation, eh? I've never heard of such a thing, though she did say it could be a genetic condition. All her evidence points to the accident itself—his own actions killed him, not Dupin."

The doors pinged closed and they travelled the short distance back down to reception.

"It's made me think of Hardesty and his situation," said Jack, as they walked across the lobby. "Pathology, I assume, has got more accurate over time. And I've got to say I'm wondering if something similar happened in his case that perhaps got missed all those years ago. And if that is the case, can I do anything about it now?"

"Yes, but Jack, the guy was a bad lad anyway. He'd probably have ended up inside anyway; if not for that then for something else. He was a career criminal."

"Maybe so, but that doesn't make him a killer directly, and that's what his sentence is for. It's on his record for life, such as it is. Just like they caught Al Capone on a technicality and stuck him inside, doesn't mean it's the right thing to do." Jack could feel himself getting hot under the collar about it, although he sensed Amanda wasn't too fussed. It was obvious she didn't share Jack's concern for Hardesty, or the fact that he was rotting in prison and maybe hadn't done the crime he'd been convicted of. That didn't sit well with Jack, and since he'd been part of the original investigation, it felt a little more personal, much closer to home than it might for anyone else.

Apart from Eddie Edwards, the arresting officer at the time.

They were almost back at Amanda's car, and Jack could see heat waves floating across the bonnet. As Amanda clicked her key fob to unlock the car, Jack stated the obvious. "It's going to be like a barbeque inside there," he said in a singsong voice. A rush of hot air like a hairdryer hit him as he opened the door and sat himself in the passenger seat. Amanda wound the windows down immediately, and Jack twiddled with the air-conditioning and wondered what his old boss Eddie was doing these days. He'd not seen the man for some years.

"I'm sure Japp will be pleased," said Amanda, as they set off back to the station, "and it's good news for the rest of the team too. I know it's been preying on people's minds; it's been quite distracting, actually."

"The press are going to go nuts at this," said Jack. "I hope that Callum Parker's family are satisfied with the results, but I can't help feeling they're not going to be. Particularly his fiancée Melissa. She'll be a right flighty set of bagpipes, that one."

"A flighty set of bagpipes?' enquired Amanda.

"You must have noticed the size of her chest, surely, and you can't tell me they're real. And she appears to be a bit of a mouthpiece about all this, so all in all, a flighty set of bagpipes. My observations are spot-on. Case rested."

Amanda had to smile. Jack was never crass or crude, but that didn't mean his eyes didn't work like those of any other warm-blooded male when it came to a woman's body. Particularly a manufactured one at that.

"So, you don't agree with plastic surgery, then?" she asked, knowing the answer.

"Nope. Make do with what you've got, and make the most of it; that's my motto." He turned to gaze out the side window as they headed back out onto the dual carriageway. As usual, it was slow-moving. She indicated to cut across into the outside lane, which was moving slightly faster, and navigated the traffic back to the station. Jack checked his watch.

"Do you fancy an ice cream?"

Amanda glanced across at him and shook her head. "You're going to be piling all the weight back on that you've lost over recent weeks if you keep eating like you are. Have a bottle of water instead."

"You sound like my grandma now."

"Your grandma's dead."

Disappointed that he wasn't going to get his ice cream, Jack turned his mind back to what they just learned from the pathologist. A sub-arachnoid hemorrhage. Who would have thought it?

"So, what's the plan then, boss?" he said. "What order are we doing things?"

"We'll tell Japp first, and then I guess we'll go and see the Parker family and see what happens from there. Hopefully, they'll accept the findings and everyone can move on."

"And if they don't move on, and Bagpipes causes a stink?"

"In my experience, I expect they'll call for another autopsy and see what that shows up," she said. "But also, in my experience, Faye Mitchell is one of the best and there will be no mistakes."

Jack grunted an agreement. He'd never known her to get it wrong in all the times they'd worked together over the years.

"She got a bit feisty when we suggested she might be swayed one way or the other. It was stupid, really; she's always been one hundred percent professional. That's why she never gives an opinion before the facts are there to support it."

It was Amanda's turn to grunt an acknowledgement; Jack was, of course, right. She glanced at her wristwatch; time was marching on, and she needed to hurry if she was to get to the flat-warming party on time. She hated letting Ruth down, but there was still work to do before she could head off home to change.

The electric gate slipped back at the station car park, and she pulled into her space and turned the engine off. She didn't immediately move, but instead turned to Jack.

"You know, this could have happened to anyone—something simple like a car accident, where neither party appears injured, and all the time deep inside someone's head nature is taking its course and silently killing them. It's quite horrendous, really. I suppose when your time is up, it's time to go." She was staring straight through the windscreen at nothing in particular, and as Jack followed her gaze, he wondered what was making her feel so maudlin.

"Then we need to make the most of our time while we've still got it," he said, reaching to open his door. The warm sun in contrast to the cold fridge of the car was welcoming, and Jack took a moment to stretch like a cat, dropping his head back for the briefest moment. He felt his neck click, the tiny bubbles of gas dissipating from around the bony joints. Thinking of what he'd just learned, he pulled his head back up slowly and followed Amanda back into the station. It had been a learning experience, although a depressing one. On days like this he was glad he had something else to do with his time of an evening that brought joy instead of pain. He was looking forward to his bowling match tonight, a spot of light relief in contrast to his somewhat melancholy though educational day.

Chapter Thirty-One

Amanda dropped her bag on her desk and, with Jack in tow, headed straight to DCI Japp's office. She rapped on his open door with a knuckle. Over her shoulder, Jack saw Japp's head rise and his eyes readjust away from the document he had been reading. Even though Japp knew Amanda, to Jack there seemed to be a satellite delay of a couple of seconds before it registered who was actually standing there in front of him.

Amanda didn't wait to be beckoned in. "Sorry to intrude," she started, "but I thought you'd like to know the news."

Japp stared at her over the top of his half-rimmed reading glasses like she had just woken him from a deep sleep. Jack wanted to rub his eyes for him. He also wanted to slap him around his jowly face. No one ever went to Japp's office uninvited unless it was important. Surely he knew that.

"What is it, Amanda?" he said gruffly.

"We have the pathology results, sir. I wanted to talk to you in person rather than on the phone."

Japp glanced across at Jack, who'd invited himself in and was standing next to Amanda. Since there was only one chair on the visitor side of Japp's desk, he let Amanda take it by offering it with an open palm hand. She shook her head lightly preferring to stand in front of the man. He was less intimidating that way.

"What's the damage?" Japp said, taking more of an interest.

"Well, that's just it, sir. Damage is probably the right word for it."

"What are you talking about, Amanda?"

"Well, sir, first of all, DI Dupin is not responsible for the death of Callum Parker. Without going into all the gory details, the pathology reports state that it was the actual car accident that caused a brain hemorrhage. I'll get the official report to you so you can read it in full, but basically the punch that Dupin threw was not the cause of death. He is in the clear."

Japp sat back in his fancy leather chair; it squeaked and groaned in protest. He took his glasses off and rubbed the bridge of his nose, looking as if he was trying to get his head around what Amanda had just told him. Eventually he spoke. "Well, that is good news. Thank you. Good news, indeed. I guess we can all rest easy again."

"Will you tell DI Dupin, sir, or shall I?"

"No, I'll tell him. It's only right. Send me the report, though. I don't doubt the press will be hounding us."

"If I may, sir," Jack began. He waited until Japp glanced his way.

"Yes, Jack? What is it?"

"I thought I should mention... The doc reckoned that the family will want another autopsy. They'll think there's a cover-up, judging by the reaction we've had from them so far. So you are aware, sir."

Japp put his head in his hands, his elbows resting on his desk in front of him.

"Is there ever any good news?" he said.

"Dr Mitchell is certain in her work," Amanda said. "Always has been. You know what she's like—I's dotted T's crossed. She had specialists take a look at Parker's brain and between them they're certain his death was not caused by a smack on the chin. If there is another autopsy, she'll be present anyway, because that's what happens. So let them request another autopsy: it will come back with the same result. Let's wait and see. Right now, getting Dupin back to work and moving forward is the important thing."

"I've been in this game long enough, Amanda, to know that the family won't take this lying down. But we'll be ready, because it sounds like the facts won't change, and while it's sad that they won't be able to point the finger, nothing will bring their boy back."

Japp folded the report he'd been reading before they walked in and slipped his glasses back into their case. "Right, then. I'm off to give the good news to DI Dupin." He got to his feet, making his leather chair groan again. Perhaps if he lost a pound or two, Amanda thought.

"Do you want me to accompany you, sir?" Amanda asked, hoping the answer was no.

"No, thank you, Amanda. I'm quite capable of telling him myself."

"Sir," said Amanda, for the sake of acknowledging him. She glanced at Jack and they both turned to exit his office swiftly, leaving Japp fumbling for something behind them. Without looking back, they headed straight to their desks and busied themselves with paperwork and emails until they were sure he'd left his office.

When he was safely out of the way, Jack rolled his chair across the carpet towards Amanda's desk and pulled alongside. "He's such a stiff old dick," he said with annoyance. "The guy just never smiles."

Amanda was replying to an email and replied distractedly, "Some folks are just like that, and I guess he's one of them." She carried on typing.

"Do you remember the movie *Good Morning Vietnam*, with Robin Williams in it?"

"Hmmm?"

"There's a scene in it where Williams is getting frustrated at his grumpy general or whoever it was, and before he walks out of the man's office he turns and says to him something along the lines of 'I've never met anyone more in need of a blow job than you.'"

Amanda raised her head and burst out laughing. "How do you remember such things, Jack?"

"Because I'm saving that saying for one day when I dare myself to use it."

"Well, may I suggest DCI Japp is not the man to use it on. I daresay it wouldn't go down too well, and early retirement without pension could be on the cards for you."

"It would almost be worth it," Jack said, waggling his eyebrows. He turned and rolled his chair back to his desk, chuckling as he went. He glanced at the time on his computer screen; it was almost 5 o'clock. Behind him he could hear Amanda gathering her things to leave.

She was almost certainly going to be late for the flat-warming.

Chapter Thirty-Two

Amanda was running late, as usual. She'd contemplated driving over to Fulham, but since Ruth's dad's flat-warming wasn't far from a tube station it made sense to let the train take the strain, to quote an ancient TV advert. She'd dashed home, dumped her work gear and changed into a slightly more casual outfit of cotton cargo pants and a raw silk shirt, with a pair of chunky heels. A light application of lipstick and some extra gel rubbed through her blonde locks and she was ready to rumble.

"It'll have to do," she said to the mirror, not entirely satisfied with what was staring back at her. She grabbed her bag again, checked for her sunglasses and headed out the front door to her car, which she would leave at the train station car park. Since it was gone 5.30 pm already, there was no way she'd be there for six.

Once on the train, she dialled Ruth. The carriage going north back into London was almost empty, so she didn't feel bad about having a conversation in a public place and being overheard. Ruth was used to her being late; it came with the territory.

"Hi, hun," she said. "Are you on your way here?"

Ruth never gave her a hard time about her long hours and the things that invariably cropped up at inopportune moments; again, it came with the territory. It was how Amanda's life had been since she'd joined the force and no doubt would continue to be. She had her eyes set on becoming a DI in the not-too-distant future.

"I've just got on the train, so I'll be there in about forty minutes if I manage to time the District line connection right. Are there many there already?"

"I got here early to give Dad a hand. Actually, the place is packed. It's a good job there's a patio outside for the overspill."

"Any sandwiches? I'm starved. I bought one for this afternoon, but we ended up back at the mortuary. I think I must have left it there."

Amanda could hear Ruth chuckle down the phone.

"Little nibbles, I'm afraid, but I'm sure I can make you a sandwich on the sly if you're that desperate. Dad won't mind. Anyway, I should go and mix and mingle, so I'll see you when you get here. It's a good job you've not driven. I don't think there's anywhere left to park."

"Right. I'll see you when I get there then," she said, and ended the call.

The train rattled alongside the ends of the skinny back gardens of houses in Croydon; the tumbledown wooden rear fences of the properties all looked the same. Overgrown brambles, discarded traffic cones, and several supermarket shopping trolleys dying on the embankment gave Amanda something to gaze at as cookie-cutter towns whizzed by and bled into each other.

She could see her own reflection if she focused her eyes on the window glass in a certain way. It was kind of eerie, almost ghostlike, watching grass banks fly by with an overlaid, stationary image of herself. It reminded her of the movie *Girl on the Train*.

The rattling journey to London Victoria took only 20 minutes. She stepped out of the carriage and headed down the platform towards the tube station and the District line. Droves of people were still headed home, back south where she'd come from, and once again she was glad she wasn't part of the daily commuter community, the herd of bored faces on the train to and from work every day. They all looked the same: men and women, all in dark suits with pale shirts, briefcases in hand.

She navigated stairs and escalators until she found herself on the correct tube platform to get to Fulham Broadway station. From there to Brompton Park, where Gordon Simpson's soirée was being held, was only a couple of minutes' walk.

The tube journey from Victoria to Fulham took almost as long as the train journey from Croydon, though with far less to see. The underground tube was one of those places that you tolerated—dirty, hot and dusty no matter what the weather was doing outside—but it was part of London life, of getting around quickly. She settled into her seat and, with nothing in particular to keep her attention, pulled out her phone and surfed the BBC news site. She was not one for Facebook; she saw it as a waste of time, and with precious little downtime in the first place, she wasn't about to spend it on trivial nonsense. So, while Ruth did her crossword puzzles or played word games on her own phone, Amanda like to keep up to date with what was going on in the real world.

A headline caught her eye: it seemed the press knew the autopsy results already. How could that be?

Family 'Scream Blue Murder'

Amanda doubted it had taken the reporter long to dream that one up. The 'boys in blue' insinuation used instead of actually saying; 'Cop Cover Up.' She scrolled the page down with her fingers, curious about what the article would say, though really, she had a fair idea, given the headline. It was nothing that they hadn't predicted might happen. But it was another distraction that the team didn't need right now, not to mention more fuel to elevate DCI Japp's stress levels. She wondered who had leaked the story. Had it been Callum's parents, or had it been the fiancée? She wasn't aware that they even knew the results as yet, and couldn't see Japp dropping in and telling them.

Given Jack's observations about Melissa Ross—the flighty set of bagpipes—Amanda suspected she'd been the one to throw the match in the jerry can. But still, how did she know if it was indeed her? Jean and Brian Parker were more reserved and too busy grieving to have so much anger. Melissa, on the other hand, seemed more upset at losing her planned inheritance now the wedding was off, and as crass at that seemed, it was plausible. She had a reason to stir things up. Amanda wondered if Callum had had a chance to make a will; it probably hadn't been something he'd thought much about in his short life. Not many young people thought about their own deaths and what they would like to happen to their bodies and belongings after they died.

No doubt now, though, that there would be a second autopsy, and even though Amanda knew Faye Mitchell's work was always accurate, it wouldn't be fun to have someone doubting it and asking for a second opinion. From their conversation earlier, though, Faye knew it would be coming; it was to be expected and was nothing unusual. And she'd attend. What happened next would depend on what the second pathologist found. She pitied Dupin and wondered about the strain he was under. Japp would have told him the good news by now, of course, and he would think he was in the clear, but this article would mean the worry would no doubt recommence. And there was still his disciplinary hearing to deal with. At the end of the day, Dupin had hit a man while off duty.

As the tube pulled into Fulham Broadway station, Amanda gathered her things and made her way to the door, waiting for the train to come to a complete standstill. The station was like a giant garden shed, with natural light streaming through the glass roof. It gave the station a less closed-in feel than some of the others on the District line. Add a truckload of plants and it could look like a greenhouse. The familiar automated warning to mind the gap sounded in her ears as she made her way out and across the platform towards the stairs, and back out up to the high street. She wanted to take a deep breath, but the air above ground wasn't much different than below it. London never stood still, not for a moment, and the street was packed with people heading home or heading out for something to eat.

Her stomach rumbled. She could smell cheap, hot pizza and greasy hot dogs as she set off for her father-in-law's place.

Chapter Thirty-Three

By the time Amanda had walked up Seagrave Road, it was almost 6.30 pm. But no one ever arrived at a party on time, so she didn't feel too bad. His new flat was in a nice part of town with plenty of green trees and wide-open pavements; Stamford Bridge stadium was almost spitting distance away. It was a pity Gordon Simpson didn't support Chelsea; he was a Crystal Palace fan through and through and had been for many years.

The big iron gates of the smart residential development where he'd chosen his flat were open; cars had been parked up and down the street. Amanda hadn't realised Gordon Simpson was so popular; he'd always struck her as a bit dour. Maybe singledom suited him. The gentle hum of conversation interspersed with male laughter and the clinking of glasses greeted her as she entered the ground floor flat. Frank Sinatra was singing lightly in the background, though she doubted if anyone had noticed. It wasn't a big flat, but it suited one person; Amanda had no trouble in locating Ruth. Her height and her heels made her relatively easy to spot in the small kitchen, and Amanda made a beeline for her.

"I'm not too late, and I didn't have to wait long for a tube connection," she said breezily.

"And you're here now. Shall I make you a sandwich and then you can relax?" Amanda nodded gratefully. "Grab yourself a drink, then, and I'll meet you outside on the patio," Ruth said, taking charge.

"You're a lifesaver. I'm famished."

Ruth nodded to where the drinks were out on display in the opposite corner of the kitchen and watched as Amanda poured a glass of wine for herself, took a long mouthful and topped it back up.

"Steady on. You'll not make the evening out if you carry on like that. Bad day, was it?" Ruth called. She was busy buttering bread and adding cheese from the fridge.

Amanda looked sheepish; god, she must have looked desperate. "On the contrary, actually, so call it a mini-celebration. It seems Dupin is in the clear, which is great news, but I don't think it's the end of it—not yet."

"How so?" asked Ruth adding salad cream and cutting the sandwich in two. She arranged the halves on a tiny plate.

"The family won't accept it, I'm sure of that, so we're expecting a second autopsy. It just means it drags on a while longer and causes more unrest for everybody, but more so for Dupin."

Ruth handed the sandwich over and nodded towards the open back door. Amanda took it outside onto the patio to eat in private and wind down a little. Ruth joined her a moment later, her own glass of wine in hand. Amanda had already devoured one half of her sandwich in the few seconds since leaving the kitchen.

"Don't give yourself indigestion by stuffing it in," Ruth admonished her. "It's only a sandwich you're eating, not the Crown Jewels." Amanda visibly slowed down her eating; she didn't want to be embarrassed if anyone saw her.

"Look, you stay here and eat that, and I'll go mix and mingle. Come out when you're ready," Ruth said, smiling. Amanda nodded with a mouthful of food and watched Ruth glide off back into the main room, where most of the housewarming guests were sipping and chatting.

. . .

Ruth caught her father's eye and he silently mouthed the word 'Okay?' She nodded, and Gordon went back to the conversation he was having with a man who looked like any other commuter who had arrived to a drinks party straight from work. Corporate. Navy-blue. She glanced around the room and noted just a handful of women, many of whom looked like they belonged in Gordon's office by day, the obvious place he'd know them all from. Ruth didn't know anybody at all in the room, only Amanda and Gordon, but as a businesswoman herself, she didn't find a room full of strangers daunting. Scanning the room, she eventually spied someone who wasn't deep in conversation with somebody else. She summed him up. He wasn't dressed like the rest; he was much more casual, in jeans and a T-shirt. Ruth estimated him to be about 20 years younger than Gordon was. Intrigued, she wondered how the two knew one another—unless the guy was a gate-crasher, or a new neighbour.

Or another long-lost child created up the toilet wall in a Croydon nightclub. Like she had been.

Figuring he could probably do with some conversation, she made her way across and introduced herself.

"Hi, I'm Ruth, Gordon's daughter."

"And I'm Liam," the stranger said, putting his hand out to shake. "I sit next to Gordon as a season ticket holder at Crystal Palace." Ruth nodded. Liam had a welcoming smile, with eyes that matched it, and was clean shaven. A small but deep pink scar about an inch long on his chin caught her eye, and she wondered how he'd got it. Liam followed her gaze and had an answer ready for her before she asked the question.

"An old soccer injury," he said. "I got kicked in the face and a boot stud cut me."

"Sorry—I didn't mean to stare. That sounds painful. I thought football was a noncontact sport?"

"It's okay. And yes, you'd think soccer was a noncontact game with all the daft new rules, but it really isn't. Far from it, in fact, though not as rough as rugby. But our university team could get a bit rowdy at times, and our opposition often took their opportunities—and my chin was one of them." He flashed his smile again as Gordon approached them from behind Ruth's right shoulder. He leaned in to give Ruth a peck on the cheek.

"I see you've met Liam already?" Her father had a comforting smile, Ruth thought, as she always did, but then again, didn't all fathers? He reminded her of a worn pair of slippers. For a fleeting moment she wondered if he was lonely on his own. She leaned into his shoulder and put her arm around his waist, pulling him in close.

"Yes, another football fanatic, just like you. I guess you'll be supporting Chelsea now, will you?" she said teasingly. She winked at Liam, knowing full well that Gordon would never change teams; she was just winding him up.

"Never in a million years. I'm an Eagle through and through! Though it will be handy when we play them at home, on their turf, I mean."

Ruth was aware that Amanda had joined them now and was waiting for a gap in the conversation. Gordon pecked her on the cheek in welcome.

"And how is my favourite daughter-in-law detective?" he asked.

"I am well, thank you, Gordon," she said. She glanced across at Liam, waiting for an introduction. Ruth did the honours.

"This is Liam, Amanda. Sits next to Dad at matches."

"A local detective?" Liam asked.

"I'm out at Croydon, actually. Ruth and I live out that way."

Liam nodded knowingly, understanding dawning in his eyes.

"Yes, we are," Amanda said, smiling, sparing him the question. Liam's face coloured slightly with embarrassment.

Ruth laughed lightly and added, "I guess we stick out like your chin scar."

"A lot better looking, though," he said, raising his glass as a toast to cover up his faux pas.

Amanda thought it best to change the subject and turned to

Gordon. "Are you settling in okay, then, Gordon? It's a lot more local for your work, and it's a beautiful flat."

"It's a lot easier to clean, too, and yes, I'm at work in twenty minutes. I should have moved a long time ago."

"I was out your way—I mean by the old house—only a few days ago. I wasn't paying too much attention, but I thought I saw some earthmoving machinery out there. Are they having some work done, the new owners?"

"They've started already, have they? They mentioned they would like to put a pool in, but I didn't think they'd be digging quite yet. Planning permission takes forever."

"Or perhaps they know somebody at the council," said Liam. "Who you know takes you a long way in this world; that's one thing I've learned in my life. All that study at uni and the people I know have got me further along than any textbook or exam."

"You're not far wrong there," added Amanda. "My job is all about connections and people. I leave the textbook stuff to the crime scene techs and the pathologists, and I spend my time playing a giant game of Who Dunnit."

There was polite laughter from Liam and Gordon, but Ruth didn't join in.

At all.

While Liam and Gordon hadn't noticed, Amanda had.

She also noticed Ruth's colour. She was as white as sushi rice.

Chapter Thirty-Four

Amanda watched Ruth but didn't say a word. She looked like corpse, a vacant expression on her face as she stood totally statuesque, silent. It seemed Liam and Gordon hadn't noticed either; they carried on chatting, oblivious. Amanda felt like she was listening with her head submerged in water; the voices around her were strangely muffled. Time stood still as she watched Ruth's colour gradually return. She took her forearm, made their excuses and gently steered Ruth towards the front door, telling Gordon she needed some air.

"Is she all right?" he asked.

"Probably an empty stomach, and the wine has gone to her head," she lied, keeping a well-meaning smile in place as she guided Ruth outside. There was a low stone wall to their right, and Amanda steered Ruth over to it to sit down for a moment. The sun was low in the sky, the horizon a beautiful shade of purplish pink with a dash of copper. She still hadn't said a word. Amanda rubbed the middle of her back in comfort.

"Are you alright? Do you feel ill?"

A shake of the head from Ruth.

"What's the matter, then?"

Ruth lifted her head and started to speak, but the words stuck in her throat.

"I... Light-headed."

"Have you eaten? Shall I get you something?" Amanda was concerned now. "Do I need to get help?"

That did the trick. Ruth turned towards Amanda in alarm.

"No!" she shouted, then lowered her voice, abashed. "I mean, no thanks. I'm feeling better now. Maybe I do need a sandwich or something. I've had a couple of wines on an empty stomach. Silly, really." She smiled at Amanda, trying to reassure her; she did seem to be coming back round. Standing now and wobbling slightly, she announced, "I'll make a cup of tea too. Want one?"

Amanda stood alongside her and their eyes locked. Even in the fading light she could see Ruth's colour was back to normal. She slipped her arm around her waist and they went back inside to rejoin the celebrations. Gordon glanced over and lifted his chin in question as they went in, and Amanda gave him a discreet thumbs-up. Satisfied all was indeed well, he went back to his conversation with another man in a navy suit. One of the many.

"Maybe we should head back when you've had something to eat?" enquired Amanda.

"I'm fine. But I am a bit tired. Would you mind if we did?" Ruth was buttering bread again, though this time she topped it off with strawberry jam. "The sugar will do me good," she explained, as if she needed to, sounding a little cheerier than she had a few moments ago.

"Not at all. No rush. We'll go when you're feeling better. I'll nip in and tell your dad," she said, and left Ruth to finish her sandwich.

Amanda could see Gordon was deep in conversation with a grey-haired man in yet another navy suit; she waited for a break in the discussion and then quietly told Gordon they were about to leave.

"Tell her I'll call tomorrow, and thanks for coming, the two of you." He beamed as he pecked Amanda lovingly on the cheek. Amanda had always found Gordon easy to get along with; everyone liked Gordon Simpson, the salt of the earth, and she was no exception. She pecked him back and gave him a light wave as she went back to the kitchen. She found Ruth staring out of the window, her hands prayer-like in front of her mouth as though she were deep in thought. The jam sandwich lay uneaten on a small plate by the sink to her side. Amanda waited; the sound of jumbled conversation carried on behind her, interspersed with bursts of laughter. It was going to be a late night for Gordon and his friends.

"All set?" Amanda enquired, making Ruth jump a little at the sound of her voice. She turned, grabbed her sandwich and, slinging her bag over her shoulder, linked her arm through Amanda's.

"Yes."

"Gordon will call you tomorrow, he said. He's busy being the social butterfly, so I told him we'd let ourselves out."

Ruth took a bite of the sandwich and they headed back outside, down through the shared driveway and out onto the pavement. The amber glow of streetlights warming up cast the world in half colour as they made their way towards the tube station. Ruth stayed silent and Amanda let her be, not wanting to intrude on whatever it was that was bothering her. Not yet, anyway.

Fulham Broadway was as busy at dusk as it had been coming up to rush hour. As they stood on the District Line platform that would take them back to Victoria station, Ruth finally spoke.

"Sorry about that. I don't know what came over me," she said. "But I feel much better now. Maybe I did just need some food and air. I hope I didn't wreck your evening after dragging you all the way out here."

"As long as you're alright and feeling better," Amanda reassured her. "I'm glad to be headed back, actually, between you and me."

A heavy breeze pushed itself onto their platform; a crisp packet blew into the air and tumbled back down onto the rails below. Their tube was about to enter the station. The mechanical roar drowned out all conversation until the train eventually came to a standstill, and the automated voice reminded travellers of the ever-present gap. The carriage was almost full, but they managed to find seats adjacent to each other. Not wanting the occupants, at least those without buds in their ears, listening in to their conversation, they opted for a silent journey, each using their own thoughts to entertain them until Victoria.

If Amanda could have looked inside Ruth's head, she'd have seen what was really troubling her.

And it was far from entertaining.

Chapter Thirty-Five

Ruth stayed quiet all the way home. Inside her head all sorts of eventualities were buzzing around, visions of what might happen if the secret came out. Her father had only just got his life back together, moved to a new flat, and things were going well for him; to have something like this come along and mess it all up wasn't fair. She herself could deal with the headaches it would inevitably bring, because she was prepared for it, but not her father. And suspicion would fall on both their shoulders, she was sure. She'd gone straight to bed when they got home and had then lain awake half the night staring up at the ceiling, knowing sleep would never come. It had been a long night.

At 4.30 AM she'd crept out of bed, eyes swollen with exhaustion, feeling like she'd been punched. She grabbed her robe and slipped down to the kitchen. The room was pitch black; it was far too early for the sun to be up. She switched on the light and filled the kettle to make her first cup of tea of the day. Looking out of the kitchen window, she could see only her reflection staring back at her—it was like looking at an image printed on a blackboard. It was a pity she couldn't rub some bits out. Her swollen eyes looked like they'd been crying, though she hadn't. Turning the tap back on, she splashed cold water on her face and dried it on the kitchen towel. She knew she looked like hell, but she could blame it on the housewarming. Her work colleagues would tease her that she'd had too much to drink, and she'd let them believe their own story. Because the real story was far more sinister, far more unbelievable, and far more serious.

Her stomach rumbled as she dropped two slices of bread into the toaster. Normally she'd go for a run, but she didn't know if she had the energy this morning, even though she knew it would help to sort her thoughts out, keep her mind in check as well as wake her up. She'd decide when she'd eaten her toast. The sound of water running upstairs caught her attention; Amanda was up. Tuning her ears to the sounds of the house, she soon heard footsteps lightly descending the stairs. In a moment the kitchen door would open, and Amanda would be standing there asking if she was okay, why she was up so early. Ruth realised she would have to go for her run in order to keep away from the awkward questions. It would do her good anyway, in more ways than one. No sooner had she finished the thought than Amanda appeared in the doorway wearing her pink fluffy bathrobe stifling a yawn, her blonde hair sticking up in all directions.

Ruth found some energy and pushed most of it into her opening sentence. "Morning," she said brightly, forcing the words to sound cheery. Amanda smiled and muttered 'morning' back. It was far too early for her. "I'll make you some tea," Ruth offered, and stood to do the necessary as Amanda sat down at the table with a thump.

"Going for a run?" Amanda enquired,

It looked like the decision had been taken out of her hands. "I fancied some toast first, then I'm off. Should I put you some in?"

"Too early for me, thanks. Just the tea," as a steaming mug was placed in front of her. Either Amanda hadn't seen Ruth looking so tired or she was ignoring it, but either way she didn't ask.

"What does your day hold for you?" Ruth asked her. "Have you got much on?"

Amanda stared into her tea and mumbled, "Hopefully Dupin is

back today. That could mean the press will be hassling us, but it will be good to have him back. It must've been hard on him. I'd have hated to be in his shoes with such an accusation hanging over me."

"I can't imagine what it would be like, being up for manslaughter or murder. Amazing how a horrible situation can arise out of something that started out so innocently."

Amanda glanced up from her tea, a questioning look on her face. "Cheery thought," she said sarcastically.

"It's true," protested Ruth. "Sometimes we have no control over the outcome, because fate intervenes. And we have no control over what others do; sometimes other people's actions force us to act out of character."

Amanda nodded and gave her a thoughtful look. It was a bit deep for so early in the morning.

"I'd better get out there," Ruth announced taking the remaining half slice of toast with her. "I'll see you in an hour," she added, and headed off back upstairs to get changed.

Amanda took a sip of tea and mulled over Ruth's last words. She knew Ruth wasn't acting normally and that she hadn't had much sleep during the night. Whatever it was that was playing on her mind, she hoped it passed soon. Amanda hadn't got much sleep either, having been fully aware that Ruth was wide awake and restless. She heard the clunk of the front door closing and hoped her run would help her manage to work through whatever was bugging her before she got back.

Chapter Thirty-Six

By the time Ruth returned home, the sky over Croydon was a pale blue with the promise of sunshine to come. Birds flitted from branch to branch in search of breakfast; some worked the ground with their feet to bring worms to the surface. Amanda was dressed and almost ready to leave, figuring she might as well go in to the station early since she was up; there was always something to do. Not to mention the fact she fancied a McDonald's for breakfast. And their coffee wasn't half bad.

Ruth's face was beet red and sweat glistened on her neck as she stood outside on the patio, a hand towel draped around her shoulders, trying to cool off. She swigged back a glass of water and tipped the last couple of inches into a nearby pot plant. She stood, panting, looking down at the herb garden. A light dew covered everything, making the plants twinkle in the early morning light.

"I must make some basil ice cubes with all that basil; there's no sense in wasting it. And the same with the coriander," she said.

On the other side of the open door, Amanda grunted absently in reply; she was only half-listening. Green-fingered she was not, nor was she a chef, but she was good at other things. Luckily Ruth had both those skills; otherwise, it would be takeaway every night and even Amanda would have to contemplate running to keep her weight under control. It was hard enough as it was.

"Right, I'm off," she said. "Speak to you later." She planted a quick peck on Ruth's cheek. Feeling a little more upbeat, she said, "I bet Gordon's got a bit of a headache this morning. The flat-warming was in full swing when we left."

"I'll call him later, see how he is."

"Good idea. He'll want to know how you are, after what happened to you last night. He was a bit worried, I think."

"I'll call him," Ruth assured her. "Well, I'd better go get in the shower before I drip sweat all over the place. Have a good one."

Amanda grabbed her keys and phone and headed out. As the front door clicked closed, Ruth was halfway up the stairs to the bathroom.

The smell of hot bacon and sausage muffins greeted Amanda's nostrils as she entered McDonald's. Rather than collecting her breakfast through the drive-through window and eating it in the car park, she decided to park up properly and head inside for a change; that way her car wouldn't stink later. It was also less messy; eating in the car, she invariably dropped something and made a grease mark. It was a habit she'd picked up from Jack; he hated eating inside with all the noisy kids and preferred the comfort of his own vehicle.

She placed her order, collected her meal and sat down. Four young boys and a man Amanda assumed was their father sat at a table a couple across from hers. The boys all looked a similar age and were dressed in their school uniforms, enjoying a greasy breakfast. She wondered if it was a birthday breakfast for one of the boys, or a special treat, or maybe their father was just short on time or patience and McDonald's fitted the bill. She hoped they didn't make a habit of it, though she was hardly one to talk, sat with her own sausage and egg muffin, a sheen on her lips that wasn't lip gloss.

She glanced again at their eager young faces as they tucked into their breakfast and realised they all looked quite similar to each other and the man with them; there was no mistaking that he was their father. She wondered where their mother was, if they had one, even; perhaps he'd taken them out for breakfast to give her a break. The boys weren't quadruplets, she realised, but they could be two sets of twins. Either way, four boys around seven years old would be a handful, tough work.

Her phone warbled out the opening bars of ELO's "Mr Blue Sky"—Jack. She wiped her mouth and fingers on a serviette before swiping the screen to take the call.

"Morning," she said brightly. "Another early bird."

"The best way to see the sunrise is to get up for it."

"And another deep thinker this morning, too, I might add."

"Where are you? You're obviously not at home. No, don't tell me: you're at McDonald's again."

How the hell did Jack know that?

"What on earth makes you think that?"

"The background noises, for one, and I know you're partial to a bacon or sausage muffin if it's early. I'm right, aren't I?"

"You're one talented detective, Jack."

"Someone's a bit cranky this morning," he said. "What's bugging you?"

"Just tired."

"A big night at the party, was it?"

"You could say that. Anyway, I'm sure you didn't ring to find out how the flat-warming went. What do you need, Jack?" She sipped her coffee.

"I'm ringing to warn you, actually. There's a bit of a crowd gathered already at the station, outside the front doors. Some are press, but there are quite a few of the public and they don't look too happy."

Amanda groaned; there was no need to ask what the gathering was all about.

"Thank goodness for rear entrances. I appreciate the head-up, Jack. Don't tell me you're at work already?"

"No, not yet, but I did go and pick up Mrs Stewart this morning because her car is in for service, and we drove by the station on the way back. I hope that mob doesn't get any bigger."

"No doubt Japp will sort it out when he gets in. He can hardly send Dupin out to do the job. I wouldn't want to be in Dupin's shoes this morning."

"Neither would I, and while *we* know he's innocent, I'm guessing the angry mob out front are on the family's side and screaming 'cover-up.' I wonder if the Parkers are with them, along with Miss Bagpipes."

Amanda couldn't help but smile at Jack's nickname for Melissa Ross. Political correctness wasn't his strong point.

Chapter Thirty-Seven

Dupin felt like a 16-year-old heading out for his first day on the job. Butterflies had been replaced by bats, and they were bouncing off the insides of his stomach as they tried to get out. He was glad to be going back to work but apprehensive at the same time, because not everyone was happy at the autopsy results. He turned the radio on to take his mind off it, but the incessant chatter of the two co-hosts grated on his nerves. He searched through stations, keeping one hand on the wheel, looking for some soothing classical music. If he was going to arrive at work in a calm state, he needed something to help that happen. Piano music filled the car as he settled on the station. He had no idea what the tune was—it wasn't one of the more popular classical pieces—but it would do for now.

The lane was clear and the leafy green trees dappled the tarmac with a lacy pattern as the early morning sun filtered through. He was lucky he could live out of town; many couldn't afford to, or didn't want the commute time, but he loved the outdoors. He and Lyn had chosen a smaller house in a green area rather than a big flat in a concrete jungle; he was not interested in keeping up with the Joneses.

It was coming up to 8 am as Dupin waited for the electric gates to roll back so he could pull into the station yard. Several cars belonging to his team were parked up already. He found a parking space, then turned his engine off and sat for a moment, just thinking. How would the team react, he wondered? While they all knew he was innocent now, he knew there had been doubt in some people's minds before the results had come in. He was aware of his nickname, that people called him Dopey behind his back, and he wondered if now they still viewed him in the same way. He'd never been dopey, not in his mind anyway, but obviously some people thought differently. It was time to go inside and pick up where he'd left off only a few days ago.

He gathered his briefcase and his lunchbox and stepped out of the car, pushing his shoulders back to stand as tall as he was able as he headed for the rear entrance. If anyone was watching on the CCTV camera, they weren't going to see a shrunken, solemn man. He had a team to run and experience to give, so it was business as usual as far as he was concerned.

Walking down the tiled corridor towards the squad room and his office, he noticed that the station seemed unusually quiet. As he entered the squad room, his team, who were all stood to order around their desks, turned towards him. Amanda caught his eye first; she beamed at him as she led a round of applause to welcome their DI back into the fold. He relaxed his shoulders and grinned despite himself as the applause got louder and his colleagues started towards him. Amanda shook his hand first, and the butterflies began to leave his stomach as each person in turn welcomed him back with more handshakes and slaps on the back. He needn't have felt so nervous, it seemed.

Conscious that people were waiting for him to say something, he gathered his thoughts as everyone took their seats. He took in the faces around the room feeling thankful for a decent bunch of work colleagues. He dropped his briefcase and lunchbox on a nearby desk and addressed his audience.

"I don't really know what to say, apart from a huge thank you. I wasn't sure what sort of reception I would get, but I certainly wasn't expecting this, and I thank you for your support from the bottom of my boots." There was a bit of polite laughter. "It's been a difficult time for me, and the journey isn't yet over, but at least I'm back at work where I can do some good. I've still got a disciplinary to face, but I can handle that, I'm sure."

A low rumble of 'Hear, hear!' spread across the squad room.

"Until I know what's what," he went on, "why don't I hand over to Amanda, who can fill us all in. Particularly me!"

He smiled and stepped aside as Amanda came forward. She stood at the front of the room and took the briefing on where they were with current cases and issued instructions, while Dupin took it all in. When she was finished, Dupin nodded his thanks and headed back to his office, where he'd most likely stay until lunchtime.

At 12 o'clock, Jack ventured out to the front of the station to see if the crowd had dissipated at all. It hadn't, but it hadn't grown from what he'd seen earlier, either. He recognised a couple of faces from his spot just inside the door: the local press, a couple of hosts from TV stations and a sizeable bunch of people waving placards. They all carried the same message in various ways, each demanding Dupin's resignation or accusing the police of a cover-up. But what did they know? They were running on passion and motivation, Jack knew—it was facts that declared a person's innocence, and facts that had declared Dupin's innocence and verified that there was no conspiracy theory.

They'd get bored eventually. And hungry. The police station was an odd place to hold a protest, a daring place to protest, but Jack figured they'd all be gone by teatime. He hoped so; he craved normalcy again.

Chapter Thirty-Eight

Jack was ready with another tin of chocolate biscuits. He hadn't seen Mac McAllister for some months, not since the man had been sentenced. He was a rough character, for sure; there was no 'rough diamond' about Mac McAllister. He wasn't even the start of the diamond; he was so far away from being a piece of coal that he was prehistoric vegetation. Jack wasn't scared of him, but he knew people who were. They say some dog owners look like their pets, and if McAllister was a dog owner, he'd be a mixture of a bulldog and a bull mastiff. Two purebreds crossed to accelerate the menace. Jack wondered how the man was doing inside prison, and if he'd met his match yet. Someone surely would have wanted to take him on, if only for a bet.

He parked in the same spot he'd used on his last visit and headed to the reception area, where the same prison officer from the previous day was on duty. He wore the same dandruff and the same vacant expression and still showed no obvious signs of personality whatsoever, and simply nodded as Jack approached the desk.

"Hello again," Jack said, not letting the man's dour persona change his own mood or manners.

"Morning," was all he got back.

"Is Mino in today, by chance?"

"He is."

"Could you please tell him I'm here? DC Jack Rutherford, in case you can't remember."

The officer made a face like Jack had disturbed him from something important—again. Making the phone call to tell Mino he had a visitor was akin to an hour of hard labour, apparently. Jack moved away from the desk while he waited. Since the officer was not going to be big on conversation, he didn't feel the need to hang around. He moved over to the window to wait. A couple of minutes later he heard a familiar voice behind him and turned to see Mino standing there. His acne seemed worse than the previous day, and it looked sore. He must have noticed Jack looking and instinctively touched his hand to his face as if to cover it. Jack held out a Sainsbury's shopping bag and, without looking, Mino accepted it, knowing exactly what it contained.

"I'm assuming he still doesn't know?" Jack said.

"I haven't told him, and since nobody else knows you were planning a repeat visit today, I'm guessing he still doesn't." Raising the carrier bag slightly, Mino added "Thanks for these. I'll tell him he has a visitor. Take a pew. I'll be back shortly."

Jack watched the youngster head out through an internal door and went over in his mind what he was going to say to McAllister when he finally got in front of him. It was a shame he couldn't start by punching him in the face, but those times were long gone. He was reminded briefly of Dupin and his recent altercation. It wasn't worth the bother.

It was almost ten minutes later when Mino waved at him to follow him through the door and down the concrete corridor towards the visitor rooms. They stopped outside a metallic grey door.

"I'll leave you to it. Just knock twice when you're ready to leave," Mino told him.

Jack nodded his understanding and slipped inside.

If McAllister was shocked to see Jack, he didn't show it. In fact, he showed no emotion whatsoever, no interest in Jack at all.

"I thought a visitor would ease the monotony of your day. I don't suppose you get too many?"

"I get my share," McAllister said curtly. "What do *you* want, anyhow?"

"Now, that's not very friendly," said Jack.

"It's a prison, in case you haven't realised," said McAllister sarcastically.

Jack ignored him. He pulled out a plastic chair and sat down opposite the big man. Prison food alters the shape of a man, but spending time in the gym had kept McAllister's bulk firm.

"This place must be agreeing with you; you look in good shape."

"I'm sure you didn't come to compliment me. What can I do for you, Detective?"

"That's more like it. Here's what I'm interested in. But you'll need to cast your mind right back."

"Oh?"

"You remember Michael Hardesty, don't you?"

"And?"

"What can you tell me about what happened all those years ago?"

"Nothing you don't already know. The guy killed my brother Chesney. And now he is doing time, as he deserves."

"Why are you so certain he killed your brother?"

"Because he was found guilty. Everyone knows he killed Chesney. Now, if that's all you want to talk about," he said standing. The metal feet from his chair scraped noisily on the floor. Chairs weren't bolted down in this room; they didn't need to be. McAllister wasn't considered a high enough risk.

"Sit down, would you?" demanded Jack. "Only I'm not so sure it's as simple as that anymore."

"What are you talking about?"

"I've been taking a look at the old case; I've just been working on a similar one that happened only a few days ago."

"You mean that dick Dupin? I saw it on the news. Serves him right."

"Well, I'm guessing you haven't seen the latest news; otherwise, you would know that he wasn't responsible for that death."

McAllister sat back in his chair with his hands behind his head and smiled up at the ceiling.

"Bloody convenient. What did he have to do to cover it up?"

"Well, nothing, as it happens. Pathology doesn't lie. You see, a pathologist deals with facts, not gut instinct; not opinion, but facts. The pathologist found Dupin was in no way responsible."

"I see where you're going with this now. You're wondering if the same thing happened and Hardesty isn't responsible."

"Something like that, yes."

"Why are you bothering? It's my understanding that he'll be out soon enough."

"I wouldn't call another two years soon enough. So, back to my original question. What do you remember about that night and the events that followed?"

"I'm not telling you a damn thing; you can go to hell. Hardesty deserves everything he got, and he'd better watch out when he gets out, because families are like elephants. We never forget."

McAllister stood abruptly, strode to the door and banged on it twice with his fist. He paced for a moment until the officer unlocked the door and he was led from the room back down the corridor to his cell. Jack sat alone, staring at the painted concrete blocks, and wondered if he'd handled it the right way. McAllister now knew what Jack was on to, and also knew that Hardesty was an inmate in the same prison, and how long he had left to serve. Jack would have been more surprised if he hadn't known. He hoped he hadn't made things worse for Hardesty, who was a damn sight frailer-looking than McAllister had been. He'd ask Mino about his health on the way out.

Chapter Thirty-Nine

Jack was back at the station a good deal earlier than lunchtime this time. His main task for the day was already done—though the job wasn't finished yet. Amanda knew where he was, so at least he didn't need to explain his whereabouts to her. And since Dupin was closeted in his office, he'd no sooner have any idea where Jack was that he would the square root of 96. Jack smiled at the thought—the square root of 96. He had no idea either, actually. He'd managed to get through school at a limp and charm his way into the force—education had been low down on Jack's list of priorities as a youngster. All he'd wanted to do was play in a band, be a drummer, but he'd never given it a chance.

Walking down the corridor towards the squad room, he caught a whiff of what was cooking in the canteen for lunch, though he couldn't detect exactly what it was. That was never a good thing; it meant it would be something mediocre and nondescript like beef casserole. Curry was always on Friday and one to look forward to; it was his indulgence each week. For the rest of the time, doctor's orders were a sandwich or a salad.

He inhaled again. Pie and chips, maybe? But try as he might, he couldn't identify the aroma.

Up ahead he saw Dupin leaving the squad room and heading his way. Jack had to admit, it was good to have the guy back at work. Dopey as he might be, the team had felt rudderless without him. Jack nodded politely as Dupin approached him, and to his surprise Dupin pulled up in front of him.

"Jack," he said, "I've been meaning to talk to you, but with everything that's been going on, it fell by the wayside. I've got to go out now, but come and see me when I get back later on this afternoon, would you? I'll be in my office later."

"Will do," said Jack, curious to know what the DI wanted to talk to him about. It was obviously something from before the accident, though he couldn't think what it could be. Dupin was already walking away, clearly in a hurry, and waved back at Jack as he went. Jack shrugged and carried on to the squad room and a fresh coffee.

As he turned the corner, Amanda leaped up from her desk and hurried towards him. She took Jack by the shoulder and guided him urgently to the coffee cupboard, which was where he was about to head anyway. She closed the door and stood with her back to it, arms folded.

"Are you going to tell me what's bugging you?" asked Jack, "or are you going to keep me a prisoner in here all day?" He was smiling, but Amanda wasn't.

She took a deep breath and let it out again.

"The second autopsy is scheduled for the day after tomorrow. Faye is aware, of course, and knows the pathologist that the family organised, as you might expect."

"So, what's the problem? We knew this would happen."

"This particular pathologist is particularly picky. I guess I'm just hoping that what we thought was all over will in fact stay all over. And I know Faye is concerned, because if the pathologist, comes back with different results, it'll be one all. Then who do we believe? Will there have to be another autopsy to decide between the two results?" Her voice was getting higher in pitch.

"I know who I would believe. But the family without a doubt would go with the latest autopsy if the results fitted their belief."

"Oh, of course they would, Jack. That's what they're hoping for."

"You know as well as I know that Faye Mitchell is our own version of Dr Picky, so I'm not worried."

"I wish I could be as confident as you are," she said, rubbing her forehead with the palm of her hand. Tiredness was catching up with her.

"Until the new autopsy results are in, there is absolutely no point in thinking or worrying about any possible outcome other than what we already know," he told her. "It will wear you down."

Amanda nodded gloomily.

"Will you attend it? Or do you want me to go?" he asked her.

"I'm not sure any police officer would be welcome, actually, Jack. But thanks for the offer." She checked her wristwatch. It was coming up to 11 am. "I need something sweet," she said. "Do you want anything?"

Jack rummaged deep in his pockets for loose change for the machine and pulled out a couple of gold coins. "I'll have a Kit Kat, please, if you're going," he said, and handed over the money. "Do you want another coffee? You look like you could use one."

She moved away from the door and nodded yes as she slipped out. As she walked through the squad room towards the vending machine, she glimpsed the crowd that was still gathered outside the front of the station. It looked like they were in for the day. But the crowd weren't her concern, and she focused on purchasing a Kit Kat and a Mars bar to tide herself and Jack through until lunchtime. The machine wasn't co-operating.

Waiting for Jack's Kit Kat purchase to complete, she glanced again at the crowd outside and took a moment to read some of the messages on the placards. Some had been quite creative in their phrasing, and others needed to learn how to spell properly, but the gist of what they were trying to say was clear to anyone who could read. As she scanned the group, a familiar face caught her eye: Melissa 'Bagpipes' Ross. She was brandishing a banner and shouting, and appeared to be the one leading the demonstration.

Amanda looked for Mr and Mrs Parker but they didn't seem to be there. Maybe Jack was right: maybe Melissa was leading this, whatever 'this' was. Maybe she felt cheated out of more than the death of her fiancé and was looking for a result that suited her needs.

The second autopsy couldn't come soon enough, Amanda thought. She hoped that Dr Mitchell's findings would be corroborated, that things would settle back down to normal by the end of the week. When something happened to someone close to you, she knew, it felt a whole lot more personal than any other case. Dupin was one of their own and still might face prison time. It would hurt everyone that knew him.

She must have been stood a while, because she felt Jack by her side.

"I'll sort it, you get the coffee."

Chapter Forty

Jack kicked the vending machine for a second time. "Damn thing," he cursed. "You never do what you say you'll do." The Kit Kat still hadn't shaken loose.

Raj was approaching the machine, counting change into the palm of his hand. "Playing up again, is it?"

"It seems you can buy one item, but the second one always gets stuck—and the second one is my Kit Kat."

"Always the way. I find if you whack it just here with the heel of your hand rather than your foot, it works just fine." Jack raised his eyebrows. "Trial and error," Raj answered, "but trust me: the heel of your hand, right there." He pointed just below the coin slot.

Jack gave it a whack and his Kit Kat fell down into the tray below. "Well, blow me down," he said. "What do you know."

"Like I said," said Raj. "Trial and error."

Jack stood aside so that Raj could get his purchase and watched as the first item came free with ease, but his packet of salt and vinegar crisps required the help of a thump from Raj's palm before the packet fell free from the machine. Raj turned and gave Jack a 'told you so' look. Satisfied they each had what they'd come for, they headed back to the squad room.

Amanda was on the phone, frowning and evidently deep in conversation with somebody, as Jack approached her desk. She waved for him to stay until she'd finished the call. Who she was talking to he'd no idea, but from the look on her face, something was afoot. He waited patiently like a schoolboy standing outside the headmaster's door.

At last, she finished her call and sat back in her chair. She stayed silent for a moment, obviously pondering whatever the caller had told her. Eventually she turned towards Jack and said, "You're never going to believe what I'm about to tell you."

"Oh? Try me." He pushed her Mars bar across the desk to her, but she ignored it—a bad sign. Clearly something serious had happened. He pulled a chair from a nearby empty desk and sat down opposite her, their knees almost touching.

He waited. And waited some more.

Finally, she turned towards him and locked eyes with him as she delivered the news.

"They've found a body."

"Right."

She took a deep breath before starting the sentence again. "They found a body, and it's in Gordon's old backyard. They were using a digger, and they've dug up a body."

It took a moment for Jack to realise exactly what Amanda was telling him. A body had been dug up in her father-in-law's old garden. Not good.

"Holy shit."

"My thoughts exactly."

"Well, I guess we'd better head over there and see what's what."

"I guess we'd better," she said, gathering her bag and car keys as though she were on autopilot.

Jack followed her uneasily out and down the corridor.

The late morning sunshine was warm on their shoulders as they slipped inside Amanda's car. Jack wound his window down as they pulled out of the car park; there was no need for air-conditioning just yet. She still hadn't said much, so Jack didn't fill the empty space with conversation. He figured her brain was working overtime about how this could all turn out. It wasn't every day a body was dug up in the garden of the house your father-in-law had just vacated. And what about Ruth?

Traffic moved relatively freely as they headed south onto the bypass, towards Caterham and a house Amanda had visited many times in the past. Not only had it been her father-in-law's house; it also wasn't the first time they'd both been there in connection with a crime. Jack wondered if it was anything to do with Des Walker, a missing landscaper they'd been searching for a couple of years ago. They'd interviewed Madeline Simpson, the lady of the house, about his disappearance, and while Jack hadn't thought there was anything to it, Amanda hadn't been as certain.

When Madeline Simpson had died in an accident a short time later, the investigating officers had been forced to put Walker's disappearance down to his simply going AWOL. He'd owed money, he was an adult, and he was entitled to leave town any time he liked and not tell a soul. And that's what Jack thought had happened.

With news of a body being dug up, however, he knew he might have to change his thinking.

"Are you thinking of the landscaper?" Jack enquired.

"I'm trying *not* to think about the landscaper. There is no reason to think it's him. That could just be a coincidence."

"We know they don't exist, not in our game."

"Alright, then. I'm hoping that we're wrong, that the Simpsons had nothing to do with this."

"I hear you. Let's wait and see."

They drove the rest of the journey in silence, each thinking of possibilities but neither voicing their thoughts. As they pulled into Oakwood Rise and headed to Gordon Simpson's old house, they could see the earthmoving equipment, along with a group of men taking an early lunch. They'd obviously downed tools at their find.

Jack and Amanda got out of the car and approached the gathering, and a man with a sunburnt face wearing a yellow hardhat stood and greeted the two of them.

"Phil Springer," the man said, introducing himself.

Jack took out his warrant card and flashed it. "Detective Jack Rutherford, and this is Detective Amanda Lacey. Are you in charge, Mr Springer?"

"I am, yes. It was me that found the body."

"Can you tell me what happened?"

"Not much to tell, really. I was digging the earth out for the pool, shifting the earth into the truck, and the next minute I could see what appeared to be a long bone sticking out of a pair of jeans, or the remains of a pair of jeans. I put the digger bucket down, had a closer snoop, and nothing has been touched since. Thought I'd better call you lot."

"Then we'd better take a look," said Jack. Amanda still hadn't said anything, leaving it all to Jack. The three of them walked over to where the digger had been working, treading carefully so anything that might be important wasn't destroyed underfoot. As soon as they'd taken a look, Jack would contact the SOCO team to come out and do their bit.

He stood looking into the hole that the digger had already excavated for the new pool. It was going to be some pool. In the jaws of the digger's bucket was what the man had described: a boot with a long bone sticking out of it and blue cloth that looked like denim. More bones and cloth were visible at the bottom of the hole.

Jack stood and stared at them. Amanda was still deathly quiet.

"I'm going to have to close this site down while we investigate," Jack told Springer, "so once we've spoken to each of your men, you may as well all go home. We will remove the body; I think it's fair to say it's a human body."

"And how long do you think that will be?" Phil asked. "I'm paying for the hire of this equipment, and I can't afford for it to sit idle."

"I'm afraid that's exactly what's going to happen, Mr Springer. That's just the way it has to be. It's inconvenient, I know, but we have a crime scene here now, and that takes priority. If I were you, I'd have a chat to your hire company. It's not your fault." Phil Springer grunted. "Why don't you carry on with your lunch, and we'll take a statement from each of you shortly."

"Right," Springer said defeatedly. The man was obviously thinking about the added cost to his project. Not to mention the homeowners' annoyance at their pool works stalling.

"Have you notified the owners of the property, by chance?" asked Jack.

"No, not yet. Do you want me to call them?"

"Yes, please. At the very least, they'll be wanting to know why you've downed tools. I'll need their details also, so we can speak to them too, though I doubt they have any involvement from what I can see here. They wouldn't be stupid enough to bury a body and then have you dig it up, I'm sure. And this body has been in the ground some time."

Jack watched as the man returned to his team to deliver the news, and then took his phone out and called the SOCO team.

He also called Dr Faye Mitchell. She'd want to take a close look at this one.

Chapter Forty-One

❧❧❧

Amanda still seemed to be in a world of her own, and Jack couldn't understand why. She was always so gung-ho when a new case came in. But today she was different; vacant, worried-looking. Yes, this was Gordon's old place, but why was that having such an effect on her? Maybe it was just the connection with Ruth, but again, why would that be so bad? Ruth and her father weren't responsible. And Madeline Simpson had been exonerated, even though Amanda had had a bee in her bonnet at the time, suspecting the woman was involved somehow. He took his vending-machine Kit Kat from his pocket and unwrapped it, then slipped a stick into his mouth while his thoughts circulated in his head. What could possibly have happened here? And to whom?

If this was the landscaper, Des Walker, in the hole, this would be a very interesting coincidence. It was well known that he had had gambling debts. And the local bookie's shop was owned by the very same Mac McAllister that Jack had been to see only a few hours ago at the prison. Jack didn't think McAllister was a murderer, but even if he had killed Walker, why would he have buried him in the garden that he was working in? Not to mention the fact that he'd never get his money back by killing the man. It was stupid and didn't make sense. As for coincidences, Jack had never believed in them.

He peeled the foil off the remaining sticks of Kit Kat and munched on them one by one, staring down into the red clay earth. The digger parked nearby reminded him of the giant orange one that had sat in this very same garden back then, awaiting its driver, the landscaper who had walked off the job and never come back.

Or maybe he had.

His stomach rumbled a little—the Kit Kat was not enough—and he wondered if Amanda wanted her Mars bar. She was standing by the group of builders and didn't look to be doing much other than gazing around, so he headed over to have a chat with her. Three of the men stared at him as he approached. The dust from the excavation covered his shoes in a thin film, turning their formal black finish into a tan colour. It was a good job it wasn't winter; he'd need his Wellington boots. He nodded sideways at Amanda, indicating for her to follow him away from flapping ears. She took the hint and moved alongside him as they headed back towards her vehicle.

"Something is wrong, Amanda," Jack said. "You're not behaving like you normally do. What gives?"

She let out a deep sigh before replying. "It just seems… it seems so, oh, I don't know…"

Jack filled in the blanks for her. "It just seems a bit close to home. Is that what you mean?"

"I guess so. It's not even my home. And I barely knew Gordon a couple of years ago; barely knew him at all."

Jack nodded, letting her find her words as she carried on. "He just doesn't seem the type to do something like this, and for what reason? Why would he have a body in his garden and then just wait for someone to possibly dig it up?

"It's most likely not Gordon, like you said. What's the motive? Why bury someone in your own garden? And he sure as hell wouldn't have bothered moving house; he'd have stayed here forever, keeping this secret buried—literally. So that leaves the only other person who's lived in this house in the last couple of years."

"Madeline Simpson."

They stood quietly for a few moments; they both knew Amanda's feelings about her.

At length, Jack spoke again. "I guess if we have an inkling of who this body might be, it won't take long to get a name. Once we've got the dental records, identification shouldn't take too long at all. Let's hope we have teeth in that skull still buried in there," he said, pointing. "There's hardly anything left of him. Or her."

"Let's hope so, but we've got to interview Gordon. And depending on what he says and how long this body has been in there, there could be others."

"Others?" enquired Jack.

"I don't mean others buried. I mean others to interview. Gordon lived in this house with Madeline for years. I can't see there being anybody else involved. You sure as hell would know if someone had dug your garden up and buried a body in it if it wasn't you or your wife. And that's another question—how would Madeline manage to bury a body without Gordon knowing?"

Jack grunted; it was feasible, but just barely.

"Look at Peter and Sonia Sutcliffe," Amanda went on. "She had no clue what he was up to. Though he said he'd wanted to confess to her. He told her himself, you know, when he was arrested. He didn't want the police to tell her what he'd done. Poor woman."

"What are you going to tell Ruth, and what are you going to do about Gordon?" Jack asked.

"We need to speak to them both, obviously, and the current homeowners."

"Why don't I talk to Gordon?" offered Jack.

"And I'll tell Ruth," said Amanda glumly.

Chapter Forty-Two

With the scene of crime officers already on their way, Amanda had no choice but to ring Ruth. She knew exactly how she would react and was dreading it. Who wouldn't be? Finding a body buried in the garden of somebody you know was bad enough, but finding one in the garden of somebody you loved was going to be doubly hard. The questions that raised their ugly heads would all need answers, and doubt could be a destructive thing. Amanda made her way to the furthest point in the yard for a little privacy for the call that she was about to make—not that anyone was within eavesdropping distance, but the seclusion gave her comfort. She dialled Ruth's number and waited for her to answer.

"Are you missing me?" asked Ruth brightly. Amanda could imagine her at her desk, sitting back in her big cream squashy comfy chair, phone to her ear with a smile stretching across her face. She was a lucky woman to have met Ruth, she thought.

"Always," said Amanda. "But I'm afraid I've got some news for you, so I'm hoping you're sat down in your office."

"Yes, I am," confirmed Ruth, worry now obvious in her voice.

"Whatever has happened? You're calling me rather than visiting, so I'm going with nothing too serious?" she asked hopefully.

There was no point stretching things out any longer than necessary, so Amanda dived straight in. "There's been a body found in your father's garden at the old house. Jack is speaking to Gordon now to let him know, but I thought you should know too."

Ruth stayed absolutely silent, to the point where Amanda wondered if they'd been disconnected. She tried again. "Are you still there, Ruth? Hello?"

"I'm here. Just a bit shocked, actually. Where was it found?"

"Workmen were digging out for a swimming pool over on the far-right side and they came across it a couple of hours ago with their digger."

"How long do you think it's been there?" asked Ruth.

"We don't know yet, but from my experience I would say somewhere between two and five years. But I can't say for sure, until someone more qualified has had a look."

"Did you say Jack has called Dad already?"

"He's doing it now; we'll need him to come in to give a statement, since he lived in the house when the body was likely buried."

"You don't think Dad had something to do with this, surely?" Ruth was beginning to sound frantic; her voice wobbled slightly now. "Because I can tell you now, he isn't involved."

"There's so much we don't know right at this moment, hun, but we have to follow procedure, and the new homeowners will be interviewed in just the same way. I just thought you should know. Gordon might appreciate your support. And I'll most likely be off the case."

"I'll call him. Speak to you later," she said, and the line went dead. Amanda was left holding the phone to her ear. She stared at it in puzzlement and then slipped it back into her pocket and reversed her mind back over the conversation she'd just had. Ruth was a strong and bright woman, and she'd taken the news in her stride, with more acceptance of the situation than Amanda would have thought. It was like she was already expecting it, somehow.

She shook her head as if to dislodge such a thought: how would the woman she lived with know about a body buried in the garden of her parents' old house? The idea was utterly ridiculous.

She looked up to see Jack picking his way towards her, trying to keep to the patches of grass that weren't covered in loose dirt. He looked like an obsessive keeping away from cracks on the pavement. She waited until he was by her side before asking how Gordon had taken the news.

"What did he say?"

"Not a lot, actually," Jack said. "He was shocked, of course. It's not every day you get news of a dead person in the garden of your old home. He's on his way to the station now. I said we'd meet him there and take his statement. The same with the homeowners. How did Ruth take it?"

"Surprisingly well, but that's Ruth for you. Not much fazes her. She hung up pretty quickly, though; said she wanted to give her dad a call, so no doubt they're chatting as we speak."

Car doors could be heard slamming over the other side of the hedge; the top of a silver van was just visible.

"That'll be SOCO," Jack said. "The sooner they start, the sooner we can get some results. I'll go and show them through." With that, he was gone.

She checked her watch. It was gone one o'clock. No wonder she was hungry. She walked around to the front of the house. The SOCO team were donning their white paper suits, masks and gloves as she approached them. Jack was already briefing them on what the workmen had found, and the condition everything was in. Dr Faye Mitchell was among them, listening intently to what Jack had to say.

Amanda heard her say, "We'll take it from here, then, Jack. I'll call you later. We could be here a while, so it might be late on."

"I'll leave you all to it, then. Amanda, let's get going," he said, Faye raised an eyebrow. Usually it was Amanda who gave the orders. For her part, Amanda was grateful, since her mind was still on

Ruth's reaction—and a feeling deep in her gut that she couldn't quite put her finger on.

"I'll drive," said Jack, and he took the keys from her fingers and slipped into the driver's side before Amanda could argue. He waited until she was sitting beside him before starting the engine and cruising out of the quiet country lane.

"It's weird, don't you think?" she asked.

"What's weird?"

"Being here again, talking about landscapers and the Simpsons."

"I wish it was as funny as *The Simpsons*," said Jack unhelpfully. "But it is a bit weird. I was thinking that if this does turn out to be the landscaper who went missing, he owed money to the bookies in town, which is owned by Mac McAllister, the very same McAllister I saw this morning. How is that for timing?"

"Hmm," said Amanda. She was quiet for a moment, pondering. "I'm not looking forward to talking to Gordon, either. Perhaps you should do it?"

"I don't think we're seriously treating him as a suspect at this stage, are we?"

"We have no choice. You saw what state the remains are in. They weren't buried yesterday. So, yes, he is a suspect, as was anybody else that lived or lives in that house."

Jack grunted; he knew Amanda was right, of course. And since Gordon Simpson was her father-in-law, she was also too close to the case. He would definitely have to do the interviewing himself.

Jack knew the case would fall back on his own shoulders. But to what result?

He'd soon find out.

Chapter Forty-Three

Jack drove them back to the station. There wasn't much they could do until SOCO had finished with the scene. They sat silent, each busy with their own thoughts. Jack wondered what Amanda's were. It wasn't going to be much fun for her observing an investigation where her father-in-law could be a suspect, and he knew that it could make things difficult for her at home with Ruth. He was glad it wasn't him, but at the same time wished it wasn't Amanda, either.

It wasn't long before they were back on the outskirts of Croydon, the scenery changing from the lush greenery at the crime scene to dappled grey concrete and graffiti. He could understand why people lived out on the greenbelts and commuted; it would be nice to go home to, spend a little time in your own back garden, maybe with a glass of wine. He had about a postage stamp's worth of grass at his place, as did the neighbours, but then he chose to live local, close to the amenities, and a postage stamp's worth was about as much as you got for your money.

He'd never left the place after Janine had passed, never felt the desire to move on. Going up at night to the bedroom they'd shared for so many years gave him comfort somehow. It had been only about a year ago that he'd dared to put some of her belongings away; her bathrobe had hung behind the bedroom door for as long as he could remember. Now it had a place in her wardrobe along with the rest of her clothes. He knew most people felt the need to clear out, to give their loved one's clothing to a charity shop so that someone else might make use of them. Jack had never felt that way, though, and until, if ever, he found someone to spend his life with, Janine's things would stay put where they were.

He pictured his leather bag of bowling balls at the bottom of the wardrobe, adjacent to Janine's own bag. They'd shared the enjoyment of the game together, Janine playing for the local women's team and Jack for the men's, but when she'd got sick Jack had given up. Then his housekeeper, Mrs Stewart, had started helping Jack out a few days a week, and over a cup of tea one morning she'd mentioned that she'd also used to play lawn bowls. Jack had found a league and asked Mrs Stewart along, and the two of them had rekindled their interest in the sport. Tonight, Jack was taking part in a local tournament.

"I must give my balls a wipe," he said out loud, forgetting where he was and who he was with.

"Really, Jack?" Amanda said, turning his way with an amused smile.

"What?" asked Jack, nonplussed. "What are you talking about?"

"You just said you need to give your balls a wipe." She was grinning at him properly now.

"Did I? Shit. I don't remember saying it, though I do remember thinking it."

"Well, I haven't developed ESP skills overnight, so you must have said it."

Jack grunted and blushed.

"Anyway," Amanda went on, "what did you mean, or dare I ask?" She grinned at him again.

"Lawn bowls tonight, a local tournament. I must polish my balls."

"Yes, I got that part. Is Mrs Stewart playing too?"

"She is, yes. She's quite good, actually." He flicked the indicator to turn into the side street entrance of the station and waited until it was clear to pull across. "What are you up to tonight, then?"

"Well, now this has happened I guess it depends on how Ruth is feeling. What happens with Gordon. There could be some family fallout. To be honest, I'm not relishing the conversations ahead."

"No, I don't blame you, but keep an open mind. You have enough experience in this game to know what's what. I don't think Gordon has had anything to do with this, though. He's the type of guy who would move a snail off the footpath so it didn't get crushed underfoot. I can't see him having the urge to kill a human, no matter how hard he was pushed, never mind disposing of a corpse. I've got more urge in my little finger than he has in his whole body." Jack pulled into a parking space and the two sat there for a moment longer.

"Now *you* need to keep an open mind," Amanda reprimanded him lightly. "You don't know that much about him, which is a good thing."

Jack reached to open his door. "I will keep an open mind, but I'm also an excellent judge of character and he's not the person we're looking for, I can tell you now. But we'll go through the process and see what happens, see what gives, and take it from there." He clicked the car lock and handed the keys back to Amanda. She slipped them back into her bag and they headed to the rear entrance. Jack carried on, "Let's see what the doctor comes back with. Maybe that body has been there a good deal longer and has nothing to do with the current or previous occupants of the house."

It was Amanda's turn to grunt; she didn't believe it for one moment.

Jack turned to her and said, "I'm going to the canteen to hunt down a stray sandwich. As dodgy as they are, they're better than nothing. Shall I get you one?"

"Please. I might be here a while yet."

Jack nodded and wandered back towards the canteen. Amanda didn't need to be at work late, not until they had something to work with, some results, some evidence. Maybe she was avoiding Ruth. Or maybe she wanted to watch Gordon Simpson being questioned.

"Open mind, Amanda, open mind," he called back to her.

Chapter Forty-Four

The sandwiches from the canteen were only just better than nothing at all. He'd started on the second half and marvelled at how the cooks had managed to do such a terrible job of a cheese salad sandwich. White bread and cheap margarine stuck to his teeth and gums, saturated from the lettuce and tomato that hadn't been dried properly before they'd used it in the culinary delight they sold as a sandwich. Smoked cheese and pale mayonnaise finished off the whole ensemble before being crammed into a cellophane packet that had been kept in the fridge since dawn.

He checked the clock on the wall while he ate, cramming the soggy mass into his mouth as he walked slowly back down the corridor. He needed a drink to wash it down, to rinse his teeth off, to get the cloying sticky wad out of his mouth and into his stomach. God only knew what it was going to do to his insides as it moved through; indigestion was likely. He sifted change out of his pocket, and when he'd found the amount he needed, he ordered a Coke from the vending machine. He punched in the relevant code number and waited for the can to roll towards him. A good few beats passed; it looked like the machine wasn't going to oblige, like it might once again need a good whack from the palm of his hand. At the last second, the red can rolled free. He grabbed it, pulled the ring open and took a long swig. A little brown tear of Coke escaped the corner of his mouth and he wiped it away with the back of his hand, belching lightly. He took his drink back to the squad room.

Gordon Simpson was on his way in, but he wasn't due to arrive quite yet. Jack decided he'd use the time to catch up on the never-ending paperwork that was stacked up in various piles on his desk, but his thoughts drifted to Vivian. She'd looked good when he'd seen her. Had that only been yesterday?

"Sod it," he said, and entered Vivian's name into the database. "I know I know," he muttered to himself, "but it doesn't hurt to know what you're dealing with." He waited a moment or two until her file came up on the screen. She'd looked different back then, when her last mug shot had been entered. She didn't sport the stylish blonde bob that she'd had when he'd met her in the sandwich shop, and she'd aged well. He'd last seen her a couple of years ago while on another case, but she'd still been a working girl back then and had inadvertently become part of a case that he was working on: she'd been about to meet the victim, before he became a victim, or in the midst of becoming one. It seemed he hadn't been able to answer the door to her either way, and so she'd gone back home, wondering. The next day, they'd discovered what had happened.

Jack and Vivian went back many years; he'd arrested her for solicitation when he'd been new to the force himself and had taken an instant liking to her. He'd looked out for her over the years, trying to help her stay out of trouble. Looking at her file now, it seemed she *was* on the straight and narrow, had perhaps even given up the oldest trade in the world. It wasn't a game for older ladies; it wasn't really a game for the young ones, either, of course, but it was the young ones who played it the most, mainly out of necessity. He'd spent a lot on warm cups of tea for them through cold winter evenings.

Jack had always got on with the street girls; he'd always liked them, though he'd never used their services. Apart from Vivian, that was. And even then, it was only after Janine had passed. He had never meant for it to happen; he'd never set out to meet Vivian in that way, but had found himself buying her a drink one night in the Baskerville pub and one thing had led to another. He'd felt so lonely at the time, and it seemed the thing to do. Afterwards, he'd felt terrible and had sworn he'd never do it again; his Janine would have frowned on it.

He closed the page down and pulled out his phone. Vivian had taken it from him outside the sandwich shop and entered her details, so she was obviously happy to meet up with him, if only for a drink.

"What harm can it do?" He selected her number and waited to be connected. She wouldn't know it was him; he doubted she had his telephone number in her phone. But she answered quickly, her warming tones like velvet on his earlobe.

"Hello, Vivian here," she said softly. Jack paused for a moment, not quite sure what to say. She repeated herself. "Hello, it's Vivian. Who is this?"

Jack cleared his throat and said, "It's Jack. Jack Rutherford, Vivian." He felt like a teenager all over again.

"Jack," she exclaimed. "I had high hopes you'd ring but I wasn't sure that you would."

"I thought you might like that drink," he said.

"I would. When are you free? How about tomorrow night?"

Jack didn't need to look into his calendar to know that tomorrow evening was totally empty, apart from watching *The Chase*. "How about tonight?" he blurted, surprising himself. He winced, glad that she couldn't see him pulling a silly face. Why had he suggested tonight? he wondered, but it was too late. The words had already left his mouth. Backtracking slightly, he added, "But it would be a bit later on. I've got something to do first. But if you're free, say at nine o'clock?" His face muscles tensed a little as he waited for her reply. He needn't have worried.

"Nine would be perfect," she replied. "Where shall I meet you?"

Then, thinking quickly, she added, "Oh, how about the Baskerville, for old times' sake?"

Jack smiled at that. She'd remembered. "Sounds perfect. I'll see you later," he said, and hung up. While he felt a little out of practice at asking a woman out, he couldn't keep the grin off his face.

Chapter Forty-Five

No sooner had Jack put the phone down than his landline rang. It was the desk sergeant, Doug, letting him know that Gordon Simpson had arrived.

"I'll be out in a moment," said Jack. It was only preliminary enquiries, but he wasn't in the habit of keeping folk waiting unnecessarily. And Gordon Simpson was sort of extended family.

Jack made his way to the front entrance and reception area where Gordon sat waiting. He stood as soon as he saw Jack, remembering him from the wedding. He put his hand out to shake and Jack greeted him warmly, or as warmly as a person could do when they were about to be interviewed about a body being found in their old back garden.

"It's good to see you again, Jack—or should I say Detective Rutherford, since we are here on official business?" Gordon had a friendly way about him, and he reminded Jack of a giant teddy bear.

"And you," said Jack. "I know what you mean by official business, but we have to follow process. I'm sure this is all a formality." He did his best to keep his tone level and not overly friendly or direct. He opened the door and Gordon followed him through down a generic-looking corridor and into an interview room. It was like any other: table, two chairs, recording equipment, cameras in the ceiling and not much more.

Jack pointed to a chair. "Take a seat," he said, and sat down opposite him. Jack spent a moment trying to analyse the man in front of him while they were getting comfortable. He seemed confident, but with a slight edge of concern, which was quite normal in the circumstances. Gordon's sandy, wavy hair looked like it needed a comb. He must've come straight to the station, anxious to get the chat over with. It was slightly damp at the temples from perspiration. It was obviously still warm outside. Or maybe it was nerves. He wasn't overly cocky, but nor was he as nervous as hell. That was a good thing. Jack prided himself on his gut, though he never relied on it exclusively for results—facts and figures were what he needed

"Let's get on with it, then," said Jack, smiling, trying to put the man at ease. There was no point riling him up from the outset, not if he wanted to his cooperation. There was time for that later if need be. Playing good cop, bad cop like they did on TV did work; it did have its place, but not in this instance. Gordon was barely a suspect.

"It's unfortunate, I know," started Jack, "and at this point in time we don't have an awful lot of information to go on. But since you were the last owner of the property until recently, we have to ask you these questions. So, let's start with the easy one. Were you aware there was a body in your garden?" Jack was deadly serious. It seemed like an odd question, but one that needed to be answered.

"Of course, I wasn't," said Gordon confidently, and then asked a question of his own. "Have you any idea when the body was put there?"

"Not as yet," said Jack, "but early estimates are between one and five years ago, so definitely during the time that you owned the property."

"I think I would have noticed if someone had dug up my garden and buried a body. It must've been from before we moved in. I can't think of any other reason."

"Like I say, just preliminary questions at the moment until we have more info."

"I don't know what else I can tell you," Gordon said. "I absolutely don't see how that body could have got there because I didn't put it there, that's for damn sure."

"Do you remember a couple of years ago when you were having a pond dug, and the landscaper went missing?"

"I do. You don't think it's him, do you?"

Jack ignored the question. He'd already told Gordon they didn't know many facts at the present time; there was no point in repeating himself.

"Do you think anybody else that lived in your house could have known, could be responsible?" Gordon shot up from his seat, his chair scraping back noisily.

"Like who? There was only Madeline and me. None of the children have lived in that house for maybe ten years. And I can't see it being Madeline, God rest her soul." He was still standing as his anger and frustration started to boil to the surface.

"Sit down, Gordon," Jack urged him. "I have to ask these questions." He waited until Gordon was sitting back in his chair and his breathing had returned to normal before he went on. "Can you think of anybody else that would have been on your property, particularly at the time when you were having the pond dug, anybody at all? Perhaps an electrician or a plumber or another workman, somebody that we haven't any knowledge of? Because if it wasn't yourself or Mrs Simpson, then we will have to explore other avenues. And right now, we haven't got too much to go on, so any help you can give us would be greatly appreciated."

Gordon sat quietly now, racking his brains to think of people who had been to the property during that time. Madeline had handled the whole project. He had been busy at work and hadn't got involved at all. Though he remembered her temper and her frustration at getting the landscaper there in the first place. The digger had been delivered a couple of days earlier, but still the man had not turned up to do the work. He remembered Madeline telling him that when the landscaper had finally arrived, he'd then cleared off shortly afterwards with no explanation and had never come back. It hadn't been long after that that Madeline herself had had her accident and the whole sorry saga of wanting a pond in the back yard had been forgotten. The orange digger had sat there for days, reminding him of her plans, before it had finally been picked up and removed by a transport delivery company. It hadn't been an easy time, and not one that Gordon wanted to revisit.

"I really don't know what else I can tell you, Jack—I mean, Detective Rutherford," said Gordon. "I have no answers, but I certainly haven't done anything wrong. I certainly haven't buried anybody in my own yard. So, I'm going to leave now, and if you've got any more questions, let me know so I can organise a solicitor." He got to his feet.

"Why would you need a solicitor, Mr Simpson?" enquired Jack.

Chapter Forty-Six

Amanda had watched Jack leave the interview room; she wondered if they were going to get any real results from the interview with Gordon. She, like Jack, knew they had nothing as yet; perhaps the questioning was a little premature. But that didn't mean they couldn't speak to Gordon Simpson again, because right at this moment, it looked like he'd been involved somehow. He'd owned that property until recently and had been there for some years, and while he might not be able to explain it now, there had to be a reason. A body had been found in his garden; whether he knew about it or not was another question.

It had been a couple of hours since they'd left the crime scene and Amanda knew that the SOCO team would be knee-deep in dirt, gathering evidence. She decided she might as well get Des Walker's dental records organised, in case her suspicions were correct, to make the process of confirmation that bit quicker. She dialled Faye's number but the call went straight to voicemail. Amanda left a brief message stating that she was organising dental records and asking if there was anything worth reporting as yet. Faye rarely gave much out before her official report, and it drove

Amanda and Jack to distraction sometimes, but it was best in the long run.

While she waited for Faye to call her back. Amanda slipped into the coffee cupboard and made herself a decaf. At least she could indulge without the caffeine keeping her awake all night. She put the capsule in, pressed the relevant buttons and waited. She'd have to talk to Ruth later on when she got home and she wasn't looking forward to it, knowing full well Ruth was going to get emotional. The woman could be tough as nails on the outside, but Amanda knew that inside she was as soft as marshmallow, although she rarely showed that side of herself in public. Amanda knew she'd be worried sick about her father and the implications of what they'd found in his old back garden.

Once the capsule had released its contents and the strong aroma of coffee filled her nostrils, she added milk and took it back to her desk to think. The squad room was almost empty. There was just herself and Raj, who sat with his feet up on his desk scrolling through his phone; she assumed he was working. She glanced up at the smeared office windows and smiled as she remembered Jack saying that they worked in a petri dish and that they needed to get new cleaners. It was odd, the things you thought about when you let your mind wander, particularly when it was wandering away from something important that you should be thinking about.

She was dragged back to the present by the ringing of her phone. It was Faye's ringtone. Amanda clicked Answer and dove straight in without any preamble.

"I know it's too early yet, Faye, but I have an inkling of who this could be, so I thought I would just see what your initial thoughts were and I can get the dental records organised."

"I understand that, Amanda, but you know as well as I do that science needs to take its time. That said, in this case, since you already have an inkling, I can probably help you with some of it."

"Like what? What can you tell me?" asked Amanda excitedly.

"What I can tell you is that the body is male, and given his state of decay and the organic evidence around him, he's been in the ground for two to three years. Does that fit with your timeframe?"

"It does, actually. If it's the person I think it is, he would be roughly five foot nine in height. Does that fit too?"

"Well, until I get the whole skeleton back to the mortuary and take some accurate measurements, I couldn't say precisely at this moment. But I can tell you that, judging by the long bones, this person wasn't particularly short and they weren't particularly tall."

"When do you think you will be able to start on the autopsy properly?" Amanda asked.

"We're still busy excavating and will probably be here until dark, so realistically I'm not going to have much to you until later tomorrow. And we may need the help of a forensic anthropologist we'll see. I have limited experience with bones."

"Okay. I'll get the dental records for my possible victim. That timeline fits, as does the height, so hopefully it will make identification that bit quicker."

"Great. I'll speak to you later on tomorrow then. Thanks, Faye," Amanda said. "Though I'm not sure if you've made my life easier or harder. I guess we'll find out."

"That sounds cryptic."

"I guess it does," Amanda said resignedly.

She finished her coffee and took her mug back to the coffee cupboard to rinse out. She left it on the draining board, ready for the following morning. There was no sense hanging around the station, so her last chore for the day was to organise getting the dental records. They'd be at the mortuary first thing in the morning.

All that was left to do now was go home and have a chat to Ruth. As she pulled out of the car park, she dialled Ruth's number to see if she was on her way home yet. Maybe they'd get take-out for dinner tonight as a distraction on what was going to be a weird evening.

Ruth picked up right away. "I've just got off the tube," she said without any preamble. "I'm not far from home. Are you on your way back?"

"Great minds think alike," said Amanda. "I thought I'd come home a bit early. To chat."

Silence filled the airwaves for a moment before Ruth said, "I suspected you would. May as well get it over with sooner rather than later."

Amanda could tell Ruth was doing her best to keep it light.

"You're not a suspect, Ruth, but yes, we do need to chat. And sooner."

Chapter Forty-Seven

Amanda had called in at Wong's on the way home for crispy pork balls and sweet-and-sour sauce. Amanda wasn't sure if she was trying to bribe Ruth or prep her or what she was trying to do with her at all, really, but it felt like a nice touch, a sort of peace offering before the peace was possibly broken. There was no reason for Amanda to think that Ruth was involved in any of this, though she was acutely aware, as she'd said to Jack, that process needed to be followed. Ruth had not lived at Gordon's old house for many years but had obviously visited. So, what could she possibly know?

The food smelled wonderful in the car, the aroma of warm pork and deep-fried batter making her drool. She hoped there was still a bottle of wine cooling in the fridge; even though it was a school night, she didn't much care about adhering to their own self-imposed rule. She pulled up in front of their house and noted that Ruth was already home, as expected. She gathered her things and the hot food and headed up the garden path, feeling a little nervous about the conversation ahead. Perhaps, in reality, she wasn't the one to do this, but then neither would Jack be. He knew Ruth almost as well as she did; he came for dinner often enough. Sometimes familiarity could be a good thing and sometimes not so much.

Amanda slipped her key into the lock and swung the door open. There was a light breeze blowing through and it nearly caught the front door, so she closed it quickly before it banged shut. That meant the rear door was open; Ruth likely out on the patio.

"Hi, it's me," she chirped breezily, hoping to take any heaviness out of her tone early on. They'd eat first before she broached the subject.

"Out here," Ruth shouted back. "I have wine." There was a singsong tone to her voice; maybe Ruth had already had a glass or two, and was well on her way to becoming merry.

Amanda tossed her car keys in the fruit bowl and dumped her bag and the food on the kitchen table before heading out the back. Ruth was on a sun lounger, eyes closed, soaking in the last few rays of the late afternoon sun. She opened one eye and raised her glass to Amanda. "Can I get you one?" she asked.

"Don't get up. I'll grab it. I need to get out of my work clothes first. I called and got takeaway from Wong's."

"Excellent," said Ruth. "Crispy pork balls, I assume?"

"I would be hung, drawn and quartered if I went to Wong's and didn't return with pork balls. So yes, we have pork balls. I'll be back in a moment."

Amanda headed upstairs to change out of her work gear. Her feet were boiling; Jack was right: her boots were far too heavy for warm, sunny days. She slipped into a T-shirt and cotton cargo pants and let her feet breathe a little, wiggling toes on the carpet as if freeing them from the confines of the stiff leather they'd been cooped up in all day. Maybe she'd add nail polish to her toenails later.

Back out on the patio, Ruth had sat up and refilled her own glass, and had poured Amanda a glass anyway.

"Thanks," Amanda said, taking a large mouthful of chilled white wine. "That tastes so good, but I suspect it's going to go straight to my head. I've hardly eaten today." She sat back and closed her eyes, feeling the warmth of the sun on her face for a moment and wondering if Ruth was going to say anything first.

"Tough day?" Ruth enquired.

"You could say that." She took a deep breath, then let it out.

"I've put the food in the oven for a moment," said Ruth. "I figured you'd want to ask me your questions first."

Amanda opened her eyes and gazed across at her. "I'm sorry about all this," she said. "I thought we'd eat first. But I don't mind either way. Maybe it's best to get the questions out of the way."

"Ask away, then," said Ruth encouragingly. "I can't tell you much, though, because there's not much to tell."

"I know." Amanda sat up fully and turned towards Ruth, her face devoid of expression. "Have you any idea who could be buried in the garden of your parents' house?"

"Absolutely not," said Ruth flatly.

"Can you think of anybody who would have reason to bury somebody in your parents' old back garden?"

"No. And I haven't lived there for a good ten years."

"Can you remember anybody that was up there when the landscaper went missing? Maybe other work people?"

"What, you think one of them offed somebody and put them in a hole?" Ruth snapped sarcastically. "And since I wasn't living there —I was here, in this very house—I've really no idea what went on up there. Have you?"

"We don't know what has gone on so far, and we won't know anything more until we have a bit more information from the autopsy. Not that there's a lot left of the body. But, hopefully tomorrow we'll have confirmation of who the victim is, and that will give us something to work with."

"So, all your questions at the moment are irrelevant, is what you're saying? Really?" said Ruth smartly.

Amanda bit back a reply. She knew if she carried on there would be one hell of a row, and she didn't want that. Amanda held her tongue and stayed silent to let Ruth calm back down. When the tense air around them dispersed and the fiery residue of her rebuke had faded, Amanda said, "I'll go and get dinner. We'll eat it out here."

It was exactly the excuse she needed to give Ruth a little space and regroup her own thoughts at the same time.

Chapter Forty-Eight

It was rare that a detective interviewed somebody that they knew in relation to a crime, and there was a reason for that. They were too close to the person, and no matter how tenuous their relationship, they had prior knowledge of them and it was difficult to stay impartial. But, Jack wondered, did he really know Gordon at all?

He'd interviewed many people over his years, various small-time crooks, people that he'd come to know, the regulars that filtered through the system. The petty thieves, the sex workers and the local gang members—they'd all been part of his life.

Jack stood in the doorway now watching Gordon Simpson leave the police station through the front door. His shoulders seemed lower, slumped even, than when he'd first set eyes on him only an hour or so ago. But that could just be the stress of it all; it didn't make a man guilty. Outside the front doors, a few demonstrators with placards saying *Police cover-up* and *Police kill* and a few other choice slogans still lingered, but they'd get bored eventually and leave. He hoped. Jack nodded at the desk sergeant and slipped back through to the squad room; it was time to go home. Tonight, he'd got a bowling match to get to and then on for a drink. He thought of Vivian, and he wondered about their 'date' later on. If it was a date, even.

By the time Jack arrived home, he had just a few minutes before he had to turn straight back around and get over to the bowling green. He'd grab his gear and devour cold leftovers from the fridge to keep him going. Perhaps he'd eat something later in the pub with Vivian. Opening the front door, he grabbed the mail off the mat and quickly sifted through the envelopes. There was nothing of interest, so he headed off upstairs to get changed into his team kit. He opened the wardrobe where he kept his bowling bag and was greeted by the perfume of lavender from the soap-on-a-rope that still hung in there. Janine had always loved lavender. He took his bag out and as usual, paused for a couple of beats before gently running his fingers across the bowling bag that sat alongside his. Janine's old brown leather bag had been keeping his own company for many years; they were like two old friends. He always paused for a moment when he took his out; he wondered, as he always did, if she was watching him now and smiling as he touched it, remembering her. She'd been pretty good at bowls, and had almost made the national team. He missed her so much that at times it hurt to breathe.

He slowly closed the door and headed back downstairs to the kitchen. Mrs Stewart had been in earlier in the day and, as usual on a bowling night, had known he'd be pushed for time. He was grateful for the yellow Tupperware box of sandwiches that she'd left in the fridge with a note propped on top: 'Open in case of emergency.' Jack grinned at her thoughtfulness. It was the older woman's idea of a joke, but one that he appreciated because it meant he could eat on the way and he wouldn't arrive out of breath or late. Mrs Stewart was a wonderful woman and a real find, and he wondered how he'd managed in all the time that Janine had been gone, struggling along on his own. In fact, he hadn't really managed at all. He'd let himself go. His appearance, his eating habits, his sleeping habits. But now with some order back in his life, he was functioning better and was a good deal happier all round.

Back in his car, he set off towards the bowling club grounds with cheese and pickle in one hand, the steering wheel in the other as he navigated the remainder of the rush-hour traffic. When he pulled up at a set of traffic lights, he rested his sandwich back in the box and fiddled with his Spotify app for a particular playlist. And a certain song. It was becoming a bit of a ritual for bowling night music, and as ELO's "Sweet Talkin' Woman" filled the car, he allowed himself to think back as he always did to his Janine. He could see her so clearly, like she had gone only yesterday. In his vision, she was dressed in white, but not as an angel: she was in her bowling gear, looking happy and radiant as she always did. Jack sang along hoping that she could hear him; it was as though the words had been written for her. He missed her every single day.

By the time the song had finished, he was pulling into the car park alongside Mrs Stewart's old beige Escort. Her car was empty, so Jack figured she must be already in the clubhouse. He took the opportunity to stuff the last of the sandwich into his mouth and swallow before anyone saw him, then grabbed his bag off the front seat and headed inside to find the rest of his team. As he walked through the doorway, he was greeted with a sea of white clothing and mainly white hair. It could have been any cricket or tennis club across the country, though with older players. Most of the members were either retired or semi-retired, with only a handful of younger players that had taken up the sport after their parents had got them interested in it. Jack was considered a younger player— his hair wasn't all white, not yet.

He caught Mrs Stewart's eye. She was chatting to a friend in the far corner of the room, and she waved back in greeting. Looking around the room for the rest of his teammates, he found Jim, who had once been the barman of a local pub that Jack had frequented, *The Jolly Carter,* and he headed over to say hello. Jim had been the landlord for as long as Jack could remember, at least 20 years, but had given it up a couple of years ago. Now retired, he still sported a huge beer gut and the ruddy face of a man accustomed to drinking copious quantities of ale each and every day. He reminded Jack of a huge garden gnome, but without the ever-present smile. Jim had always been a bit of a sourpuss during his time as a landlord and had been single for most of his life, probably because of his demeanour, but he was now finally stepping out with a woman. Jack assumed it was this particular lady friend that was putting a smile on his face now; he greeted Jack warmly with a firm shake of his hand. Sourpuss had turned into someone a little sweeter. Retirement and a woman were agreeing with him.

"Are you ready for this, Jack?" Jim enquired. "It's going be good tonight. I can feel it in my water."

"I hope so," said Jack. "I could do with something to take my mind off work. Though there's got to be something a little more entertaining for my mind than your waterworks."

Jim guffawed, the sound filling the small room. When the noise level had settled back down, he carried on. "Busy, are you?" the big man asked.

"Always am, it seems."

"What are you working on?"

"Ah, you know, the usual. Dead bodies." Jack didn't really want to talk about it, but he didn't want to appear rude either.

"You all must be sick of the grief outside your station with all those demonstrators, I expect. A bit noisy, I shouldn't wonder."

"You've seen them, have you? Pain in the sodding backside."

"Well, I can see why the family might think there's a cover-up—an off-duty police officer hits out and the man dies? It's not a good look."

"No, it's not," said Jack.

"It reminds me of that case some years ago—do you remember it, Jack? It must be fifteen or so years ago now, when that Eddie guy worked with you—what was his name?"

"Eddie Edwards, and you're going back a bit, Jim."

"That I am. I can't think of all the details, but they'll come to me."

Jack knew exactly what case Jim was referring to. While he'd have liked to say 'Great minds think alike,' he wasn't sure the rule applied in this instance. Why had Jim remembered such a case from so long ago?" he wondered.

"You must be thinking of Michael Hardesty and the McAllisters."

Jack watched as recognition dawned on Jim's face and his podgy eyes opened wider in excitement.

"That's it! Whatever happened there?"

"The man is still inside, actually. Still got some time to go. And McAllister's inside too, though nothing to do with that case. He was always in trouble, that one. The whole damn family were, in fact."

The clubhouse started to empty out towards the green now, ready to start play.

"We'd better get going," Jack said, "but let's talk about this again, if you don't mind. Perhaps I could buy you a pint?" Jack's gut was good for one thing, and that was knowing when there was more to a tale than was being told.

Jim had been thinking about the same case as Jack. But why?

Chapter Forty-Nine

It seemed it wasn't going to be Jack's night—not for winning at lawn bowls, anyway. Jim tapped him on the shoulder as he was about to leave.

Turning in surprise, Jack said, "You scared me half to death, Jim," and placed his hand dramatically across his heart.

"Sorry. I didn't mean to, but I was thinking about what we were talking about earlier. You know, with that old case, that Hardesty bloke. Maybe I could have a chat with you tomorrow? Maybe I'll come to the station?"

"What's on your mind, Jim? There's not many people volunteer to come to the station to talk. Wouldn't you rather meet for a coffee somewhere?" Jack was even more intrigued now, and by the look on Jim's face, he was bothered by something.

"Yes, probably. Yes, coffee. Let's have coffee," he stammered.

Jack couldn't help but notice Jim seemed nervous, a bit unsure of himself, unsure of his words or what to say. He wasn't making clear, coherent sentences. Something was buzzing around in the man's mind.

"I'll call you tomorrow," said Jack. "There's a decent greasy spoon not far from the station. They do great bacon sandwiches. I don't get to go often. Amanda hates the place; she prefers McDonald's, though heavens knows why."

"Right. I'll wait for you to call me. The thing about being retired is I've got plenty of time. So whenever is good for you will be good for me."

"I'll call you tomorrow, then," said Jack. Over Jim's broad shoulders he could see Mrs Stewart walking towards him; she paused a moment, not wanting to intrude in his conversation, no doubt.

He was conscious of the time—it was coming up to 9 o'clock already. Now he needed to get across town and meet up with Vivian. He hated being late.

"I must go," he said. He bade Jim goodbye and readied himself to walk Mrs Stewart back to her car, as was his custom.

"Hot date waiting?" called Jim. Jack had to smile at that; the man couldn't possibly know, and while he wasn't so sure quite what it was, he was excited about it anyway.

"Something like that," he called back, smiling, and focused on getting himself and Mrs Stewart back to their cars.

He waited for her to unlock her own vehicle.

"Good night, Jack," she said gracefully.

"I just want to make sure you're okay," said Jack.

"I'm quite alright, Jack. I appreciate your concern, and thank you anyway. And have a nice evening."

He waited until she'd pulled away before getting in his own vehicle and heading over to the Baskerville. Ten minutes later he was parking the car once again. He flicked on the interior light and checked his hair in the mirror.

"What on earth are you doing, Jack?" he asked himself. "You look fine. She knows what you look like. This is not a blind date. In fact, it's not a date at all. It's a drink." It didn't stop him double-checking himself again anyway. Satisfied, he flicked the light off and made his way to the pub entrance feeling like teenage Jack again—on his first date.

It had been a good long time since he'd met up with a woman for a drink, or for anything, and he felt somewhat out of practice.

He opened the door and walked inside. Since he was a few minutes late and the place was heaving, he strained to look over people's heads to spot Vivian. He couldn't see her anywhere, and a surge of disappointment filled his chest. She'd changed her mind.

"I'm here," she said from behind him, making him startle. Relief replaced the disappointment, and he felt himself smiling.

"I'm sorry I'm a few minutes late," said Jack apologetically. "I've just come from the bowling club and one of the members was intent on chatting to me. But I was really conscious of getting over here and not keeping you waiting. Of all the times to want to talk, but I didn't want to be rude. I'm sorry." It came out in one long, exhausting string. He knew he was rambling, but couldn't seem to slow it down.

"It's fine, Jack," she said, smiling back at him. "I've only just arrived myself. Now," she said, calmly placing her hand on his forearm, "slow down. It's me—Vivian. You've known me for years, remember? Can I suggest you take a deep breath and start again?" Her eyes twinkled even in the dim light of the bar.

Jack knew she was right, knew when he was beaten, so did as he was told, inhaling a deep breath and letting it out again, feeling his shoulders drop an inch or two and his heart rate slow down slightly.

"Does that feel better now?"

"It does, yes. Thank you. Sorry about that." He needed to move on and stop being so silly. "Let's get some drinks in, shall we? What can I get you, Vivian?"

"I'll have a gin and tonic please," she said, and they both edged over to the bar to order. It was only then that Jack realised what was playing on the sound system—"Last Train to London." It was on the same playlist that he'd listened to on the drive over. Another of his ELO favourites.

"Did you win?" she asked.

"We didn't, actually, not tonight. But that's how it goes sometimes: you win some, you lose some. Anyway, what have you been up to today?"

"Not a lot, as it happens, actually, Jack. To tell you the truth, I think I need to get a part-time job. Since I've given up full-time work, I appear to have far too much time on my hands, and I need to do something with it."

Jack passed her drink to her and paid the barman for the round. "Have you any thoughts on what you might like to do?" he asked before he took a sip of his beer.

"Not really, no. I've been self-employed for so long. I don't really fancy working for somebody else, being told what I can and can't do, part-time or otherwise. And while I'm getting a bit older, I don't have the skills to work in a do-it-yourself store like people my age seem to be doing these days to stretch their pension out a bit."

Jack smiled as they turned away from the bar. "I can't see you in B&Q. Not sure you'd fit in. Too classy," he said, smiling.

She blushed and smiled back. "So, I've got to figure something out, though I haven't got a clue what as yet."

Jack scanned the room for an available table and chairs. There was one left and Jack nodded with his head that that's where they were headed. When they were both sat comfortably and Jack had taken a long swig of his beer, the conversation carried on.

"Have you thought about doing some voluntary work?" he asked. "Is it that you need the money, or are you just trying to fill your time?"

"Fill my time, really," she said. "I've done all right for myself over the years, so as long as I don't go mad spending, cut back on the caviar, I'll be fine." Her eyes twinkled as she teased him. "But I can't rattle around my place all on my own doing nothing all day, so I've got to find something."

Jack fell thoughtful for a moment. "You know, you've got a lot of knowledge to give back," he said. "You know your industry inside out, and how it's changed over the years, so here's an idea. Why don't you get involved with the girls in a support role, on a voluntary basis, educating them on personal safety, and maybe even health issues? If they are going to carry on with their career choice, why shouldn't they also have access to support and training like anyone else?"

Vivian's brows knitted. "And how would that work with law enforcement, with all you coppers? Soliciting is an offence. I don't need to tell you that."

"Easy. You wouldn't be running or encouraging them—you'd be *supporting* them. There's a huge difference. The sex trade will never go away as long as there's a demand. Anyway, it's only a thought off the top of my head; it may be absolute bollocks." He concentrated on his beer for a moment, but from her posture, Jack could tell Vivian was mulling it over.

Conversation between the two of them was as warm and easy as freshly baked jam tart and custard, and they spent the next hour or so reminiscing and talking about their individual future plans. Jack surprised himself with how much conversation he had to offer that wasn't actually work-related. The extra activities he'd taken up were proving useful.

Eventually, he needed a pee.

"I'll be right back," he said, standing, and headed over to the gent's toilets near the front door. Idly he wondered how many men had used the toilet excuse for a quick exit on a disaster date and skipped out, leaving the poor unfortunate woman sat there like a lemon waiting for him to return.

Jack didn't intend to do the same. He was enjoying himself too much now he'd settled his nerves. It might be too early on in their friendship to wish the night would last forever, as ELO had sung when he'd ordered their first drinks, but like with Jim at the bowling club, a good woman was now putting a smile on his face.

And it felt good.

Chapter Fifty

Jack studied himself in the mirror. White foam covered half of his face. He set about shaving with downward strokes, first one cheek and then the other, then more gingerly around his chin. He looked at his moustache protruding through the foam and wondered whether he should shave it off. It had been there for so many years it was part of his being, and he couldn't remember a time without it. He wondered if it had tickled Vivian as he'd kissed her cheek last night. Perhaps it was time for a change. Turning his face first to one side and then the other, he decided his moustache could stay for another day at least; there was no need to rush into a decision. He stepped into the waiting shower, and soon the tiny bathroom resembled a Turkish bath house as steam ballooned around the ceiling like warm storm clouds.

He'd had a good time last night; there'd been no shortage of conversation with Vivian, and they'd both agreed at the end of the night that they'd had a nice time and would do it again. Maybe he'd take her for dinner. Maybe they'd meet for morning coffee or brunch on Sunday. Maybe it was the start of a new friendship, or a rekindling of an old one.

Once dry, he dressed in a pale blue newish shirt and tie, but before he went downstairs, he dashed back to the bathroom cabinet for his bottle of Brut. He wasn't in the habit of wearing aftershave, so he slipped the top off and tested the fragrance with a deep sniff. It didn't smell too bad. Maybe aftershave didn't go off. He splashed some on to his face and neck, washed his hands and headed down for breakfast. His bathroom smelled like the locker room of a soccer team—thirty years ago.

Amanda was already at her desk in the squad room, and she looked up as Jack walked in. He noted she didn't look too happy, and he immediately felt bad for not having called her last night to see how it gone after her conversation with Ruth. But his mind had been elsewhere; he'd had a fairly full social calendar for a change. He wandered over to her desk and sat on the corner of it.

"How did it go?" he asked

"Not so good," said Amanda gloomily. "Things got a little heated. She certainly didn't appreciate the questions, even though she knows I've got to ask."

"How is she this morning?" he asked.

"Quiet, but at least we're speaking. I guess she's worried about Gordon, too, so I'm trying to give her some space, cut her some slack. She isn't a suspect, Jack. It's nothing to do with her, really." She changed tack. "And Gordon? Did he have much to offer?"

"Much the same. Nothing he could say, so we're left hanging out for the autopsy results, see what they throw up." He was about to get up to leave when Amanda put her arm out to stop him. "Jack," she said questioningly. "Are you wearing aftershave?" There was a tiny smile on her lips.

"So what if I am?" he said indignantly.

"It's just that I've never known you wear it. It smells like Brut."

"That's the detective in you, DS Amanda Lacey," he said, then stood up and headed for the coffee cupboard for his first of the day. When he'd set his own coffee brewing, he called around the corner of the door to Amanda, "Do you want another?" She waved a hand no and he moved back in to add the milk. When he was done, he started to take his mug back to his desk, but then decided on a quick detour back to Amanda's. He popped himself back on the corner, mug in hand.

"I had a bit of a weird conversation last night at the bowling club," he began. Amanda was finishing off an email and hardly paying attention, but Jack carried on. "It was with a retired barman. I've known him for some time, but since he retired and I don't go to the pub much anymore, I only see him occasionally—at the club that is."

"And what did he have to say that was so weird or interesting?" She was still talking to the screen rather than Jack.

"Jim—that's his name—mentioned the protesters out front and the whole police cover-up angle and the dead man, and then he brought up the subject of the Hardesty case."

"And you think that's a bit weird?"

"I do. What would jog his memory about that case, like it did mine? Why would the average guy on the street think about Michael Hardesty from all that time ago? That's what doesn't make sense."

"I have absolutely no idea Jack. Are you going to tell me?"

"Well, that's just it. I've no idea. But I am meeting him for a cuppa later on this morning, so I'll let you know how it goes."

"Have you found anything out about that case? Because you've probably spent enough time on it now."

"I haven't as yet. Let's see what Jim has to say later on, though."

"You do that, Jack," said Amanda, then returned her full focus to the screen in front of her. Jack was dismissed. Amanda was in full-on boss mode.

Jack walked round to the café; he'd texted Jim the name of the place earlier. It was 10 AM, the perfect time for a mid-morning bacon roll, and that's exactly what the small café smelled of. Jack sat down at a vacant table, positioning himself so he could watch the door and see Jim when he arrived—not that you could miss him. He was built like a gorilla with a balding head. Jack didn't have long to wait before the door opened and said gorilla wandered in and sat down at the table opposite him.

"Morning, Jim. Can I get you tea or coffee with your bacon roll?"

"A mug of tea, thanks," Jim said, and smiled. Jack called their order across to the counter. He was a regular; the Polish owners, two brothers, knew him well. That done, Jack started off the conversation.

"So, Jim. You've got me thinking, got me wondering. What's on your mind about a case from fifteen years ago?"

Jim picked up the ketchup bottle and started to examine it; it was something to look at other than Jack. A silence separated them until Jim was ready to speak. "There'd been quite a bit of controversy about that case when it went to trial, and I'd always wondered why. Then afterwards, when it was all finished and the guy had gone to prison, it got me thinking. Mac McAllister used to come into the pub quite a lot, but there was somebody else that used to come in the pub quite a lot, too, as well as your good self, that is."

"Oh? Who are we talking about?"

"It was that Eddie guy, Eddie that used to work with you. Edwards."

"I thought he used to go to The Rose. I didn't think your place was his watering hole."

"Well, that's just it. The Jolly wasn't his hole. And he only came when the McAllisters were there. He never stayed long, usually just had a shot of whiskey. A quick conversation and off he'd go again. But obviously when you weren't in drinking either. Don't you think that's odd, a copper drinking with the McAllisters?"

"I don't suppose you ever overheard a conversation?"

"No. I wish I had now. But it was around that time when the case was in the news. I'd say he met up with Mac McAllister probably half a dozen times in the back of the pub. Probably thought no one would notice or think much of it, but I did."

Jack touched his moustache, fiddling with the whiskers. He found stroking it therapeutic.

It could stay a while longer, he thought. Call it a moustache reprieve.

"And you think there's something in it?" Jack enquired.

"Oh, hell, I've no idea. I wondered about it afterwards, but what could I do? I'll tell you what—a big fat nothing. It was way too late. I had no evidence of anything going on; it could have been totally innocent."

"And there's not a lot I can do about it now, either, to be fair, Jim. But I tell you what I'll do: I'll open the case notes and have a quick look—and when I say open the case, I mean I'll get the file out and have another look." Jack had already had a look, but he couldn't think of much else to tell Jim. Nevertheless, Jack's antennae were working hard and waiting for further signals.

Two mugs of tea and two bacon rolls arrived and Jack tucked in straight away, leaving Jim to pour ketchup all over his. Devouring the bacon roll gave Jack's brain some space to think about what Jim had just told him.

Eddie Edwards, his sergeant at the time, having somewhat clandestine meetings with the McAllister boys in the back of a pub at the time of the trial. Did he or the McAllisters have anything to do with it? Jack would have to dig a bit deeper, maybe pay McAllister another visit, shake some trees, as they said on TV, and see what fell out.

He concentrated on his bacon roll as he thought about his next move. He would need to track Eddie down—wherever he was these days.

Chapter Fifty-One

Jack always did his best thinking to music while he was driving someplace, and that's exactly what he did now. He wasn't quite sure where he was headed, but with "Mr Blue Sky" he didn't really care. He sang along with it, each word as familiar to him as his morning routine. He belted down the bypass, headed out towards the edge of the county and some greenery. It was only when he reached Caterham that he realised he was headed in the direction of the old Simpson house. Funny how the mind worked when you were on autopilot, he thought. He hadn't intended to drive there, hadn't intended to go anywhere—he'd just intended to drive and think.

He turned off Stanstead Road, headed to Oakham Rise and pulled up outside the house. All was quiet in the cul-de-sac; everyone was at work—as they would be by mid-morning midweek. He turned his engine off, rested his head back against his headrest and closed his eyes, thinking. Why would Eddie have been meeting up with the McAllisters, so publicly and so regularly? And especially at that time, with the trial going on. Was it even legal? He doubted it was innocent. He picked his phone up and called Raj.

"Can you do me a favour?"

"Sure thing, Jack. What do you need?"

"Can you get me the details of the solicitor and the barrister that handled the Hardesty case? It would be fifteen years ago, so a while back, not an open case. I'll give you their names. Got a pen and paper?"

"Fire away," said Raj.

"The solicitor was Howard King and the barrister was Mrs Maxine Keppel. Can you find out for me whether they're still in business? And whether they are or not, can you tell me where I can find them today, maybe get me their home addresses?"

"Sure. Can I ask why?"

"Just putting old dogs to sleep while I'm in the area. I thought I might pop in." There was no point advertising to anyone else what he was working on, on the quiet.

"They local, are they?"

"Well, they used to be; I assume they still are. Anyway, text me their addresses when you find them, would you? I'm headed their way now."

Jack rang off, then stepped out of his car, went up to the front door of the old Simpson house and knocked. If the owners were in, he'd tell them that he needed another look around. And if they weren't in, he planned to sneak round the back and have another look for himself. Sometimes just visiting the scene of a crime for a second time, when all the hubbub had left, allowed him to spot something, some tiny thing that could be insignificant, but when added to the other pieces of information, could be a vital piece of the puzzle. It was kind of like fresh eyes, even though those eyes were his own.

Nobody answered the door. There were no cars on the driveway, so he slipped down the side and through the back gate into the garden. The digger sat silently beside the huge hole. Crime scene tape covered off some of it, and Jack picked his way across the lawn again and slipped underneath the blue and white plastic. There was really nothing to see; the remains of the body had gone, of course.

It was just a hole, subsoil with a red tinge and nothing more. He turned back to look at the rear of the house. It was an impressive detached place, and he knew from past enquiries that it sported five bedrooms and was spacious and modern inside. Gordon Simpson was obviously doing well for himself to have afforded such a place on the edge of town.

Turning back towards the rear of the garden he looked out onto open fields. A woman with a small white poodle walked along the cinder path, no doubt headed home from her walk into town. It was peaceful; there was just the sound of birdsong and not much more. He could understand why Gordon hadn't been in any rush to sell up after the death of his wife, like he hadn't with his own place. Coming home of an evening or weekend to a country view of rolling hills and open green spaces was a privilege not shared by many.

His phone chirped with a message from Raj. Maxine Keppel, the barrister, was still in business. It seemed, though, that Howard King had since retired. He sent a thumbs-up emoji in reply.

He looked at the address; it was on the way back into town. King lived in Purley, just off the main road, so Jack decided he'd drop in on him on his way back through. Hopefully he would be pottering in the garden as other retired people did on a sunny day. Turning back towards Gordon Simpson's old house, he scanned the part of the neighbourhood that he could see from his spot on the edge of the garden. There were no overlooking windows from other properties providing a view into the garden; the whole area was completely private, the perfect place to bury a body without anybody noticing.

He turned back around towards the path where the woman had been walking; it was now empty. He wondered how busy that path was throughout the day. Could somebody have seen something and not realised what they'd observed at the time? It was perhaps worth questioning the locals who used it, at least.

There was nothing else to see, and since he was there without the current owners' knowledge, he slipped back down the side of the house towards his car. The other houses in the cul-de-sac were as silent as they had been when he arrived. There was nobody visible, no nosy neighbours who could see somebody coming or going. If a visitor had been at the Simpsons' place at the time the body had been buried, it would have gone largely unnoticed.

Jack drove to the end of the cul-de-sac to turn around, then slowly drove back past the house again, looking at it from a different direction. He paused for a moment, waiting for inspiration or an explanation, but nothing presented itself.

He headed back towards town, taking the A22 towards Purley and to see Howard King. He pulled into the driveway of number 4, stepped out of the car and headed towards the house. It was a traditional semi-detached two-story home, with UPVC windows, a satellite TV dish on the roof, and a stained wood front door. It looked like every other one along the road. A small lawn at the front was edged to one side with a path that led to the entrance door. The flower beds were empty, except for a couple of Coke cans and an empty pizza box. Jack figured the guy wasn't a gardener, and neither was his wife if he had one. He noted the windows needed a good clean, and he thought again about the ones back at the squad room. King also lived in a petri dish. What was it with his sudden window fascination?

He knocked on the door, then noticed the buzzer and pressed it. On the other side of the door, he could hear someone calling, 'All right, all right, I heard the knocking,' and Jack half-smiled. The door swung open, and a man of around 70 with long grey hair tied loosely in a band glared cantankerously at him.

"Morning. Mr King, I presume?" enquired Jack.

"Yes," the man said abruptly. "Who are you? If you're selling, I'm not buying."

"DC Jack Rutherford," he said flashing his warrant card. "I wonder if you've got a moment?"

"What is it about?"

"An old case, actually. I was just passing through, and I thought

I'd pay you a visit. I would normally call first, but as I say, I was passing. From Caterham."

King didn't look convinced, but he stood aside. "You'd best come inside, then," he said, in not a particularly friendly manner.

Jack followed King down the dingy hallway and into a side room that appeared to be the lounge. It didn't look like it had been cleaned for the last 20 years. A thick grey layer of dust covered every surface, and cobwebs hung from the ceiling corners. He thought he heard a faint rustling in the corner by the wood basket, though there didn't appear to be an open fireplace.

"Want some tea?" King asked. Jack wanted to say no—he didn't fancy a cup—but it was always good to share refreshments when you were after information.

"Please. No sugar, thanks," said Jack.

He watched Howard King leave the room. His greying hair reached the middle of his back and Jack wondered when it had last been cut. Or washed. It reminded him of rats' tails.

Chapter Fifty-Two

❦

When Howard King returned with two mugs of tea, Jack was beginning to wish he had refused. Dark treacle-coloured drip marks ran down from the rims from previous beverages; the mugs had obviously never been cleaned sufficiently in between times. He wondered who else's bacteria he might be sharing when he took his first sip. Petri dish, he thought again.

"Sit down, will you," Howard directed, pointing to the sofa that Jack was trying to avoid. There were more grey dog hairs on it than there was clean space.

"I'm good standing. Thanks," said Jack.

"Suit yourself," Howard said, and sat down in his chair.

Suddenly it didn't feel right to Jack that he was still standing; it put King at a disadvantage. If King was going to be forthcoming with information, Jack needed to be on the man's level, literally. A wooden chair in the corner of the room caught his eye; it would be a safer bet. He pulled it a little closer and sat down. Howard King raised an eyebrow, as if to say "Why aren't you sitting on the comfy sofa?" Jack was as perceptive as he was quick on his feet.

"Bad back. I'm better on a hard surface," he lied. He glanced at the mug and the pale brown liquid within. Something white and lumpy floated on its surface and Jack hoped it wasn't sour milk. He took a sip. It tasted like dishwater and he put it down on the old glass table that separated the two men. He'd done his bit, taken a sip, and now it didn't matter if he didn't drink any more.

It was Howard's turn to speak. "What's this all to do with? You mentioned an old case?"

Jack was pleased to be getting down to business, he didn't fancy lingering in the man's home for too long. He imagined fleas jumping up and biting his ankles, making their home in his socks. "It's about a case that you worked on with Maxine Keppel some years ago. Michael Hardesty and Chesney McAllister."

King nodded his recognition. He reminded Jack of one of those bobbing dogs that you saw at the back of people's rear windscreens.

"You remember it, then?" enquired Jack.

"I certainly do. Unfortunately," said Howard. "It's one of those cases that I guess I'll always remember."

"Oh? And why is that?"

"We should have won that one, but we didn't. Hardesty should never have gone down for murder, but it all seemed to get out of hand very quickly. One minute he was driving along, minding his own business, then a car accident and a man is dead. And it wasn't from the actual car accident."

"So why did that stick with you?" asked Jack.

"Because whatever we did, we seemed to hit a brick wall at every turn. Pardon the pun."

"So, what do you think actually happened that night?" Jack asked.

"It was a simple altercation and nothing more. But those boys had a history together. Their families had a history together and not a good one. And somehow McAllister won. Maxine did her best, but like I said, every turn we seemed to hit a brick wall. I suspected something was going on at the time, but I could never get to the bottom of it, never prove it."

"Like what, exactly? You think somebody was buying somebody else off?"

"No, not so simple as that. Though I daresay somebody would have tried it." Howard was quiet for a moment, looking out through the smeared window. Not that there was much to see through the grime.

Jack waited.

After a few moments, without looking at Jack again and still looking towards the window, Howard said, "I'd been out for a drink one night. I'd had a bit of a skin-full. Actually, truth be told, it was a stressful trial, and the whiskey bottle and I were good friends for a good proportion of that time. Only in the evenings, you understand, not during the day. I do like a drink; I'm not embarrassed about telling you. I still do, but that aside, nothing to do with it.

"So, I was on my way home one night and I was desperate for a piss, so I pulled over up a side road and snuck behind a bush. There were a few houses along there, and a pub a bit further down, so the bush came in handy. Once I'd done my business and was zipping myself up, I heard voices. They were raised, like they were having an argument. I listened, and I recognised one of them. It was one of the McAllister brothers—Mac, the big guy. I wouldn't want to meet him in a dark alley. I couldn't tell what he was saying, but it was heated, sounded threatening. I stayed where I was to listen, keep out of his way. Since it was almost dark, I peered my head round to see what I could see." King went quiet again, either reliving what he'd experienced that night, or wondering how much to tell Jack.

"Go on," Jack urged impatiently.

"I can't be sure, exactly, but when I looked out, I could see the back of McAllister and he had somebody pushed up against the wall. I couldn't hear what he was saying, but I guess he was reminding him of who the boss was."

"And did you get a good look at who he had up against the wall?"

"Well, I couldn't be one hundred percent sure. Like I say, it was almost dark. But I thought I knew who it was, although I wasn't totally sure. I couldn't follow the guy, but it's stuck with me all this time."

Jack tried again. "Who was it? Who did you think you saw?"

"The foreman from the trial. I only caught a fleeting glimpse of him, but it would all fit, looking back. If McAllister had bought the foreman off, that guilty verdict would have worked well in his favour."

"And you didn't have enough evidence to go to the judge." Jack was beginning to understand King's predicament.

"Correct. What could I do? Tell him I *thought* I saw something, but it was dark and I couldn't be sure? He was hardly going to call a mistrial or sack the foreman because someone may or may not have seen something, no matter who the person was.

"So, when the verdict came back guilty, that was it, the end. Hardesty got sent down, and he should never have. Not for murder, anyway. Accidents happen, and even if he had a hand in that man's death, he didn't murder him. He didn't set out to do that. That was all fabricated after the fact."

"What about Maxine Keppel? Did you tell her?"

"Of course I told her, and she said the same as what I've just said: we couldn't really go to the judge without any evidence and with just a maybe. It was pointless. We had to just do our best from then on and hope we got Hardesty off."

"Are you still in touch with Maxine?"

"No, our paths don't cross anymore now. I'm retired, spend all my time in here, though she still practices. She's still a barrister." Howard looked at Jack's mug. "You've not finished your tea," he said. "You want a splash of malt in it?"

Even though it would make it more palatable, Jack never drank during the day, not on duty. "Sorry, I guess I've had enough tea for one day, thanks," he said, standing. "You've been really helpful. Thanks, Howard." Howard nodded from his chair. "I'll see myself out," Jack said, and headed back down the dreary passageway to the front door. He opened it and stood briefly on the step. The world smelled a whole lot sweeter than the air inside Howard King's house. It was as if the man had imprisoned himself, the way he lived. In fact, the prison where Hardesty was residing smelled a good deal sweeter than King's lounge, with that odd rustling in the log basket. He shuddered and pulled the door closed behind him, then wandered back to his car, deep in thought.

"Poor sod," Jack said out loud to himself.

He was talking about Hardesty.

Chapter Fifty-Three

When Dr Faye Mitchell was satisfied that the skeleton was laid out correctly on the trolley, the photographer stepped in and readied his camera. The remains of the body from the hole at the Simpsons' old place, unlike many other skeletons they found, were complete. All the pieces had been retrieved; there was nothing missing. That was a plus, because one hand missing or the head missing or even a leg missing usually meant that the killer had tried to prevent identification. Even now, identification would be difficult unless there were any other distinguishing marks on the bones, and that was where a forensic anthropologist was required. Had the body been found earlier with flesh still intact, they might well have been able to find distinguishing features such as scars or tattoos, but in this particular case, they'd been far, far too late.

On the trolley next to the bones lay the other items that had come from the makeshift grave—the remains of a pair of jeans, what looked like a short-sleeved cotton shirt, and workmen's boots. There were no personal effects—no wallet, no watch, no telephone, nothing of any personal significance except a cufflink that had been recovered from the soil on top of the body. It had an eagle engraved on it.

"Let's start, then, shall we, Quentin?" she said to the photographer. All the bones had been catalogued and measured; all the data written down in the report. The individual was male and five feet, nine inches tall. The skull was missing its second molar on the upper left side, and that fitted with the dental records of one Mr Desmond Walker—the missing landscaper. At last, they could give him a name.

"Can you get closeups of this please, Quentin?" she said, pointing to a visible fracture on the right temple. The photographer snapped away from various angles, taking pictures of the crack alongside a small tape measure to make it easy to see the length of it. There were some flaky parts around the crack that indicated something sharp-edged had hit Des Walker's right temple.

"There are no signs of callus formation or remodelling, so this injury was peri-mortem, around the time of his death. It hasn't started to heal at all. Fractured skull by blunt force trauma, by some sort of instrument at the temple, is what killed Mr Walker," she said to Quentin. "It's a linear fracture and, looking at the angle and damage around it, I'd say it was sustained from behind." Quentin snapped away as Faye looked closer. "It's not a typical depressed fracture. It's not from a baseball bat or something similar. The marks are all wrong. And it's not sharp force trauma, either, like you'd see in a machete injury. But I would say it was consistent with something in between, like the edge of a spade, possibly."

Satisfied that the skull could tell them no more, she carried on down through the vertebrae, the ribs, the pelvis and the rest of the bones of Des Walker's body, examining each one for tiny nicks or prior breakages or anything else that could say what had happened to him. Apart from a broken ankle that had healed some years before, the only mark on Des Walker's skeleton was the fracture at the temple—the cause of his death.

When she was satisfied that the remains could tell her no more, she instructed Quentin to photograph each of the items of clothing so they could be used for further identification. Everything had to be logged, even though the dental records were a perfect match.

It was coming up to lunchtime when they finished. Knowing that Jack and Amanda were anxiously awaiting her results, she went back to her desk and made the call before finalising her report. She dialled Amanda's number first, and she answered almost immediately.

"Hello, Faye. What have you got for me?"

"I'm good, thank you, Amanda. How are you?" She was being sarcastic. "No time for pleasantries today, then?" Faye asked.

"Sorry. How are you, Faye? Are you well?"

"I am, thanks, and yes, I have some news for you. It is Des Walker. We confirmed it from his dental records, and everything else agrees with that. So that was a good guess; it made my job rather easy, for a change. And as you would expect, he didn't die of natural causes but from blunt force trauma to the head. He had a fracture on his right temple from an object that was likely sharp on the edge. So, something like a spade."

"Right," said Amanda, breathing out. She sounded a bit despondent even to her own ears. What had she been expecting? What had anyone been expecting? "That gives me something to work with. Thank you, Faye. Now I've just got to find out who killed Des Walker. And who put him in the ground."

"One last thing. We found a single gold cufflink, with an eagle on it. Not actually in the grave with him, a little higher up in the soil. Maybe whoever was digging the hole, lost it after the initial coverage? Apart from the remains of his clothes, that was it."

"Interesting, thanks."

"I'll leave that with you, then," said Faye struggling out of her lab coat while she held the phone with one hand. "It's time for lunch."

"I don't know how you can eat lunch in your job," said Amanda.

"I've still got to eat, you know, and the skeletal remains of a dead body are a lot easier to eat lunch after than someone that's jumped off London Bridge. They make a bit of a mess of themselves. Not the prettiest way to go."

"Spare me the details," said Amanda, "but I get your point. And thanks again," she said, before hanging up.

Amanda sat back in her swivel chair and nibbled on the index finger of her right hand, not something she did normally.

"So, he was murdered, hit by a spade or something like it," she said to herself out loud. "Now who could have done that? And why?"

"I have no idea," said Raj, coming up behind her. Amanda turned and looked at his handsome face. "Any idea where Jack is?" she asked.

"Haven't seen him all morning," said Raj. "So that man who was dug up was murdered, possibly by a shovel?" He balanced himself on the edge of her desk, legs crossed, hands clasped and resting on his thighs. She spied his well-manicured fingernails; Raj always looked after himself. His appearance was obviously important to him, though she wouldn't call him vain. Perhaps his colleagues could take a lesson from him.

"The timeline fits. Des Walker was there digging a pond when the Simpsons were in residence, so I guess now we have to revisit and ask more questions. With Mrs Simpson dead, that only leaves Mr Simpson, and I've seen Jack's interview. There really wasn't anything there. I really do believe the man had no clue about this."

"So, what's next then?"

"I'll tell you as soon as I know," said Amanda.

Chapter Fifty-Four

Jack was almost back at the station when his phone rang. It was Amanda.

"I'm nearly there now. Two minutes away," he said, pre-empting her question of 'Where are you?' He was aware he had been incommunicado all morning. That wouldn't sit well with his boss. He hoped Japp hadn't noticed too.

"Right, thanks. I've got some news from Faye. It is Des Walker in the mortuary. She's confirmed it with his dental records, as well as his height and age. That's a positive ID."

"Great. That gives us something to work with. Anyway," said Jack, "I'm not surprised, really. You always thought something had happened to the guy. I just figured he'd gone off and left his debts and his sister behind. I guess you were right all along."

"Question is, though, who killed him? Apparently, he's got a hole in the side of his head by his right eye, so he was hit with something heavy and with a sharp edge."

"Did Faye say what she thought he could have been hit with?" He was casting his mind back to what he just seen at the Simpsons' old place: a few odd tools lying about, though no workmen. Obviously, Des Walker had been there originally, digging a hole, and would have had all his tools with him."

"Well, she did mention a spade. What are you getting at, Jack?"

"I don't know. I'm just thinking. I've just come back from the Simpsons' old place. I'm thinking what tools you would use to dig a hole. What would be lying around for an opportunist?"

"Well, he had a digger, but if you were whacked on the head by the side of a digger there probably wouldn't be much of your skull left."

"Exactly," said Jack. "I wonder if a shovel or a garden fork would have done the trick, as Faye suggested?"

"But surely Des would have seen that coming and defended himself? If you've got somebody stood in front of you with a shovel and they pick it up and swing it at your skull, unless your hands are tied behind your back, you'd lash out, probably put your hands out and stop it." She paused. "Hang on a minute," she said. "He was hit on his right temple, so that means two possibilities. One, that the person that hit him was left-handed."

Jack could see where she was going with this and interrupted her. "Or he was hit from behind, which would fit with your question of whether he would have seen it coming and stopped it. He *didn't* see it coming: he got whacked from behind by someone right-handed."

"Let's go over the timeline again," she said. "Because if Des Walker went missing on the day that he turned up for work, that's got to be the day he was killed. Stands to reason. I doubt somebody would keep him tied up in the shed and risk him getting out or calling attention to himself. But Madeline Simpson had said that he'd gone off in his car and never came back."

"Do you think she could have done it?" asked Jack, incredulous.

"You know as well as I do it takes all sorts to do all types of things, so I'm not surprised at anything anymore in this job. Question is, if it was her, why? What was her motive?"

"Whoever it was, whether it was Madeline or Gordon, how did

they then bury the body? That digger was there for ages, long after the funeral."

"I know. That's perplexing me too, because when we questioned her, that hole was still empty. We looked at it. So where was she, or whoever did it, storing him in the meantime?"

"Was there anything else in the grave with him? His wallet or any other personal belongings?"

"Faye mentioned a cufflink with an eagle engraved on it, but it wasn't directly with the body apparently. It was in the dirt above him. She wondered if whoever was burying him, had lost it then."

"Odd. Well, I'm not far away now. Let's do as you say and look back at the timeline and who else could have been involved. Then maybe we can figure out where the hell the body was kept before they buried him."

"Maybe we need to look at Gordon's movements over those couple of days as well as Madeline's. There's one thing that is puzzling me," said Amanda.

"And what's that?" inquired Jack.

"When Madeline had died, that digger was still sat there and that hole was still empty, and yet Des had been missing a few days by that stage. If Madeline had done something on her own, say, and stored the body in the garden shed, for example, surely somebody, Gordon perhaps, would have found it at a later date and wondered why it was there. Wouldn't he?"

"You would think so," said Jack. "Unless the person who found the body was also in on it. They'd have had plenty of opportunity to use the digger and bury the body."

"Well, that poses another problem, then, because after the funeral, when they took that digger away, the driver himself filled the hole in, and there was no body in it then."

"So, we've got a body that somehow found itself in the ground. Is that about right?"

"That's kind of how it looks on the surface, Jack. It's almost like a magic trick, don't you think?"

Chapter Fifty-Five

Amanda sat at her desk, perplexed. There had to be a simple explanation as to how the body had got in the ground. The worrying thing now was that her father-in-law could now be part of a murder investigation, which was a whole lot more serious than a random body being found in his garden. But how could that be? She knew Gordon. He really was a softy, and as far as she knew, he had absolutely no motive to kill and bury a landscaper. Madeline, on the other hand, had been foremost in her mind at the time of the original investigation—and long before she knew of her connection to Ruth.

She needed space to think, and the office wasn't doing it for her, so she grabbed her bag and headed out to her car, figuring a drive would do her good. She drove to a small park just on the outskirts of town, pulled up at the curb and headed over to a park bench in a quiet corner in the shade of an old oak tree. As she walked over, she spotted a man playing fetch with his Alsatian.

She sat and breathed deeply as she tried to think the problem through. The investigation was becoming a little bit too close for comfort. What was she going to tell Ruth? That her father and stepmother were prime suspects in a murder? There was no other plausible explanation so far, and she thought of Occam's Razor: "Other things being equal, simpler explanations are generally better than more complex ones."

A body is found on a property where you lived, meaning you likely have some knowledge of how it got there. Surely?

She dialled Ruth's number and waited, but Ruth didn't pick up. Not bothering to leave a message, she hung up and left the phone on her lap, figuring she'd try again soon. Ruth would call back when she noticed the missed call on her screen. But after another five minutes of sitting there, Ruth still hadn't done so; that was unlike her, Amanda thought uneasily. Her mind wouldn't settle on the issue at hand, so she decided maybe a slow walk around the park would help her sort it out in her head. She thought of Fred and Rosemary West. They had filled their garden with bodies, because their basement was already too full. Amanda shivered involuntarily, wondering if there were any more bodies on the Simpson property. But why would there be?

She watched as the Alsatian chased the ball again, retrieving it and carrying it back to his owner.

Ruth had been keen on buying her father's old property. But Amanda had wanted to look around if they were going to spend such a chunk of money on a house. It was also a bit too far out of town for both of them, really; it wasn't practical. She had always wondered about that, wondered about why Ruth had made such a fuss about it when she'd only lived there a handful of years herself; she'd lived with her natural mother some miles away for most of her life. Madeline Simpson hadn't been a part of her life until relatively recently.

She tried to call Ruth again. It went to voicemail, and again she didn't bother to leave a message. Ruth must just be busy, she told herself. She'll call back later.

One thing she did have to organise now was to get Gordon Simpson back in for further questioning, and that meant she'd have to involve DI Dupin. Des Walker's sister, Rose, needed notifying too, something else to put on the to-do list. It was another nasty part of the job, but a task she could probably do herself. At least it would give the woman closure, and she'd know why her brother had vanished so suddenly.

Her phone rang but she instantly knew it wasn't Ruth. The opening bars of "Mr Blue Sky" told her it was Jack.

"What's up, Jack?"

"You stood me up for one. Where are you?"

"Fresh air. What's up?" she asked again.

"I've tracked down the foreman from the Hardesty case, so I'm going to go and have a chat with him."

"Hang on a minute. What do you mean?"

"The foreman from the Hardesty case. Did I not say?"

"I guess not. We were talking about finding Des Walker."

"Sorry, I thought I'd mentioned it. Well, I went to see Hardesty's solicitor this morning, an old guy called Howard King who's now retired, and he told me something rather interesting. Apparently, King was coming back from a drinking session one night and got caught short, so he pulled over to take a leak. As he was coming out from behind a bush, he heard a commotion coming from a nearby pub on a backstreet and he clearly saw Mac McAllister having a rather heated discussion with another bloke. The light was almost nonexistent; it was nearly dark, but the streetlamps were on, and so he could see McAllister but he only got a glimpse of the other guy's face. And whatever they were talking about was getting heated, because he clearly heard McAllister shouting in a threatening voice."

"And so?" asked Amanda, rubbing her temples and wondering what it all had to do with anything.

"And so King thought he recognised the bloke that McAllister was roughing up." Jack paused for effect before going on. "Get this —it was the foreman from the trial."

"Right." Amanda's brain was clunking into motion now, but it was slow going.

Jack carried on, "So my take on it is that somebody probably

McAllister bought the foreman off for a guilty verdict. Why else would the two of them be together?"

"So why didn't King do something at the time?"

"My thoughts exactly, but when I asked him, he said, 'How could I? I had no evidence.' He wasn't one hundred percent sure it even *was* the foreman, but thinking back now, it all fits. Wise after the fact, like it's easy to be."

Amanda continued to rub her temples, trying to think it through. Her brain felt like it was fit to burst.

"Right. Go and talk to the foreman then. I'm sure he'll deny it, though. Why wouldn't he?" Then she said, "I just can't take any more in at the moment, Jack, so deal with it on your own, would you?"

Jack detected the overcooked tone in Amanda's voice. It was unusual. She sounded scared, worried and stressed to high heaven. He changed tack. "Hey," he said softly. "Do you want to talk about it?"

Amanda felt her shoulders relax a little and was tempted to confide in him, but not over the phone. "I'll be back at the station a bit later. Perhaps we'll have a chat then."

"As you wish," said Jack, trying to keep things upbeat.

Amanda ended the call as a white poodle dashed in front of her feet, chasing a stray tennis ball. Its blonde owner ran along behind it, waving, and apologised to Amanda for disturbing her. The woman looked vaguely familiar, Amanda thought; they'd perhaps crossed paths before. She raised her hand and replied that it wasn't a problem, then stood to make her way back towards her car. Her little outing hadn't done much for her thoughts apart, from perhaps depressing her a little further.

What was about to come? she wondered uneasily. And how much anguish was about to fall on Ruth's shoulders? Nothing good for either of them, she suspected.

The first thing she had to do was get Gordon back in for DI Dupin to interview, and take it from there.

It wasn't a day she was going to look forward to.

Chapter Fifty-Six

His visit with the foreman had been a waste of time. He'd expected as much, as had Amanda. As Jack entered the station through the back door, he nearly collided with DI Dupin, who was exiting. He took a quick backward step to avoid it.

"Jack," said Dupin. "I've not seen you around much. Been busy?"

"You know me, always got my nose to the ground like a bloodhound following something." Jack smiled and carried on his way inside, not wanting to stop for a conversation.

"I could do with a minute later on," Dupin called after Jack, who raised his left hand in the air in acknowledgement and carried on walking. He didn't dare look back or stop; this way, he'd won his silly game. One day, though, it would get him in trouble; of that he was sure. Still, it made him smile.

He was almost at the squad room when he remembered the vending machine further up the corridor. He fiddled for change in his pocket, hoping he had enough for a Kit Kat. He should be giving them up, he knew, so he decided to share it with Amanda. He put money into the machine and was waiting for his chocolate bar to fall into the tray when something to the right caught his eye. Through the glass in the fire safety doors, he could see through to the front lobby and beyond, where the protesters were still hanging around, though there were now fewer than there had been. He tilted his head to get a better view and counted about ten people still with placards. The ensemble were obviously getting bored now, though Melissa 'Bagpipes' still looked enthused, waving her placard and shouting at anyone who passed by. Jack grabbed his Kit Kat and headed back to the office.

"I've got the Kit Kat. Why don't you make the coffee," he called across the room to Amanda. She glanced up at him with a scowl and Jack wondered if he'd been too casual with her; she didn't seem too happy. Sensing something was off, he wandered over.

"Well, you look like you've lost a pound and found fifty pence," he said.

"That's about how I feel, actually," she said glumly.

"You don't have to tell me," he said. "I gather it's something girly?" He put both hands up in mock surrender. He knew Amanda well enough to know when something was work related and when it wasn't. This wasn't. Something was definitely playing on her mind, and he wondered whether it concerned Ruth. He didn't want to pry, though, so he let it be. He knew she'd say something when she was ready.

"I figure I'll make the coffee, then?" he said, pulling the Kit Kat out and breaking it into two.

"Okay, you win. I could do with the break," she said, and headed into the coffee cupboard. Jack followed her, starting on his side of the Kit Kat.

"I've just seen Dupin heading out," he said. "He wanted to stop and chat but I said I was on a mission. But I'm sure he'll catch me later."

"I don't know why you avoid him so much. He *is* your DI, you know, and he's going to be the one that interviews Gordon Simpson again, because I can't. I'm family, sort of."

"I'll do it," said Jack.

"No offence, Jack, but I think seniority here will help. You've already interviewed him once plus the fact you were at my wedding, remember—so you're probably too close as it is."

"But I'm not family."

"That may be so, though a court would argue that, so it's better if Dupin does it, I'll brief him later. Did he say where was going?"

"I didn't ask. Didn't hang around long enough," Jack said.

"I'll call him in a minute. We need to get Simpson back here as soon as possible. He is the only obvious suspect in this at the moment; we have nothing or no one else to work with. Or should I say, you don't."

"It's a bugger, isn't it?" said Jack. "There's no evidence against him apart from the fact it was his garden. But I think anybody would argue that a body found in the garden of a house that you lived in was down to one of the inhabitants of the house, and since there were only two of them, and Madeline Simpson is dead, that leaves Gordon. And I don't believe that Madeline Simpson could have done it all on her own."

"I agree with you, Jack," she said. "But this is going to bring a whole heap of shit down on Ruth, and that means me too. And while I can cope with it, I'm not sure Ruth can. It's her father, after all."

"Talking of Ruth," Jack said. "How is she taking this so far? You said you were speaking, but only just."

"Well, I thought we were speaking," she said, "but I've tried her three or four times today and she hasn't picked up at all, which is really unusual. So I guess she is taking a break from me for a while. Maybe she needs some breathing space."

"I'm sure it's only temporary measures," said Jack. "And changing the subject slightly, I notice the protesters are still out the front. When is the second autopsy scheduled for? I thought it was today."

"It is—it's probably in progress as we speak," said Amanda, looking at her watch. "So hopefully everything will be put to bed and that one will be cleared up once and for all. I suspect the only reason the family asked for a second one is to provide ammunition for a civil suit. So fingers crossed that Faye and the second pathologist agree on the results and there is no need for any further mayhem with all this."

"Do you think she'd do me a favour?" Jack said thoughtfully. Amanda passed him his mug of coffee and he took a sip before speaking again. "Only, having seen the solicitor from the Hardesty case yesterday and the fact that the foreman could well be involved, I'm just wondering what the autopsy photos showed, whether Faye could take a look and see if she can make anything from them. The whole case just seems too similar to what Dupin's gone through, and now we know that there was something else going on in the background, a cover-up, possibly, I'm wondering about other evidence. You and I wouldn't make any sense of the autopsy photos, but Faye might."

"We can but ask," Amanda conceded. They walked with their coffees back to their desks, just as Dupin put his head round the squad room door and called across to Jack.

"Have you got a minute now, Jack?"

Jack looked at his coffee and considered taking it with him. Dupin, as if reading his mind, said, "Bring it with you."

It seemed people knew Jack all too well. He wasn't sure if that was a good thing or a bad thing. Once Dupin was safely out of the door frame, Jack glanced at Amanda and rolled his eyes before following him to his office. Dupin sat down in his own chair. Jack took the only other chair on the opposite side of his desk.

"I had a telephone call this morning, a rather interesting telephone call."

"Oh?" said Jack.

"I believe you went to see Mac McAllister at the prison."

"I did. yes."

"Is there a problem. Jack?"

"I was curious about something, that's all."

"What has McAllister got to do with anything that you're working on?"

"A line of enquiry. Actually, sir," said Jack. figuring he'd better put some formality into it, "I've been working on something in my own time, a case that was very similar to what you've gone through yourself. So, I thought I'd take a closer look, since the guy has been rotting in prison for the last fifteen years."

"And who is that?" asked Dupin.

"Michael Hardesty. You might remember the case from back then, a local battle between Hardesty and Chesney McAllister. Hardesty went down after a car accident and McAllister was killed." Dupin nodded in confirmation. "There were certain similarities, so I thought I'd take a closer look. And certain anomalies too, I might add. Is there a problem with that?"

"No, no problem. What anomalies do you mean?"

Jack sensed Dupin's interest had been piqued further. "It seems the foreman and McAllister might have been up to something together. They were seen outside a pub one night. McAllister had the man up against a wall, and they were arguing. Odd, don't you think? Then a guilty verdict and that's the end of that."

Dupin seemed lost in thought, his left hand playing with his lower lip, and merely grunted.

"That's that, then," said Jack, standing. "Anything else?" Jack tried again, itching to leave.

Dupin raised his head, still miles away. "No, carry on."

"Thanks." Jack shrugged his shoulders and left him to it, perplexed at the strange conversation he'd just had.

But his coffee was getting cold, so Jack headed back to his desk and concentrated on that instead.

Chapter Fifty-Seven

"What sort of mood was Dupin in?" Amanda enquired when Jack returned to the squad room.

"He seemed distracted, actually. He was fine at first. He asked me why I'd been to the prison, about my visit to McAllister, of all things. I don't even know how he knew I'd been."

"Odd. I wonder how he did know?" Amanda said. "Oh well, mine is not to question why," she said. "I may as well tell him about questioning Gordon Simpson and get it over with. Then I'm going to head out for some lunch. Back in a minute," she said, and wandered off in the direction of DI Dupin's office.

As she approached his doorway, there was no obvious sound of conversation. His door was wide open, so she knocked lightly but he was engrossed in something, staring at his desk, oblivious to her presence. She knocked a bit harder on the door and he raised his head this time.

"What is it, Amanda?" he said tersely. Then, as if realising his curtness, he repeated himself in a gentler tone. "Sorry. What can I do for you, Amanda?" He waved his hand for her to take a seat and she obliged.

"You're aware of the body that was found at the Simpsons' old place," she said, "and I'm sure you're aware that Gordon Simpson is my father-in-law. But we have reason to believe that he could be connected to the body in the garden, and so we need you to interview him formally. Jack is happy to do it, but again he knows Gordon, though not as well as I do. So it's over to you."

Dupin appeared to be looking right through her, and she found it unnerving. She gave him a moment to gather his thoughts.

"Right, okay. Yes, I see your point. When is Simpson coming in? Have you told him yet?"

"No, sir. Raj is on to it, but I wanted to give you a heads-up."

"What evidence do we have on him? asked Dupin.

"Well, that's the problem, sir," she said. "We don't have anything tying him to the body, apart from the fact that he owned the property at the time when the body was buried, and with only two inhabitants in the house, one of whom is now deceased, we're suggesting that Gordon Simpson was part of whatever happened, either solely or along with someone else. The only other explanation is that Madeline Simpson herself disposed of Walker's body, but we find it hard to believe that she could do that all on her own."

"And why is that?" asked Dupin.

Amanda filled him in on the details: the empty hole at the funeral and everything else they knew that suggested that somehow the body had miraculously found its own way into the ground.

Dupin sat back in his chair with his head back and said, "I see your point. It's almost unbelievable that either Simpson or his wife or both of them were involved, but we have to believe it because Walker's body didn't just appear there by magic. And you're right: his body was put there when Mr and Mrs Simpson lived in the house, so it would be too far-fetched for somebody else to go in and dig a hole, dump a body and cover it back over and neither of the Simpsons be aware of it. I gather they were both in the country when this happened?"

"Yes, sir. We questioned Madeline Simpson for some time when the landscaper went missing, but we got nowhere. We also questioned Gordon, but he was at work, and since no body had been found at the time, Walker was listed as a missing person."

Dupin checked the time on his watch and said, "I need to be somewhere just now, but organise Mr Simpson for late on this afternoon. He'll want his solicitor, no doubt. I will see what we can shake loose."

"Yes, sir. I'll check in with Raj." She stood to leave.

"And Amanda?" he asked. "What do you think about Gordon Simpson's involvement?"

"Personally, sir, I can't see how he'd have any involvement. I know him well. He really is a timid kind of individual, a real gentleman, and it just doesn't fit with what I know of him. But I couldn't be so sure about Madeline Simpson. I didn't know her; she died before I met her officially as Ruth's stepmother. I'd had an interest in her at the time of Mr Walker's disappearance, but again, nothing ever came of it, no evidence of anything. And then she had her accident and was killed. So, to answer your question in a roundabout way, no, I don't believe Gordon Simpson is guilty, but I have no other explanation."

"Let's see what the questioning throws up, then, see what his alibi is. Now that we have a time period to work with since Walker was last seen alive, it might be wide but it's something." He stood to dismiss Amanda and get on his way to wherever he was headed. "It's the right call, Amanda, for you not to be involved in the interview. We need somebody who's going to be impartial, and you're clearly not."

Amanda knew that he wasn't being harsh; this was simply the reality of the situation, and she was happy that somebody else was taking the task off her hands.

"I'll be back later," Dupin said. "Keep me posted."

Amanda walked back to her office, but just before she turned back into the squad room, she checked back over her shoulder to see Dupin heading out towards the car park. She wondered where he was going, but she'd got enough to think about without adding trivia. He was probably going for his lunch—she needed the same.

She decided to try Ruth again. She still wasn't picking up her phone, so Amanda tried her office directly. Her PA answered.

"I'm afraid she's not here," the woman said.

"Any idea where she might be? She's not picking up her mobile."

"I'm sorry, no. She didn't say. She left about half an hour ago. She's probably just gone for lunch."

"Okay. Please tell her I called, that I was worried."

"I will," the woman said, and Amanda ended the call. If Ruth had only been gone half an hour, at least she was okay, but why hadn't she returned her earlier calls?

You know the answer to that, Amanda, she said to herself out loud.

She is avoiding you. She blames you already.

Chapter Fifty-Eight

Ruth had hardly done any work. She sat staring at the screen in front of her, her mind elsewhere. All she had done all morning was drink coffee and distract herself from what was really going on in her head. A body had been found at her parents' old place and her father had been questioned. Gordon wouldn't hurt a fly; he wasn't that kind of guy. But her stepmother Madeline? Now she'd been something else. And two years ago, on a warm summer's day as they'd lain together on sun loungers on the patio, Madeline had confided in her after Ruth had pieced together some rather strange events that had gone on and linked them all back to Madeline. You couldn't make up what she had done—a series of pranks that had gone horribly wrong and resulted in several people losing their lives.

And Ruth knew that Des Walker had been one of them, had always known.

Her head felt like it was full of bees. She rested her elbows on the glass desk and closed her eyes.

The clock on her computer said it was almost 1 o'clock, and since she was doing nothing productive at work, she grabbed her bag and informed her PA that she was going out for a while.

Green Park was bustling with folks out seeking their lunches. Ruth didn't feel much like eating, but she did feel like a drink. And a long one. She walked into the first bar that she came across and ordered a cold white wine. The barman, sensing she was in no mood for conversation, didn't even try; he delivered the glass with a knowing smile, looking up at her from under hooded lids, and set it down in front of her. She took a long mouthful and then another, draining half the glass down. The cold liquid shot straight to her empty stomach, but it felt good as it went. The barman had since moved on to serve somebody else, but she could see that he was keeping an eye on her. Ruth picked up the glass and downed the rest of it in two long gulps, and the barman again wandered over to her.

"Can I get you another?" he enquired.

Ruth still hadn't looked up at him. She couldn't have described him to anybody, had no idea what he looked like.

He tried again. "Another?"

This time she did look up, and her gaze lingered on his face for just a moment, though she wasn't entirely sure why. He wouldn't be able to solve the problem that was about to unravel, the problem that could tear her world apart.

"Yes, please," she said.

"Coming right up," he said and refilled her glass. "If I may say so," he said mildly, "you might want to order some food with that." He nodded at her drink. "It will make the headache less severe when you get it later."

Ruth just gazed at him, not entirely sure what he was saying and not entirely sure how to respond. Was he being nosy or was he simply a caring barman? Deep down, though, she knew he was right. And since she hadn't eaten anything since toast at breakfast, she could already feel the effects of the first glass on her system. And it felt great.

"You're right," she said. "I'll have a sandwich, whichever type you choose." She picked up her glass and took it across to a vacant table by the window. She knew she was probably coming across as rude, and that while that would have bothered her normally, today it didn't. Today she didn't give a toss about anybody else's feelings, only her own.

The bar was bright and airy, and the window seat gave her a good view of the outside world bustling by—mainly navy suits and a few tourists. Idly, she wondered what Amanda was doing, how the investigation was going and what her next move was, but she hadn't the guts to ask her since she was avoiding her calls. But she knew she couldn't do so forever. They'd have to talk, and soon. She was dreading going home, and she was dreading her phone ringing again. Amanda had eventually left a message, sounding concerned, and Ruth didn't want to worry her, but until she'd sorted things out in her own head, she couldn't bear to talk to Amanda—or anybody else.

Part of her wished that Madeline had never confided in her, though it had been Ruth that had pushed the confession, having figured things out fairly early on. A spate of silly deaths, deaths that couldn't be explained but were all linked back in various ways to her stepmother, who turned out to be suffering from a manic menopause. Ruth didn't know the details about what had happened to the landscaper, but she knew that her stepmom had been responsible for his death; Madeline had refused to tell Ruth where he'd been buried, to keep her out of it. Keep her out of trouble.

But then Madeline had died, and on the day of her funeral, Ruth had gazed out of the kitchen window at the big orange digger sitting idle on the far side of the garden. The hole by the side of it had looked shallow and uneven, and realisation had come quickly after that.

Ruth grimaced at the seriousness of what she was now involved in. Both she and her father could go down for their part, however small, in one woman's silly and selfish actions. The shit was about to fly, and her father would be caught in the crossfire. Ruth needed to keep him out of harm's way, somehow. They had no actual evidence that her father was involved, yet, but it was his garden, so unless he had an alibi... There was nobody she could ask for help or advice. Oh, what the hell was she going to do?

A sandwich was pushed in front of her and she felt the barman hovering by her side again.

"Can I get you anything else?" he said, his voice full of concern.

Ruth was tempted to ask for a lawyer, but refrained. With a weak smile, she gave her thanks and he left her be. She was halfway through the first sandwich when her phone rang again— Amanda. She stared at the image of her that flashed up but didn't answer.

"I want to pick it up," she whispered miserably. "I want to talk to you. I want to ask you some questions." Her voice broke as the first of her tears slid down her cheeks.

But how could she talk to Amanda without giving the game away?

She let the call go to voicemail again and watched the world outside go about its business without her.

Chapter Fifty-Nine

Lawrence Dupin wasn't stupid at all, despite what people thought of him. As soon as Jack had left his office, he'd put two and two together and come up with a four. If Jack had been out to the prison to see McAllister and discuss an old case, he'd also then found out about and seen Hardesty. It didn't take the brains of the Archbishop of Canterbury to put together what Jack had been working on in his own time. His own personal situation was similar to that old case, and that's where Jack had made the connection. No, Dopey he was not. Auguste Dupin, however, he *could* be.

Jack Rutherford was wasted as a DC, Dupin knew. He should have been promoted to a DI long ago, but he'd never wanted to climb the ranks, was always happy to be an excellent detective solving cases rather than playing politics and doing paperwork. It was Jack's dogged detective work in deducing that the two cases were similar that was sending Dupin on his journey to a certain address now, surprisingly, one not that far away from his own. In fact, as the crow flies, it would be less than a mile on foot through nearby fields.

He drove out of Croydon and its grey concreteness and on to

Caterham, which had seen its fair share of police interest over the past week or so. He tossed thoughts around in his mind, wondered about all the possible reasons for why he was headed there at all, and kept arriving back at the same one. He had to be sure, though, and that meant seeing the whites of his eyes when the man admitted it.

Narrow, leafy lanes came and went as he turned up to what had once been a council estate on the edge of town. Many of the residents had since bought their own places when the government had sold them cheaply years back. Others had turned their homes into flats to rent out privately, and it was one of those flats that he was headed to now. He cruised slowly down the road to the address at the end. There wasn't a house that he passed that didn't have a Sky dish on the front wall. Some homes had flowers outside and neat postage-stamp-sized lawns. Some had menacing-looking dogs chained up, pink wet tongues dangling from their mouths. It was a real mishmash of inhabitants: those who couldn't afford to live in the more salubrious part of the village and those who chose not to.

He pulled up outside what looked like a semi-detached property but was in fact four flats. A discarded shopping trolley lay on the front pathway; it sported only three of its four wheels. Dupin checked the address even though he knew he was in the right place. He locked the car door and headed up the path. There were four buzzers, three of which had names on and one that hadn't. It didn't matter. He needed flat 1A, which he assumed was on the ground floor. Kids' graffiti and the smell of urine filled the porch, and Dupin wondered why at least one of the four residents hadn't bothered to clean it up. The ammonia smell burned into his nostrils. Dupin held his nose while he waited for someone to answer the door. Eventually it cracked open, held back on a security chain, and half of a face belonging to a man he recognised peered out. Even half hidden, there was no mistaking, even after all these years, the haggard face of Eddie Edwards.

"I wondered when you'd find me. What took you so long?" Edwards said through the partially opened door. The man's voice sounded like a work boot rubbing on gravel. Too many cheap cigarettes.

"Let me in, then. I think it's time we talked."

The man stared back at him, deciding what to do. Finally, the door closed momentarily while the chain was removed. Eddie reopened it about six inches and moved away from it. Dupin touched the bottom of the door with his boot to save his fingers coming into contact and did the same on the other side to close it. He didn't want his fingers touching anything in the place unless they absolutely had to. The odour in the dark hallway wasn't much better than the porch he'd just been stood in, though there was an added fragrance of stale curry lingering in the air. He wanted to open a window; the smell made him want to gag. He followed Eddie Edwards through to the tiny kitchen at the end and took a quick glance around, noting the squalor the man was living in. The offending smell lingering in the air was the remains of several takeaway containers still lying on the draining board. They'd been there some time; a once-red smear of tandoori was now a dull dried dark brown, looking more like blood from a crime scene. A baby cockroach wiggled its antennae at him.

Dupin stayed standing; he wasn't going to risk his clean clothes by sitting down, and since Eddie was hovering by the back door, arms loose like he was about to flee, he got straight down to it. This wasn't a social call.

"How have you been keeping, then, Eddie?" Dupin asked.

"How does it look like I've been keeping?" said Eddie sarcastically. "It's hardly palatial, is it?"

"You could tidy up a bit," said Dupin. But Eddie wasn't interested in his domestic advice. "Anyway," he carried on, "did you think I wouldn't bother to find you?"

"Oh, I thought you'd find me. I just didn't think it would take you so long." There was a sly grin on the man's thin lips; a cold sore in one corner looked angry and red. "So, what did take you so long to put it together?"

"It doesn't matter. I want to know why. I want to hear it from your own lips why you set me up," Dupin said, more calmly than he felt inside. If he could have his way, he'd have punched Eddie in the stomach by now, but it would serve no purpose, except maybe to make him feel better.

"I took advantage of an opportunity that came my way. It wasn't planned. I was merely out for a walk, minding my own business, then lo and behold, there you were in the middle of a punch-up. And it must have been my lucky day when that young guy died. I thought I should go and buy myself a lottery ticket because you, Dupin, were so far in the shit it wasn't funny. Well, not to you, anyway. Was for me, though. So, I did my neighbourly bit and told them who and what you are. I thought you'd be off to prison yourself."

"Just like the old days, eh? And someone keeping their mouth shut at another man's expense?"

"I couldn't resist it; it was laid out ready for me to take, and I did."

Dupin wasn't surprised; he'd figured as much. But what did surprise him was Eddie's ugly attitude and the venom of his words. He would happily have let Dupin go to prison for the death of the Parker boy. Had the pathology results been different, he could well be on his way to awaiting trial—all at Eddie's hand.

"Well, I'm not going to prison. I didn't kill that man; it was a freak accident."

"It was a damn cover-up, and you know it," screamed Eddie suddenly. His eyes blazed and spittle gathered at the corner of his mouth. "It's all a load of bullshit."

Dupin leaned in as close to the man's face as he dared. "Like Hardesty? Was that bullshit, Eddie?"

Eddie pulled back, a look of confusion on his face. "What made you bring that up?" he spat.

"It was the exact same thing with Hardesty: guy gets into a simple traffic accident and ends up in prison—except he should never have gone to prison, should he, Eddie?"

Eddie fell quiet. Dupin stumbled on. "So, tell me, how much did

McAllister pay you? Or was it the foreman that got the verdict over the line for you all? Which of the two of you was playing rugby with a man's life? Eh?"

Eddie looked up from his boots at the mention of the foreman.

"Yeah, I know about him, too," Dupin said. "Well, I hope it was worth whatever you got for it, because Hardesty is still rotting in prison. I managed to save my own ass, no thanks to you. But I wanted to see your face so you knew I was on to you. And to think I'd believed your tale of woe back then! You spun me a line, and I sucked it up like the novice DI I was. But not any longer." Dupin started for the front door; his lungs needed clean air. Eddie Edwards and the foreman had been up to their arses in it and Dupin had let it happen on his watch. He needed to figure out how to put it right.

Eddie called after him, but his voice failed to hold any power. "Well, if that's all you've come to say, you've done it. Now get the hell out of my house." Eddie's attempt at kicking him out was as pathetic as the bitter man he'd allowed himself to become.

At least Dupin now had the confirmation he needed. But could he do anything about it?

Chapter Sixty

Dupin's blood was boiling in his veins by the time he made it back into his car. His wheels squealed as he left the quiet avenue and the filth and squalor of Eddie Edwards behind. He felt as dirty as the man's kitchen, if that were possible. So, it had been Eddie Edwards who'd dropped him in. But he was only confirming what he already knew deep down. And all the mess that had followed was over money and Eddie's greed years ago when he'd needed to pay off his debt. He'd got mixed up with McAllister's mob, and then everything had got out of hand.

Eddie had been pissed that Dupin had been promoted to DI when it should have been his position for the taking, and he'd never let it drop. Dupin had known what was going on in the McAllister case—that the foreman had been bought and that Eddie had been bought—but for the sake of his own career he hadn't reported it. He'd only been a DS at the time, the same as Eddie, and had then been promoted over him. He hadn't wanted to rock the boat at the time; he'd been more eager to get on and please his new bosses than to punish Eddie. And he was just as far in the wrong as Eddie was, he'd known, for not speaking out. So, he'd made DS Eddie Edwards a deal: kicked off the force with no pension in exchange for no prosecution over tampering with the case. Added to the burden on his conscience was the fact that an innocent man lay in prison. It was less grief all round if Eddie simply resigned with immediate effect. It hadn't taken the man long to decide; he had left the same day.

Dupin had figured that would be enough to serve him right. What he hadn't expected was for Eddie to take a chance and dredge it all back up, tit-for-tat, as the opportunity presented itself. Judging by the squalor the man lived in and his obvious ill health, the lack of pension had hit him hard, but that was not Dupin's concern. The problem now was if it all came out—if Jack could place him back in the case, or if he found Eddie and spoke to him for some reason. Eddie would be bound to tell Jack of his involvement, and smile doing it. Dupin was up to his eyeballs just as much as Edwards was.

The stress surrounding his pending disciplinary hearing and the protesters outside had been hard enough, and he was also tired of Lyn moaning on about it. He couldn't deal with it. And he didn't want to remain under scrutiny himself; even if he resigned his post now and called it quits, there'd still be an investigation. No one liked a dirty copper.

He didn't feel much like going back to the station yet. Glancing at the clock on his dashboard, he noted it was a little after 2 PM. He estimated he'd have to be back for around 4 pm to do some catch up on the landscaper body case before he interviewed Gordon Simpson later. So, he still had a couple of hours to burn. Knowing Lyn would be out at work, he turned towards home and pulled up in his own driveway. The silence of his house was what he needed now, a place to sit and close his eyes and think things through. He let himself in, poured a finger of whiskey and sat in his chair in the lounge to mull things over.

He was woken by the front door slamming and a woman's voice calling him—Lyn was home. He glanced at the clock on the mantelpiece. It was nearly 5.30 PM. He'd fallen asleep.

"Bugger, shit, bollocks!" he shouted as Lyn came through the living room door.

"That's no way to greet your wife," she said caustically.

Dupin was out of his chair, searching for his car keys and ignoring her remark. He hadn't the time or the inclination.

"I've got to go. I'll call you later," he said, and flew out the front door towards his car. He'd call Amanda on the way and let her know that he wasn't far off, that he'd been delayed; he'd figure it out. He'd make something up. It was not her concern.

He hadn't been in the car for five minutes when his phone rang. He looked at the caller ID and groaned. He had no choice but to take the call and clicked the button on his steering wheel to accept.

"Yes, Amanda," he said in as normal a voice as he could muster, hoping that the sleepiness had left his vocal cords.

"Are you on your way somewhere? Only Gordon Simpson is waiting for his interview, and his brief isn't fond of hanging around."

"I'm twenty minutes out. Keep them entertained," said Dupin. "But since I'm running late, you'd best fill me in. I hate going in without proper preparation, but sometimes needs must." He listened while Amanda ran through what they knew, which wasn't much different than what Jack had already said earlier on. They were banking on the fact that either Mr or Mrs Simpson or both of them had committed the murder. One of them. And since Madeline Simpson was herself lying in a grave, that only left Gordon. It was far from ideal, and it might be tough to get through the CPS, but if Gordon had no alibi and no reasonable way of explaining how the body had got there, he would be the favourite and would no doubt be arrested. At the very least it cleared another case off, ticked another box. The commissioner would be grateful.

It felt like old times. Almost.

Chapter Sixty-One

Jack slumped down in his swivel chair and twiddled with the whiskers of his moustache, deep in thought. How the hell had Dupin known what he was working on? And how the hell did Dupin know that he'd been to the prison? There was obviously a grass, somebody on the inside who'd felt it necessary to call the DI and let him know that he'd been. The box of chocolate biscuits had not been enough, apparently, and someone hadn't been able to keep their gob shut.

He swivelled slightly from side to side, staring at the keyboard in front of him. He'd never looked at it in so much detail before; it had dirty brown smudge marks over the well-used keys. He wondered why he had never noticed just how dirty it was. But now he looked at it, he was disgusted with it. It reminded him of the rest of the office and his new fascination, wherever it had come from, with living in a petri dish. Maybe it was Mrs Stewart's influence? He had the sudden urge to clean the dirt and grime off his keyboard, and while he was at it, his monitor. The mundane task would help him think, allowing enlightenment, he hoped, to fill his skull. He glanced over at Amanda, who was busy doing something on her own computer, head down, fingers tapping away furiously. She'd have something he could use.

He sidled over to Amanda and said, "I don't suppose you've got a packet of wet wipes in your bag, have you?" Amanda looked at him over her right shoulder. From the look on her face, he'd dragged her from deep concentration, and she was struggling now to comprehend what he was saying. "Wet wipes," he repeated.

"Yes, that's what I thought you said. Hang on."

Jack watched as she pulled her bag up from off the floor and passed him a little green packet without another word.

"Thanks. I'll return them when I'm done."

Back at his desk, he pulled out a wet wipe and got to work first on his monitor and surround, then worked his way down the keyboard. There weren't going to be many fresh wipes to return to Amanda; he'd have to buy a new packet for her. He carried on dutifully cleaning the rest of his desk, wiping it free of coffee stains, chocolate biscuit crumbs and general debris. All his files and belongings were now in a neat pile on the floor. Several of the other officers watched him with interest. Maybe he'd start a trend, he thought. Maybe he'd pass the remaining wet wipes round and they'd all have a go cleaning the place up a bit. Maybe somebody would organise that window cleaner he'd been on about.

Standing back looking at the clean space he'd created, he thought it was a shame he had to put all his stuff back on his desk. Now was the time to have a sort-out and throw away the things that were useless, things he didn't use, the things he didn't need any longer and create some order in his work space. His nostrils filled with the perfume of baby oil and talcum powder and he breathed deeply. It was the same smell of a newborn baby.

Jack and Janine had never had children; they'd never been blessed. So he hadn't any first-hand experience of infants, but he thought back to a case he'd been on about the same time as Hardesty was going through his troubles. A newborn baby had been found that Christmas on a snowy church porch and he remembered visiting the tiny little bundle when she'd first been taken to hospital. Mary, she'd been called by the nurses who'd cared for her. He'd taken her a little pink rabbit and kissed her tiny head, and she had had the same smell that was lingering on his desk now. He wondered what had happened to her, to little Mary. Perhaps he'd follow up and find out where she was living; she'd be a young woman now, he thought with some surprise.

He began sorting through the files and loose bits of paper and post-it notes, stacking some things back on his desk and others in file 13—the rubbish bin. He was almost finished when he saw Amanda approaching.

"Does that feel better now?" she enquired, reaching to pick the almost-empty packet of wet wipes.

"I'll buy you some more. I've almost used them all," Jack said apologetically.

"I don't think I've ever known you to scrub your keyboard," she said.

"Me neither. But I seem to be on a bit of a bacteria-fest at the moment. I keep washing my hands too. Maybe I'm coming down with OCD," he said, smiling.

"I don't think you 'come down' with OCD."

"I read somewhere that when you've got something whizzing around your head and you're trying to work it out, a mundane task, like tidying something away or clearing a cupboard out, for instance, gives your brain something else to chew on and the answer will spring forward on its own. So, I thought I'd give it a try. That and a little inspiration from Marie Kondo."

Amanda raised an eyebrow. "And did it work? Did it bring you joy?" Her lips twitched in a quick smile, and she began fiddling with the package of wet wipes. Jack watched, mesmerised. Perhaps he'd do the windows next.

"Do you know," he said, "watching your fingers fiddling with that green packet, I think it just has."

"So, what shook loose?"

"I was wondering who told Dupin about my visit to McAllister and the prison, and I just realised," he said, nodding at the green packet. "It will be Kyle Greenly."

"Now where do I know the name Greenly from?" said Amanda, looking up at the ceiling as if hoping the answer would be written on the water-stained tiles.

"Well, you know the name because Max Greenly is a local businessman, but he's also the father of Kyle Greenly, who is also the nephew of one DI Lawrence Dupin."

"He grassed you up," said Amanda.

"He certainly did," said Jack resignedly. "He must think I'm as green as grass."

Chapter Sixty-Two

Satisfied with his newly cleaned and Kondo-ized desk that now smelled of newborn babies, Jack picked up the file that was on the top—the Hardesty case. He knew every piece of paper that was in it, he'd been through it so many times, but he pulled out the autopsy photographs again and spread them out on his clear desk. They had been taken almost 15 years ago and the quality was poor compared to what he was used to seeing now—grainy and hard to discern.

He picked up the autopsy report again. Again, he knew most of the wording by heart now, and he also knew the pathologist who had performed the procedure—Charles Winstanley. He'd worked with him on many cases in the past; the old man had only recently semi-retired. He was one of those characters who, even when he had been 40 years old, looked like he should have been in retirement. He was famous for his wispy white hair that stood straight up like Don King's. Jack had always found him a decent person, talented, accurate and inquisitive, but looking at the photos now, he wondered if there was any chance of a mistake in Winstanley's work on the case.

There was only one way to find out and that was to ask Faye Mitchell if she'd be willing to take a second look. He picked up the phone, selected her number and waited for it to connect. When she answered, it was obvious she wasn't in her office. He could hear traffic close by. Maybe she was out grabbing a bite to eat for lunch and walking back to the lab.

"Yes, Jack?" she said. "What can I do for you?"

"I'm hoping I can ask a favour, actually, Faye," Jack said.

"You can always ask. Can't promise I can do, though."

Jack was used to the woman's occasional abruptness, and as usual he ignored it. She was wired differently to him, and that was fine. He carried on, "You're obviously familiar with Dupin's case and your findings, and I just wondered what the possibility was of you looking at some photos from a cold case that might be related. Actually, it's not strictly a cold case—it's more of an old case, but it's the same sort of setup."

"What happened in that case, Jack? Why the interest now?"

"Well, a chap is in prison—he was charged with murder, actually—but I'm just curious. Given the recent experience with Dupin, I wondered if the same thing might have happened with this man, Michael Hardesty?"

"It's not like you to get involved in old solved cases, Jack. Are you underworked at the moment?" She tittered lightly; it was her way of being amusing.

Jack wasn't sure how to answer, so he stayed silent, pondering his next move. But Faye realised what he was doing and filled in the gap anyway. She knew Jack well enough; they'd been on too many cases in the past together, and she respected his judgement.

"Why don't you bring the photos over," she said. "I'm just headed back to the lab now. Who did the original autopsy?"

"It was Charles Winstanley, actually," said Jack. "Fifteen years ago."

Jack heard her sharp intake of breath. The man had a reputation, and a good one.

"The revered Dr Charles Winstanley," she said, putting emphasis on each word. "I spent time training under him myself, and I guess you know his daughter works in the lab here too."

"Yes, I do know, so I guess if there's any way of keeping this between you and me that would be best. I'd appreciate it."

"I hear you," she said.

"I'll bring in them round now," said Jack. "I'll be over in twenty."

Jack hung up, pushed all the photos back into the folder and hurriedly left the squad room before anybody could ask questions, Amanda included. At least Dupin was out, wherever he'd gone, and as he pulled out of the car park and the electric gates closed behind him, he wondered what Faye would make of this. As she'd said, Charles Winstanley was a practised pathologist and wouldn't appreciate having his work mulled over by a former student. But getting a second opinion was a common part of the job these days, and Winstanley would no doubt know that, and so be it. It had to be done.

The lab reception area air-conditioning always seeming to be just one degree too cold for Jack's liking. He approached the young woman on the desk and told her that Faye was expecting him, then waited by the lift doors, knowing that she would come out through them shortly. When they eventually pinged open, he stepped straight in to greet her and they headed back upstairs to her office, via the fish tank and her PA, who glanced at Jack disapprovingly. She'd remembered his belching from his last visit.

They were sat at her desk.

"So, what have you got, then, Jack?" asked Faye.

"Take a look at these, if you wouldn't mind, and see what you make of them," he said, handing her the file. "I know they're a bit grainy, but obviously you're the expert here, not me and I've no idea what I'm looking for. But you might see it, whatever 'it' might be."

Faye lifted her eyes to Jack as if to say 'no shit, Sherlock,' but the twinkle in her eyes told him she wasn't offended. He smiled, though he wasn't sure if it was an apology smile or an 'I'm sucking up to you' smile. Jack watched the top of her head as she perused the photos in turn, studying each one intently. When she got the image of a section from the man's neck, she removed a magnifying glass from a drawer and took a closer look.

"They aren't terribly clear, are they, Jack?" she said, sounding disappointed.

Jack kept quiet; he didn't want to agree with her in case she gave up too soon.

"I wonder if the original files are still with Winstanley," she mused. "He might have the master copy that we can get better copies off?" She was thinking out loud.

Jack didn't need to reply, and the silence went on for what felt like a couple of minutes but was probably only seconds in reality. He felt like he was sitting on the edge of his chair, eagerly waiting for good news about test results.

Finally, Faye put the magnifying glass down and looked straight at Jack.

"Tell you what I'll do," she said. "I'll contact Charles Winstanley's office, and when we've had the second autopsy on Callum Parker later on, I'll ask the pathologist to see what he thinks. How does that sound?"

"I can't say fairer than that, can I? Thanks."

"If we can get a better resolution of the photos, we might see things a bit clearer," she said, pointing to a particular one. "For instance, in this area, that would be where I would be looking at if it was the same sort of event, but there isn't enough detail visible. It's too grainy." She picked the photos up and put them back in the folder. "Can I keep these for now?"

"Please, yes," said Jack. "Any help you can give me would be appreciated." He rose to leave, not wishing to take any more of her valuable time.

. . .

Shortly after Jack had left, Faye made the call to Charles Winstanley's office. It seemed they did have the original masters, so she asked for the higher-resolution image files to be emailed on to her as soon as possible.

Chapter Sixty-Three

In high-profile cases, it's not unusual for there to be a second autopsy. Often lawyers defending clients on murder charges call for another one just to be doubly sure of the facts, and many pathologists have their work re-examined in this way. Anyone who finds themselves accused of murder, for instance, would want a second opinion too. Nonetheless, this is never pleasant for the pathologist—one never liked being second-guessed, and Dr Faye Mitchell was no different. She'd met the second pathologist many times at conferences and medical get-togethers, and though she wouldn't exactly have referred to him as a friend, she certainly regarded him as a colleague, though not from the same team.

Dr Kevin Douglas worked in Surrey and had a solid reputation; he was a regular in courtrooms and in the expert witness box. It helped to know who was going to be rechecking your work, and the fact that it was Dr Kevin Douglas gave Faye some heart. While it wasn't required for the first pathologist to be witness to the second autopsy, it was normal procedure. And Faye was interested in his findings as well as wanting to see how the man worked.

There was little sense in moving the body to another venue across town; it was much easier for Douglas to go where he was needed. Faye had already sent specimen samples and photos across to him and given him a heads-up about what they were looking at. She could do no more at this stage apart from wait for Dr Douglas to arrive and try to steady her nerves. Everything was ready and waiting to be confirmed.

Dr Kevin Douglas was a distinctive man to look at—tall and dark, though not particularly attractive. She'd heard colleagues politely refer to him as having a face for radio. Standing at around 6 ft 6 in height, he had dark hair that started from his temples and hung down to touch his collar. The dome of his head, however, was as shiny as a new coin. He reminded Faye of Herman Munster.

He smiled directly at her as he entered the office, and once again, she was struck by how slim he was; he looked like he could snap at the waist at any moment. She stood and greeted him with her outstretched hand, which he took gently; his was almost twice the size of her own. His fingers were so long and thin they resembled the plastic skeleton's that hung on a stand in the corner of her office. She wondered if he played the piano.

"Dr Douglas, it's good to see you again," she said, tilting her head back to connect her eyes to his. He stood nearly a foot taller than her.

"Please, just call me Kevin," he said, smiling. His eyes were an intense hazel and reminded Faye of the glass bead eyes on a teddy bear she'd had as a youngster. Clear and wonderfully warm.

"And obviously I'm Faye Mitchell."

"It's good to see you again, too. How have you been keeping?"

"Well, apart from being second-guessed in this case, I've been great, thank you. And you?" She wasn't trying to sound smart, and instantly regretted voicing her nerves at Douglas.

"The same here, thanks. And I wouldn't worry about being second-guessed, Faye, because from those photos and samples you've sent me already, I can see what the outcome will be. But I have been tasked with performing a second autopsy, so that's what I'm here to do, and it's good to have you alongside me."

You can tell so much about a man by the way he speaks, Faye

thought, and Dr Kevin Douglas was a gentleman. He might not be a poster boy, but he was warm, friendly and well mannered. She felt herself relax; her shoulders settled back at their normal angle. Somehow, she felt reassured that the work she'd already completed and the conclusion she'd come to would not be disputed.

"Shall we?"

Faye couldn't help smiling; it felt like he was asking her to dance. He led her out into her own autopsy suite, where she grabbed disposable aprons and gloves and passed a set to him.

For Faye, it was always a pleasant experience to see another pathologist at work, particularly someone as esteemed as Kevin Douglas. As the body of Callum Parker was examined once again from head to foot, all Faye could do was stand back and watch and answer any questions he had of her and her findings. When it came to the main areas of concern—the brain and the neck bones—he referred back to the photographs and the reports that she had already given him.

"You've done a very thorough job, Faye, and from what I've seen so far I'm inclined to agree with your results. I see no congenital aneurysm that could have caused the haemorrhage, and when I look at the vertebral arteries, I can clearly see a rupture. Obviously, I'm going to have to write up a full report, but your summation is correct—that it wasn't the sudden braking but rather the forced turning of the steering wheel so frantically that dislocated his spine, which in turn ruptured the artery, resulting in the haemorrhage." He turned and smiled at Faye reassuringly, knowing himself how unpleasant it was to be second-guessed.

"Well, I am relieved that you agree. I was certain of my findings, of course, and it's unfortunate that the family wanted this, but I can understand why."

"Oh, me too. Like I say, I'll write up a report saying that I concur with what you have found, and add in the fact that all the smoking and arguing and fighting could well have accelerated it. We'll never know for certain if it could have been avoided."

"I wonder what the family will do next. Will they let this go now?"

"Faye, your guess is as good as mine," Kevin said. "In my experience, many are satisfied, but others just won't let it lie. The Parkers may file a civil case against the officer involved, but the evidence is clear, Faye. You and I both arrived at the same conclusion; there would be little point in a third autopsy. It's one of those freaky things that happened. The human body is a complex machine, and sometimes we have no control over what it can do. In this case, Callum Parker died from his own actions and nobody else was to blame."

"I agree."

"I think we're done here," he said, checking the clock on the wall and pulling his gloves and plastic apron off at the same time. "I don't know about you, Faye, but I'm rather peckish. Have you got time for coffee somewhere? I saw a small café not far away from here, on the way in."

"I know the one, and they bake the best muffins if you fancy one." His smile told her he was interested. "And I also have something else for you to take a look at, if you don't mind?"

"Not at all. I am at your disposal," he said, smiling down at her.

Faye felt herself get a little warm around her face and neck.

She was blushing.

Chapter Sixty-Four

While she'd been in with Kevin Douglas doing the second autopsy on Callum Parker, better copies of the files had landed. And because her PA knew she was waiting for them, she had printed them out and placed them on her desk ready. Faye eyed them as she and Kevin passed by.

"Just give me a minute, would you Kevin? I'll be right with you." Gathering up the photos, she glanced at them quickly, noting that they were in fact somewhat clearer. She stuffed them into a nearby folder to take with her. When being asked for a second opinion, or asking someone else for one, Faye liked to have her own already established first, but in this instance, there hadn't been time—she'd explain along the way.

The two doctors walked the short distance to the café around the corner. The smell of freshly roasted coffee beans and warm muffins hung on the air.

By way of conversation, Faye said, "This is my favourite café, so I'm very lucky it's so close to work." Kevin held the door open for her and she slipped inside. It was modern in décor—glass, slate, concrete, tiled floors, bare walls—but filled with local artists' depictions of trendy local scenes in various muted shades. She noticed Kevin glancing around the walls, looking at the various pieces.

"They look quite good to me," she commented. "I've often thought about buying one myself." Kevin was gazing at one in particular, an impression of the old asylum that had been knocked down to make way for the prison. "It looks a bit creepy, don't you think?" said Faye. "It was knocked down only fairly recently. The local loony bin, as it would have been called years ago, though you wouldn't get away with calling it that these days. And not everybody that got locked up in there was officially loony." Kevin raised his eyebrows in agreement. "Medicine has come a long way in a very short space of time, don't you think? And we're much more open to discussing some illnesses. It's okay to talk about mental health and depression, for instance, but certainly not back then. It was easier to medicate and hibernate. Except they didn't wake up again in the spring."

Kevin gave her his strange, sad smile again. "I often wonder what happened to all those people," he mused. "Sad, really. I guess they are out in the community somewhere, struggling."

They placed their order and took seats at a small table by the window. It was always busy there, with mainly local workers buying food to go. It was a bit far out for local shoppers, so people tended to pop in grab what they needed and dash off again. It was good business for the café owners. No one sat lingering with laptops, making a single coffee last all day.

Faye pulled the file out while they waited for their drinks to arrive. "If I could impose on your brain a while longer?" she enquired.

"Absolutely. What is it?"

"I haven't seen these new photos myself yet, but I'd be interested in your opinion anyway. So I'm not going to say anything, but I'll hand them over and let you peruse them, tell me what you think." She nudged them towards him across the table and watched Kevin pull his reading glasses out of the top pocket of his jacket and slip them on the end of his nose. The brown tortoiseshell rims made the honey of his eyes look even richer. She felt herself blushing slightly again at the thought of what she just envisaged. While Kevin wasn't the most attractive oil painting in the world, she found herself drawn to him for some reason, and in particular his honey-coloured eyes. She pulled her gaze away quickly before he noticed—she hoped he hadn't done so already.

Faye sat quietly while he looked over each photo in turn, picking them up and holding them closer to see. He didn't say anything. A waitress arrived at Faye's shoulder with a tray carrying coffee and their muffins, and Faye could immediately see the girl's predicament—where should she put their order down? She also saw the young woman turning pale as she realised she was looking at autopsy pictures. Kevin perceptively became aware at the same time and hurriedly gathered all the photos together, placing the one he was most interested in on top, allowing the young woman to put the tray down. She scurried off like a mouse escaping a cat's grasp. When she had gone, Kevin burst out laughing and Faye couldn't help joining in, their eyes meeting across the table.

"Oops," said Kevin. "That'll put her off food for today."

Faye pushed Kevin's coffee across to him along with his muffin and took a sip of her own while he studied the photograph on the top of the stack. She broke the crunchy part off the top of the muffin and began to eat, giving the man time to gather his thoughts.

"I'm guessing this is an old case, and I'm also guessing you have no samples?"

"Correct."

"I'm also guessing you think this could be a similar case to what we've been working on this morning?"

"Correct again," she said, taking another bite. Icing sugar gathered on her chin and self-consciously she wiped it off with her napkin.

"Well," he said, "it's hard to be sure from this printout, but I'd say you could be looking at the same thing. Look," he said, pointing to a particular area. "That could be dislocation. I wonder why the original pathologist who performed the autopsy didn't spot it?"

Faye had another idea come to her.

"Or maybe it was the photographer who inadvertently *did* spot it, with the camera angle perhaps?"

"That's possible, I suppose, and perhaps the pathologist simply overlooked it or wasn't aware of the photographic outcome, having already seen what he'd seen with his own eyes and made his decision. It's possible. And maybe fifteen years ago it hadn't been seen before? I'm guessing, of course. You'd have to do some research."

Faye sat back and chewed quietly, deep in thought. The implications were massive—life-changing, in this case.

"This person is very likely to have experienced the same outcome: a ruptured artery, just like our friend Mr Parker. What's the situation with this case now?" Kevin asked.

"He's been in prison for murder ever since."

Kevin raised his eyebrows. "Murder?" He sounded incredulous.

"Yes, apparently so. DC Jack Rutherford remembered the case from when we started working on the current one, and he had a look into it. It seems a bit over the top. Don't you think?"

"I certainly do."

"So how can we prove otherwise with what we've got here? And what can we do to help the man?"

"We find the original pathologist, first off. After that, there is only one way as far as I can see."

Faye felt she understood what he meant but needed to be sure. "Exhumation."

"Got it in one," he said. "Let's hope we don't need to go that far."

Chapter Sixty-Five

No one liked a dirty copper, and no one liked a dirty pathologist either. Faye's head was swimming with reasons why the great Dr Charles Winstanley had made such a catastrophic error, one that had resulted in a man being imprisoned for nearly fifteen years. How she approached it was going to be awkward—he was her old tutor, no less—but meant that an innocent man had gone to prison. Someone had to help put it right. Winstanley was pretty much retired now, but fifteen years ago he would still have been extremely competent. Not that retirement meant you weren't competent, of course, but age sometimes dulled the mind; there was a reason why people retired from such a technical job.

As Kevin and Faye left the café there was a comfortable silence between them and she assumed Kevin was thinking along the same lines—and feeling glad it wasn't him that had to do the deed in confronting the great doctor. Traffic whizzed by as though nothing traumatic was going on in the drivers' heads, and in truth most of them probably hadn't much to worry about, save for the usual—paying the mortgage, getting the kids to school on time or what to have for dinner. She doubted anybody was wondering about how to get an innocent man out of prison and how to approach a revered pathologist about the fact that he'd made a grave error.

Kevin broke the silence and said, "I can help where I can, if you'd like me to, but I totally understand if you don't want me anywhere near it. It's your case, Faye."

"I appreciate that. Thank you," she said, still facing forward as they walked. "The first thing I need to do is talk to Jack and see what's what, and then someone needs to pay Mr Winstanley a visit. I'm not relishing the job, not only because he was my teacher, but because I work with his daughter here in the lab. This is not going to go down too well, is it?"

"No. I see what you mean. I know that his son is a pathologist up in Manchester too. I've worked with him a couple of times, actually. He's a decent bloke."

"The whole family are, which is why I wonder about this slipup. How could he have missed it?"

"Well, maybe in his head, he already had the answer and didn't need to see the images, what was *really* in the photographs, because he'd done the autopsy. He knew with his own eyes what he'd seen, but the angle that the photographer managed to capture inadvertently is all we have to go on. Luckily, we have that. It's photographic evidence now over memory."

"But surely Winstanley looked at the photographs afterwards. You know, during the trial?

"But if he didn't see it the first time in the lab, he wouldn't be looking for it when giving evidence. And the image printouts were not very clear because of the low-resolution copies. They are clear now, because we know what we're looking at and we have the much bigger master. They didn't email that size of file back then; the computers probably couldn't cope with the sizes. I know it sounds like I'm making excuses, but it is quite feasible that that's what happened and it's just something that got missed by chance."

"I need to go and see Jack and Amanda urgently," she said. "They'll know what to do, because now we have evidence of a wrongful imprisonment. Maybe one of them will go and see

Winstanley. Getting the man out now could be quite a task, but this is new evidence, so hopefully they'll be able to use it. It doesn't matter why the pathologist missed it; it matters that it's put right. Don't you think?"

"I absolutely do. Yes, figure out Charles Winstanley later, but let the police know now."

They were back at the building now and as they entered the lift to go back upstairs, they let the subject drop and turned to small talk. Faye knew there was nothing more she could do until she'd spoken to Jack, though she thought maybe she should go through it again and try to find another possible explanation. She couldn't mention this to anybody within her office; she had to keep it to herself.

The doors opened on Faye's floor and they walked past the fish tank and headed back to her desk, where they said their formal goodbyes.

"Do you want me to take a copy of this file away?" Kevin enquired.

She couldn't immediately see why he'd want to copy, but he was offering; it could come in useful in the future, she surmised.

"I'll get a copy made if you can hang on for a moment," she said, and took the file out to her PA to be copied. The two walked slowly back to reception together, just passing time while her PA did the necessary and caught them up. Once at the entrance door again, Faye thanked Kevin once more for coming in and for corroborating her results on the Parker case.

"No corroborating needed, really, Faye," he said. "You are correct in your summation, as I said. That's exactly what happened, and I found the same thing. The guy killed himself, in effect—an unfortunate, freaky accident that nobody could have seen coming and nobody but Callum Parker could have stopped."

The PA came over and handed over the copies Faye had requested. Faye passed them to Kevin.

"It was nice meeting you, Kevin," she said.

"And you too, Faye. Maybe if I'm passing, we could sample

another muffin together. What do you think?" His eyes twinkled like warm, clear honey again, and Faye couldn't help but smile. And agree.

Walking away back to her office, she couldn't understand why she was smiling and then she realised—she quite liked Kevin.

But she needed to motor on with this now and call Jack immediately. She dialled his number and he picked up right away.

"I have some news for you, Jack. Are you able to come this way?"

"What's up, Doc?" he said. He sounded like Bugs Bunny.

"I've got something I'm sure you'll be interested in, and I don't want to leave it any longer, or say it over the phone. I've got stuff I've got to get on with here, but I'm hoping you're a little freer?"

"I'm on my way," said Jack. "I'll be there in twenty."

Chapter Sixty-Six

Jack couldn't believe what Faye was telling him. It was like music to his ears, like "Mr. Blue Sky" on full blast on a Bang & Olufsen sound system bouncing around in his car. It was everything he wanted to hear.

Michael Hardesty had not been responsible for the death of Chesney McAllister.

Now all he had to do was figure out how to get the man out of prison—no easy task. Rather than waiting until he got back to the station, he called ahead to Amanda to tell her the good news. But while he didn't expect her to be as ecstatic as he was, he had hoped for a more upbeat response.

"What's the matter, Amanda?" Jack asked. "I thought you might sound a bit more enthusiastic."

"Sorry, Jack," she said distractedly. "But Gordon is here waiting with his solicitor and Dupin seems to have gone AWOL. I'd have thought he might like to prep since he doesn't know much about the case, and apart from a quick phone conversation with me, he appears to be leaving it to the last minute. I'm not impressed."

"I'm sure he'll be back in time."

"Well, you can't do the interview and I can't either, not really." Jack picked up on her low tone, it wasn't like Amanda to be like this. "Hey, Amanda, don't be so down about it. I know that's easier said than done, but nothing has happened as yet, so the best thing is to try not to worry until something, if anything, happens." Jack winced at his own words; they sounded hollow even to his ears, but what else could he possibly say?

"It is easy for you to say, Jack, but it's Ruth I'm concerned about, too. She's going to blame me for this, and that's going to be hard on both of us. I can't believe this is happening. Gordon is a family member and I just can't comprehend that he'd be involved in a murder!" Her voice was a good couple of octaves higher now than when she'd picked up the phone call.

"I know what you mean," said Jack. "But have you spoken to Ruth yet?"

"She's still not picking up; she's obviously avoiding me. And I suspect Gordon has called her this morning anyway, so she's probably keeping her distance. I'll be enemy number one, the police detective on the case. I'm dreading going home later."

"You can always come round to mine if you need some space," said Jack. "There's always a spare room if it helps."

"I hope it doesn't come to that. Whatever happens, we've got to work through this together, and separate houses aren't the answer. But thanks anyway."

Jack sensed she was ready to talk about something other than her personal life, so he obliged. "Just by way of a change in the subject for a moment, have you spoken to Des Walker's sister, Rose? Has she been informed now that we have her brother's remains?"

"Yes, she is aware now. Raj went over earlier on. At least she won't always be wondering and worrying and trying to figure out where he'd been all these years. It should bring her some peace now, even though he's dead. It can't be easy when someone goes missing; all sorts of things would remind you of them. But at least she's got closure now. That's one good thing for this case."

"Indeed. Well, I've got to make a quick detour before I get back in, so I'll be back in an hour or two."

"That's not a quick detour, Jack," she said.

"Okay, I lied. I've got to pay a visit, and I'm not referring to the gents' toilets. If Dupin asks after me, keep him amused, eh?"

"I don't think that's an issue, to tell you the truth." She sounded lower than an oboe; all the fight had drained out of her voice as she resigned herself to the fact that something could happen to Gordon. And that meant to her and Ruth as well. With a shudder, Jack realised just how much crap could fall upon her family. He hoped she had a tough umbrella to shelter under.

It didn't take Jack long to find Eddie Edwards' current address, which was where he was headed now. He wanted to find out for himself just why he'd been drinking at the Jolly Carter so often, and more importantly, why he'd met up with Mac McAllister in the back room. What Jim had told him over bacon rolls had been playing on his mind, and something had niggled away at him. Now things were becoming a little clearer as time wore on, but he needed to hear it for himself. Add that to the evidence that the pathologist had somehow got it wrong, and it seemed that maybe something bigger *was* going on. It wouldn't be the first time corruption had been involved in a trial.

He wasn't surprised, then, when he turned into Eddie Edwards' road that his address wasn't far from the crash scene—if you were a sparrow. Or on foot.

Nor from Dupin's house.

He pulled up outside Eddie's flat and took in the surroundings. It was a far cry from the days when Edwards had been driving around in a brand-new fire-engine-red Jaguar with a woman on each arm, and Jack wondered what had happened to the man's luck since he'd left the force. He hadn't invested his ill-gotten gains wisely, that was evident.

Jack pressed the buzzer and waited for the door to open. When it did, he was taken aback by the first words out of Eddie's mouth as he peered from around the cracked door, where the security chain was holding the fort.

"You as well?"

His words weren't lost on Jack. He let them filter into the back of his brain and linger until later, when he could figure out who else had visited.

"Let me in, Eddie," he said impatiently. The door closed again and the chain rattled as it was taken out of its socket, and then the door reopened, allowing Jack to walk inside. He'd never been to Eddie's house, had not kept in contact with him since he'd left the force so suddenly; they hadn't been best buddies at the time. As Jack surveyed the squalor that the man now lived in, he was saddened at how the man's life had obviously hit rock bottom. It was nothing more than a glorified squat.

"I'm obviously popular station conversation," Eddie said.

Jack ignored him, but filed it with the other snippet that was rattling around his head. Someone else was interested in the man, but who? What else would Eddie come up with if he let him speak?

"Then you'll know why I'm here," said Jack. "What can you tell me about the pathologist in Hardesty's case?"

Eddie's eyebrows raised and furrowed all at the same time. Jack noticed his surprised look; it seemed genuine.

"Not a lot. I'm no expert, am I? Why the interest?"

"He got it wrong, Eddie. Michael Hardesty is in prison and he's innocent. He wasn't responsible for McAllister's death."

"Well, shit happens," said Eddie, sounding bored.

"That's all you can say? 'Shit happens'?" Jack paced up and down the tiny, filthy kitchen area, rubbing his forehead with his fingers as if stimulating his brain somehow. "How much of a part did you play in it? I know you were in the McAllisters' pocket."

Eddie glared at Jack but said nothing. It was obvious he didn't really give a stuff anymore.

"I don't have to answer your questions, Jack," shouted Eddie, suddenly angry. "I'm not a copper anymore, I'm a civilian, so I'd like you to leave my house. Now."

Eddie's irises were blazing, though the whites stayed a dirty yellow, the colour of diluted mustard. The man's kidneys were not functioning as they should.

"What are you afraid of, Eddie? What happened back then? Why did this pathologist get it so wrong?"

"I know nothing about the pathologist," said Eddie, averting his gaze towards the far wall. Wallpaper was peeling from the top corner and had drooped down, giving the impression the tired room had sagged.

"Maybe not, but you know about other stuff. What else happened, Eddie? Because this all stinks—stinks like a pig farm at swill-out time."

"Can't help you with that, Jack. Now, if that's all you came for, I think you should leave now. I've already said my bit."

But Jack wasn't ready to leave just yet, even though he was being edged towards the front door. "I'm assuming that it was you that set Dupin up. You can almost see the Parker house from the top of the hill outside."

"Get out! I don't have to answer your questions. Now sod off, will you?"

"No, you don't Eddie," Jack said, resignation in his voice. "Sometimes it's what you don't say that gives me the answer."

Jack was back at the front door. He opened it and stepped out, then turned back. He could see Eddie's outline against the light coming in from the kitchen window. The man was reed thin.

"I hope the money you got was worth it," Jack shouted. "How much was it, exactly? A new Jag every year? If you've got a conscience, Eddie, you'll do the right thing. I'll leave you with that thought. Help me put it right, then maybe you'll sleep a bit easier at night. You look like you need it."

He slammed the door closed, and stormed back towards his waiting car.

. . .

Eddie slumped down on a ripped vinyl chair and started to cry. In reality, no, it hadn't been worth it.

But it was too late now.

Chapter Sixty-Seven

Doug at the front desk rang through to Amanda to tell her that Gordon Simpson and his solicitor, were still waiting. "Show them through to the interview room, would you, please?" said Amanda. "DI Dupin is on his way back, so he won't be long. Make him a cup of tea or something."

"I'll get the tea boy to do it," said Doug, "and that ain't me."

Amanda rolled her eyes in frustration. She didn't need the petty grief when there was so much crap already colliding inside her skull. It was about time that man retired. She put the phone down and sat back in her chair, disappointed that Ruth still hadn't called her back. Amanda had stopped trying; there was no point making it more and more obvious what was happening. She'd deal with it later, face to face, when she got home.

Dupin was on the case now, not her, and Amanda resigned herself to hearing what went on second-hand when the DI eventually arrived. And Jack still wasn't back either; his little detour had taken the longest hour in human history. Still, in another few minutes, everything would be well underway and hopefully Gordon Simpson would be back home as if nothing had happened. Deep inside, though, Amanda knew that that was unlikely to happen, and an overnight spell in a police cell could be part of the DI's plan.

Half an hour later Dupin blustered into the squad room and cocked his head at Amanda for her to follow. She noticed he'd got the folder in his hands, so at least he looked like he knew what was going on.

"Anything else I should be aware of, Amanda?"

"Not to my knowledge. But I'm off the case now."

"Right, yes, of course." Dupin carried on towards the interview room, file swinging in his hand. She was about to head back to her own desk, then had second thoughts and slipped into the viewing room so she could watch her father-in-law's interview take place.

Gordon Simpson looked ill at ease. Who wouldn't be, in his situation? His solicitor sat beside him, and even though Amanda had no prior knowledge of his work, his body language looked competent and his neat, tailored suit gave him an air of authority. The one-way mirror and the computer screens feeding images from the camera told her little else about the man. Maybe after the interview she'd know more.

DI Dupin had his back to her and started off gently by asking some basic questions. Either he was leading Gordon into a false sense of security or he was frantically trying to reorder things in his own mind, having only just blustered into the office. He didn't strike Amanda as fully prepared for what was about to go on in the interview room. But that was how he was at times: Dopey—hence his nickname. And the pressure he'd been under himself of recent probably hadn't helped his focus. Maybe it would work in Gordon Simpson's favour. Maybe not.

Eventually Dupin reached the time period when Des Walker had actually disappeared.

"So, Des Walker came to do some work at your property. Is that correct, Mr Simpson?"

"Yes, correct."

"And that was on Wednesday, 10 August 2016?"

"I believe so."

"You believe so?" questioned Dupin.

"I didn't write it in my calendar, since I wasn't involved."

"Where were you the day that the landscaper started work at your property?"

"I was at work—with plenty of witnesses."

"What time did you get to and leave work?"

"I arrived just before nine, and I left just after five, like I do every other day, like clockwork. Anybody at work can vouch for me. The only time I left in between times was to get my sandwich at lunchtime, and I slipped out the office for maybe ten or fifteen minutes."

Gordon was starting to sound and look a little more confident, thought Amanda. At least he had an alibi for the timeline in question.

"What did you do that night when you got home?"

"Same as always. I had my dinner and watched TV."

"On the following day, Thursday, 11 August 2016, what was your routine?"

Amanda noticed Gordon's head drop a little. She wondered why.

"Mr Simpson?" Dupin pressed on. Where were you on Thursday, 11 August 2016?"

"I was actually on a course that day."

"You were on a course?"

"Yes, continued education. We have to do so many hours each year. I was on a course."

"Where was this course, and what time did it start?" asked Dupin.

"It was out over Ealing way, and it was a full day, from memory. It started at nine AM and finished at four PM."

"And I'm guessing again you have people who can verify that you were there for all that time?"

Gordon took a deep breath while he seemed to figure his words, and Amanda was curious as to what was going on his head. She pressed her tongue up against her top teeth, willing his answer to keep him out of further trouble.

"That morning there was a delay on the tube," said Gordon resignedly. "Somebody decided to commit suicide, and the trains were all backed up. So we sat in the tunnel for a good hour before things got moving again."

"Is that right?" Dupin said, smiling. "So, you weren't there on time, is that what you're telling me, Mr Simpson?"

"I was delayed, but I got there later that morning. There's plenty of people who could confirm that, I'm sure. We left at four PM for home as usual, in time for dinner."

"Was your wife, Madeline Simpson, at home that morning?"

"I would expect so, though she'd be getting ready to go to work herself. I left at the usual time, so I've no idea. It was the tube that was delayed, not me."

Amanda noticed that Gordon was getting anxious; his voice was rising slightly and getting snappier with each response. His solicitor hadn't said anything yet, but then Dupin hadn't asked any questions that Gordon couldn't answer simply. She watched Gordon wring his hands nervously on the table in front of him; the questioning was starting to bother him.

Amanda was aware of the door into the viewing room opening behind her, and turned to see Jack slipping in.

"Thought I'd just see how it's going," said Jack.

"That depends which side you're on," said Amanda. "Gordon seems ever so worked up now, and I don't blame him, but he's just said that he was delayed getting to his course on the Thursday morning. There was a suicide on the line, and the detective in me says that would have been on the news. He could have used that excuse and not been on that tube at all. He could have been at home, disposing of a body."

"You're beginning to sound like you don't believe him either," said Jack.

"No, I'm not. I'm saying that's what Dupin will be thinking too. The chance of tracing anybody that could confirm he was on that tube is pretty remote. Yes, the CCTV cameras down there could be scrutinized. But it would be like searching for a vegan in a butcher's shop— a long shot— and he is hardly someone that stands out in a crowd during rush hour.

"Good luck with that one," Jack grunted in reply, hoping he wasn't going to be the one to have to trawl through the footage to prove otherwise.

"Dupin's taking it easy at the moment, but I can feel where this is going. It could be a long night," said Amanda. "And until Dupin is satisfied with his replies, he'll want to keep working on him. And that means an arrest."

Jack didn't know what to say, and settled for "It'll all work out in the end, Amanda." He hoped it sounded encouraging enough, because right now as he looked at Gordon Simpson, it didn't bode well. Even if Simpson had been on that tube, there had still been plenty of time the previous evening to dig a hole under cover of darkness and bury Des Walker.

"Do you recognise this?" Dupin asked, pushing a photo across the table. It showed the gold cufflink.

Gordon stared at it before speaking. "Yes, it's a cufflink."

"Of yours?"

"I had some like this, yes. Madeline bought them for an anniversary present one year, but I lost one somewhere."

"We found a single cufflink not far from the remains of Mr Walker. Can you explain how that could have happened, Mr Simpson?" Dupin sat back in his chair, smug.

"I'm sorry, no, I can't. Maybe I lost it in the garden and with the digging, it's turned up." Gordon's voice faltered slightly, as he undoubtedly realised where this was heading. An item of his had been found near a dead body in his old garden. Anyone would start to feel frightened at the implications and Gordon couldn't explain it any further. His solicitor finally spoke.

"Since they are Crystal Palace supporter merchandise, many pairs of these cufflinks would have been sold, so it hardly means my client is responsible for a man's death, Detective Inspector." He stood to leave. "Now, if that's all you've got, my client has been more than generous with his time. And we're leaving."

Gordon stood, too, confusion evident on his face.

Dupin got to his feet as well, and Amanda and Jack watched intently, knowing in their hearts what was about to happen. They'd seen it so many times before.

"Not so fast," said Dupin. "Gordon Simpson, I'm arresting you for the murder of Desmond Walker. You do not have to say anything..."

Amanda dropped her head with a mixture of anguish and worry. Only Gordon himself knew if he had anything to do with the landscaper's death, but his arrest had just made things a whole lot more official. She hoped he wouldn't be charged, not Gordon. She had to do something, but what? Her hands were well and truly tied behind her back now.

"I need some air," she said, and left Jack watching the proceedings.

Jack, for his part, knew what this would now mean for Amanda, his friend and colleague, and his shoulders sagged under the realisation.

"Damn it!"

Chapter Sixty-Eight

Jack watched as the small group in the interview room split up. Gordon Simpson and his solicitor huddled together deep in conversation, while Dupin left the room for a moment. He wondered about Ruth and whether Amanda would give her a call now, although since Ruth appeared to be avoiding her, it was unlikely. While it was tempting as a friend of the family to call her himself, it wasn't the done thing. And Gordon hadn't been charged with a crime as yet; he was still merely answering questions under caution. Still, it meant they could hold him for a full 24 hours, and because this was in regards to a murder investigation, that could be extended if need be. Jack hoped it wouldn't come to that. Why Dupin had arrested the man quite so soon Jack wasn't sure, but Dupin had other things on his mind, so maybe he wasn't thinking clearly.

Jack thought back to his earlier conversation with Eddie, and the mention of his previous visitor. It had to have been Dupin, thanks to Kyle at the prison. But why would Dupin be involving himself in an old case, one that he'd only just found out that Jack was working on, and nothing to do with Gordon Simpson at all? The fact that Dupin's mind was evidently elsewhere could be a good or bad thing, depending on your outlook and whose side you were on, but in this case, it didn't bode well for accuracy and open-mindedness.

He glanced at the clock on the wall; it was getting late and there was nothing more for Jack to do here. He made his way out of the viewing room in search of Amanda; she needed his support right now. When things got personal, rationality went out the window, and he only hoped that she wasn't going to do anything stupid. He made his way towards the back door, figuring that was where she'd headed when she'd announced her need for air. There'd be no point going to the squad room or out the front, where protesters were still waiving their banners and shouting at anyone that might listen.

"It's about time they buggered off home," he mumbled to himself.

He found her outside, perched with one bottom cheek on a concrete step, shoulders bent forward and her head in both hands. He hoped she wasn't crying—he'd never seen her cry, and he wasn't good with other people's tears. Jack sat down next to her and put his arm around her shoulders, feeling a little uneasy at the contact. While they were mates, she was still technically his boss and they were at work, but still, she was human and so was he, and if she needed some support, he was the one to give it. If prying eyes didn't approve, tough shit.

He rubbed ever so gently in between her shoulder blades with his left hand, something his mother had used to do to him when he was upset as a young boy. He'd appreciated the comfort. Amanda responded by lifting her head and turned to him with moist eyes. Her tears were about to spill over, but she fought them back with sheer will, and so far, they were staying put.

"Well, there's nothing more you can do here tonight, Amanda," said Jack. "Why don't you head home, go and talk to Ruth?"

"The fact that I'm so close to this makes me want to *be* involved. He's my father-in-law, Jack. I'm supposed to be able to help him, protect him, protect Ruth from bad things happening. I feel so helpless."

"I'm sure this will all wear out soon enough. There's got to be something positive that can help him if he's innocent, and he's not been charged yet."

"You know as well as I do, it doesn't matter about that. If the CPS thinks there is a case beyond reasonable doubt that he is the person who did it, or at the very least disposed of the man's body, then he'll be charged shortly. And then it's going to be hell."

They both knew that Gordon's being charged with murder meant time in a remand centre while awaiting trial, followed by a lengthy prison spell if he was found guilty.

"Let's hope it doesn't come to that," said Jack. "Let's not get ahead of ourselves. Being arrested just means Dupin can formally question him, and until we've got something a bit more concrete to present to the CPS, he won't be charged. This time tomorrow he could be back at his own house."

"Don't get my hopes up, Jack. I know what you're trying to do and I appreciate it, but just don't, okay?" She stood, brushing his arm off her shoulders, and headed back inside. Jack was tempted to follow, but figured he'd give her some space. She was probably going to get her bag and head home, as he'd suggested. He hoped she would; there was nothing she could achieve here.

It was time he was heading out himself, but Dupin might need him, so he headed back inside to see what the man's next move was. He found Dupin in his office, seated behind his desk, deep in thought. Jack rapped on the door with his knuckle and walked in.

"What's your plan?" said Jack. "Leaving him to stew before you go back for more questions?"

Dupin didn't bother to raise his eyes. "Something like that. Do you need something, Jack?" he asked.

"I was just going to head off home, but I don't know if you need me, what with Amanda out of it."

"Amanda? Oh, yes. Father-in-law. No, she can't be involved. "

"I guess Raj is going to be working with you on it? Not me?"

"Yes, I'll stick with Raj, keep things clean. I've had it up to my back teeth with people pointing fingers at procedure and cover-ups.

I don't need any more crap. Go home, Jack. I'll call you if you're needed, if anything transpires."

Jack was about to head out the door when a question occurred to him. He wrestled for a moment, debating whether to ask it or not. What the hell.

"Do you think the CPS will go for it on what little we have—a body in his old garden and a cufflink nearby?"

Dupin finally looked up at him. "Quite probably."

Chapter Sixty-Nine

If Amanda thought she was dreading going home before, the dread had now doubled. It felt like broken concrete slabs thrown together in her stomach, jagged edges pushing out from her insides. She wasn't looking forward to facing Ruth. She slipped her key into the lock and went inside. The house was deathly quiet, yet she knew Ruth was home. She could smell her, sense her; her perfume lingered in the hallway and Amanda could feel her presence somewhere close by. There was no point calling out; she doubted if Ruth would answer.

Amanda glanced around the lounge door to check if she was there, but the room was empty. She carried on down to the kitchen and peered inside. Ruth was standing looking out of the kitchen window at her herb garden, but didn't say a word as she heard Amanda come in. Her body language conveyed how she was feeling; her shoulders visibly sagged. Amanda waited patiently, knowing that Ruth needed her space; having never been in such a delicate situation herself before, she hoped that staying quiet was the right thing to do. She stood motionless in the doorway and willed Ruth to turn around and say something.

It felt like a lifetime later when she finally did, though it was probably only a minute or two. Ruth's eyes were pink around the edges from crying, her make-up slightly smeared, and she looked terrified. Her bottom lip was trembling as she tried unsuccessfully to steady her voice.

"Why didn't you call and tell me?" she asked in a voice that was barely audible.

"I wish I could've, Ruth, you know that, but it's not my place. And you hadn't returned any of my previous calls. I'm assuming you've spoken to your father?"

"His solicitor called me, said he'd been arrested. It's serious, isn't it, Amanda?"

"I hope it's not Ruth, but you know I can't discuss an ongoing investigation, particularly when it is one that involves a family member. And I'm off the case so I don't know how much help I could be anyway. I can only tell you what I suspect will happen, and that is if Dupin feels he's got enough evidence, he'll go to the CPS and your father will be charged. If not, arrest means just a formal questioning, so he may well be home in a few hours. It really depends on Dupin, the evidence and the CPS. It's totally out of my hands."

At least they were talking, and Amanda wanted to ask again why Ruth hadn't returned any of her calls, but now didn't seem the right time. There were clearly more important things worrying Ruth; Amanda hated seeing her so distressed. Abandoning caution now, she walked over and took her in a warm embrace, rubbing her back like Jack had rubbed hers not long ago, hoping it gave her comfort too. Whatever happened, it would be a trying time for both of them.

"Do you think Dad did it?" asked Ruth.

"I don't think so," said Amanda. "I know what people are capable of, but I hate to think that Gordon did do it."

"And what if he didn't?" said Ruth, struggling to keep her tears at bay.

"Then hopefully there'll be some evidence to say that he didn't do it, but right now it doesn't look good. To anyone looking in, a body found in your garden can only mean one thing: the occupant or occupants put it there."

"But two people lived in that house—Madeline was there as well." Ruth sniffed loudly.

"Unfortunately, Madeline is not here to answer questions, though, and the CPS will think that one of them couldn't have done it without the knowledge of the other. That they were accomplices."

"So, you're saying that just because it was found in Dad's garden, he is now responsible even though he might not have done it?"

"For some of it at least, unless evidence proves otherwise. Concealing a crime, particularly one as serious as a murder, still holds a sentence."

Ruth turned back to the window and wiped her cheek with the back of her hand. "How long will we have to wait to find out if Dad will be released tonight?"

"Again, I can't comment, Ruth but I would suspect that he would be held overnight for questioning. That's normal tactic. Your best bet is to talk to his solicitor. Do you have his name and number?"

"I do," she said. "I can't bear to think of him lying in a prison cell overnight."

"He's at the police station, Ruth, not in prison."

"It's the same thing!" Ruth shouted as she swung round. "He'll be lying in a cold concrete room with a plastic mattress and a sink if he's lucky. And he didn't do anything—it's not fair!"

Tears were running freely down her cheeks now, and Amanda could do nothing but give her another hug. Ruth's body shook as Amanda tried to console her, and she sobbed as though her heart would break. Ruth rarely got upset over anything, and while Amanda knew she was worried about her father, she couldn't help wondering what else was on her mind to have elicited such a powerful reaction. Perhaps it was the stress of work added into the fact.

When Ruth's sobs subsided slightly and she pulled away,

Amanda tore a piece of kitchen roll off the dispenser nearby and handed it to her to dry her eyes.

"Let's see what the morning brings," said Amanda, in as soft a voice as she could muster. "We may well be worrying about nothing. Try and remember that."

Ruth nodded as she dabbed, then turned back and resumed gazing down the garden. Her shoulders shook slightly and Amanda knew that she was crying again.

Stress affected everyone differently, she thought, but Ruth's display was wildly out of character.

No, something else was up, Amanda knew.

She didn't have to wait long to find out what it was.

Chapter Seventy

While Amanda was off the case and sleeping fitfully through the night, another team were going through Gordon's new flat, armed with a search warrant after his arrest. Every drawer, every cupboard door, every nook and cranny was looked into as they searched for something that could possibly link Mr Simpson to the body in his old back garden. Since he'd recently moved house, a lot of his belongings had been sold; not everything from the five-bedroom place would fit into his one-bedroom flat. But he'd kept sentimental things for his new life as a widower.

It was Raj who found the missing link—quite literally. He had been tasked with searching Gordon's bedroom. Gordon it seemed, was a tidy man, a formal man, and looking through his wardrobe Raj stood to admire his array of neatly pressed shirts and nice suits. They weren't overly flashy, but they were nice nonetheless. Appearance was important to Gordon. Raj ran his hand down the sleeves of the shirts, and even through his latex gloves, he could feel the quality of the cotton. They weren't the finest Egyptian, but they weren't high street either—and they were quite possibly made to measure, to boot. Each shirt had double cuffs rather than the regular single button that most men opted for; Gordon really did like the formal feel. But double-cuffed shirts need to be fastened by something other than a button, and it was the cufflink box on the top of his dresser that gave Raj the final clue to Gordon's involvement in the burial of Des Walker. As he tipped the contents out onto the top of the bureau, there were several pairs that he matched together. But there was an odd one left over, and he'd seen it before in a crime scene photograph. The eagle looked straight at him.

"Mr Simpson, what have you been up to?" Raj said to the empty room.

It was identical to the one that had been found in the grave. He slipped it into an evidence bag and labelled it, then alerted the officer in charge of the search.

The search of the rest of Gordon Simpson's flat turned up nothing more of use, and the team went back to the station. Gordon was still in police custody but wouldn't be questioned again until the morning. Raj wondered how he'd react to the news that the mate to the mystery cufflink had been found in his own trinket box. It didn't bode well.

Raj felt sorry for Amanda; this wasn't going to be easy to weather. While it wasn't her fault, she was going to feel somewhat embarrassed that her father-in-law had been charged with murder; it was only natural. And as she was close to the case, he knew there'd be people with suspicious minds and gossipy mouths.

Ruth had barely touched her plate at dinner time; Amanda wasn't surprised. She wasn't particularly interested in food herself, but her stomach had grumbled regardless and she'd forced herself. Ruth had then retired to bed early, saying she'd got a banging headache; after her tearful outburst earlier, this was understandable. Amanda had stayed downstairs catching up with work. After that, she watched a little TV and went up to bed just after 10 PM. Ruth had been already fast asleep, which was a good thing. The rest would help her recover and deal with whatever else was to fall on her shoulders. She knew it wasn't over yet.

When Amanda awoke the following morning, Ruth had already gone, but that was not unusual since it was her early morning running time. She wrapped herself in her pink robe and went downstairs to make the first cup of tea of the day. While she'd managed to sleep herself, she had been aware of Ruth's restlessness, but there was little she'd been able to do to help. The clock on the kitchen wall said it was a little after 6 AM, and the first thing that Amanda thought of was Gordon and how he'd taken his first night in a police cell. After his arrest, she knew there was no way Dupin was going to let him out until he'd used the allocated time to question him. What would today bring, she wondered? Would the CPS charge him? Oh, how she hoped that it wasn't Gordon, that there was another explanation, though what, she couldn't think. Ruth had mentioned Madeline last night, but again Amanda thought there was no way one woman on her own could have disposed of Des Walker's body; he'd have been a dead weight—literally—and far too heavy for even a muscular man to move, let alone Madeline Simpson. And even if she could have moved the body, there was no way she could have done it all without her husband knowing what was going on. No way. At the very least he had to be an accomplice, and that was a chargeable offence.

By 7 AM Amanda was at work, anxious to find out if anything significant had happened during the night. Even though she wasn't on the case, there was no harm in asking. Whatever the outcome was, she needed to be able to support Ruth as best she could. Forewarned was forearmed.

By 10 AM, Gordon Simpson had been charged with the murder of Desmond Walker. He would appear in the Magistrates Court the following morning. It wasn't the news she wanted to hear.

But the day was about to get worse. At 1:35 PM, Jack walked into the squad room, where Amanda sat staring at her blank computer screen, and informed her that Ruth was in reception and wished to talk with the officer in charge of Gordon Simpson's case.

"What?" she said, her voice full of astonishment. "What is Ruth doing here, and what does she want with Dupin?"

"It's highly unusual, I know, but get this. She says she's got something to discuss, something that will prove Gordon's innocence." Jack shook his head in disbelief.

Amanda rose up, ready to head out the door, but Jack put himself in front of her and placed his hands on her shoulders. "Now, you know you can't do anything, so stay put and let me find out what's going on."

"But Jack, I need to find out for myself!" Her anguish was audible.

"And I will tell you when I know," he said firmly. "You'll be the first to know. But right now, find something else to do to take your mind off this and trust me. All right?" Jack locked eyes with her, hoping his authority as a friend and colleague would make her see sense. She sat back down.

"I'll be back shortly," he told her. "Stay put."

Jack knocked on Dupin's door and walked straight in without being invited. He didn't wait for Dupin to ask him what he wanted this time; he ran straight with it.

"I guess Doug has told you already that Gordon Simpson's daughter is here to talk to you. Says she's got something to discuss, some evidence?"

"Apparently so. I'm on the way to talk to her now, so we'll see what this evidence she says she has is. Though the CPS have charged Mr Simpson, so she may be grasping at straws. She'll probably tell me it was her, trying to save her old man. It wouldn't be the first time it's happened."

"You are going to hear her out, though, aren't you? Take her seriously?"

"I'll see what she says. Yes."

Dupin stood, gathered up his notepad and checked his breast pocket for a pen before marching out in the direction of the interview room where the desk sergeant had deposited Gordon's daughter. When Dupin walked in, Ruth met his gaze and watched as he sat down opposite her. A striking woman on any other day, but her swollen eyes and blotchy face told him of her despair and upset.

"I'm DI Lawrence Dupin, and you're Ruth McGregor, is that correct?"

"It's Ruth McGregor-Lacey, actually, but yes, Ruth. I'm Gordon Simpson's daughter."

"I've been told that you have something I need to hear."

"I do," she said, taking a deep breath and letting it out slowly. Her hands shook with nerves as she rubbed them together in front of her. Her voice sounded like she was talking across a vibrating telephone line; the tension made her words hard going.

"This isn't going to be easy for me," she began, "because of the upset it's going to cause when it comes out." She paused to catch her breath and carried on. "But I can't let my father take the rap for something he didn't do. It wasn't him; he is not responsible for the death of the landscaper, or his body being in the garden back at the old house."

"I see," said Dupin, not convinced but happy to dig further. "So why don't you tell me what you know from the beginning, and let me be the judge of that." He wore a slight smirk on his face; he'd seen family members lie before to get others out of trouble. How convincing could this woman be, he wondered?

"Can I ask you a question first?" Ruth said. She was gaining control a little more, her voice strengthening as she forced herself to be the tough, direct woman she normally was.

"Go ahead," said Dupin.

"If you knew that a murder had taken place, but you'd no idea where the body was or any actual evidence that a certain person had killed someone in the first place, is it an offence not to report it?"

"There could be charges, yes."

"But if I could tell you about the deaths of two people, do you think that would negate any charge of knowing about the body you found? In other words, if what I tell you would help you clear up another case, help your resolved case figures, would that mean the other charge might be dropped? Hypothetically, of course," Ruth added hurriedly.

"It might be considered. It depends on the information that you have. By the way, have you spoken to a lawyer yet? Hypothetical questions are not much protection."

"I haven't, no, and perhaps I should, but I've got to get this out either way, so a solicitor is immaterial. This is at great personal expense to me, you understand. Dad had nothing whatsoever to do with the body being in the garden, and whether a solicitor advises me to say anything or not, I've got to help Dad. Tell the truth of what really happened."

"Then why don't you tell me what's on your mind, Ruth?"

"Can I have your word you'll take my information into account if you charge me?"

"Yes, you have my word. Now, why don't you fill me in?"

With another deep intake of breath, Ruth began to tell the story of how she had come to know about the deaths of at least two people and the poisoning of another.

"I remember that summer well, because Madeline Simpson, my stepmother—had an accident. She had a collision with a truck and ended up breaking her arm and spent some time in hospital. When she came out and was recuperating, we were sat having a drink out on the patio. Some strange things had been going on around that time; there just seemed to be too many coincidences. Anyway, I put two and two together, because I always enjoy puzzles, and confronted Madeline to see what she'd say."

"Like what? What are we talking about here?" said Dupin, leaning forward.

"There was a local man in the news who had terrible food poisoning; he used to go into the café where Madeline worked. And then somebody else died in hospital after a car accident. The accident had been on the road where there was a garden centre that

Madeline used to visit. And then there was the death of a man called James Peterson. He was from her book club, I think."

She paused again to gather her thoughts and to give the detective opportunity to ask questions about anything she'd said so far. He kept quiet.

"I know who killed him. Accidentally. And I'm not just making this up to get Dad off, either, because if you take a close look at the toxicology report from James Peterson's autopsy, you'll find Viagra in his system and smoked mackerel pâté in his stomach. The drug was administered via the food as a prank by my stepmother, Madeline Simpson. A prank that went terribly wrong. She didn't know about his heart condition, or I doubt she'd have done it."

Dupin was now scribbling furiously on his pad, making notes so that he could double-check what Ruth was saying. There was no way that Ruth McGregor-Lacey or whatever she was called could know about stomach contents and tox results unless she'd either had some involvement or *knew* somebody who'd had some involvement in those cases. It would be an easy one to check. She lived with a detective from the case, after all.

"And how does all of this help your father, Ruth?"

"Because it was Madeline Simpson who buried the landscaper in the garden. She killed him and buried him single-handedly, all on her own. Actually, with the help of a digger. She wasn't strong enough to do it alone, obviously; the digger was useful and convenient."

"And you expect me to believe that she could, indeed, do all that on her own? How did she kill him, exactly?"

"She whacked him with a shovel, I believe. She told me the whole sordid story of what she'd been up to, how menopause was a constant raging fight inside her and she'd decided on retribution one day. It was the landscaper that she killed first. She didn't mean to hurt anyone. These were all supposed to be simple pranks to teach each of them a lesson for annoying her so much." She took another breath and ploughed on. "That afternoon while we sat on the patio, she told me about all of them, but she wouldn't tell me what had happened to the landscaper's body. She said it was her way of keeping me out of any trouble: if I didn't know, I couldn't tell. No one else knows her secret, and I'm only telling you today to help my father." Tears started to fall afresh down her already swollen face. "And this is probably going to be the end of my relationship with Amanda. The fact that I've known this all along... Her trust in me is going to be smashed to smithereens now. Amanda has no clue, no involvement in all this. She didn't know my stepmother." Ruth pulled a clump of tissues out of her sleeve and blew her nose loudly.

"How did she do it, then? How did she bury the body?"

"Well, I could never say for sure *where* she buried it, and it was actually our old cat Dexter that showed me."

"I'm sorry?" asked Dupin incredulously.

"I know it sounds stupid. It was the morning of Madeline's funeral and Dexter was digging a hole to do his business on the dirt pile where the digger still stood. Then at the last minute, he changed his mind and decided to dig another hole at the side of it. That covered the original hole up, and then he squatted down and did his business there. And watching him, that's how I knew it was exactly what Madeline had done. That digger had sat there for a week on top of a pile of dirt. People came and went, investigating Des Walker's disappearance, and all they could see was an empty hole, a rather crude empty hole, if you looked at it closely enough. Not one that an experienced landscaper would necessarily have dug, but it was certainly one that a middle-aged woman with no prior knowledge of operating a digger could have hastily dug after she'd already buried a body in the original hole. A hole the landscaper had originally dug. That digger stood on top of the grave for ages with the fresh hole to the side. The whole thing was very smart, wouldn't you agree?"

Dupin sat back in his chair, not quite sure if he believed what she was saying, but it fitted perfectly. It was too far-fetched to have been made up. He scrutinised her face, her pleading eyes, her strained body language—she looked like she was telling the truth.

He'd interviewed enough people in his time and knew when someone was lying or not. Her body language and anguish were genuine. The story, though far-fetched, was certainly plausible.

"I'm going to leave for five minutes; I need to check on something. Please, stay where you are."

Dupin hurried out of the interview room and headed towards the squad room. He needed a computer.

In the tiny viewing room, Jack stood open-mouthed. Ruth's story was indeed plausible, and it would fill in an awful lot of missing pieces. But her revelation was going to wreak holy havoc on her life with Amanda—and here at work. Amanda and Jack had investigated that disappearance together, and now it turned out that Ruth had known the details since Madeline had died.

He hoped Ruth and Amanda were strong enough to weather the tsunami that was surging their way, because they were going to need more than a tough umbrella to withstand this one.

Not a religious man, Jack crossed his chest silently anyway.

Chapter Seventy-One

Amanda paced impatiently up and down the squad room, wondering what was going on, what Ruth was here to talk to Dupin about. She hoped she wasn't going to get herself into trouble, perhaps even make something up just to save her father, though that would be unlike Ruth in the first place. But Amanda knew Ruth was extremely close to her father now; she'd only reconnected with him in her late teens and they'd since become close. She could only hope that whatever it was she was telling Dupin, it was of dire importance. Ruth wasn't soft or stupid enough to think that she could come and plead with Dupin for her father's release; she knew it didn't work like that. So, what on earth could she be saying to him?

As she paced the squad room, wearing the carpet out, she saw Dupin surging past the doorway on his way down to his office. He looked in a rush, and since he was obviously out of discussions with Ruth, she figured she could follow, ask him what was going on. The worst that could happen was he'd tell her to mind her own business. She was almost at his door when he came blustering back out and collided with her in the corridor.

"Not now, Lacey," he shouted, and hurried passed her mumbling an apology as he went.

"What the hell was that?" said Amanda to herself, and attempted to pace after him. But Dupin was ahead of her and obviously on a mission. He shouted for Raj as he approached the squad room door, then slipped inside. Amanda followed and saw that the two men were already deep in conversation, and it looked secretive. Dupin obviously didn't want the rest of the team to hear whatever they were talking about. Raj was nodding up and down, his head bobbing like a doll's with a spring in its neck.

Dupin then flew back out of the room towards the interview room, and Ruth.

She approached Raj's desk, but got a similar brush-off from him, which was unlike Raj.

"Not now, Amanda. I'm sorry," he said, as he stood in front of his computer, trying to block her view. "Top secret," he said jokingly.

Amanda tried to get a glimpse of his screen but caught only some of it. It was an old case, a death she had investigated with Jack a couple of years ago. Raj turned, still keeping himself between her and the computer, and scanned the screen. Then he closed the page down and ran from the room.

What on earth was this all about, she wondered? The room was empty now, apart from one civilian researcher, who was looking curiously up at Amanda from over the top of her own computer screen.

Amanda raised her eyes to the ceiling, grasped her hair in both fists and screamed, "Will someone tell me what's going on?"

The researcher averted her gaze and resumed her work as Amanda stormed from the room, headed towards the back door and fresh air. She was tempted to go and see what was happening in the interview room, but at the same time something told her to keep well away, that she might see something or hear something she wasn't meant to. It seemed everybody in the station was involved in whatever it was except for her.

Out in the car park, Amanda stood blinking in the sunlight, bewildered and suddenly very nervous. She wished she had a cigarette—not that she smoked, but it would give her something to do and perhaps calm her down. Maybe pacing up and down the tarmac would have the same effect, she thought, so she focused on her breathing as she walked from one end to the other. But after a full five minutes, she was still as stressed as ever. She needed something else to occupy her mind.

She dialled Jack's number, and he answered almost immediately.

"Where are you?" she blurted.

"Not too far away, actually," said Jack, wincing on the other end of the phone. He was still in the interview observation room. It wasn't a lie as such; he wasn't that far away. "What can I help you with?" he said. "Anything in particular?"

"I just thought since no one will tell me what's going on with Ruth, I might as well crack on with something else and be productive, take my mind off things. I thought I'd go and see Charles Winstanley, see what he says, perhaps help you out with the old case. At least I can put my skills to use trying to get a possibly innocent man out of prison. I'm not allowed anywhere near the landscaper case, or Ruth either, it seems."

"Good idea," said Jack. "I was going to call him myself and go and see him with Doc Mitchell, but it may as well be you."

"Where's his details, then?"

"The file is on my desk. It's all there, so knock yourself out. I'll speak to you later."

They rang off, and Amanda had turned to walk back inside when she noticed out of the corner of her eye that Jack's car was actually there, parked in the car park. "What the—?" she said. She marched back inside as fast as her booted feet would take her and stormed into the squad room. It was still empty, except for the researcher who was startled by her presence once more. There was no point making a scene to one person, so, mumbling to herself, Amanda grabbed her bag and then went over to Jack's desk to get the notes. When she'd got what she needed, she headed back out towards her own car. She'd ring the pathologist on the way and hope that he could see her, because there was no way she was staying in the building and being treated like a damn mushroom.

Being kept in the dark and fed bullshit was far too stressful.

Chapter Seventy-Two

It was an easy half-hour journey for Amanda down from Croydon to Leatherhead. She drove past Epsom Downs racecourse and on to Ashtead, where she picked up the A24 and heavy roadworks. It wasn't far from there to the hospital where Dr Charles Winstanley was still working part-time. She'd called his assistant on her way down and told the woman it was of vital importance that she speak with him today, and he had agreed he could spare a few moments later on in the afternoon. She'd sit and wait until he had those moments, but she needed to put her energy into something. Unfortunately, Dr Winstanley was probably going to get more than he bargained for, given the mood she was in.

She parked her car and made her way towards the building, forcing her shoulders down in an effort to stop her insides from churning. She felt like a pent-up steam engine.

"Slow it down," she coaxed herself. There was no point going in guns blazing and upsetting the poor man. If they were going to get Michael Hardesty out of prison, then they needed the good doctor to be on their side rather than going on the defensive straight off. He might also have a simple reason for having missed what they'd seen in the photos.

She called at reception and asked that Winstanley be notified of her arrival, and said she'd wait in reception till he was free. No sooner had Amanda taken a seat than the receptionist called her brightly back over and gave her directions on where to find him. The woman's ponytail bobbed up and down with each syllable she spoke, though why Amanda noticed it when her brain was so overloaded she had no idea; nonetheless, it amused her just the same. The bobbing ponytail was just the mundane thing she needed to get herself back on track, and she felt herself relax a little more.

She headed down corridors that looked the same as the corridors in any hospital and finally reached the offices of the autopsy suite. She pressed the buzzer and waited. An older woman opened the door and welcomed her into a smaller reception area.

"You must be Detective Lacey," she said with a bright smile. "Dr Winstanley won't be long. Can I get you a cup of tea, perhaps, or a coffee?"

"A glass of water would be good, actually. Thank you," said Amanda. She made herself comfortable to wait. Moments later the woman returned with a glass that she plopped down on a glass coaster beside her. Amanda looked through the file notes and photographs again and rehearsed what she was going to say to Winstanley. She dreaded upsetting him, but at the same time they needed to find out what had gone on back then. It was a shame she hadn't brought Faye Mitchell along—too impatient to get on and do something.

A few minutes later a man appeared in front of her with his hand outstretched. He was no more than five feet tall, with wispy grey hair that stood straight up. She had heard the man looked like Einstein but hadn't quite realised just how accurate that description was. His friendly smile stretched from one ear to the other, and she took an instant liking to him; he reminded her of everybody's cuddly grandad. She stood towering over him, even though she wore flat boots, and shook his hand briskly.

"DS Amanda Lacey," she introduced herself. "Thank you, Doctor, for seeing me at such short notice."

"Not at all. If I can help in any way... Come on through," he said, pointing to his office door. It was one of the nicest working environments she'd ever seen. The room was modern minimalist, and the walls were covered in bright abstract art. She'd assumed, given his age and position, that his office would be more leather and walnut. Attracted to a large painting on the far wall, she wandered over and stood looking at it for a moment. She had no idea who had created it, but it was striking—not that she was an art expert but she knew what she liked. Winstanley stepped up alongside her.

"Do you like it?" he enquired.

"I do, actually. I'm not really one for art, but I am drawn to it, yes."

"My granddaughter painted it. Can you believe she is only seventeen years old? She's going to go a long way."

"Well, she's very talented," agreed Amanda.

Pleasantries over, they turned and headed over to Dr Winstanley's desk. He indicated a chair in front of it, then seated himself in his office chair.

"So, what can I help you with, DS Lacey? Because I'm sure you didn't come to admire my granddaughter's artwork." There was that smile again, making her feel comfortable and at home.

"It's a bit of a delicate matter, actually, Doctor, but there is no easy way to do this. So I'm just going to tell you what we've found out. Please forgive me before I start."

"Ah, that sounds ominous," he said. "Tell me more, then. Don't keep me waiting."

Amanda first explained the old case that Jack had been investigating. She then mentioned DI Dupin and his own experience, then the first and second autopsies on Callum Parker, and concluded with how it had come to be that this old case was now back on their desks. When she got to the subject of the details that had been missed during his part of the investigation, he grew visibly concerned. She pushed the photographs across to him and watched his bushy greying eyebrows knit together like two fluffy mice joined at the tail. She sat quietly, waiting. It was important to let him digest, let him think; not daring to speak or interrupt him, Amanda wondered what was going on his head.

Was he horrified that he'd made a mistake?

Was he horrified that it had come to light?

Or was there another answer?

She waited—and stayed silent.

Chapter Seventy-Three

Amanda was an excellent reader of body language. After many years on the force, she relied on that instinct to give her clues to a subject's honesty, or lack of it. She could see by Winstanley's paling face, the slight quiver of his lower lip, that the old man was mortified. His flyaway grey hair moved gently as he brought his head back up fully from the images laid out on his desk. He directed his gaze somewhere over Amanda's shoulder, towards one of the windows, and she wondered what was going on in that brain of his.

She also needed to broach the next subject that was on her agenda: that Jack had learned about the possible corruption involved in the McAllister case. Perhaps the great pathologist himself had succumbed, had been asked to do something that he hadn't wanted to do at the time. It could happen to anyone, she knew; money was too tempting for many people to resist. She cleared her throat, and the sound brought his gaze back to meet hers. He looked rather uncomfortable, disappointed and upset. She had a feeling she already knew what his answer to her question would be, but she needed to ask anyway.

"Dr Winstanley, I have another question for you."

"I'm in shock," he said. His voice was barely audible.

"There was some talk during the investigation that perhaps the McAllister family had gotten to people on the case, and I wondered…"

She got no further before Charles Winstanley put his hand up to interrupt her. "I know what you're going to ask," he said with his hand still up, "but absolutely not. On my heart," he said, placing his hand on his chest. "I have never taken and will never take a bribe on a case. Absolutely not. You have my word on that." He said it with such authority, such force, that Amanda knew instantly he was telling the truth. His eyes were full of concern that he could have been responsible for a miscarriage of justice, however unintentionally.

"I'm sorry, but I had to ask. Things were different fifteen years ago, as I'm sure you're aware—and remember that it's only because of this current case that we are even looking at the older one."

"And what happened to the man, the man in the old case?"

"He is still in prison, I'm afraid. He's still got some more time to go."

The doctor hung his head in obvious despair and stayed silent. When he raised his head again, he looked directly into her eyes. "What can I do to help now?"

"Well, if you agree that there was in fact an error, we may well have grounds to get the murder charge quashed. There is more work to do yet, and it won't be a short process, but it would be the quickest option."

"Whatever I can do to help. I can't believe it; this is my worst nightmare come true. Never in my career has something like this happened, and now, just as I'm coming to the end of it, I'll be known for such a grave mistake. And a man has lost the best part of his life."

Amanda reached out and placed her hand on top of his. "I'll keep you informed, Doctor," she said gently, and stood to leave. "And thank you for your candidness. Now let's focus and put this right, eh?" She gave him a weak smile, hoping to encourage him.

"I'll show myself out," she said. She gathered her things and reached a hand out to shake his. He gave her a distracted shake in return, not half as strong as the one he'd given on her arrival only a few minutes ago. All the power had left the man's body; he seemed to shrink like a balloon losing its helium.

As soon as Amanda was back outside, she called Jack to tell him what she'd found out and relay the good news. She couldn't help notice that he was distracted when he answered his phone, not his normal jovial Jack self. Obviously, something was happening at his end, something she wasn't privy to and couldn't ask about. Not yet, anyway.

"So, you were right, Jack," she said, as breezily as she could manage under the circumstances. "It looks like Hardesty is an innocent man. And I would say I believe the doctor. I don't think he was involved in any bribe or backhand or whatever you want to call it. I think it was a genuine mistake. The poor man is mortified, totally horrified, by what that has meant to Hardesty. As you would expect."

Jack was quiet for a moment, pondering. "But if that's the case," he said, "maybe the foreman didn't have anything to do with the verdict after all. Maybe he was bribed, but it could also be that he simply got lucky because of the evidence that was presented. Hell, Dr Winstanley might not have even known the outcome of the case; he'd no reason to hang around after his testimony. Most doctors don't. And the same with Eddie—he got lucky, too. Although I know he did accept bribes—that was evident in the way he lived, the flash cars and women. It was pretty obvious that money was coming from somewhere, and the job didn't pay that well. And that money's definitely dried up, given how he's living now. He's a real has-been."

"I think there's been some grounds in the past," said Amanda. "Eddie was obviously up to something to get money, like you say, but maybe in this case they all did just get lucky. You spoke to the foreman, didn't you?" She remembered that he said he was going to call in and see the man.

"Sort of," said Jack. "The guy wasn't particularly friendly; he denied everything. It was a very quick conversation, and basically, I got thrown off his property. So, there wasn't a great deal I could do, and I haven't been back for more. I've got no evidence, just an insinuation. People don't tend to respond well to insinuation, so I had to leave it."

It was Amanda's turn to think while she put the pieces that she knew of in order. At least being involved in what Jack had been working on was keeping her mind off what was really going on back at the station and in particular with Ruth. She'd got that yet to come.

"I'm on my way back now," she said. "Is it worth me popping in to see this character Eddie?"

"No, I doubt it," said Jack. "There's little point. He was up to no good, and the guy's rotten to the core but this is down to the pathologist's mistake, not Eddie's hand. And by the look of him, he won't be around for much longer, either. I suspect he's got kidney disease or something like it; his eyes look like Mrs Stewart's bananas and custard. He had diabetes when I worked with him, not that he looked after himself then. Same now, I'd say."

"Right, then," said Amanda. "I'm on my way back, then. You can fill me in what's been going on back there perhaps?"

Jack grunted noncommittally and said, "I'll see you later," before hanging up.

Amanda stared at the disconnected number on the dashboard screen. She didn't like the sound of that.

"Yep, I'm a mushroom."

Chapter Seventy-Four

"Not now, Jack," said Dupin distractedly as Jack rapped on his door with his knuckle.

"I think you'll want to hear this," said Jack. He needed to be persistent.

Dupin looked up over his reading glasses and glanced at Jack like he was something that had just crawled out from under a rock and bitten him. "I'm a bit busy," he said, a tad more forcefully this time.

Undeterred, Jack stepped into the office. "It's about the old case, actually, the one I told you about, with Eddie and Hardesty. It seems the pathologist made a huge mistake with it—the blunder of his career, I'd say."

Dupin looked up from the note that he was writing. "What do you mean?" he asked, only half interested.

"Amanda has just been out to see the doctor, Charles Winstanley. She showed him some photographs that Faye had looked over, as well as the other pathologist that did the second autopsy for the Callum Parker case. He took a look and confirmed it too. And get this. It seems the cameraman in the old case that day was quite clever and caught the whole thing on film. It's the same situation as Callum Parker—they both died of a freak haemorrhage."

Jack let it sink in with Dupin for a moment and stood watching the man's reaction with interest. "Hardesty is innocent," he said, "and is rotting in prison, and it's all because the pathologist got it wrong. It had nothing to do with a foreman or bribes. Not in this instance, anyway."

Dupin sat back in his chair, clasped his hands behind his head and closed his eyes. Jack watched the colour drain from his face. Was he imagining it, or was Dupin breathing rather shallowly?

"So, it seems whatever Eddie or the foreman were doing with the McAllisters, it was the pathologist all along—simple, though it's cost the poor sod fifteen years of his life."

A grin seemed to spread over Dupin's lips, which Jack regarded as highly inappropriate. But when the man opened his eyes and looked directly at him, he saw something else there. Relief.

Jack's brow furrowed as realisation began to dawn: his thoughts raced back through what he knew of Eddie and his ways from back then, and what he knew of Dupin both then and now. Sure, the pathologist had got it wrong, but something else had been at play, he was sure of it. Jack's gut was rarely wrong. Suddenly it was as though a light went on in his head. He could have smacked himself —it was obvious.

"You knew, didn't you?" he said accusingly. "You damn well knew!" He banged his fist on Dupin's desk, making his coffee cup rattle in its saucer.

Dupin leaned forward. "I'd advise you to remember who you are talking to, DC Rutherford," he said warningly.

Undeterred, Jack ploughed on. "You knew Eddie was on the take. That's why when you got promoted to DI, he was the first one that you got rid of. It was all a bit quick, from my memory, all a bit hush-hush. And that's who shopped you with the Callum Parker death— Eddie sodding Edwards, to get you back!" Jack's fury rose as it all fell into place. "Why didn't you say anything back then when you had a chance?"

"What exactly are you accusing me of, Jack?" Dupin asked.

"I'm accusing you of knowing that Eddie put somebody away wrongly and doing nothing to stop it. You bettered your own career and got a tick in a box at the same time for the commissioner's figures, and a man lost fifteen years of his life because of it. You make me sick!" shouted Jack.

Dupin stood up and pushed his chair back noisily. "Jack, you don't know what you're talking about," he boomed, "and I'll thank you to show some respect."

"Respect?" Jack spat. "I've never had much respect for you, and I certainly didn't have any respect for Eddie. And whether the pathologist made a mistake or not is immaterial. What you did, what you and Eddie did, is far worse than what the pathologist did. You could have stopped it; an innocent man is in prison for case-closed ticks and blood money between the two of you. You disgust me." Jack's lip curled in a sneer, and he turned and stomped out of the office. "I can't be in the same room as you!" he bellowed over his shoulder.

Dupin sat back down heavily in his chair. Deep down, he knew Jack was right. Dupin had been aware of exactly what had happened back then, and had left it be. The truth about the pathologist was something new to him, though. All these years, he'd contemplated what Eddie had done and his own part in it, but had chosen to let the dogs stay sleeping. But the recent events he'd found himself involved in had brought it all home again—what he'd helped cover up and what it had meant for an innocent man.

Sitting in the police cell himself after his own arrest had been the most frightening episode of his life—the not knowing, the uncertainty about his future. But he'd been lucky in the end: the evidence had shown he was not to blame, and the relief that had powered through every sinew of his body at the welcome news was something he'd never forget. But Michael Hardesty had not experienced that welcome news, he knew: only the terror of his life ahead

—behind bars. And all for his own career and a few lousy boxes ticked.

"What the hell am I going to do now?" he mumbled to himself.

Jack wasn't quite sure what he could do as yet, but whatever he decided, it wasn't going to involve Dupin. He knew he should talk to Japp, but would he believe the DI's involvement? Jack had no actual proof about what the two men had done back then, and he was well aware Dupin and Edwards could deny it all. At least he had the pathology evidence, though, and he hoped that would be enough to help Hardesty.

At any rate, he now had some work to do; he needed to put together a plan for getting him out, and that wasn't going to happen overnight. He hoped the pathologist didn't backtrack on his admission, that he'd cooperate to help Hardesty and secure his release; it was the least he could do. A tough way for the old man to end his career if the news broke, which it would.

Even if Charles Winstanley did decide to change his mind and chicken out for whatever reason, at least Faye and the second pathologist concurred that the images showed another freak haemorrhage. It beggared belief that it had got messed up in the first place at all, but with fresh evidence Jack could now do something about it.

He also needed to talk to Amanda, but as a friend, not a colleague. However, that would have to wait a while. Ruth's confession had meant she'd been placed in police custody for now, and that was another mess that was going to need cleaning up. Jack knew the fallout was going to break Amanda's heart. All he could do was be there, as impartially as possible, for whatever happened between the two women he loved the most in his life.

It was going to be an emotional time ahead all round.

Chapter Seventy-Five
TWO DAYS LATER

DI Laurence Dupin resigned the day following Jack's accusation, which surprised the entire station—except for three people close to the truth. DCI Japp had been informed of the miscarriage of justice and had accepted Dupin's resignation immediately, though Jack and Amanda both saw it as the chicken's way out. Conveniently, it tidied away the need for the disciplinary that was still hanging over Dupin's head. As with Eddie, there'd be no pension forthcoming, and the wrath from his wife Lyn would be halfway to the punishment he deserved. That and his own conscience, reminding him that he'd left an innocent man to rot, a fate that he himself had narrowly escaped. Since Charles Winstanley's admission alone would be enough to get Hardesty's conviction quashed, there seemed little point dragging Edwards and Dupin back into an already messed-up case with no actual evidence of either of their involvement in it. Whether it was fair was a matter of opinion, however.

The squad room resembled a wake rather than a hive of activity now. With the news of Dupin's sudden departure and Amanda taking sudden sick leave, tongues had started wagging about her own possible involvement in the Des Walker case. Surely Amanda herself would have known of Ruth's involvement. Surely they shared secrets with each other? Sadly, some of the team had indulged in sly homophobic, misogynistic remarks on top of it all, which saddened and infuriated Jack.

DCI Japp had eventually intervened with strong words and physical threats, and things had calmed back down. Jack had spoken to both Ruth and Amanda individually by phone, simply to check on them; but fearing they might not welcome his wisdom at the moment, he knew he had to wait at the sidelines until normal play was resumed. He was sure it would be. Amanda wasn't due back on the job for a couple of weeks, she was taking some time out on the Cornish coast while she sorted through her feelings. Until then, Jack was being the best support he could be for her while she struggled to come to terms with it all. Ruth and Amanda had a lot of work ahead of them if they were going to stick together through this, he knew.

Meanwhile, Jack admitted he was relieved with the quiet atmosphere in the squad room; it was a welcome change from the pace of recent days.

His phone chirped with an incoming text.

Still on for dinner? VV

Jack smiled at his phone as he typed his reply. He must ask Vivian why she always signed off with VV, since her surname didn't start with V.

You bet. Come for 7pm. It's coq au vin.

Tres bon! Je vais apporter du vin.

Excellent. Au revoir.

Vivian. It was good to have the friendship of a female companion again, and though his Janine would always be in his heart, Vivian brought a warmth to him he hadn't realised he had been missing. She was also quite clever at French, and he looked forward to sharing some of Mrs Stewart's chicken casserole with her; she made it just the way he liked it, with half a bottle of wine in it.

Jack placed his phone on the desk in front of him and turned his chair so he could see out of the window. The sky was filled with thickening grey clouds that looked like cotton wool balls that had been soaked in dirty water. The sombre weather matched the sombre day, and his mind changed tack to Amanda and Ruth—the only other women in his life. Ruth had been charged with assisting an offender, but with the critical information that she had provided on the other two cases, she was unlikely to see any of the three- to ten-year jail term the offence carried. He hoped a suspended sentence would be it.

Gordon Simpson had of course been allowed to walk free; all charges against him had been dropped. Nobody could say for sure how the cufflink had ended up in the soil; maybe Madeline herself had found it and it had fallen into the hole accidentally that day. After Gordon's initial shock at the truth, he'd decided to take a break from work, giving himself some time to digest what the woman whom he'd known since childhood almost, had shared a bed with for so many years, had done. And his daughter had kept secret.

Jack knew that disappointment didn't come close to what Gordon felt. "You think you know someone, but really—do you?"

"Talking to yourself again, Jack?" said Raj as he balanced on the corner of Jack's desk, mug of tea in his hand. He carried an air of despondency, like the others in the room.

"It's the only way to get any sense around here," Jack said, smiling.

Chapter Seventy-Six

THREE MONTHS LATER

Jack and Howard King stood waiting by the prison gates, like a scene from the *Blues Brothers* movie. In his head, Jack was running through the words of one of his favourite ELO songs, "Last Train to London." It had been playing in the car on the way in, and on the night he'd first bought Vivian a drink at the Baskerville pub. As it turned out, that particular situation was bubbling along nicely for Jack. He had wanted that night to last forever, of course, but since there had been many more, he was happy enough. She was now filling her daytime hours with the new support group she'd started.

Howard nudged Jack as the doors opened and a slightly built man exited through them. He didn't appear to be in any rush, and both men watched as Michael Hardesty ambled slowly toward them, drinking in the lunchtime autumn sunshine on his face as he moved, a small bag of belongings in one hand. By the time he'd reached his welcoming committee, he wore an exuberant grin from ear to ear.

"Tell me I'm not dreaming," he said, a slight tinge of worry in his voice.

"You're a free man, Michael, and no one can take that away

from you now," Jack assured him, returning a smile matching Hardesty's in size. "Have you decided where you want to go first?"

Michael looked at the bunch of notes in his hand, all £46 of it. "It's not a great deal they give you, is it?" he said.

"Enough for a pint and a bag of fish and chips," Jack said brightly. As a man released from prison, even though he had been wrongly convicted in the first place, £46 was all Hardesty was entitled to. Not even an apology. He'd have been better off waiting until the end of his sentence in many respects; at least he'd have been entitled to support, or got a halfway house provided to him for a while. But who would want to hang around in prison when they didn't need to? Not Michael.

"And I'll buy," added Jack. Hardesty's bit of money had to last him until benefits could be sorted out, and that could be some weeks away.

"I had hoped Barbara and Cassy might have been here," he said solemnly, as the three of them headed slowly over to Jack's car. Both Jack and Howard King were keenly aware of the man's physical limitations. Prison time hadn't been good to him, and his strength was failing him. "But I guess they didn't get the memo, eh?"

There was nothing for Jack or Howard to say to that. Both women had moved on many years ago, not wanting the family name to bring either of them further trouble. Jack had done his best to trace them both, and had found Barbara. She had remarried, however, and didn't think it right to contact Hardesty again. 'It was for the best,' Barbara had told Jack in a letter, but Michael's disappointment was obvious.

"I'll get the first round in," offered Howard as they climbed into Jack's car. "You save your money."

Jack started the engine and they set off out of the prison grounds.

"What are you looking forward to doing with your new freedom?" Jack asked over his shoulder.

"As odd as it sounds, I'm looking forward to making my own

decisions again. The small ones, like when to turn the light off at night and when I'll eat my breakfast. Do you know, I've not turned a light switch off in fifteen years? Or watered a plant."

Jack turned to the frail-looking man beside him; his grey, pasty face was starting to change slightly to pink as his excitement increased. It was the best feeling in the world to see the man with hope in his eyes. Jack reached for his phone and his playlist, tapping the start icon. ELO ticked over in the background, carrying on from where it had been when they'd arrived at the prison. He hummed along as they drove, and Michael wound the passenger window down to sniff the air like a dog riding in a car along a country lane.

In fact, the whole story had started in a leafy country lane.

"Turn it up, Jack, would you? I feel like singing," Hardesty said, sounding stronger with each word as he joined in with the lyrics he knew. Jack obliged and turned the volume up as high as it would go. He wound his own window down, and Howard, in the back, followed suit. With his long grey ponytail getting caught in the wash, he looked like an old rocker, as Jack's car headed towards first the chip shop then the Baskerville pub for Michael's first pint in fifteen years.

"I'll think I'll head into London afterwards," Hardesty announced. "On the train maybe." He fell silent again for a moment, listening to the words in the song, and then the three men picked up the chorus and sang like a trio of out-of-tune geriatrics on a coach day trip to Brighton.

The last train to London, Jack pondered. Where would Hardesty go after that?

He had sod all.

But he did have his freedom.

∼

Want to continue on to the next book in the series? Click here to start reading Butcher Baker Banker now.

Did you enjoy Scream Blue Murder?

Want to continue on to the next book in the series? Click here to start reading.

Butcher Baker Banker is available now

Acknowledgments

This book is a work of fiction, though some physical places are indeed real. The characters however are most definitely a figment of my imagination.

I'd like to thank Graham Bartlett, a police procedural advisor who makes sure the correct process is followed when it comes to the technical stuff. That said, any variation from procedure is for creative purposes because in reality some tests take weeks to get the results back from. That would mess with the story timelines too much and we'd be all day waiting.

Thanks to Dr. Ben Swift who is the easiest forensic pathologist to work with in the whole wide world, along with Dame Sue Black, professor of anatomy and forensic anthropologist. Thanks to you both for your tissue and skeletal advice in keeping it real.

And thanks to Sarah Waters, and her help with the legal beagle.

And thanks to you, the reader because if you didn't buy my books, there would be little point me writing any more.

And last but not least, hubby Paul, for your enthusiasm, constant support and ideas.

Also by Linda Coles

If you enjoyed reading one of my stories, here are the others:

The DC Jack Rutherford and DS Amanda Lacey Series:

Hot to Kill

When a local landscaper vanishes, Madeline Simpson knows she was the last person to see him alive – because she killed him.

With a serial sex offender on the loose, Detectives DC Jack Rutherford and DS Amanda Lacey already have their hands full. It's only when another death occurs that a link between the two cases comes to light, and Madeline finds herself the focus of their investigation.

While attempting to keep her deadly secret, Madeline stumbles upon clues that point to the true identity of the sex offender. She's closing in when tragedy strikes, and the death toll increases.

But DS Amanda Lacey has no idea how close she is to the killer as her work and personal lives collide.

How long will she have to wait to find out the full truth?

If you like interesting characters, imaginative story lines, and British crime drama, then you'll love this captivating story.

The Hunted

The hunt is on...

They kill wild animals for sport. She's about to return the favour.

A spate of distressing big-game hunter posts are clogging up her newsfeed. As hunters brag about the exotic animals they've murdered and the followers they've gained along the way, a passionate veterinarian can no longer sit back and do nothing.

To stop the killings, she creates her own endangered list of hunters. By stalking their online profiles and infiltrating their inner circles, she vows to take them out one-by-one.

How far will she go to add the guilty to her own trophy collection?

Dark Service

The dark web can satisfy any perversion, but two detectives might just pull the plug...

Taylor never felt the blade pressed to her scalp. She wakes frightened and alone in an unfamiliar hotel room with a near shaved head and a warning... tell no one.

As detectives Amanda Lacey and Jack Rutherford investigate, they venture deep into the fetish-fueled underbelly of the dark web. The traumatized woman is only the latest victim in a decade-long string of disturbing—and intensely personal—thefts.

To take down a perverted black market, they'll go undercover. But just when justice seems within reach, an unexpected event sends their sting operation spiraling out of control. Their only chance at catching the culprits lies with a local reporter... and a sex scandal that could ruin them all.

One Last Hit

The greatest danger may come from inside his own home.

Detective Duncan Riley has always worked hard to maintain order on the streets of Manchester. But when a series of incidents at home cause him to worry about his wife's behaviour, he finds himself pulled in too many directions at once.

After a colleague Amanda Lacey asks for his help with a local drug epidemic, he never expected the case would infiltrate his own family...And a situation that spirals out of control...

Hey You, Pretty Face

An abandoned infant. Three girls stolen in the night. Can one

overworked detective find the connection to save them all?

London, 1999. Short-staffed during a holiday week, Detective Jack Rutherford can't afford to spend time on the couch with his beloved wife. With a skeleton staff, he's forced to handle a deserted infant and a trio of missing girls almost single-handedly. Despite the overload, Jack has a sneaking suspicion that the baby and the abductions are somehow connected…

As he fights to reunite the girls with their families, the clues point to a dark secret that sends chills down his spine. With evidence revealing a detestable crime ring, can Jack catch the criminals before the girls go missing forever?

Scream Blue Murder

Two cold cases are about to turn red hot…

Detective Jack Rutherford's instincts have only sharpened with age. So when a violent road fatality reminds him of a near-identical crime from 15 years earlier, he digs up the past to investigate both. But with one case already closed, he fears the wrong man still festers behind bars while the real killer roams free…

For Detective Amanda Lacey, family always comes first. But when she unearths a skeleton in her father-in-law's garden, she has to balance her heart with her desire for justice. And with darkness lurking just beneath the surface, DS Lacey must push her feelings to one side to discover the chilling truth.

As the sins of the past haunt both detectives, will solving the crimes have consequences that echo for the rest of their lives?

Butcher Baker Banker

A cold Croydon winter's night and pensioner Nelly Raven lies dead and naked on the floor of her living room. The scene bears all the hallmarks of a burglary gone wrong.

It's just the beginning.

Ron Butcher rose to the top of London's gangland by "fixing things". But are his extensive crooked connections of use when death knocks at his own family's door?

Baker Kit Morris will do anything to keep his family business alive. Desperate for cash, he hatches a risky plan that lands him in trouble. As he struggles to stay out of prison, he forges an unlikely friendship with an aging local thug.

And then there's the Banker, Lee Meady, a man with personal problems of his own.

Just how does it all fit together?

As DC Jack Rutherford and DS Amanda Lacey uncover the facts surrounding the case, the harrowing truth of the killer's identity leaves Jack wondering where the human race went so badly wrong.

The Chrissy Livingstone series:

Tin Men

She thought she knew her father. But what she doesn't know could fill a mortuary…

Ex-MI5 agent Chrissy Livingstone grieves over her dad's sudden death. While she cleans out his old things, she discovers something she can't explain: seven photos of schoolboys with the year 1987 stamped on the back. Unable to turn off her desire for the truth, she hunts down the boys in the photos only to find out that three of the seven have committed suicide…

Tracing the clues from Surrey to Santa Monica, Chrissy unearths disturbing ties between her father's work as a financier and the victims. As each new connection raises more sinister questions about her family, she fears she should've left the secrets buried with the dead.

Will Chrissy put the past to rest, or will the sins of the father destroy her?

Walk Like You

When a major railway accident turns into a bizarre case of a missing body, will this PI's hunt for the truth take her way off track?

London. Private investigator Chrissy Livingstone's dirty work has taken her down a different path to her family. But when her upper-class sister begs her to locate a friend missing after a horrific train crash, she feels duty-bound to assist. Though when the two dig deeper, all the evidence seems to lead to one mysterious conclusion: the woman doesn't want to be found.

Still with no idea why the woman was on the train, and an unidentified body uncannily resembling the missing person lying unclaimed in the mortuary, the sisters follow a trail of cryptic clues through France. The mystery deepens when they learn someone else is searching, and their motive could be murder...

Can Chrissy find the woman before she meets a terrible fate?

The Silent Ones

An abandoned child. A missing couple. A village full of secrets.

When a couple holidaying in the small Irish village of Doolan disappear one night, leaving their child behind, Chrissy Livingstone has no choice but to involve herself in the mystery surrounding their disappearance.

As the toddler is taken into care, it soon becomes apparent that in the close-knit village the couple are not the only ones with secrets to keep.

With the help of her sister, Julie, Chrissy races to uncover what is really happening. Could discovering the truth put more lives at risk?

A suspenseful story that will keep you guessing until the end.

Also by Linda Coles

Jack Rutherford and Amanda Lacey Series:

Hot to Kill

The Hunted

Dark Service

One Last Hit

Hey You, Pretty Face

Scream Blue Murder

Butcher Baker Banker

Book set 1

Book set 2

Book set 3

Book set 4

Book set 5

The Chrissy Livingstone Series:

Tin Men

Walk Like You

The Silent Ones

About the Author

Hi, I'm Linda Coles. Thanks for choosing this book, I really hope you enjoyed it and collect the following ones in the series. Great characters make a great read and I hope I've managed to create that for you.

Originally from the UK, I now live and work in beautiful New Zealand along with my hubby, 2 cats and 6 goats. My office sits by the edge of my vegetable garden, and apart from reading and writing, I get to run by the beach for pleasure.

If you find a moment, please do write an honest online review of my work, they really do make such a difference to those choosing what book to buy next.

If you'd like to keep in touch via my newsletter, use this link to leave your details:
https://geni.us/lindacolesnewsletter
Enjoy! And tell your friends.
Thanks, Linda

Keep in touch:
www.lindacoles.com
linda@lindacoles.com
Follow me on BookBub

Manufactured by Amazon.ca
Bolton, ON